D0041700

the dead and the dark

the dead and the dark

courtney gould

This is a work of fiction. All of the characters, organizations, and events portrayed in this novel are either products of the author's imagination or are used fictitiously.

First published in the United States by Wednesday Books, a division of St. Martin's Publishing Group

THE DEAD AND THE DARK. Copyright © 2021 by Courtney Gould. All rights reserved. Printed in the United States of America. For information, address St. Martin's Publishing Group, 120 Broadway, New York, NY 10271.

www.wednesdaybooks.com

Designed by Omar Chapa

Library of Congress Cataloging-in-Publication Data

Names: Gould, Courtney, author.
Title: The dead and the dark / Courtney Gould.
Description: First edition. | New York : Wednesday Books, 2021. | Summary: When Logan, the adopted daughter of reality television ghosthunters, teams up with Ashley to search for missing teens in Snakebite, Oregon, they find themselves falling for each other as they uncover a hidden evil.
Identifiers: LCCN 2021008146 | ISBN 9781250762016 (hardcover) | ISBN 9781250762023 (ebook)
Subjects: CYAC: Ghosts—Fiction. | Gay fathers—Fiction. | Fathers and daughters—Fiction. | Lesbians—Fiction. | Good and evil—Fiction.
Classification: LCC PZ7.1.G68634 De 2021 | DDC [Fic]—dc23
LC record available at https://lccn.loc.gov/2021008146

Our books may be purchased in bulk for promotional, educational, or business use. Please contact your local bookseller or the Macmillan Corporate and Premium Sales Department at 1-800-221-7945, extension 5442, or by email at MacmillanSpecialMarkets@macmillan.com.

First Edition: 2021

10 9 8 7 6 5 4 3 2 1

For Mom, who taught me that love is what holds back the Dark.

Some of the thematic material in *The Dead and the Dark* involves child death and endangerment, violence including strangulation and drowning, and homophobia and homophobic slurs. For a more detailed description of sensitive content, please visit gouldbooks.com/books/tdatd.

the dead and the dark

Interlude

For the first time in thirteen years, it snows in Snakebite.

The snow is a gentle thing, lilting like dust on the early-January wind, coating the rocks along the Lake Owyhee shore in thin slush. The lake water is black and seeps like ink into the snow-hazy sky. It is nighttime, the people of Snakebite warm in their homes, fingers pressed to their windows while they nervously watch the snow fall. For a moment, the world is silent; it is only the wind and the shifting trees and the hushed pulse of water against stone. It is held breath.

A boy stumbles to the lakeshore.

He thinks he is alone.

He holds his hands in front of him, palms up as though the snow is only a figment of his imagination. Flecks of it stick to his eyelashes, in the navy netting of his basketball shorts, in his hair the color of the golden hills that border town. He pauses at the water's edge, looks out at the horizon, and sinks to his knees. He is far from home, far from the light, far from anything.

The Dark watches the boy. It is tucked into the body of a new host, staggering across dead grass and juniper boughs for a better view. This new body is unwieldy to the Dark. It will take time to adjust to this skin, to these eyes, to the anxious beating of this new heart.

What are you afraid of? the Dark asks, quiet as the whispering wind. *You have a plan. Act.*

The host tenses. His fingers are clenched at his sides, lips pressed together, eyes wide. He is a wild animal frozen in fear. "Something's wrong," the host whispers. "Why's he on the ground?"

Does it matter?

"I don't know." The host does not move. "What do I do?"

Go, the Dark breathes.

The host nods. He inches from behind a thick juniper trunk, standing closer to the boy, just out of sight. The boy does not notice. Does not move. Through the flickering snowfall, the boy's face is tear-streaked, red with grief, hollow. He stares out at the black horizon, but he stares at nothing.

The host hesitates again.

The boy pulls a cell phone from his pocket. The glare of the screen washes over his face, the only light in the unending dark. He taps out a message, and then stares at it in silence. Tears are still wet on his cheeks, rivulets of white light.

All at once, the host is overtaken with the idea of marching forward, grabbing the boy by his collar, pressing thumbs to the column of his throat. He feels skin under his fingertips, the tangy scent of iron mixing with the snow. For years, he has imagined this. He pictures death running through him like a current.

As quickly as he imagines it, he chokes the vision.

The Dark has dealt with this kind of hesitation before. It slithers through the host, coiling around his heart until it finds the black rot of hate it knows well. This host craves death. The desire has bubbled under his skin for as long as he can remember, but he has been too afraid to claim it as his own.

Do you want me to help you? the Dark asks. *Do you want me to make you strong?*

The host scowls. "I do."

It is the truth.

Then do this, the Dark breathes. It simmers in the shadows, the water, the sky. *It is the truth you have been hiding from all these years.*

"The truth," the host whispers. He clenches and unclenches his fists, fingers fidgeting at his sides. A silent moment passes, then another.

And then the host moves.

By the time he crosses the distance to the boy, the snow is falling in heavy sheets. The sky is a blur of gray, closer than it should be. Stifling. The host grabs the boy and there is no going back.

The boy's eyes catch the host's for a moment, flashing from sorrow to surprise to recognition. He does not scream. Above them, the sky is gray, then black, then nothing.

The Dark slides deeper into the host, sinks its claws in, roots itself in the rot.

After thirteen years, the Dark has finally come home.

1

Love, Hollywood

BRANDON VOICEOVER: We're back in the basement of the Calloway House in New Prague, Minnesota. Local legend says that Agatha Calloway once used this basement for satanic rituals, but no evidence to back up such claims has been found. While the daytime tour of the house turned up no unusual readings, Alejo and I return to the basement at night to see what spirits might linger between these walls.

ALEJO: Brandon, did you feel that? It was here.

[Alejo shakes his head, eyes color-inverted by the infrared camera. He waves a hand through the air in front of him, clutching his chest with the other. Brandon tentatively approaches. He adjusts his spectacles and powers up a clunky device.]

BRANDON: What did it do? What did it feel like?

[Alejo is silent.]

BRANDON: Alejo?

[Alejo's grip tightens on the stitching of his cardigan. His eyelids flutter shut and he collapses against the wall.]

ALEJO: It went through me. God, it's so cold.

[Brandon takes Alejo's hands. The ThermoGeist Temperature Detection device flashes a startling shade of blue between their fingers, detecting an anomaly nearby. The two men look tenderly into each other's eyes.]

BRANDON: We'll survive. We've been through worse.

Logan scoffed and shoved another balled-up turtleneck into her suitcase. *We've been through worse.* She seriously doubted it. She'd seen every episode of this show, from the haunted windmill to the satanic rock museum to the toilet that doubled as a portal to hell, and this was the corniest one yet. *ParaSpectors* never shied from melodrama, but as the show crawled into its sixth season, these cheesy tear-jerker moments seemed to come every other episode. Logan wasn't sure if it was the network's idea or just her fathers' penchant for drama.

She pulled two packed suitcases from the pyramid of bags at her feet and walked them into the hallway. Other than Brandon and Alejo muttering back and forth on the TV, the house was quiet. Logan sulked back into her bedroom and stood at the second-story bay window. White morning sun glinted off the surface of the swimming pool. Beyond her backyard, sprawling geometric houses rolled down the valley one after the other. She pressed her fingertips to the window and closed her eyes.

She *really* didn't want to leave LA.

Behind her, boots crunched the loose popcorn kernels littering her carpet. Alejo Ortiz—*the* Alejo Ortiz of ghost-hunting fame—leaned against her bedroom door. Between his half-up black hair and lanky frame, he looked like he'd been plucked right from Logan's TV. He surveyed her luggage, holding his phone walkie-talkie style. The real Alejo held himself differently than the one on TV. He was quieter, less dramatic, always slouched like he was trying to hear a little clearer.

"The lady of the house is in good shape," Alejo said into his phone. He swept the popcorn kernels out of the doorway with the edge of his boot and raised a brow at Logan like the mess was their little secret. "We've got a few more suitcases to load up, then we can hit the road."

"Nice." Brandon's tinny voice crackled on the other end of the line. *"No bodies under the mattress?"*

Alejo chuckled. "The dirty clothes put up a fight, but we showed them who's boss."

Logan rolled her eyes and kept packing. The cheesy FaceTime chats had been a daily fixture for the last six months. Every year, when *ParaSpectors* wrapped shooting for the season, Brandon and Alejo flew straight home while the production team set off to scout newer, "spookier" locations. But this year, Brandon had different plans.

"How's Snakebite treating you?" Alejo asked.

"Same as always. It's like nothing's changed in thirteen years." Brandon cleared his throat. *"Except the snow. That's finally cleared up, though."*

Snakebite, the rural Oregon ranching town where Logan's fathers grew up, was the kind of place with no pictures on Google. It was a blip on the map, a tiny scratch of farmland torn into a sea of yellow hills. According to Brandon, it was the perfect place to film the next *ParaSpectors* season premiere. But what started as a week of location scouting turned into a month. The network threw the *ParaSpectors* wrap party for season six and Brandon wasn't there. Alejo celebrated his forty-second birthday alone. Logan graduated from high school and Brandon watched from a spotty FaceTime call. A month turned into six and Logan wondered if Brandon planned to *ever* come home.

She was no expert on location scouting, but she was pretty sure it didn't take six months for a single episode.

Something was off.

And then, last week, Alejo had announced that if Snakebite was keeping Brandon away, they would just take themselves to Snakebite. LA wasn't home by any means—they'd only been in this house for a few years—but she'd lived here longer than she'd lived anywhere else. Just as she'd gotten used to the city, it was being snatched away.

It *sucked.*

Logan put a hand on her hip. "If you're gonna stand here, can you help me move some of these?"

"Sure thing," Alejo said. "Hold your dad."

He passed his phone to Logan and grabbed a suitcase in each hand. Logan gave Brandon a brief glance; his short crop of dark hair was a bit more unruly than usual, but his thick-rimmed glasses and perpetual semi-frown were unchanged. He looked just as half dead as she remembered. He flashed a tense smile. *"Hey, you."*

"Hi."

"Enjoying summer vacation?"

Logan blinked. "It's not really vacation. I graduated. It's kinda just . . . summer."

"Right."

Logan stared at Brandon and Brandon stared back. She grasped for something else to say but came up blank. With anyone else, conversation came as easy as breathing, but with Brandon it was always harder. She glanced at the hallway, then back at Brandon. "I should help Dad."

She tossed the phone on her naked mattress and grabbed another handful of bags.

Brandon cleared his throat. *"The drive will be worth it. I forgot how scenic it is up here. Lots of space."*

"I'm super looking forward to seventeen hours of bluegrass on the way up," Logan groaned.

"Hey," Alejo snapped from the hallway. "Don't diss my music. And it's nineteen hours to Snakebite. We have time for show tunes, too."

"Even better."

Logan pictured Snakebite: big trucks, one-story houses, twangy country music thundering from every direction. She was sure her family was going to increase the queer population by 300 percent. It would be just like the hundreds of other small towns she'd been to growing up. Until she was fourteen, their little family hadn't actually "lived" anywhere. They'd been creatures of the road, setting up camp in town after town while Brandon and

Alejo busted ghosts and channeled the dead for small change. And while Brandon and Alejo peddled their services, Logan was by herself. From one motel room to the next, she was always alone.

That was the thing with the Ortiz-Woodleys. Even after her dads made it big with *ParaSpectors,* even after they bought the LA house for "stability," even after Logan settled in and went to a public school for the first time in her life, it was like one extended base camp. Even if Alejo and Brandon promised that Snakebite was only temporary, packing up and leaving LA was a reminder that this had never been home.

Logan knew better than to think any of this was permanent.

"When do you think you'll head out?" Brandon's muffled voice asked.

"I'd say we're about ready," Alejo said. He scanned the room for his phone, raising a brow at Logan when he spotted it on the bed.

"Is it too late to run?" Logan nudged her backpack with the side of her boot. "I've got granola bars and fizzy water in here. I think I could make it in the wilderness."

"The wilderness of West Hollywood?" Alejo scooped his phone from the mattress and turned to face the TV. "God, I wish you wouldn't watch these."

BRANDON VOICEOVER: With Alejo down for the count, I'm forced to continue the investigation on my own. I use the SonusX to detect any ghostly voices in the basement.

BRANDON: Spirit, we're not here to hurt you. Please don't attack us. Don't attack my husband. We're here to help you move on.

GHOSTLY VOICE: Who are you that disturbs me?

BRANDON: Brandon Woodley.

[Brandon kneels beside Alejo, placing a hand on his shoulder.]

BRANDON: And my husband, Alejo Ortiz. We're here to—

"Okay, off," Logan said. She snatched the remote and turned off the TV.

In only a few trips, she and Alejo moved the last of the suitcases to the minivan in the driveway. Alejo tucked his phone into the back pocket of his jeans, Brandon's hairline just visible on a sliver of the screen. In the summer sun, the lime-green *ParaSpectors* logo tattooed on the side of the van was almost blinding.

Alejo slammed the trunk closed and slapped the top of the van in classic dad style. "All packed. Logan, any last words for your dad before we rock 'n' roll?"

He extended the phone to her and the screen lit up expectantly.

Logan leaned in close. "See you in nineteen hours."

Alejo took the phone back and walked to the other side of the van. Quietly, he asked, "Have you found anything else?"

"Not yet," Brandon sighed. *"There's, uh . . . People are getting nervous.* I'm *getting nervous. The timing isn't ideal."*

Logan narrowed her eyes.

Outside the van, Alejo nodded. He whispered something

unintelligible into the phone, then turned the screen to face Logan. "Well, as our extremely eloquent child said, see you in nineteen hours."

"Love you," Brandon said, though it wasn't clear if he meant both of them or just Alejo.

"Love you, too," Alejo said. With a half smile, he ended the call.

Logan shuffled through her phone and queued up nineteen hours of her favorite podcast before slumping into the passenger seat. Alejo pocketed his phone and climbed behind the wheel.

Once they were situated, he sighed. "So, before we take off, I feel like I need to clear the air. Snakebite isn't like LA. They're . . . *insular* is a good word for it. When we get there, we have to remember that family's the most important thing."

Logan blinked. "Okay? We've been to small towns before."

"Yeah, but this is a little different. I know things aren't always easy with you and your dad, but in Snakebite it's really important that we all try to get along."

Logan gave a dismissive hand-wave. "What're they gonna do, send a mob after us?"

Alejo frowned. He turned the ignition and backed the van out of the driveway without offering an answer. The hazy morning sky opened up behind the house, blue-green and bright as freshwater. Logan thumped her head back against the seat.

"It's gonna be tough, but it's only a few months," Alejo said. "Just . . . try to have fun."

"I will try my *very* best."

Logan stuck her earbuds in and turned the volume high enough to drown out the van's stammering engine. Alejo was right—Snakebite would be just a few months. Just another spot on the map. Like LA, it would be just another base camp on the road.

But this time was different. In a few months, she'd be eighteen and she could go wherever she wanted. In a few months, she could pack up all her things and set out to find a place that was real. Somewhere that would last longer than just "a while." A *home.* Snakebite was just another stop on the road, but for her, it would be the last one. Alejo pulled the van around the corner and the sharp angles of the LA house disappeared. Logan closed her eyes.

It was a few months, and then she'd find a place she could call home.

2

A Viking Send-Off

"I appreciate you putting this together, Ashley. It's beautiful." Mrs. Granger gripped her husband's wrist and dabbed at her smudged eyeliner with a wadded Kleenex. "Tristan would have loved it."

The sun was high over Snakebite Memorial, cutting jagged shadows across the yellow grass. The weird thing about the cemetery, Ashley thought, was that it actually had the best view in town. The hills around Snakebite were rugged and misshapen, shadowed by passing clouds and golden with clusters of dry dirt and rabbitbrush. At the base of the hill, blue-green Lake Owyhee met the gravelly shore and twisted on for as far as she could see. It didn't seem fair that the only people with a view like this were the ones who couldn't take it in.

But maybe you *had* to die to see the valley like this.

Tristan Granger wouldn't see it. He had no body to bury.

"I hope it helps," Ashley said. She pulled her black cardigan tight around her chest to block out the wind. "I just thought if

Tristan knew we were still looking for him, maybe he'd come home."

Mrs. Granger nodded. "I hope you're right."

A stand at the front of the vigil held a photo of Tristan for everyone to see. It was Ashley's favorite picture of him—unkempt sandy blond hair, a ratty black hoodie, and the same basketball shorts he'd worn every day since freshman year. His chin rested on his hands, his smile easy and warm. The picture would be cheesy if it was anyone else, but nothing looked cheesy on Tristan. Ever.

Today marked six months since Tristan's disappearance. Five months since the application deadline for the University of Oregon closed. Three months since Owyhee County police stopped looking for a person and started looking for a body. A month and a half since Tristan missed his high school graduation. One month since Sheriff Paris had called the disappearance of Tristan Granger a cold case.

Today was their four-year anniversary.

Ashley tried not to think about that.

"You two were so good. I know he loved you," Mrs. Granger said. "You've got your mom's spirit, though. I wish I was that strong."

Ashley said nothing and looked across the vigil. Tammy Barton stood at the refreshments table with a plastic cup of lemon water in hand, gently managing several conversations at once. It wasn't the first time today someone had compared Ashley to her mother, but each time she was reminded of how untrue the comparison was. Tammy's expression was a careful balance of warmth and grief, her stance inviting and solemn all at once. Ashley wished she had even half her mother's poise.

As if on cue, Tammy turned and caught her gaze. She made her way from the refreshments and delicately placed a hand on Ashley's shoulder, softening her practiced smile into a small, sympathetic frown for Tristan's parents. "Greg, Susan, I'm so sorry about all this. You know we're praying for you and your family every day."

"Tammy," Mrs. Granger said. "Thank you for everything."

By *everything,* Susan Granger meant money. Whatever Tammy Barton couldn't provide in emotional support, she made up for tenfold in financial support. Over the last decade, Barton Ranch had almost completely taken over Owyhee County. The vigil, the food, the decorations—it was all on Ashley's mother's tab. Tammy reached out and took Mrs. Granger's hand. "We were practically family. I wish there was something I could do."

"There's nothing *you* can do," Mr. Granger said. His gaze shifted to Sheriff Paris, who stood alone at the front of the vigil, quietly eyeing Tristan's photo. "There's something he could do, though."

"Frank is doing everything he can with the evidence he has, Greg." Tammy put a hand on his shoulder. "People can point fingers all they want, but he has to prove it."

Ashley grimaced. Since Tristan's disappearance, she'd had this exact conversation a thousand times. The vigil was supposed to be a time to just think about Tristan, but even here, people only wanted to talk about Brandon Woodley. Until a few months ago, Ashley had never heard of the Snakebite-resident-turned-TV-ghosthunter, but the moment he arrived in town, it was like everyone forgot how to breathe. Like everyone forgot how to talk about anyone else.

Some of the suspicion made sense. Brandon Woodley was apparently here to film an episode of his show, but he refused to tell anyone what mystery he was here investigating. He hadn't brought any cameras or crew. As far as Ashley could tell, he'd just been wandering around Snakebite for the last six months with no intention of leaving. That might not make waves somewhere else, but Snakebite wasn't the kind of town where people lingered. In Snakebite, you were either fleeting or permanent. People who came to town always left, and people who left didn't come back.

Except Brandon Woodley. According to her mother, Brandon had been gone for almost thirteen years and no one had paid him a single thought since the day he left. He was an unknown entity—a ghost from a version of Snakebite that existed before Ashley. Just the thought of him made Ashley uneasy.

And then, a week after his return, Tristan vanished.

"I'm gonna get some water," Ashley said.

"Careful, the lemons aren't great. I think they might be old," Tammy said. She gave Ashley's shoulder a single pat.

Across the service, Fran Campos and Bug Gunderson chatted quietly. Ashley drifted toward them and it felt as if she were finally coming to shore. Everyone else here was bent on asking her a thousand questions about Tristan—*When was the last time you saw him? Did he say where he was going? Did he ever mention Brandon Woodley?*—but Fran and Bug were better than that. They were her best friends and the only comfort she'd had in the last six months, like twin beacons in a night that refused to end.

Fran spotted Ashley and pulled her into a tight hug, honey-colored curls bobbing at her slender shoulders. Bug hovered behind them with a glass of lemonade clutched between her fingers. Her freckle-smattered face was distant, her little mouth a frown, eyes trained on the lake.

"Say the word and we can go," Fran said. She tucked a wisp of Ashley's hair behind her ear. "You don't have to stay the whole time."

"I kind of do." Ashley squished a dandelion under the toe of her black flat. "It would look weird if I left, since I planned it."

"Yeah, you planned it, so they already owe you."

Ashley groaned. "I can't just—"

She was interrupted by a car door slamming at the base of the hill. A white minivan was parked haphazardly at the side of the valley highway with one tire on the road and the other sunken into the gravel shoulder. Ashley couldn't quite read the lime-green writing on the side of the van, but she was almost positive it involved a cartoonish drawing of a ghost. A lanky man with brown skin and dark hair stepped out of the car, stretching his arms to the sky. He leaned into the passenger window, muttered a few words, and ambled to the gated dirt patch at the bottom of the road with a fistful of lilies.

Ashley had lived in Snakebite her entire life, but she'd never seen someone visit Pioneer Cemetery on purpose. Where Snakebite Memorial was a rolling hilltop of gold grass and neat headstones, Pioneer Cemetery at the bottom of the hill was nothing but mounds of gray dirt over unnamed bodies. It was a historical landmark, a dedication to those who died on the Oregon Trail more than anything else. A stone slab stood at the front of the lot with an approximation of who was buried there—*Gunderson Baby, Mattison Girl, Anderson Boy*—but no one really knew who they were. Anyone who belonged to Snakebite was buried at the top of the hill, beneath supple lawns, facing the wide-open valley.

The man knew exactly where he was going, though. He strode past the stone key and approached a mound of dirt somewhat isolated from the rest. He paused there, eyes closed in a silent prayer, before gently laying the flowers over the dirt.

The graves were only names without memory, but the man mourned.

It twisted in Ashley's stomach like a knot.

"Who's that?" Bug asked.

She wasn't looking at the grave or the lilies or the mystery man. Ashley traced Bug's gaze back to the parked van. A girl had climbed out of the passenger seat and now stood in the road, propped against the car door to pop her back. Ashley tried to get a better look, but the girl's face was half obscured by a pair of overlarge sunglasses. Her hair was a shoulder-length straight crop with the black sheen of crow feathers. Even from a distance, it reflected the thin sunlight overhead.

"This is so rude," Fran said. She folded her arms over her chest. "Not really the time for a pit stop."

"I don't think it's a pit stop," Ashley said. She watched the man at the grave. His posture was solemn; it was grief. "Maybe he knows someone buried there?"

"Who?"

Ashley shrugged. "I don't know."

"It's like they don't even realize there's a funeral up here," Fran said.

Ashley gritted her teeth at *funeral.*

Around them, there was silence. The sound of the crowd mingling was gone, replaced by the hushed hissing of the wind.

The rest of the vigil had stopped talking and joined them at the edge of the cemetery, peering down the hillside at the newcomers with an eerie sort of knowing. It was like Brandon Woodley's arrival all over again. The silence was pointed like a weapon. These strangers weren't strangers at all.

They were enemies.

The girl on the road noticed the crowd. She stiffened and stared up the hillside, frozen for a moment like an animal who'd just realized she was on display. She called something to the man at the grave then quickly clambered back into the van.

The man turned and looked up the hill, but he was unfazed. He looked at the crowd like it was a challenge. Like he dared someone to say something. The man's face was familiar. Ashley was sure she'd seen him before.

The man remained in the cemetery for a few more moments before wordlessly making his way back to the van. The strangers pulled away from the highway shoulder and puttered south toward Snakebite itself.

"Well, there's a face I didn't expect."

Sheriff Paris stood next to Ashley, but he wasn't talking to her. His uneasy smile was aimed at her mother.

Tammy pursed her lips. "Yeah."

"Who was that?" Ashley asked.

Paris and her mother eyed each other. After a moment, her mother shook her head. "We'll talk about it later."

Whispers erupted around them and Ashley felt sick. This was all wrong; the vigil was supposed to be about Tristan. It was supposed to be a way to bring him home. Even if everyone here thought he was dead, Ashley knew he wasn't. She could still feel him here, like there was a line connecting them. Wherever he was, he just needed someone to find him. He just needed someone to bring him home.

"Mrs. Granger," Ashley said, sharp enough to cut through the crowd. "I know you asked everyone to bring a memory of Tristan. I think we should share now."

For a moment, all eyes turned to her. The morning smelled like soil and hurt, and the inside of Ashley's mouth was swollen with unspent tears. The crowd slowly gathered around Tristan's photo. Shakily, Ashley pulled a notecard from the pocket of her dress.

Before she could speak, Sheriff Paris cleared his throat.

"Ashley," he said, "I hope you don't mind if I start us off."

Ashley blinked.

"Right. This isn't so much a memory as a promise. I know we're a pretty small town and when something happens to one of us, it happens to all of us. And I know it's easy for us to point fingers at people who're different." Sheriff Paris cleared his throat. His blond hair was bright and slick in the summer sun, eyes clear and blue as the sky behind him. "I love Tristan like he's my own kid. Even if we've officially called the case cold, I'm not done looking. I won't stop until we find him alive. I won't stop until he's home."

Ashley took her mother's hand. In front of her, Mr. and Mrs. Granger nodded solemnly. They had their problems with the investigation, but Sheriff Paris was right. He couldn't arrest someone on suspicion alone, and even if he could, arresting Brandon Woodley wouldn't solve Tristan's disappearance. No one wanted to find a killer—no one wanted Tristan dead. Ashley just wanted Tristan home.

Paris gave a tight-lipped frown and a terse nod, then motioned to Ashley.

"All yours."

Ashley took a deep breath. The crowd of people in the cemetery turned to face her. Ashley shakily held up her notecards and studied them. She'd practiced her speech all night in front of her bedroom mirror, but with dozens of eyes trained on her, the words suddenly felt far away.

This wasn't for the crowd. This was for Tristan.

"I hope you guys don't mind if I, uh . . . if I say something *to* him." Ashley looked up and caught her mother nodding at her. She cleared her throat. "Tristan, when we were in second grade, you asked me to marry you. You took me out to the field behind the track and made a ring out of dead grass. I turned you down because we were too young and because I said if I was gonna marry you, it had to be for real."

The crowd laughed softly at that. Cool lake wind brushed Ashley's ponytail across her back. She stared at the words on her notecard until they swam and she had to stitch the memory together.

"You didn't give up. That's how you are—you see the way things should be and you make them happen. You asked me to marry you again in third grade, fourth grade, fifth grade. In eighth grade, you compromised. You said we could just go to the spring social together. I would've said yes to you then, but my mom said I was too young to date."

Tammy Barton sheepishly raised her hand and took a long sip of lemon water.

"It didn't matter to us. We didn't have to be on a real date. I went to the dance with my best friend and had the night of my life. Freshman year, you asked me out to dinner. No marriage, no dances, just cheeseburgers and milkshakes. I sat in that booth across from you and we laughed for hours. You and me were just two people who already shared everything. It was the easiest thing we ever did."

Tears stung the corners of her eyes. It wasn't a memory, it was an ache. The memories were Tristan, but more than that, the memories were everything she was. Mrs. Granger pressed her face into her husband's shoulder. Sheriff Paris held his cap against his chest and looked at her, face steely with grief. Fran and Bug eyed her, wiping their faces.

Ashley closed her eyes.

"Some people might think you're never coming back, but the Tristan Granger I know would never give up. Snakebite is our home. This is where you and me started and it's where we'll end. So Tristan, wherever you are, please come home."

3

The Murder Hotel

In a sad but unsurprising turn of events, Alejo parked the mini-van outside a rundown motel. The sun glared through the front windshield as the van's humming engine finally puttered to sleep.

"Wow," Logan groaned. "The motel looks great. I feel like a kid again."

"You are a kid." Alejo gave her a look. "Your dad's waiting outside. *Please* smile when you see him."

Logan turned in her seat. Brandon Woodley, her second and all-around less effective father, waited for them in the center of the motel parking lot, hands shoved in his pockets as he paced the sun-bleached pavement.

A towering, rusted sign in the parking lot read BATES MO-TEL. The name was promising, though the motel wasn't nearly creepy enough on the outside. The marquee on the dilapidated office building flickered the word VACANCY; the NO looked like it'd never been lit. An abandoned pizza stand was squat in the center of the parking lot with its window permanently boarded up. The letter board simply read WELCOME TO THE BATES. COME HAVE A SLICE.

"My family," Brandon called, strolling toward the minivan like he'd spent the last six months at sea. "Together at last."

Alejo hopped out of the front seat and met Brandon halfway across the parking lot, pulling him into a hug so tight Logan was surprised it didn't break him in half. She thumped her head against the passenger seat and closed her eyes. Maybe she was being overdramatic. If she was, it was because she'd learned from the best. Brandon and Alejo looked into each other's faces like they hadn't seen each other in years, never mind the fact that they'd FaceTimed every night they were apart.

It was like they were back on TV; their reunion was one violin solo short of an Academy Award.

Logan paused her podcast and climbed out of the van. The sun felt hotter in Snakebite than in LA. It felt closer, as if it were only feet overhead. Logan patted the back of her neck with her sleeve to soak up the sweat. It was the kind of weather that would usually call for a dip in the pool, but Logan doubted she'd find one here. The Bates hardly seemed like the kind of motel that had *amenities*.

"I hope there's blood in the shower," Logan said. "They can't just waste a name like that."

Brandon looked over Alejo's shoulder and smiled uneasily at Logan. Surprisingly, he looked better than he had on FaceTime the day before. More awake. His dark brown stubble had lost its usual peppering of gray hair and his cheeks were fuller. He scrunched up his nose and cupped a hand over his brow to block out the sun.

Logan hadn't seen him look this alive in years.

It was unsettling.

Brandon scooted around Alejo and stood in front of Logan without offering a hug. His loose-fitting button-up was patterned with palm trees and pineapples that glared in the summer sun. He cleared his throat. "How's it been down south?"

"Boring," Logan said. "This is where we're living? I thought Oregon was supposed to be green."

"Oh, uh, yep. This part of Oregon is more like . . . well, it's kind of its own thing." Brandon motioned to a pair of doors on the inside corner of the motel's L-shape. "We're rooms seven and eight. The *deluxe* suites."

"Deluxe . . ." Logan muttered. She pulled off her sunglasses and cleaned them with the hem of her shirt. The outside of the motel was painted white, clouded with brown rust stains. The parking lot was half gravel and half pavement, riddled with potholes and the butts of used cigarettes. This wasn't the kind of place that people sought out, Logan guessed. It was more the kind of place where people crash-landed when they couldn't make it any farther down the road. She'd stayed at hundreds of these places over the years. At a certain point, they all blurred into one.

"I get my own room, right?"

"I don't know," Brandon said. "I thought the three of us sharing a room sounded fun. Like a nonstop sleepover."

Logan stared.

"He's joking," Alejo cut in. He joined their triangle and put an arm over Logan's shoulders, laughing the strained laugh of a man who'd just prevented a bloodbath. "Take the girl out of the city and she suddenly forgets what jokes are."

Logan offered a half-smile. She wished that Alejo didn't

always have to translate for them. Talking to Brandon was supposed to be easier than this. Before they sat her down for the *you're adopted* talk, she'd just assumed Alejo was her birth father. They had the same dark hair, the same sharp sense of humor, the same coolheadedness. Alejo had always made sure that, no matter where they were, Logan felt wanted. Even if she was alone.

But everywhere they went—Flagstaff, Shreveport, Tulsa—she was an afterthought. To Brandon, she was sure she was another ghost lingering just out of sight.

An elderly woman emerged from the office building of the motel, leaning on a knotted wooden cane. When her eyes locked on Alejo's, she melted. "Chacho, you better get over here."

"¡Ay, Viejita! Hermosa como siempre," Alejo cried. He bounded across the parking lot and gave the woman a kiss on both cheeks.

"Mentiroso," the woman said. "¿Que pasó, Chacho?"

Logan smiled, but it was strained. Alejo fell into Spanish so easily, but it'd never come naturally to her. Alejo had tried to teach her growing up, but thanks to the show, he was hardly around long enough to practice with her. It was always stilted for her. She shifted awkwardly from one foot to the other, suddenly untethered from the conversation and from Alejo. Next to her, Brandon was entirely tuned out. His gaze was miles away.

"And this is Logan," the woman said. It was a statement, not a question. She released Alejo and made her way to Logan, planting a firm kiss on her cheek. Her long ponytail was pepper-gray and streaked with silver. She wore a T-shirt that read THIS TOWN BITES BACK. "I've seen all the Facebook pictures, but she's even prettier in person."

Alejo smiled. "Logan, this is Gracia Carrillo. She's mi tía."

"Your daddy lived here when he was little," Gracia said, motioning to Alejo. "We told him to come back and visit whenever. I didn't think he'd wait until he was an old man."

Alejo scoffed.

Logan put on her best pleasure-to-meet-you smile and returned Gracia's hug. "Thanks so much for letting us stay here. It's beautiful."

"A liar, too." Gracia laughed. "Come with me. I'll show you your room."

While Brandon and Alejo started unloading suitcases from the van, Gracia led Logan to room 7. The door caught on the frame, knocking chips of white paint to the pavement. Inside, it was a standard motel room—hideously patterned wallpaper, matching queen-size beds, a mini fridge, a TV mounted on the long wall. A door connected her room to Brandon and Alejo's room. Not a feature she was particularly enthusiastic about, but the room was *fine*.

"Home sweet home," Gracia said. She gave the breakfast table a hearty slap. "You don't hate it too much, do you?"

"It's perfect," Logan lied. "Am I allowed to make changes?" Logan wasn't sure how long they planned to stay in Snakebite. She needed one of those TV makeover guys—the ones that her fathers referred to as the "bane of reality TV"—to bring her aesthetic to life.

"Of course."

Quietly, Gracia stepped inside and closed the bedroom door. She peeked through the curtains at Brandon and Alejo, who were only halfway through the unloading process, then turned to face Logan. "I'm so happy you and your dad are finally here. Happy the three of you are together again. I think Brandon has been very . . . lonely."

Logan arched a brow.

"He wanders around here all day. He's always gone at night. I sit there all the time and wonder what he's doing. People ask me what made him come back here. I tell them I don't know."

"Location scouting." Logan inspected her nailbeds. "For the show."

"Uh-huh. That's what he told me. I thought you might know something else." Gracia smiled, warm and bright. "It doesn't matter anyway. People might not be happy to see the three of you here, but I—"

Logan squinted. "What do you mean they're not happy?"

She thought of the crowd at the funeral, gathered like crows at the edge of the hill, silently staring down at her. It'd been so eerie she almost thought she'd imagined it. They'd looked at her like she was trespassing. Like she'd stumbled into their town from outer space.

Gracia waved a hand. "I have been wishing your dad would come home since the day he left."

Dad. *Singular.*

Maybe Brandon was a mystery to Gracia, too. If she'd hoped to get the inside scoop, she'd picked the wrong source. Logan had spent years trying to get some kernel of truth out of Brandon. Gracia wasn't the only one who found it easier to talk to Alejo.

"Can I ask you something?" Logan asked. "I saw a funeral on the way into town."

"Oh." Gracia's voice was sharp. "It's their service for the Granger boy."

Logan perked up. When she'd asked Alejo what exactly they were investigating in Snakebite, his answers were vague at best. *The usual stuff—dead crops, cold spots, strange noises.* A dead kid was the kind of creepy small-town thing he should've mentioned. She leaned forward and propped her chin on her fist. "How'd he die?"

"He's not dead, just missing," Gracia clarified. "He probably ran away. Anyone you ask around here will tell you he was a good boy. They don't think he would leave like that. The group he ran with, though . . . they're not nice kids. They're all rotten."

Logan was silent.

"I hope he's alive," Gracia continued, "but a part of me hopes they don't find him. If they finally lose one of those kids, maybe they'll stop acting so high and mighty."

Logan blinked. Gracia's expression wasn't warm anymore, but Logan couldn't figure out what it was. The way the people at the vigil had looked at her like she was arriving by UFO, and now this strange, whispered blood feud. Something was wrong here, and not in the usual small-town way.

Outside, Logan could just make out her fathers' voices.

"You want my advice? Ease up on the jokes."

"*You* always joke with her. Why can't I?"

Logan turned away from Gracia and peered out the window through the blinds. Alejo pulled a suitcase from the back seat of the minivan and tossed it onto the pile in the parking lot. Brandon stood next to him, fiddling with the latch on one of his bags. His expression was hard to parse—maybe embarrassment, maybe discomfort. He looked more out of place than usual, like the sun and the hills and the wide-open sky somehow disagreed with him.

Alejo paused and wiped sweat from his brow. "It's just the three of us now. Just family. Everything's gonna be okay."

"You know I was never good at that."

"At what?"

"Being okay."

Alejo laughed, short and tense.

Gracia stood at Logan's back and put a hand on her shoulder, silver-gray brow furrowed as she watched Brandon unpack. She watched him like the crowd at the vigil watched them. Like she wanted to disassemble him just to study his parts.

Alejo spotted them through the blinds and rolled his eyes. "What was it you said back home? If you're gonna just stand there, can you at least help?"

"We're just catching up, Chacho," Gracia said loud enough for Alejo to hear. She gave Logan a single squeeze on the shoulder and, quieter, said, "Go help your dads. And if you ever need to talk, remember I'm in room two."

Logan swallowed and nodded. Gracia left the motel room and Logan was alone with nothing but the sputtering air conditioner and the quiet. Just like every other motel on the road, she would get used to these walls. She would get used to the silence, to the absurd heat, to the loneliness. But there was something different about Snakebite. She'd spent years tuning out Brandon and Alejo's "mysteries," but something about this one tugged at her. It begged her to dig deeper.

It didn't matter. Even if there was something different in this town—something *wrong*—it was only a few months. She'd spent years enduring places like this.

This wasn't a home. It was just another place, and she would survive it.

4

Into the Wild Abyss

Ashley Barton had lost people before.

When Tristan first disappeared, all of Snakebite thought they were detectives. Everyone could've sworn they'd *just* seen him; Mrs. Alberts from homeroom saw him down at the lake, Debbie who ran the Laundromat said Tristan came and picked up his mom's linens just that afternoon, Jared from the gas station drove past Tristan playing catch with his little brother. All forty-three students at Owyhee County High joined the search parties. Finding Tristan seemed inevitable to Ashley at first—there were only so many places a kid from Snakebite could go. Up until a month ago, the search parties had been going strong. But once Sheriff Paris declared the case cold, the parties began to dwindle. Now, a week after the vigil with no new leads, Ashley doubted this could go on much longer. Soon, she'd be the only one left looking. She tried to stamp down the desperation in her chest.

Ashley made it to the parking lot outside the Lake Owyhee campground at half past five in the morning, armed with a travel mug of hibiscus tea and her best walking shoes. The sun was minutes from breaking the horizon, warming the dark sky with a hazy pink glow. Sheriff Paris stood in the center of the parking lot with a map of the Lake Owyhee wilderness splayed over the hood of his police cruiser.

"Morning," Ashley said, stifling a yawn. "It might be just me today."

Paris shook his head. "John was just brushing his teeth when I left the house. He'll be here with the rest of your pack any minute."

Ashley took a long drink of tea. Gray mist sat low on the water, obscuring the woods across the lake. They'd searched the area around town three times over, but the other side of the lake was untouched. A strange, cloying dread churned in her chest when she looked at the trees across the shore. She was sure something was there. It watched her, dark and hungry and waiting. Some mornings, she heard a low hum that seemed to echo through Snakebite. Bug and Fran swore they didn't hear it, but even now, if Ashley closed her eyes it was there.

She focused on Paris.

"The vigil kinda felt like a funeral." Ashley twisted the end of her ponytail between her fingers. "I was worried people would stop showing up to these."

"Do *you* feel like he's gone?" Paris asked.

Ashley pressed her lips together. She couldn't explain *what* she felt. Some days, it was like the memory of him followed her just out of sight. She'd thought it was grief—conversations where she swore she heard him answer, the faint smell of diesel fuel right before she fell asleep, the constant anticipation that she would see him standing on his front yard mowing the lawn when she drove past. She'd felt grief when her grandma died, when they'd put down her first cat, when her father left town when she was in the first grade and never came back. This was different. She'd never felt this kind of longing before. It was like Tristan was standing next to her. She thought of him and a sadness filled her up, deeper and colder than any she'd ever felt. It was a sadness that breathed. It wasn't final.

"No," Ashley said.

"That's what I wanna hear." Sheriff Paris checked his phone. "Other people might give up, but you kids still care about him. That's what'll help you find him. And as long as I've got mornings off, I'll be out here, too."

"Thanks."

Down the highway, an engine roared. John Paris pulled into the campground parking lot with Fran, Bug, and his best friend, Paul Thomas, crouched in the bed of his truck. Like usual, the five of them gathered around Sheriff Paris's map for a rundown of the ground they'd be searching, and like usual, they split into two groups to cover more ground. For weeks, it'd been John and Paul in one group and the three girls in the other.

This time, Fran immediately latched onto John's arm. "I feel like we should mix it up. See if we come up with something new."

There was no arguing with Fran, so Ashley and Bug trekked into the hills beyond the campground alone. Once they were far enough up the steep incline of the nearest hill, Bug let out a sigh like she'd been holding her breath since she arrived. She plopped down on a rock and tied her hair into a bushy red ponytail. "She's being weird, right?"

"Fran?" Ashley asked.

Bug nodded. Ashley cupped her hand over her brow and

looked out at the next hill over. Fran and John walked side by side, playfully shoving each other back and forth while Paul tagged along behind them. They weren't searching for Tristan; they weren't searching for anything but a way to lose the third wheel.

"She likes him," Ashley said. "It's whatever. I wish she wouldn't use searches to flirt."

"You could say something."

"So could you."

Bug ran her heel through a loose patch of gravel. "But you're better at it. She'd probably listen to you."

"She'd listen to you, too."

"She *never* listens to me," Bug groaned.

Ashley tightened her ponytail. "I'll talk to her later. Maybe."

They both knew she wouldn't say anything. Ashley had been friends with Bug since she was in diapers and Fran since the Camposes moved to Snakebite in first grade. There weren't a lot of other kids her age in town, which meant that knowing everyone was a default. But as soon as Fran came to town, their trio was so much more than friends by default. They were a three-headed beast. There was no Ashley without Fran and Bug. Every party at the cabin across the lake, every summer road trip, every greasy dinner at the Moontide—it wasn't Snakebite without Bug and Fran by her side. It wasn't home.

Now, things were changing. It wasn't just Tristan. Fran was drifting away, hanging at John Paris's side, finding ways to be alone with him. Which left Bug either jealous of John, jealous of Fran, or jealous of some combination of the two. Ashley was sure there was a piece of Bug that wanted to fuse them all together and stop the drifting before it stuck, but it wasn't that easy. College was on the horizon for Fran, and the ranch was on the horizon for Ashley. Bug still had two more years of high school, and she was looking at facing them alone. Quietly, the three of them were pulling apart. It wasn't anyone's fault. It was just time. Maybe that was worse.

Ashley looked across the hilltops at Fran and John. They'd successfully broken away from Paul, tucked behind a lone juniper tree, apparently under the impression that no one could see them. The early morning sunlight caught them there and Ashley felt a pang of longing in her stomach. She and Tristan had stolen moments like this before, ducked just out of sight. When she closed her eyes, Ashley could still hear the raspy sound of their breathless laughter.

When she opened her eyes, something was different. There was a third shadow with John and Fran. Ashley narrowed her eyes. It was another face, wedged just between them, staring across the hills. Staring at Ashley.

The world was too calm, too still, too silent.

A voice breathed in her ear. *"I am—"*

"Ashley," Bug said.

The world snapped back into focus. Ashley blinked and the shadow between John and Fran was gone. The morning was as wide and bright as it always was. Ashley's heart raced, her lungs aching for air. It was just her imagination, but for a moment, she had been sure the shadow was shaped like Tristan.

"Sorry," Ashley said, rubbing her eyes. "I spaced out for a second. I . . . I think I'm just tired."

Bug gave her a sympathetic frown. "I have some of my mom's melatonin if you wanna try that."

"I'm okay," Ashley said. "Thanks, though."

The morning rolled on, but they found nothing. Ashley and Bug scoured their assigned area, turning over every rock, rifling through every cluster of Scotch broom, checking every dusty ravine, but Ashley knew without searching that Tristan wasn't in these hills. She knew the sound of his heartbeat, the pattern of his footsteps, the small *hush* of his breath when he was about to speak. If he was this close, she would feel him.

He was just out of her reach, but he still *was.*

He still existed.

He wasn't gone yet.

5

Eat The Blues

A knock sounded from the door between Logan's room and her fathers'.

She'd successfully converted her bed into a comforter cocoon, surrounded by an array of her favorite depression snacks. Most hardships only called for one: embarrassment was chips dipped in pickle juice, anger was vanilla ice cream drizzled with soy sauce, and loneliness was bananas covered in Cheez Whiz.

But tonight was a true rock bottom. Tonight required all three.

"Come in," Logan groaned.

She minimized her tab of US road trip ideas and clicked off the TV. They walked into the room—Alejo with Brandon at his heels—to survey the damage. The motel room was stuffy and hot with the smell of mold and sweat.

"The holy trinity all at once, huh?" Alejo whispered, eyeing the snack buffet. He sat on her mattress and popped a slice of Cheez Whiz banana into his mouth. Instantly, his nose wrinkled up and he forced himself to swallow. "Kids today have no standards."

"I have standards," Logan said.

"We heard Judy through the walls," Alejo said. "Judy *reruns.* And don't tell me the plot sucked you in. You and me already watched them all."

Logan flopped back against her pillow and the stifling scent of dust clouded up around her. "We're in the middle of nowhere with a bunch of MAGA hat–wearers. Everyone is creepy and weird and I don't wanna leave my room. But also my room sucks. I'm literally gonna die."

She'd only been in Snakebite for a week and already felt like she was in the vacuum of space. There was nothing to *do* here. The walls of her room were too close. Her mattress was too hard. The night sky outside her room was too big and she was sure she'd fall into it if she wasn't careful. She was going to suffocate here without people to talk to. The next closest town was hours away and probably just as bad. She was miles from help, and tonight Logan felt every mile like fingers closing around her throat.

"I did tell you it was gonna be hard," Alejo said. He brushed a strand of Logan's hair from her face.

"Why are we here?" Logan asked.

Alejo and Brandon looked at each other with identical half-frowns. It was a kind of telepathic communication that Logan had never been privy to, even back in LA. Even crammed in this tiny motel together, she was stuck on the outside. They didn't mean to shut her out, yet here she was.

"We're here to help people," Alejo said.

"I thought we were here for the show."

"We are," Alejo said. "And the show is gonna help people."

"How?"

Brandon adjusted his glasses. "I know you might not believe in what we do, but there are things wrong with this town. You can feel it, right? Even when your dad and I were kids, things were wrong. Now we're here to figure it out."

"Is it the missing kid?"

"I don't know."

"No offense," Logan said, "but you guys never *solve* anything."

Brandon grimaced. "This is different. It's personal."

"That sounds so creepy."

"Not creepy." Alejo laughed. "More like you grow up in a place and think it's normal because it's all you've ever known. We never really planned to come back, but with everything we've learned since leaving, we thought we might be able to do some good here. It'll be like saying a real goodbye, anyway."

"Okay," Logan said.

Alejo squeezed her hand. "I promise, that's all it is."

Behind Alejo, Brandon looked at his hands.

"I wish you left me in LA," Logan said.

Alejo pulled Logan into a hug. "I know it sucks. We can't leave, but your dad and I will do whatever we can to make it better."

Logan burrowed deeper in her comforter. The patterned floral wallpaper, the '70s wooden tables, the chipped crosshatch ceiling, the buzzing fluorescents—it was going to drive her crazy. She cast her arm over her forehead dramatically. "I need art or something. String lights. New pillows."

Alejo eyed Brandon and nodded. "Decorations. We can do that."

He lay back against the pillows alongside Logan. On the end of the bed, Brandon sat up straight. He eyed them wistfully and Logan thought he looked so lonely it hurt. He leaned in for a moment like he meant to lie down next to them but couldn't. This was how it always went. He was always simultaneously here and a thousand miles away. She'd seen him make this face more times than she could count, and it felt like this every time.

"Hey," Alejo whispered. He reached for Brandon's hand.

Brandon stood and offered a pained smile. "It's getting late. I'm gonna turn in for the night. You're better night owls than me."

Alejo said nothing. The door between rooms shut behind Brandon, and the two of them were left in an uneasy quiet. Logan cleared her throat. It wasn't too late to make an appeal. "I feel like we don't *have* to stay here."

"No. We don't."

Alejo's sweater rustled as he sank deeper into the mattress. Getting him to admit even that was a small victory. Alejo's palm was pressed over his eyes, lips pressed in a taut frown.

Logan sat up. "Then what are we doing here? Like, *really?*"

"What do you mean?" Alejo asked.

"It's been six months. What are you still trying to figure out?"

"Sometimes," Alejo sighed, "it's not about figuring things out. It's about being a family. Your dad's been dealing with this place all alone. The least we can do is come here and support him."

"Oh yeah, because he's been super supportive of us."

It was the wrong thing to say. Alejo stared at the ceiling with a difficult expression. After a moment, he rolled over and pushed himself from the bed. As if to reassure her he wasn't mad, he smiled, but it was mournful.

"It'll look good in here with the string lights," Alejo said. "Maybe we'll go shopping tomorrow."

Logan nodded. It was like she was drowning, but these weren't waters she'd ever been in with Alejo. He wasn't Brandon—they'd never had this wall of silence between them. She wanted to ask why Brandon had been here for so long. She wanted to ask about the missing boy. She wanted to beg him to leave.

Instead, she said, "Good night, Dad."

Interlude

The Dark is not a monster.

It simply is.

It enjoys this world and its sorrows. It tastes the tang of fear on the wind. It has seen great and shining cities by the sea, lush forests absent of human life, deserts so wide they turn horizons to gold. But it likes Snakebite best of all. Snakebite is where the Dark was born. Snakebite is the Dark's home.

The Dark is hungry tonight.

It is starving.

The host sits alone. He often sits alone, silently oscillating between guilt and apathy. The TV is on as it always is, playing a sports game that the host does not watch. The host cannot watch. He thinks about blood between his fingers. He thinks about the sounds of strangled gasps and crunching bones. These things didn't used to plague the host's thoughts, but now death is the only thing on his mind. Not fear of death, but desire for it.

The host needs death like he needs air to breathe.

You want it, don't you? the Dark whispers to the host when they are alone. *You're strong, but not strong enough. Why not do what you want?*

The host winces. "I will. Later. People are still scared."

It's been plenty of time, the Dark breathes. Its voice gusts through the room like a warm breeze. *No one is looking anymore. No one cares. They have moved on. The same will be true of the next.*

The host leans back in his chair. He doesn't like being pressured like this, but the Dark has waited long enough for him to strike. It grows weaker with each passing day. It ebbs and flows in the shadows, swimming to stay alive while its useless host sits around and *thinks.*

"What're you getting from this?" the host asks. He kicks his feet up on the coffee table and closes his eyes. "Is this making you stronger?"

It has nothing to do with me, the Dark reminds him. *I came to you because* you *need help. Hosts before you have been too afraid to understand what I offer. Do not run away from yourself.*

The host looks at his hands.

This is only temporary, the Dark says. *As I told you in the beginning, when you have the strength to stand on your own, I will leave you. When your heart tells you what it wants and you no longer hesitate to act, you will not need me.*

The host likes this idea. He imagines himself roaming the country on a spree, too smart to be caught. He imagines news stations decrying his actions, horrified and fascinated by him in equal measure. He imagines the news articles written about him, trying to understand how he did it; how he got away with it. The Dark's claws are sunken so deep into him he cannot feel them there. The host makes a contemplative click with his tongue. "What if you want me to do something I don't wanna do?"

Impossible. I can only want what you want. That is my nature. The Dark encases the host—he feels its warmth and is comforted. *For as long as you carry me, I* am *you. I can be nothing more.*

The host clears his throat. "Partners, then."

Partners, the Dark agrees. To a certain extent, the host is not wrong. They *are* partners. The Dark presses into him, pulling at the piece of his heart that aches to strike again. Beneath his skin he is a viper, and vipers are not meant to spend their days waiting. The Dark breathes, *Shall we do it again?*

The host smiles.

6

Country Roads

When Logan imagined a shopping trip, this wasn't what she pictured: cramming into Brandon's rented Dodge Neon, peeling her knees from the dash in the boiling heat, puttering down Main Street to find a dinky antique shop that just happened to sell some art. Since arriving in Snakebite, Logan had learned that the center of town was the farthest a person could get from a McDonald's in the contiguous US, the town proper was a whopping 1.5 square miles, and the nearest *anything* meant it was at least two hours away in Idaho.

Satan himself couldn't create a more perfect hell.

Brandon stayed quiet on the drive into town, eyes fixed on the flat gold hills that rolled out on both sides of the valley. It'd been years since they went anywhere without Alejo along to mediate. Given the months they'd been apart, Alejo apparently thought a trip into town—just Logan and Brandon—might generate some warmth between them. Maybe Alejo didn't know them as well as he thought.

Brandon had one hand on the wheel while the other hung

out the driver's side window, carelessly ducking under and over the current of the wind. Without turning, he asked, "When was the last time it was just us?"

Without hesitation, Logan said, "Tulsa. When I was on the show."

"Ah," Brandon said. He adjusted the square black sunglasses that sat over his regular glasses. "That's right."

That's right. Logan tried not to let the cool carelessness in his voice creep under her skin. To Brandon, Tulsa was just another spot on the road. It probably didn't weigh on him like it did on her, hanging heavy in the silence between them. It probably didn't linger at the back of his thoughts every time he closed his eyes. He probably didn't see it like she did—the brick-walled tunnel under the city, the smell of garbage and fried food, the flat horizon that felt like everywhere and nowhere all at once.

She'd only been allowed on *ParaSpectors* once in her life, and Brandon had made sure the opportunity never came up again. Maybe she'd asked too many questions, been too annoying, or maybe he'd just never wanted her there in the first place. At night, when it was quiet enough for Logan's thoughts to really run wild, she could still hear his voice echo like a thunderclap from the alley walls. She pictured the way Brandon turned to her, stare full to the brim with hate, and said, *Get out, Logan. Go home and leave me alone.*

And then nothing. He stared until the production team swarmed in, offered Brandon a water, a moment to sit, asked if he wanted to start over on the episode. They'd led Logan away from the set, back to the motel, and said, *That was weird. Maybe another time.*

After that, it was radio silence between them. He didn't say a word to her the entire week they filmed in Flagstaff. In Shreveport, he booked a room in a different motel so he wouldn't have to be around her. Logan couldn't wrap her head around how casually he'd moved on like the hurt didn't rot under his skin. Brandon hadn't spent sleepless nights scrolling through *ParaSpectors* forums, reading speculations about why Logan Ortiz-Woodley never returned to the show.

- **She probably annoyed the shit out of them**
- **No one wants to babysit a whiny kid when they're working**
- **Bralejo is perfect. Adding a kid would just make it weird**

For years, Logan had craved an explanation. Some kind of apology for the outburst and the subsequent silence. She'd expected Brandon to at least say it was an accident, it had been a long day, he was nervous without Alejo, he'd directed his anger at her on accident.

But Brandon had said nothing.

Even now, gliding along flat roads to nowhere, Brandon said nothing. Mired in humid, uncomfortable silence, he said nothing. Maybe he kept her at arm's length on purpose, just waiting until she was eighteen so he could get rid of her for good. Maybe he wanted it to be just him and Alejo again. Maybe he'd regretted adopting her the whole time. Before Tulsa, their relationship had already been awkward and distant. But after, Logan had stopped trying to fix it. If Brandon didn't care, Logan wouldn't, either. She would live her life, and he could be a part of it if he wanted to.

They parked outside Snakebite Gifts and Antiques and

Logan went to work. She'd visualized how to improve her room, and had it down to a few well-placed art prints, some string lights, a new comforter, and a couple of potted plants. Gracia had a policy against candles in the motel rooms, but herbal incense and a stick lighter would do the trick. The store wasn't exactly what she'd pictured—mostly old shelves littered with dust-coated antiques that hadn't been touched in years—but she could make this work.

Brandon wordlessly followed, quiet as a ghost. He perused the shelves they passed, badly pretending that he was looking for something.

"Do you have something else to shop for?" Logan asked.

Brandon laughed, quiet and dismissive. "Nope. I'm committed to the hunt."

Logan groaned.

They made their way to a small section of art prints. Logan paused at a canvas photo of a rural road. It was a bit country for her taste, but it tugged at her. She pulled the canvas from the shelf and brushed her thumbs over the stitching. It was the kind of picture she would've made fun of someone for having back in LA—generic and impersonal—but its loneliness spoke to her now.

"I like this one."

Brandon stepped to her side and admired the photo. "Not what I would've picked. How much?"

"Twenty-five," Logan said. She tilted the photo and narrowed her eyes at it. "I don't know—is it ugly?"

"No." Brandon took the photo delicately and looked it over. In his sweater and glasses he looked like an art critic appraising a masterpiece, not a manufactured print from some random store. "What do you like about it?"

"Um, I don't know, I just feel like I get it," Logan tried. Brandon was so casual now, like shopping together was a normal thing that they did. Logan pursed her lips. "It reminds me of when we lived on the road. I mean, it sucked. But there were moments. I remember Dad took me down to this river for an afternoon. I used to think . . ."

Logan clenched her jaw. She used to think that home wasn't a place, it was family. But the family she had then—their strange, broken trio of misfits—hadn't felt like home in a long time. They were still three lost things, but they were infinitely far apart. Home wasn't family now. Home was nowhere.

Brandon looked at her, but his gaze was distant. He looked beyond her.

"It doesn't matter," Logan said. "I want it."

She took the canvas print from Brandon's grasp and tucked it under her arm. They carried on through the store, methodically working through Logan's list of aesthetic improvements. In a few months, she would be loading this same haul of decorations into boxes before she left Snakebite behind.

Brandon paused next to a shelf of tattered dolls.

"Do you feel . . . *safe* in Snakebite?" he asked.

"I don't love it," Logan mused, "but I haven't seen any pitchforks yet."

"I mean more like . . ." Brandon stared into the cart wistfully. "I think about memory sometimes. How our mind rewrites our memories from scratch every time we think something up. If we wanted, we could forget a piece of our lives completely. Just . . . write over it."

Logan unloaded her pile of artwork with a scowl. "I hope I forget Snakebite when I leave."

"Fair enough." Brandon was quiet. "Sometimes I wish I could forget it, too."

The gift shop front door rang. Logan stood on her toes to see over the shelves. A group of kids around her age wandered into the store, laughter following them from outside. It was three girls and two boys, all clad in summer dresses and cargo shorts and sunglasses, shoulders sun-kissed, hair damp with what Logan assumed was lake water. They weren't like the kids from LA, but a sharp pang of longing still struck Logan at the sight of them.

Next to her, Brandon's expression darkened.

"Someone you know?" Logan joked.

"We should probably buy these and get home."

The group of teens rounded the nearest shelf, each of them idly touching items without really considering them like wandering through this store was just a standard part of their day. Logan couldn't blame them—on her brief trip through Snakebite's "downtown," she hadn't seen a single thing for kids her age to do for fun.

A boy at the front of the group paused when he spotted Brandon. Sunlight filtered through the dusty store shelves, streaking the boy's pale face sickly yellow. His lips twisted into a grimace.

"They multiplied," the boy said. He motioned to Logan, unnervingly square jaw clenched. "What're you doing here?"

Logan looked to Brandon for an explanation, but Brandon only stared. He adjusted his glasses, then turned like he meant to leave.

"Hey," the boy said again. "I asked what you're doing here."

The other teens gathered around the boy were silent. Logan recognized them from the vigil the day she'd arrived. This was the same group of kids who'd stared at her and Alejo like they thought their glares could kill. Logan began to understand Brandon's quick retreat, but she wasn't one to run away.

"We're shopping," Logan said. "What's *your* problem?"

The boy's glare shifted from Brandon to Logan. "My problem is this guy shows up here and my friend goes missing. I wanna know why."

Maybe she'd spoken too soon on the pitchforks. Logan looked to the front of the shop for backup, but the woman behind the register only watched the argument unfold with vague interest, like it was a bit of theater on a slow afternoon. Truck engines stammered outside, voices trickled in through a crack in the door, and Snakebite carried on. No one was coming to their defense.

"How about you mind your own business?" Logan snapped. She adjusted her art prints under her arm, but she didn't budge.

The boy at the front of the group took a step forward.

Before he could say anything, another of the teens slipped in front of him. Her bright blond hair was pulled up in a high ponytail, cheeks dappled with freckles, eyes unnervingly wide. She'd been standing at the edge of the cemetery on the day of the funeral; Logan recognized her same blue-eyed stare, like the girl was trying to pull her apart.

"We don't want a fight," the girl said, voice obnoxiously appeasing. "Why don't you two just go?"

"Who're you supposed to be?" Logan asked.

"Stop." Brandon put a hand on Logan's shoulder like he meant to quiet her. He wasn't focused on the group of kids harassing them. His *stop* was meant for her, not the bullies. In classic Brandon form, he was already on the run, retreating from the situation like he retreated from everything else.

"Why should *we* have to leave?" Logan asked. "We're not—"

"Logan," Brandon warned. His lips made a tight frown. He looked at the blond girl and said, "We're going."

Gently, he tugged Logan to the cash register. From the other aisle, the kids whispered and laughed. Humiliation crashed like a rockslide in Logan's stomach. Even when she was defending him, Brandon wasn't on her side.

He gave the gift shop cashier his card. "Sorry for the trouble."

The cashier shook her head.

Wordlessly, Logan gathered her decorations and made her way out of the store. If it had been Alejo, he would have stood up to them. Or he would have been proud of her for saying something. But Brandon had done nothing. Logan couldn't look at him.

She climbed into the car and buckled up, searching for the right words, but only came up with, "What was that?"

Brandon thrummed his fingers over the steering wheel without turning on the car. "It's not worth arguing."

"You could've said something."

"It wouldn't matter." Brandon fixed his glasses. "Those kids . . . you saw the blond one? She's a Barton. The Bartons own everything in this town. The lumberyard, the ranch, all the restaurants, all the parks. They're in charge of the whole thing."

"She doesn't scare me," Logan scoffed. "I can handle redneck Barbie."

Brandon shook his head. "Not her. It's her mom that's the problem."

"Whatever."

"It's best to just . . . do what they say."

Logan rolled her eyes. "Even if what they say is wrong?"

"I get that it's hard. But this is just temporary." He fired up the Neon and crawled away from the curb, leaving Snakebite in a cloud of exhaust. After a moment of aching silence, he sighed. "We'll finish the show, then the three of us can leave for good. It won't be that much longer. Sound like a plan?"

Logan grimaced. She swallowed the argument brewing in her chest and nodded. "Sure. Sounds like a plan."

7

What's Done In The Dark

"We had salmon and asparagus last week," Tammy Barton said, neck strained so that she could see her weight-loss app over her reading glasses. "Low calorie, but no flavor. Let's try the stir-fry this week. I can make a big batch of that. It'll be good for lunches."

"I hate stir-fry." Ashley longingly eyed a packet of instant mashed potatoes. "I can make my own dinner."

"When you buy groceries with your own money you can."

Ashley groaned. It had only been a few days since her argument with Brandon Woodley and his daughter at the gift shop, but it still scratched at the back of her mind like a dog trying to come inside for dinner. Defusing the fight was the right thing to do, but the way the girl had looked at Ashley—angry and wounded—wouldn't leave Ashley alone.

Her mother compared boxes of brown rice, silently weighing the pros and cons of long grain and short grain. She was on a health kick that meant only fresh veggies and seafood were suitable for dinner. Even before the diet, she had been a nightmare to shop with. Before Tristan's disappearance, Ashley would've avoided it at all costs. But lately, she didn't want to be alone. Things had felt different in Snakebite for months, even beyond Tristan's disappearance. The sun felt different, relentless and hot as rage. Something boiled under the surface of their little town.

Snakebite Mercantile was mostly empty this early in the day. Carrie Underwood swirled from a single overhead speaker, echoing from the green-and-beige-checkered linoleum. Somewhere behind them, shopping cart wheels squealed. A man turned the corner into the dry foods aisle, shopping cart suspiciously loaded with nothing but microwave meals, Cheez Whiz, and a jar of pickles. When Tammy spotted him, she tensed, tossing the long-grain rice in her cart like she meant to make a quick getaway.

The fluorescents overhead flickered in anticipation. The air was stiff with the threat of battle. The strange man's dark brow furrowed, jaw clenched, fingers gripped tight around the handle of his shopping cart. Tammy's eyes narrowed, but she didn't back down. She pushed a blond curl behind her ear, donned a cutting smile, and simply said, "*Alejo.*"

The man, surprisingly, returned the smile, though his was easier. Unlike her mother, Ashley thought there was a part of him that meant the gesture. His black hair rested at his shoulders, half tied-up in a knot at the back of his head. It took Ashley a moment to recognize him as the man from Pioneer Cemetery on the day of Tristan's vigil.

Ashley's stomach sank. That made him the gift shop girl's other father. Maybe he was here because he was angry. His expression was hard to read, but he was surprisingly intimidating for a man wearing a knit sweater that read WHO'S AFRAID OF THE DARK.

"Tammy," Alejo said, "fancy meeting you here."

Tammy cleared her throat. "What a coincidence. I feel like I see *you* everywhere."

"I'm sure you love that."

Barton women didn't back down and they certainly didn't lose. Tammy exhaled sharply. "How are you and your family settling in?" she asked. "I heard you're staying at the Bates. Bit of a downgrade from a Hollywood mansion, but you're used to living on my property, so I'm sure you've made yourself at home."

"*Mom,*" Ashley breathed.

The man turned to Ashley and his expression warmed. "This must be your daughter? Ashley, right? It's been a long time."

Ashley blinked. She was sure she'd never met the man before, but something about his smile was familiar.

"Don't talk to her," Tammy said, stepping in front of Ashley.

Alejo rolled his eyes. "Oh, please. I'm just trying to have a conversation. You're the one turning this into a thing."

"I'm not doing anything but getting my groceries."

"Right," Alejo said. He eyed Ashley again. "I heard you met my daughter the other day."

Tammy scowled. "I said don't talk to her. How would you like it if I went and talked to *your* daughter?"

Ashley looked back and forth between the two of them. Her mother was usually a master of mitigating situations like this. She was supposed to be the picture of poise and calmness. This untethered version of her was unsettling. Ashley held her breath. Guilt over the fight in the gift shop welled up in her like a balloon.

"You don't have to," Alejo said. "Your daughter and her friends already harassed her. It was apparently quite the Snake-bite welcome."

"Hmm." Tammy briefly eyed Ashley like she meant to ask for clarification, but she steeled herself. "Maybe if she kept her head down, she wouldn't—"

"Logan isn't hurting anyone by shopping for *candles,* Tammy."

Tammy paused for a moment, eyes narrowed. "Logan . . . ?"

Alejo cleared his throat, but said nothing.

Tammy shook off whatever surprise the name had given her. She spun her cart around to leave. "We'll just get our groceries later."

"You don't have to—" Alejo dragged his palm over his mouth. His lips pressed together in a thin, desperate line. "Can we talk?"

Tammy closed her eyes and exhaled, slow and measured. Without looking at Ashley, she smiled. "Can you go get some broccoli for the stir-fry? I'll just be a second."

Ashley nodded. She took the shopping cart and walked as briskly as she could to the next aisle. She had no intention of missing their conversation. She'd never seen her mother act so unnerved by anyone, let alone a lanky forty-something in a knit sweater. From between the candy bars and the soda, she could just make out her mother's tense voice.

"Okay, five minutes."

"Tammy . . ." There was a moment of silence as someone walked through the aisle. Once they were gone, Alejo continued, "You're not happy we're here—I get that."

"Apparently you don't. Otherwise you'd leave." Ashley could hear her mother's scowl from an aisle away. "What do you want?"

"You know we haven't had it easy here."

"Yes, I know the loss was hard on you. And I'm sorry, really." Tammy was quiet for a moment. "But I thought you two leaving was more of a permanent thing."

"I did, too," Alejo said, "but the three of us have just as much a right to be here as anyone else."

"Hmm," Tammy said. "Her name is in really poor taste, by the way."

Alejo was quiet. His quiet was a wounded thing, tense and cold all at once. "You can say whatever you want to me and Brandon—I really don't care—but Logan doesn't have anything to do with that."

"You know how Snakebite is. Why bring her?"

"Because we're a family," Alejo said, voice bordering on desperate. "What're we supposed to do—leave her home?"

"Alejo," Tammy said, softer than before. "I'm serious. What are you doing back here?"

"We're location scouting. For the show."

"You're going to make a joke out of us."

And then neither of them said anything. Ashley leaned further into the candy bars, listening for more. Her head swam trying to keep up. It occurred to her how strange she'd look to anyone browsing the aisle, but she didn't care. This was about more than what John had said to Logan at the store. She'd never heard her mother talk like this. She'd never heard her sound so unsettled. This was the same Tammy Barton who chased fast food chains and superstores out of Snakebite without batting an eye, who commanded the entirety of Barton Ranch with ease. She was Snakebite's sole protector. Nothing rattled her. But something about Alejo apparently crawled under her skin.

He cleared his throat.

"It's not a joke. You don't think things have been weird? You don't think there's something *off?*" Alejo asked. "After . . . there was a lot of stuff happening here when we left. Problems we never got to resolve."

Tammy's heel clicked on the tile. "I'm one of these problems?"

"*Real* problems," Alejo clarified.

Her mother said something else, but it was drowned out by an elderly couple making their way down Ashley's aisle. Ashley eyed them with a scowl, but the couple didn't notice, fixated instead on store-brand seltzer. The overhead lights buzzed and the frozen aisle groaned and under it all, her mother's voice continued, soft and low as a hum. Ashley closed her eyes but she couldn't make out the words.

Finally, a bit of the conversation filtered through.

"You didn't have to do that," Alejo said, "but you knew it was right."

"And now what? You want me to pretend?"

Alejo was quiet. "Logan doesn't know anything about her. Brandon and I decided it was best. We wouldn't even know where to start."

"Fine."

"Thank you," Alejo said, and he sounded like he meant it.

"And when you're done, you'll leave? For real this time."

"Of course. As soon as we've figured it all out, you'll never see us again."

"Oh, thank god." Her mother's voice was a flood of relief.

It was the usual Tammy Barton, sure and easy. "If it means you'll leave, I'll do whatever. I'll even invite you back to Sunday brunches."

Alejo laughed, more relieved than Ashley expected for someone who'd just been asked to self-exile. In an instant, the atmosphere changed from tense and miserable to amiable. Friendly, even.

"I *do* miss Sunday brunches." The squeaky wheels on Alejo's cart swiveled. "God, I hate this town."

"You didn't used to."

Alejo was quiet. "No, I didn't."

The silence between them stretched so long, Ashley wondered if they'd quietly parted ways. She leaned into the aisle and closed her eyes. This wasn't right—her mother shared everything with her, but she'd never heard of Alejo. She'd never heard of Brandon or their family or all this apparent history. Ashley hated secrets. They were needles pricking at her skin, small and sharp and constant, reminders that there were some truths she still didn't deserve, no matter how hard she worked to live up to her name.

"Well, until you disappear again," Tammy said, almost too quiet to hear.

Alejo's wheels screeched. "Can't wait."

Ashley scrambled to the produce aisle and grabbed a bag of broccoli florets. Her mother rounded the corner with an odd, knowing smile. She took the broccoli and dropped it into the cart, but her eyes were fixed on Ashley's face.

"How much did you hear?"

"All of it?" Ashley bit her lip. "I'm sorry about the whole fight with that girl. John just started going off at her, and I tried—"

"Don't worry about it." Tammy shook her head, but she

wasn't angry. She pushed a piece of Ashley's hair behind her ear. "I would've done the same thing if I was you. I've known that family for a long time. Some people are just determined to be victims."

"Who was that guy?" Ashley asked.

Tammy shrugged. "No one important."

"Are you friends?"

Tammy turned the cart around. For a while, she wheeled in silence, chewing on an answer before spitting it out. "At one point, sure."

Ashley nodded. Further down the aisle, Alejo pulled a bag of potato chips from a tall shelf. His expression was distant and glassy. Ashley couldn't tell if it was anger or adrenaline that still wracked him, but whatever it was, Alejo's hands shook when he moved. If Tammy noticed, she didn't bat an eye.

"A Barton's job is to make sure Snakebite stays safe," Tammy said, navigating her way to the checkout.

Ashley wasn't sure she understood. But she nodded and followed her mother without another word, secrets dogging her steps like shadows.

8

A Necessary Fire

It had taken Ashley until seventh grade to realize that it was called Snakebite for the shape of the lake. On a map, Lake Owyhee didn't look like a lake at all. Instead, it looked like a wide-mouthed river that stretched deep into the dry and empty Owyhee wilderness. It twisted through the bald hills like an uncoiling serpent, forking at the north end into a snake's mouth. And inside the mouth of the viper was Snakebite, laughably small and unnervingly alone.

The last time she'd waded into the lake at night, Tristan was with her.

Now, Ashley stood waist deep, staring at the point where the warm black water met the hills on the horizon. Away from the light of town, the night sky was a paint stroke of mauve clouds and speckled starlight. The water pulsed against her stomach, asking her to step just a little farther into the depths. She'd never liked swimming at night before, but there was something comforting about the dark now. It gently pulled her into the nothing.

"Ash."

Ashley turned just in time for a thick wall of lake water to crash over her face. Bug stood knee deep only a few feet away wearing a mischievous smile. She stooped to splash again, but Ashley buckled her knees and ducked under the surface, turning the world to nothing more than the sound of churning waves.

When she came up, Bug was standing next to her.

"You okay?"

"Yeah," Ashley exhaled. She wrung out her ponytail. "I'm fine."

She wasn't, but it wasn't worth explaining anymore. The world since Tristan's disappearance was like a fist pressed into wet clay. She felt the impression of him in her chest. Her new version of okay would just be this. It was a hard thing to swallow.

She hadn't really wanted to come out tonight, but she'd spent weeks trying to get the search party to this side of the lake. A piece of her thought, once she got here, she would feel Tristan's presence. She would know where to look. The answer would fall into her lap. But she'd been here for hours and she felt nothing.

On the lakeshore, John Paris hunched over a pile of juniper brambles. His bright red swim trunks glared in the cool dark, massive shoulders bobbing as he attempted to start a fire. They'd packed kindling and a lighter in the back of the truck, but as usual, John was determined to do it like the movies. Just a stick and furious motion. Fran and Paul sat behind him on the picnic table only halfway paying attention.

"I thought we were supposed to be swimming," Ashley said.

Bug shrugged. "Guess they changed their mind."

"You can go hang out with them if you want." Ashley popped her neck. "Maybe you and Paul can talk about his dad some more."

"Oh my god, no thanks," Bug said. "If he—"

Before she could finish, John's fire roared to life. He sprung backward, tumbling to his back. Fran and Paul jumped up behind him with a cheer. Ashley and Bug made their way toward shore.

While the others settled, John sat on the log next to Ashley. For a moment, he stared into the dirt between his feet in silence. "How're you holding up?"

Ashley blinked. "Oh. You know."

"Yeah." John wiped his nose. "I know."

Ashley nodded. Compared to her friendships with Fran and Bug, she and John had only ever been as close as two people raised in the same pocket-sized town. But on nights like this, when Ashley looked into John Paris's face, it was like he was the only one who got it. He was the only other person with a Tristan-shaped impression in his chest. The only one who looked out at the black horizon and wondered if Tristan was looking back. The emptiness was suffocating him. It was suffocating Ashley, too.

In a way, it was nice to know she wasn't alone.

Usually, there were six of them. There was a gap in their circle, just between Ashley and John. She hadn't expected the empty air to feel so cold.

Eventually, the night softened into a blurry semblance of the way things used to be. Fran playfully fed s'mores to John, wiping stringy bits of marshmallow on his swim trunks. Bug slipped on her favorite green hoodie and buried her fists in the front pouch. Paul grasped at the dark, trying to catch flecks of ash between his fingers. It was almost right.

"I wish I could see their faces when they find it." Paul laughed, part of a conversation Ashley had long since tuned out. He nudged John.

"I don't care about their faces. I just want them to admit it," John said.

"That, too," Paul relented.

Over the last year, all of them had changed. But John Paris had changed the most. Instead of the scrawny pale boy he'd been junior year, he was now six feet tall with shoulders as wide as a horse's and a square jaw that made him look just like his father. He was colder now, too. He wasn't the boy who rode ATVs around the hills all summer with Paul and Tristan. He was more serious, like over the course of a single school year he'd turned into an adult. In a few years, he'd either be at Barton Lumber or training to join the police like his dad.

"Needs more wood," John said, ignoring Paul completely. He slapped his knee and stood to face Fran. "Wanna help?"

Fran's eyes widened. "Oh, yeah. Cool."

John smiled at her and they made their way toward the trees, leaving Ashley sitting opposite Bug and Paul. The fire popped and crackled, licks of orange flashing against the velvety night. A pile of firewood was stacked next to it—more than enough to last for hours.

So they'd been ditched.

"I'm gonna get a truck," Paul said, angled toward Bug. Puberty may have blessed John, but it'd done the opposite for Paul. He'd grown at least six inches in the last year, but his limbs were still gangly, eyes sunken so deep they looked bruised. He flashed a toothy smile at Bug and the firelight sank into the deep crevices of his face. "Well, I'm *probably* getting one."

Bug's eyes remained on the fire. "Awesome."

"Yeah. My dad says if I can fix up this old Tacoma he got from the tow lot, I can have it. He's teaching me how to fix the radiator."

"Nice."

Paul kept talking, oblivious to the way Bug avoided eye contact. This was usually when Ashley and Tristan would meet eyes and Tristan would shake his head. Ashley would have to bite her lip to stop from laughing. Later, when everyone else had gone home and it was just her and Tristan in the back of her truck under the stars, she would put on her best Paul voice and say, *My dad taught me how to change oil the other day. A truck with a fresh oil change? That's art.* And Tristan would laugh until he wheezed. He would pull Ashley against his chest and they would be a tangle of laughs and kisses until her mom called and they had to race back to town before sunrise.

Ashley pressed fingers to her lips and traced the small smile there. She was sitting at the fire mourning the person she was supposed to be sitting with. She opened her text message window with Tristan—his last message was too bright. Too short.

T: I can wait.

She rubbed at her eyes and tried to rope herself back into the conversation.

Then she saw it.

At the edge of the trees, just beyond where John and Fran had disappeared, a figure sat on a severed juniper trunk. At first glance, it looked like it could be a shadow. But it didn't *feel* like a shadow. Its limbs were too long, chest too still, face too empty. It pulled at her, just like the black lake water had pulled at her. It watched her, unmoving. In the dark, Ashley thought it grew, fusing into the dark between the trees.

Bug stiffened. "What's wrong?"

"Do you see someone?" Ashley asked. "Sitting on the tree."

"There's no one there," Paul stated, matter-of-fact.

Bug squinted. "I'm trying to see—"

The figure stood, but its movement wasn't right. It was jagged, abrupt, pained. The figure didn't approach them. It only watched. Ashley felt sweat bead at the nape of her neck. Her chest was cold and tight, heart thumping a slow, fearful march.

"How do you not see it?" she asked.

Bug clutched her hoodie closer to her chest. "I'm . . . what does it look like?"

"It's right there."

"Ash," Bug said, quieter, "I don't see anything."

The figure turned away from the campfire and made its way into the trees. There was something familiar about it. It was the same figure she'd seen during the search a few days earlier, but even more familiar. She'd seen its back before—she knew the shape of it. Ashley stared into the empty shadows and it hit her. "Oh my god."

"*Ashley,*" Bug hissed.

She ran.

In a few strides she hit the tree line, and then she was in the dark. Everything was different here, like the trees had tugged her out of the world of open water and night skies and into an empty void. There was an electric buzz to the woods. Footsteps pulsed against the packed dirt from all directions. She ran deeper into the dark, clinging to the sound because it meant she wasn't imagining him.

He had been here the whole time.

The trees fell away and she came to a small clearing. Moonlight sifted through the trees, streaking the dirt silver. Ashley leaned against a tree to catch her breath. For a moment, she thought she'd lost him. The footsteps were gone. There was no more wind, no more stars, no more crickets or rustling branches or water lapping lazily at the shore behind her.

Instead, there was the black silhouette of a cabin, stark against the night.

And there was breathing.

It was measured inhales and calm exhales. She recognized the sound from years of comfortable silence—it was *Tristan's* breathing. It was as familiar to her as the shape of his back disappearing into the trees. She smelled him here, coating the trees in the scent of diesel fuel and mowed grass. He was here, but the clearing was empty.

"Tristan," Ashley croaked.

Tristan's breathing changed, quickened like he was afraid. Ashley scrambled to the middle of the clearing, but Tristan was nowhere. She'd seen him by the lake. She heard him here. There was no way she was alone.

The breathing changed again, faster, rattling like there was something caught in his throat.

"*I . . .*" Tristan's voice crackled.

"Tristan?" Ashley fell to her knees and the trees spiraled around her.

"Ashley."

Not Tristan. Ashley looked down at her trembling hands. Dirt crumbled between her fingertips. She whipped around, searching the shadows.

Behind her, there was a flash of red.

"Ashley, what's . . . ?"

Ashley blinked. A figure emerged from between the trees,

but it wasn't Tristan. Fran knelt next to her and put a hand on her wrist. Her sweatshirt was bunched up, hair mussed like hands had been knotted in it. John stood a few feet behind her with his arms folded over his chest. His red swim trunks glared in the dark.

"Did you say Tristan?" John asked. "Where is he?"

Ashley shook her head. Her heart hammered. She sucked in a ragged breath, trying to find her footing.

"Ashley, Tristan isn't here." Fran's grip on her wrist tightened. She turned to face John. "She's freaking out. We should take her home."

"Where did you see him?" John asked again.

"*John,*" Fran snapped. "She's—"

Ashley shook her head and it was like the world shifted with her. She wanted to stand—to keep looking for Tristan—but her chest ached. She doubled over into Fran's arms and cried. Tristan was here, but she couldn't reach him. Something kept them apart, cold and dark and lonely. Ashley was looking, but she couldn't reach him.

She was afraid.

9

The Choking Light

Logan is in the kitchen.

The lights are off and the kitchen is dark, save for the searing green numbers on the microwave that read 2:34 a.m. The windows stretch from floor to ceiling so that the night spills onto the black tile floor. The San Fernando Valley unfurls into a basin of noise and light outside. It isn't lonely here like it is on the road. But it's still empty.

The front door clicks open.

He ambles into the kitchen without turning on the lights, stumbling like he's drunk. He glances at the microwave and sighs. Even with all the lights outside, he doesn't see her. He only sees the dark. Sometimes, Logan thinks it's all he wants to see.

Alejo is already in bed. She should be in bed, too. Brandon throws open the refrigerator and absently stares inside, looking for something he never finds. The white light from the fridge pours over Logan's face, but even then, Brandon doesn't see her. He isn't looking for her.

When he spots her, his gasp is small and nervous, the sound fluttering like moth's wings from the linoleum. "I didn't see you there."

"Just getting water," Logan says. Her words echo like she's underwater. She is too close to her own voice. "Where were you?"

Brandon adjusts his glasses. Logan looks at him, but she can't see his face.

"Research for work," Brandon says.

"What kind of research?"

"Ah." Brandon leans against the granite island and folds his arms. The room darkens around them. "It's pretty late. Shouldn't you be asleep?"

"Okay." Logan slumps. "Good night."

But Brandon's posture changes. He puts an arm against the wall and blocks her from standing. When he speaks, his voice is deeper. It comes from everywhere at once.

"You know where you sleep."

And then the kitchen is gone.

Logan is lying down. Fear rises up in her like bile. She is lying in a hole so deep the only thing she can see above her is the night sky, black and freckled with starlight.

Brandon reappears over her.

"Goodbye, Logan," he says. He shovels a mound of dirt and tosses it over the hole. The dirt slaps across her face, and—

Logan woke with a gasp.

Urine-colored light glared through her closed blinds. The motel room was muggy and warm and smelled like mildew. Logan rolled to her side and her sheets stuck to her skin, hair plastered to the back of her neck. She choked until her throat was raw, until her mouth tasted like iron, until the crawling dregs of soil left her cheeks, until she was sure she was awake.

"Not real," Logan whispered, tenderly massaging her neck.

She touched her comforter, her nightstand, the wall behind her bed, and breathed, "Real."

It wasn't an entirely new nightmare. She'd dreamed of the kitchen a thousand times, but that last part—the burial—was a twist. She massaged her throat, gently reminding herself that here, in the motel room, she could breathe.

A knock sounded at the door.

Logan scrambled from her bed and pressed herself to the wall. She pried an opening in the blinds and searched the dark, but she couldn't quite angle enough to see the door of her room. The motel sign flickered against a thin layer of fog, but otherwise, nothing moved. The parking lot was eerily still.

"Is anyone awake?" a voice called from outside.

Logan approached the door and peered through the eyehole. She didn't recognize the boy on the other side of the door. He shifted awkwardly from one foot to the other, wearing a beanie, a flannel, and half-framed glasses that sat too low on his nose. Against her better judgment, Logan opened the motel door. Cool wind snuck under the hem of her sleep shirt.

"What?" she snapped.

The boy's hands were clasped in front of him, fingers twisted into frantic knots. "Sorry. I, uh . . . you should come look."

Logan rolled her eyes. The boy backed up and motioned to the wall between her room and room eight. At first, she couldn't see it. She rubbed her eyes, blinking away the sleep, and the spray-painted letters shifted into focus.

The first word was one she'd seen a hundred times in the comment sections under her fathers' videos. In person, it burned. She approached the slur; it stretched the full width of the wall between their doors, red paint glaring at her. Only four letters, but each one was a punch to the gut. Whoever had left it had the forethought to make it plural.

The phrase below it was what snatched her breath away. YOU KILLED HIM.

The door swung open. A pajama-clad Alcjo stepped into the threshold and stifled a yawn in the crook of his elbow. Logan's stomach dropped. She was overcome with the sudden urge to throw herself over the door if it meant he and Brandon didn't see it, too.

"What's going on?" Brandon asked, joining them outside.

Alejo rubbed his eyes and followed Logan's gaze to the wall. When he saw it, he said nothing. The night smelled like old garbage and laundry.

"Bran, I don't think you should—"

Brandon adjusted his glasses and stared at the slur. Wordlessly, he ambled back into the motel room, hand perched to cover his face.

"We should talk to the cops," Logan said. "People can't—"

Alejo turned and put his hands on her shoulders. His expression was impossible to read—concern, fear, anger, pity—and he shook his head. "No. Don't worry about that. We—Gracia will come help us cover it in the morning. It's not . . ."

"It's not *what?*" Logan asked.

Alejo looked past her at the boy who'd woken them. "Elexis. I almost didn't recognize you in the dark."

The boy nodded. "I'm sorry, Tío. I tried to wake you up first, but—"

"Thank you for letting us know." Alejo sucked in a sharp breath. "Why don't you get back to sleep? We'll take it from here."

Elexis made his way back across the parking lot, ducking

into the motel room on the far end of the building. Logan made a mental note of it—if Alejo was his tío, that made Elexis her family, too.

Logan furrowed her brow. "You were gonna say it's not a big deal."

A hate crime *was* a big deal, actually. Logan was no expert, but she was pretty sure hate crimes were illegal. She was pretty sure the police were supposed to *do* something about them.

Alejo looked over his shoulder, eyes fixed on Brandon, silhouette outlined in the pale light of the motel room. He didn't seem surprised or angry or even disappointed. He was just . . . quiet. He looked like he had in her dream, broad and emotionless. Unreadable.

"No cops," Alejo said. He pulled her into a hug, cupping her head against his shoulder. "Just us. Everything's gonna be okay."

Somehow, she doubted that.

10

From The Beginning

"Where's Paris?"

Ashley slapped her palm on the front desk of the Owyhee County police station, startling Becky Golden out of her usual cheery daze. The station lobby was eerily quiet at nine in the morning, the silence broken only by the hum of an outdated computer and the fridge in the break room.

The world spun too fast. After Fran and John had taken her home, she hadn't slept. It was a miracle she hadn't woken her mother with her restless pacing. It didn't make sense—she'd seen Tristan in the woods, heard his breathing, been close enough to reach out and touch him. Her voice echoed from the brick walls, reverberating back at her like a slap.

Becky blinked. "Ashley? Are you okay? You look sick."

"I'm fine. Where's Paris?"

"At home, probably. I can call him if it's an emergency."

An *emergency*. Ashley wanted to laugh. She didn't have words to describe what this was. Emergency definitely didn't cover it, though. The rasping, gurgling sound of Tristan's breathing was branded into her. Even after sleep, it was all she could hear. It was beyond an emergency.

"Tristan was in the woods," Ashley said. "I think he's hurt."

"Oh my god," Becky said. She took Ashley's shaking hand in hers and reached for her desk phone. "Where is he now? At the ranch?"

"No. I think he's still out there."

"You left him?"

Ashley wavered. "I . . . I don't remember."

"You didn't see where he went?"

Ashley shook her head. She eyed the mustard-colored countertop. "He was hurt, though. He probably didn't get far."

Becky narrowed her eyes, finger paused on the dial pad. This was the same Becky Golden who had started out as Barton Ranch's receptionist. The same Becky Golden who'd sold Ashley her first horse. Who still stopped by the ranch for chardonnay and gossip on a weekly basis. She had been a family friend since before Ashley could walk, but right now she looked at Ashley like she was a stranger.

"Ashley, I'm a little confused."

Ashley cleared her throat. "Me and my friends were across the lake and I saw him. I followed him into the trees, but then it was like he just . . . wasn't there. I could still hear him. I don't know how, but I know he was there."

Becky gave her a pitying once-over. Ashley hadn't bothered to change into clean clothes—her shirt was smattered with dirt, fingertips black with grime, shoes coated in a layer of muck. She was sure she looked crazy. Maybe she *was* crazy.

"Ashley," Becky said softly. "Does Tammy know you're here?"

Ashley shook her head.

Becky leaned in like their conversation was a secret. "I know this has been so hard for you. I have a cousin over in Ontario. He's a counselor. Maybe you could talk to him about all this."

"What?"

"I thought therapy was only for weirdos, but I tell you, it really helped Tom since he lost his mom." Becky pulled a sticky note from her desk and scrawled out a phone number. She handed it to Ashley with an over-proud grin. "For when you're ready."

"Wait," Ashley said. "I don't need this. I need Paris."

Becky sighed.

"I'm not making it up."

"No, of course not." Becky frowned and brushed a thumb over Ashley's knuckles. Her skin was soft and smelled like rose lotion. "Grief can do strange things to your head, though."

"I wasn't hallucinating."

"Sounds like a ghost," someone said.

Ashley traced the voice across the lobby. A girl sat in one of the plastic lobby chairs with a home-improvement magazine sprawled across her lap. Ashley's eyes widened with the realization that she wasn't alone. It was the girl from the side of the road the day of Tristan's vigil—the girl from the gift shop—slouched in her chair like she'd been there for hours, eyebrow curiously quirked.

Ashley turned back to Becky. "How long has *she* been here?"

"Literally the whole time," the girl said, folding her arms. "Just ignore me."

Ashley blinked. She immediately retraced everything she'd said since storming into the station. Had she been so tired she hadn't seen someone sitting there? "You've just been eavesdropping?"

"It's not eavesdropping when you're yelling." The girl put down the magazine. "A person randomly disappearing into the woods sounds like a ghost, though."

"It wasn't a ghost." Ashley straightened her posture and fixed the girl with a cool glare. "Ghosts aren't real."

"Okay."

"If it was a ghost, that would mean Tristan's . . ."

Dead, she thought.

"Dead?" The girl asked. "Maybe. I think my dads did an episode with a lady who saw ghosts of people who were alive, though."

"Ashley," Becky said quietly, "ghosts aren't real. She's just trying to promote their show. If you wait for Paris to come in, we can do an official report."

Ashley kept staring at the girl. This was the daughter Alejo had been discussing with her mother at the grocery store. "Is that why you're here? Just waiting for people to come in so you can make them watch your show?"

The girl scoffed. Her black hair was gathered up in a sleek, short ponytail, eyes murky with the half-lidded stare of a person who hadn't slept well.

"No," the girl said. "The show sucks."

"Then why are you here?"

"Same reason as you. I'm here to see the sheriff." The girl inspected her nails. "And I'm first in line."

"What do *you* need him for?"

"I'm here to report a hate crime." She flashed a tight-lipped smile. "You wouldn't know anything about that, right?"

Ashley pursed her lips. She'd only heard a bit of John and Paul's conversation the night before, but she was sure they were the guilty party. Outside the front window, the sky was gray as marble. The rest of Snakebite was probably waking up. She would have to explain what she'd seen to Bug and Fran. To her mother.

They wouldn't believe her, either.

"Can we talk outside for a second?" Ashley asked.

The girl eyed her suspiciously. "I'm good. Don't wanna lose my spot in line. I've already waited two hours for someone to take my statement."

Ashley turned to Becky, who pointedly avoided eye contact. "You can't just write down what happened and let her leave?"

"She said she wanted to talk to Paris," Becky said.

The girl shook her head. "No, I said I wanted to report a crime. I'm totally happy to let *you* help me."

Becky offered a thin smile. "Of course. Logan Woodley, right?"

"*Ortiz*-Woodley," the girl clarified. "It's hyphenated."

Logan Ortiz-Woodley. Ashley chewed on the name while Becky took Logan's information down. Ortiz was a Snakebite name—relatives of Gracia Carrillo, she thought—but Logan wasn't a Snakebite kid. She was an outsider. She didn't know the woods or the lake or the rolling hills. She wasn't burdened with the years of history this town was built on. When Becky promised that Paris would be in touch soon, Ashley wondered if Logan knew the boy who'd done it was the sheriff's son. She wondered if Logan knew that this report would amount to a "stern talking-to" for John and nothing else. She wondered if Logan understood how things worked in Snakebite at all.

Logan, apparently satisfied, turned to Ashley and arched a brow. "That was shockingly easy. You have my attention."

Ashley motioned to the door.

They stepped out into the pale morning. The wind was sweet with the scent of lake water, cool and gentle as linen. Ashley inhaled the summer air and felt a little clearer. A little more present. The foggy haze of the night before slowly began to burn away.

"Just so you know, I don't actually know if ghosts are real." Logan fidgeted, placing a hand on her hip and then down again at her side. Her eyes were sunken with exhaustion, trained on the lakefront highway that stretched beyond the parking lot. "I don't know if that's what you were gonna ask. But yeah."

"The thing I saw last night wasn't a hallucination," Ashley said.

"You think it was something paranormal?"

"I don't know. Have you ever seen anything paranormal?"

Logan grimaced. "No. Never."

"Oh."

"But you don't want it to be paranormal," Logan said. "You wanna find this Tristan dude, right? Alive?"

Ashley nodded.

Logan mulled over it for a moment. Her expression was difficult to read, both pensive and worried. She rubbed her palm over the back of her neck, eyes trained on the pavement.

"The F-word wasn't the only thing on my dads' door last night." Logan closed her eyes and exhaled. "It said *you killed him,* too."

Ashley sucked in a breath. John and Paul were the ones who'd done the graffiti. Writing *you killed him* meant John and Paul thought Tristan was dead. Anger boiled up in Ashley's chest. All the searches, all the vigils, all the times they said *we'll find him soon* . . . they didn't believe any of it. It was all for show.

Logan cleared her throat. "Do people think my dads hurt someone?"

"I don't know who put that on—"

"I'm not saying you know anything," Logan said, hands raised in surrender. "I'm asking about what it said. Do people think my dads hurt that guy, or is this how you guys greet all gays?"

Ashley blinked, briefly staggered by how casually Logan said it. "I don't really have an opinion."

"Oh my god. I'm not asking your opinion. I'm asking if everyone in this town thinks my dads *killed* someone."

"Yeah. I guess so."

Logan exhaled. "Why?"

"Tristan went missing in January. A week after your dad got here." Ashley cleared her throat. "You have to admit, it's kinda . . ."

"I don't have to admit anything," Logan said. "Where did people see him last?"

Ashley closed her eyes. "I was the last one who saw him. He was over at my place. And then he disappeared."

"Oh." Logan's eyes widened. "Were you two—"

"Dating. Yeah."

"Yikes."

It was the most inappropriate reaction to the disappearance that Ashley had heard so far. And somehow, it was the most refreshing. Logan bundled her arms into her sweater sleeves and crossed her arms. "You've been looking for him?"

"Yeah," Ashley said. "It's weird, but it's like I still *feel* him here. I have these flashes of him, like he's right next to me. And then last night . . ."

Logan pressed her fingers to her lips, considering. Warm

wind buffeted along the highway, warmer than it should be this early in the morning. Beads of sweat pricked at the back of Ashley's neck. After a moment, Logan exhaled.

"You want help finding him?"

Ashley paused. "Why would you help me?"

"Because if we find him, he's not dead. And everyone will know my dads didn't do anything."

Ashley nodded. "That makes sense."

"It doesn't have to be a whole thing," Logan said. "Let's just go to where you saw him last night."

Ashley's eyes widened. "Now?"

"Why not?" Logan asked. Her half-smile was unsettlingly amused. "I help you, you help me. And once we find your boyfriend, my dads can finish the show and leave."

Ashley extended a hand. She wasn't sure if this was the kind of arrangement where you shook hands, but it felt right. The wind that slipped between them was soft as a whisper.

Logan took her hand and shook.

"Temporary partners," Logan said.

Ashley smiled. "Sounds good to me."

11

The Piano-String Woods

Logan sat in the passenger's seat of Ashley's truck in the gravel driveway of Barton Ranch.

Sunlight glinted from the perfectly square windows of the ranch house, framed by pristine white siding and gray trim. The walkway to the black front door was lined with hedges, each one packed with blooming white flowers. Beyond the house were stretches of pasture that looked as if they went on forever. The horizon was a patchwork of green and gold. It looked like the kind of place she'd see on HGTV, pretty and sprawling and nondescript. At least there was no picket fence.

She tried to shake off the weight of her night. The last few hours were a blur—the nightmare, the slur on her fathers' door, the police station, and now *this.* Now she was waiting for Princess Snakebite herself to emerge from her quaint ranch house in clean clothes so they could investigate her missing boyfriend.

Logan couldn't make it up if she'd tried.

Finally, Ashley stepped out of the house in a baseball cap and a faded yellow T-shirt that read BARTON LUMBER. She looked a thousand times more awake than the girl Logan had met in the police station an hour ago, but shadows still circled her bright blue eyes. She was putting on a happy face, but there was only so much it could cover.

Ashley climbed into the driver's seat. "Ready?"

Logan threw on her sunglasses. "Is this your dad's truck?"

"Nope," Ashley chimed. "She's all mine."

"This is the car that *you* drive?"

Ashley scoffed. "Tell me the last time you hauled something in a Tesla." Her voice was more rural when she said *Tesla,* like the word itself was a rusty tool she'd pulled from her belt for the first time in years.

"You're so full of shit. I'd never drive a Tesla."

"Should you tell your dads where we're going?" Ashley asked.

"They won't care." Logan eyed the ranch house. "Did you tell your parents where we're going?"

Ashley grimaced.

"Cool. A secret mission." Logan smiled. "Let's do it."

They pulled away from Barton Ranch and followed the dusty highway until the single-story houses of Snakebite fell away and only golden hills and divots of gravel remained. The landscape was miles from Logan's visions of the northwest. She'd spent years imagining emerald forests and misty mountain ranges and lonely, tree-tunneled roads. Instead, she got hills that looked like clenched knuckles, rolling one after the other into nowhere.

That was where she was now: *nowhere.*

Ashley yanked the truck across the two-lane highway without warning, veering onto a road that followed the lakeshore. The Ford thumped from pavement to gravel, momentarily upheaving the clothes and textbooks from the back seat. Logan gripped the dashboard and closed her eyes to keep from puking, but Ashley was unfazed. She commanded the truck as though she were a cowboy breaking an unruly steed, one hand firmly on the reins, leaning into each bump and skip with ease.

"So, the spot is a ways past the turnout," Ashley said. She flipped her visor down and plucked a pair of pink sunglasses from its grasp. "I hope you have walking shoes."

Logan inspected her strappy leather sandals under the glove box. "I'll be fine. Anything's a walking shoe if you believe in yourself."

"Ha," Ashley huffed, humorless.

The truck skipped over a pothole and Logan's sunglasses toppled to the floor of the truck. Ashley smiled at her smugly, as if she thought handling bumps in the road was something only girls from Snakebite could do. The Ashley Barton who drove the Ford was different from the one Logan had met at the police station. She was unbothered, casually slouched in her seat, T-shirt shifted carelessly above her belly button. The sun-kissed skin of her stomach was dappled with light brown freckles.

Logan stared for a moment too long.

She sat back up and focused on the road ahead. She was gay, but not thirst-after-straight-horse-girl gay.

After half an hour, the gravel road spilled into a makeshift turnout at the edge of the woods. Lake water pulsed at the shore to their left. Darkness gathered in the junipers ahead of them where the trees huddled too close to see between. Something about the quiet made Logan feel ill.

"This is where you guys go for fun?" Logan asked.

"Not here," Ashley said, hopping out of the truck. "Follow me."

Logan did. The nausea she'd felt in the truck only deepened as they crossed the tree line. It wasn't fear so much as unease. The woods were quieter than they should have been. But maybe this was how woods always were—she wasn't a frequenter of the great outdoors. A gentle clawing dread rummaged in her gut, warning her that something waited here.

Ashley strode along, touching each trunk as though the bark held secrets. Her lemon-blond ponytail, tucked through the gap in her baseball cap, bobbed between her shoulder blades with each step. Logan couldn't help imagining her in a granola bar commercial.

When Logan and her fathers lived on the road, they'd spent nights between towns parked on highway shoulders along woods like this. Bugs and passing cars were bad, but the isolation was worse. In the woods, there was no exit. People who died weren't found for months, if at all. She'd imagined the branches like misshapen fingers beckoning her into the dark, waiting to snatch her away. Maybe it was the woods that had snatched Tristan Granger.

"Here," Ashley said suddenly. "This is where we were."

Logan walked down to the water where the dirt dissolved into dust and rock. The shore formed an alcove just large enough to swim in without being seen from the lake proper. A few feet away, half submerged in water, a black bikini top was snagged on a rock. It swayed along the incoming waves like a solemn flag.

"Cute," Logan said. She hooked her toe under a strap and picked it up. "Yours?"

Ashley flushed. She snatched the bikini top away and flicked the water out before tying it to her purse strap. "It's not mine, it's my friend's."

"Your friend had a good night," Logan said. "Better than you, I guess."

Ashley turned to face the lake. She stepped up to the water line and closed her eyes, one hand on her hip, the other clasping the bikini top as if she were channeling it for clues. Logan was tempted to stand in the same pose and see if any visions of missing boyfriends came to her, but she wasn't feeling quite that mean. Not today, at least.

"What are we looking for?" Logan asked.

Ashley marched up the bank, back toward the trees. "I was by the fire when I saw him. He went into the trees."

"You followed him?"

Ashley didn't answer. She kept walking, disappearing into the trees. Logan half jogged to catch up. The woods were quieter the deeper they went. They reached a clearing where the trees fell away and the lake was only a distant line of blue beyond the branches. A battered cabin stood a few feet ahead of them. There was a sound under the silence. Logan closed her eyes to hear it better.

The woods weren't quiet. Not completely.

Music drifted between the trees. It was a piano song trickling through the quiet somewhere nearby. The sun filtered through the bare branches, dousing the world in lonely magic. The piano played a ghost song, haunting and strained; unbearably sad, but beautiful.

"You guys have a lot of pianos in the woods?" she asked. Her laugh was breathy, uneasy, because joking about the ghost song was easier than trying to wrap her head around it. It was the kind of thing her dads would investigate on TV. But Brandon and Alejo weren't here now. Whatever this was, it was real.

"I know where it's coming from," Ashley said. She moved toward the cabin. She was too casual about all of it, like it was normal to dive headfirst into the paranormal. Because that was what the piano in the woods had to be—*paranormal.* As far as Logan could tell, no one lived out here. Aside from the crumbling cabin, the woods were empty.

Logan moved in front of her, hands raised to slow her down. "You want to go *toward* the ghost piano?"

"It's not a ghost piano." Ashley scooted around her. "But get your, uh . . . stuff ready. I don't know who'd be playing it."

Logan froze. "Wait, what stuff?"

"Like from the show. The thing that finds ghosts."

Logan blinked.

"You're supposed to be the ghost hunter," Ashley snapped.

"Why would I have gear on me? We didn't even stop at the motel."

"I thought you guys just carried that stuff with you." Ashley grimaced. "You don't have *anything* on you?"

"I don't even know if the stuff my dads use is real." Logan laughed. "Besides, I was only on the show one time. I barely know how to use it."

Ashley rolled her eyes. A warm breeze sifted through the junipers and the sunlight through the branches was thick as gold. The piano music continued, soft and sweet and lilting on the wind. Ashley looked at Logan, then turned toward the cabin. Logan's heart skipped a beat. There was something familiar about it, just like there was something familiar about the trees. It was just beyond her reach, a hair fainter than memory.

"It's coming from in here," Ashley said. Her voice was so soft it sounded like she was in a trance. "I'll show you."

They hiked to the front of the building. *Cabin* was a generous word. The structure was completely broken down, wooden planks that once stood upright now bent as though the sky had pressed its palm to the roof and slanted the whole thing. The windows were smashed, fractals of broken glass sticking jagged from the rotten frames. Pillows of moss coated the corners of the roof.

"Do you smell that?" Ashley asked.

Logan closed her eyes. There was a distinct smell coming from the cabin, like spiced cider and wood smoke. It was a smell she remembered, though she couldn't place it. It conjured up memories of laughter she couldn't quite hear. She tasted blackberries on her tongue. The bones of a memory were scattered before her, but she couldn't bring them to life. It was suffocating, this familiarity.

"You've been here before?" Logan asked.

"Yeah . . ." Ashley trailed off. "We come here sometimes to hang out. I've never been here during the day, though. It's . . . different."

They made their way to the front door. The piano music continued, following them all the way to the rotting front porch. When Ashley pressed the door open, the music stopped, replaced by the groan of old wood under their feet. The inside of the cabin looked less surreal than the outside; the floor was littered with beer cans, spent cigarettes, and dusty footprints. The walls were etched with names. A ratty gray sofa was pressed into the corner of the main room, and beside it, a dirt-stained cloth covered what Logan assumed was a piano. She didn't need to uncover it to know it hadn't been played in years. She'd have been surprised if it could still make music at all.

"What is this?" Logan asked.

Ashley paced along the main room, running her fingertips along the walls. "I don't really know. John found it when we were in eighth grade. It was on one of his dad's maps. We started coming out here on weekends so our parents wouldn't find us."

Logan nodded. "Tristan came here, too?"

"Yeah."

Logan turned to the window facing the lake. Fragments of broken glass littered the dirt outside, catching specks of white sunlight. Down the bank, Lake Owyhee ebbed at the shore. This place was beautiful once. Logan could almost picture it.

Behind her, Ashley gasped.

She faced the front of the room, staggered like she meant to run. Her eyes were fixed on the empty space in front of her.

"What's—"

"*Shhh,*" Ashley hissed. "Do you not hear that?"

Logan listened, but aside from the standard sounds of the woods and the cabin, she heard nothing. Ashley's eyes were wide with fear. She backed up slowly until her shoulders met the wall.

"They're coming inside."

"Who?" Logan whispered.

Ashley looked at Logan, blue eyes teary with panic. She turned back to face the door, and her expression changed from fear to confusion. "It's . . . your dad?"

It was Logan's turn to be confused. She watched the front door, following Ashley's gaze, but there was nothing. Not even a shadow she could mistake for a person. She heard no voices. No footsteps. It was just the forest and the cabin and the nothing.

"I don't see anything."

Ashley kept staring, palms flat against the wall.

"Ashley," Logan tried.

"He's . . ." Ashley closed her eyes. "I'm trying to . . . he's yelling at someone. He just keeps saying he doesn't know."

"Who?" Logan demanded.

"Your dad," Ashley said again. "Oh . . . uh, Brandon."

Another handful of silent moments passed, Ashley's glassy eyes fixed on a point in the center of the cabin. Logan closed her eyes, tried to hear, but there was nothing. "What's happening?"

"It sounds like someone else is talking to him, but I can't hear them. Brandon says he's sorry. He says he doesn't know what to do."

"There's no one here."

Ashley's gaze snapped to Logan. "You *have* to see him. There's no way it's just . . ."

Logan stared at the entrance to the cabin, but it was empty. Her stomach sank. The whole cabin was empty. There was no way someone was in this cabin and she couldn't see them. This wasn't the kind of thing that happened in real life. Invisible people were the kind of thing that happened on a filler episode of *ParaSpectors* when they didn't have the budget for special effects.

Logan swallowed. "What's he doing now?"

"Just standing there." Ashley said. She narrowed her eyes. "It's like he's listening. Not to us. He says they have to go. He says . . ." She paused and looked at Logan. ". . . He says people will find out. He says no one can find the body."

"What?" Logan asked. "What body?"

"I don't know," Ashley said. "I'm just repeating—"

She went silent again.

Logan sank to the sofa and closed her eyes and listened, but there was nothing.

"You really can't see this?" Ashley asked.

"*No,* I can't see it," Logan snapped. "I can't tell if you're . . . is this a prank? There's no way this is real."

Ashley shook her head. "I can't really see him anymore."

Logan pressed her face into her palms. The cabin spun around her. It was like she was stuck in a nightmare again. This had to be a joke, some ruse to make fun of her, but Logan couldn't understand the punch line.

"He's gone," Ashley murmured. "I don't understand. I—"

"Who was he talking to?" Logan asked quickly. "My dad?"

"I don't know." Ashley ran a shaking hand through her ponytail. "I don't know what I saw. I don't—"

Logan checked her phone, but they were miles from service. She wanted to ask Alejo about this. She needed *real* answers, not Ashley's *I don't knows*.

"Do you think your dad is the one who lived here?" Ashley asked. "He said something about 'the house.'"

"Here?" Logan gestured to the ruined living room. "This place has been abandoned for decades at least. There's no way he lived here."

"Then why would he be here?"

"It wouldn't make any sense to live here," Logan said. "It's miles from anything. It's completely isolated. He'd be completely . . ."

". . . alone," Ashley finished.

Ashley joined Logan on the sofa. They sat in silence, Logan with her face in her hands and Ashley facing the front door. The breeze through the cabin was colder now, though Logan suspected that was because of the anxiety churning in her gut. Brandon had been right when he said that things in Snakebite were wrong. But the disappearance, the ghosts, they weren't supposed to involve him. She came out here with Ashley to clear Brandon's name, not tie him to the mystery.

First Ashley had seen the ghost of her boyfriend. Now she'd seen Brandon. It would be impossible to convince her the two weren't connected.

"What do we do now?" Logan asked.

Ashley leaned back. Her hands still shook. She looked out the cabin window and closed her eyes. "You come with me. We have . . . a lot to talk about."

12

Herd Of Black Sheep

They drove back to Snakebite in silence.

Ashley led Logan into the Chokecherry, Snakebite's one and only pub. She wondered how the Chokecherry looked to an outsider. She'd grown up ogling the walls packed with old records and toy trains and football jerseys and acoustic guitars. It smelled like wing sauce and grease, the air coated in a film of oily kitchen heat. Pictures of cattle farms and rusty tractors were nailed haphazardly into the wood paneling. An old shotgun was mounted behind the bar, complete with gold antlers engraved on the handle. There wasn't a building in Snakebite that was more quintessentially *Snakebite.* The history of their little town was recorded here in piles of memorabilia.

Today, the pub was empty, which was unsurprising on a weekday. The sky outside careened toward dusk, and Ashley's stomach moaned for some old-fashioned bar food. They slipped into an old vinyl booth, Logan on one side and Ashley on the other. Gus—the Chokecherry's owner, bartender, waiter, and janitor—made his way to their booth with a notepad in his hand.

"Hey, Gus," Ashley said. "Just the Black Butte and some fries."

Gus nodded and turned to Logan, who looked from Ashley to Gus and back again like the whole setup was a trap. Finally, she took a look at the menu and cleared her throat. "Uh, I'll have the drink she said, plus some wings? And can I get those to go?"

"No, she's staying," Ashley said. She still had a thousand questions, and Logan wasn't leaving until she got some answers. "Everything is for here. I'll pay."

Gus eyed Logan. "You over twenty-one?"

". . . Yes?" Logan tried.

Gus shrugged and made his way back to the kitchen, leaving them alone. Never in the history of the Chokecherry had Gus actually checked someone's ID. It was an unspoken rule—every teen in Snakebite came here for cheap beer and fries, and as long as they promised not to drive and paid their check in full, Gus had no problem serving. The police in Snakebite didn't care, and the type of police who *did* care would never set foot in a town this far from civilization.

Logan settled into her side of the booth. She wore her discomfort plain on her face, and Ashley wasn't sure if it was the bar or the ghosts or that she just didn't want to be here with the girl who'd just told her that her father's ghost had rattled off a bunch of incriminating things. She couldn't blame Logan if it was all of the above. A Johnny Cash song blared from the jukebox across the pub. A gnat buzzed by Ashley's ear.

She leaned forward until Logan met her eyes. "I think we should talk about—"

"Yeah, I know," Logan snapped. "I just . . . can I have some time to, like, *process?*"

"Sure, yeah," Ashley said. She looked at the etched tabletop and studied the woodgrain. "I'm freaked out, too. I'm the one who saw it. I guess I'm just confused. I mean, your dad isn't dead."

"Right."

"So that's two now."

Logan arched a brow.

"Two ghost-spirit things I've seen of people that aren't dead."

"Two?"

"Tristan," Ashley clarified. "This means he's probably alive."

Logan pressed her face into her palms and dragged her fingertips down her face, stretching the skin under her eyes. "It doesn't make any sense. I am so confused."

Ashley was confused, too. Seeing and hearing Tristan was one thing, but this was something else entirely. Tristan was only a glimpse. He was moments of familiarity, there and gone as quick as a flash of lightning. Seeing Logan's dad was *real.* He'd been so lifelike it seemed impossible that Logan didn't see him, too. Brandon Woodley had been there in the cabin, standing in front of her. She could've reached out and touched him if she hadn't been so afraid.

"Your dads never said anything about the cabin before?" Ashley asked.

A shadow passed over Logan's expression. Ashley got the sense that she'd stepped on loose terrain. She didn't know much about Brandon Woodley or Alejo Ortiz. She didn't know anything about who they were before they left Snakebite, or who they were now. Why they'd disappeared for so many years. She ran her thumbnail along a crack in the table, searching for the right words.

Ashley leaned in. "I just wanna understand what I saw."

"Okay."

"I'm not gonna tell anyone about it. If that's what you're worried about. It's probably good we saw it, though. If someone else saw what we saw—"

"—what *you* saw," Logan clarified.

"—they might think it looked bad."

Logan's eyes narrowed. "Are you blackmailing me?"

"Oh my god, no." Ashley ran a hand through her ponytail. "I just meant, could you tell me a little more about him? Both of your dads, actually. You know more than anyone else."

"I didn't even know they were from here until a few months ago." Logan rolled her eyes. "Why are you asking? So you can go snitch? I know they didn't kill anyone."

The door to the kitchen swung open, effectively ending the argument. Gus placed their food and drinks on the table and disappeared back into the kitchen. Ashley stared at her fries in silence. She didn't want to be friends with Logan, but they both had a stake in this. They both needed answers. Logan tentatively took a sip of beer and her nose wrinkled up; apparently she was put off by the taste. She slid it away and folded her arms.

"I'm not gonna snitch," Ashley said. "No one would believe me, anyway."

"They'd believe you more than my dads." Logan picked apart one of her wings, delicately avoiding getting sauce on her fingers. "Everyone already hates us. It wouldn't even be that much of a stretch. They'd be happy you gave them a reason."

Ashley frowned. It was a fair point.

"I don't want a killer. A killer means that Tristan's . . ." Ashley pointed at Logan with a fry. "We want the same thing. We just want things to go back to normal."

"Normal," Logan scoffed.

Ashley rolled her eyes. "I'm not blackmailing you."

"Sure."

"You really don't like me, do you?"

Logan stopped dissecting her wings and looked up. "It's not personal. I hate literally everyone in this town."

"It feels a little personal."

"Probably because you're used to everyone liking you."

Ashley huffed. "I'm not . . . never mind."

Logan cleared her throat and smiled. "So, what's next in the investigation? We know the cabin is haunted. It's *maybe* connected to your boyfriend."

Ashley frowned. "We find out more about the cabin, I guess. I can ask my mom. You ask your dads about it, too. Once we figure out what it is, we can plan next steps. We should definitely go back, though."

The bell on the Chokecherry's front door rang and Ashley froze. Fran and John strode in, eyes locked on Ashley's table like they were on a mission. Ashley looked for Paul trailing behind them, but for the first time since she could remember, they were alone. Logan turned around and eyed Fran and John with casual interest.

"Ashley," Fran said, leaning onto their table. "Where have you been? I texted you, like, a million times this morning. Are you feeling better?"

Ashley smiled. "Sorry, it's been a weird day."

"Apparently." Fran shot a skeptical look at Logan. "I'm Fran, and this is John."

"Yeah, we've met," Logan said coolly. "Heard you were missing a bikini top."

Fran flushed. She turned back to Ashley and snatched a french fry off her plate. "Looks like you're almost done. You can give us a ride home."

"I . . ." Ashley looked to Logan.

Logan shrugged. "I'll be fine. Just give me your number and we'll meet up later."

Ashley tapped her phone number into Logan's phone, then followed Fran and John into the night.

The air was warm and sweet outside the Chokecherry. On most summer nights, the dry wind down the main road smelled like barbecued meat and whiskey, but tonight it carried the strange, pungent musk of grief, too.

Ashley climbed into the driver's seat of the Ford, and John and Fran both crawled into the back seat. She felt uncomfortably like a chauffeur. Fran playfully shoved John, and he shoved her back before slipping his hand into hers. They laughed, quiet and warm, and the whole display punched Ashley in the stomach. It was stupid to be jealous, but she wasn't sure what else to be.

"So, is this a thing now?" Ashley asked.

Fran cleared her throat. "Yeah, uh, I guess it is. We made it official last night. I should've told you."

"I don't know. Ash didn't tell you she was hanging out with what's-her-name," John noted.

They pulled away from the Chokecherry, away from the buildings on Main Street into the unlit rows of houses along the lake. The Ford rumbled in the night and Ashley kept quiet. She should care about Fran's dating life, but her thoughts were snagged on the cabin. On the ghosts. On Logan.

"You're lucky we saved you." Fran laughed. "God, your face. You have that face you do when you're pretending to listen, where your eyes get all wide. You were doing it *so bad* talking to what's-her-face."

"I was not. She's actually kind of interesting."

"You're just too nice," Fran said. "We were randomly walking by and I was like, John, oh my god, she's way too nice for this. She doesn't know how to leave. We *have* to rescue her."

"And we did," John added. "You're welcome, Barton."

Ashley was glad they were shrouded in dark, because she was *sure* the face she made would start a fight. She wasn't sure what was happening to her. Ashley Barton didn't start fights. She didn't argue with people. She didn't have meltdowns in the woods.

They kept driving until they came to John Paris's house. It was a squat, green house that fit neatly between two identical houses in different colors. John climbed out of the back seat and made his way to the door, but Fran walked quietly to the driver's side window.

"Hey," she whispered. "You know I love you."

Ashley smiled. "Thanks. Love you, too."

"I know you've got a lot going on. All of this . . . is it still Tristan?"

Ashley looked out the windshield. It was Tristan in a way that she couldn't explain. It wasn't just that he was missing. He was still here, lingering like a shadow at her every step. It was that she was seeing things she shouldn't be able to, and no one would believe her if she tried to explain it.

No one but Logan, and Logan was a whole different problem.

"I don't want you to feel left out 'cause of me and John," Fran continued. "Like, you're my everything. You and Tristan were such goals. I remember looking at you and him and thinking I *had* to find something like that." Fran ran her shoe through the gravel at the side of the road. "We're gonna find him and get him back. But . . ."

Ashley cleared her throat. "But if we don't find him."

". . . if we don't find him, or if something happened to him. I don't know—you're my best friend. Are you gonna be okay again?"

Ashley blinked at the porch light. It was a fair question, but it struck a place in her that felt like an endless pit. She felt for an answer, but there was only this dark, empty feeling. She put on a smile. "I'll be fine eventually. Just . . . give me some time."

Fran nodded. "Yeah . . . I mean, yeah, of course. It really sucks. But I'm here for you no matter what."

"I think I just need something to feel normal again," Ashley said. She pursed her lips. An idea bloomed in the back of her mind. She could hit two birds with one stone—get more investigating done without disappearing on Fran and the others. She could still make this whole thing work. "We should do something at the cabin. Like we used to."

"That sounds really fun."

"And I can bring Logan."

Fran narrowed her eyes.

"I think you'd like her," Ashley mused. "You're both kind of . . . I don't know, she reminds me of you. Kind of. If you hate her, I won't invite her again."

Fran considered. "Okay, fine. But only because you're going through it."

Ashley beamed. "Good night, Fran."

"Good night, Ashley."

Fran disappeared into John's house and Ashley was left alone in the night. Her phone pinged in her pocket. She unsheathed it and studied the new message alert.

UNKNOWN: lol thanks for paying for dinner btw

Ashley thumped her head back against her seat.

AB: Sorry I forgot.

After a few seconds, another message popped up.

UNKNOWN: You have reached your limit for messages from this number. You will need to purchase one (1) dinner before receiving any further correspondence.

Despite herself, Ashley laughed. It wasn't much, but it was a start. She and Logan weren't going to be friends, but they were going to get to the bottom of this. They were going to get Tristan back. She was going to stop seeing things she wasn't supposed to. Everything was going to go back to the way it was.

Ashley started the Ford and drove into the dark.

13

A United Front Of Losers

Logan stood in the center of the Bates Motel parking lot with a to-go box of wings, mozzarella sticks, and chili-cheese fries—all things *she'd* had to pay for, since Princess Put-it-on-my-tab ditched her. It would be easiest to just duck back into her room, but that meant another night of staring at Twitter by herself. It meant turning the TV all the way up to drown out the screaming in her brain. Because everything was very suddenly too much: ghosts were maybe real, Brandon maybe had something to do with Tristan Granger's disappearance, and she was maybe the only person who could clear his name.

At least, she was the only person who wanted to.

Instead of swiping into her room for the night, Logan clutched her to-go box to her chest and made her way to room one. It was the room she'd seen Elexis duck into the other night. After Ashley and her friends, Logan was desperate to talk to someone her age who was also not evil.

She knocked once. There was shuffling inside the motel room, then the door opened a crack. The beanie-clad boy from the night before peered out like his motel room was a front for a den of criminals.

“Hi,” she said. “I’m Logan, in case you forgot.”

Elexis blinked at her.

“I hear we’re family. We met the other night.”

Elexis’s eyes widened. “Yeah, I know. I didn’t write that. I was just—”

“I know you didn’t write it.” Logan shook the to-go box, rattling the mozzarella sticks against the cardboard. “Elexis, right? Are you busy? I come bearing gifts.”

“Oh,” Elexis breathed. He eyed the to-go box in her hands and his brow furrowed. Reluctantly, he opened the door the rest of the way and motioned Logan inside.

The inside of Elexis’s motel room was worlds different from her own. The floral-patterned wallpaper was almost completely covered with video game posters. He’d gotten rid of one of the full-size beds and replaced it with a gnarled brown futon. The other bed was pushed into the corner of the room, over-burdened with pillows of all shapes and sizes. The focal point of the room was a TV stand that acted as a shrine to his PS4. The TV was paused on what looked like some kind of cowboy shooter game.

At least *someone* was having fun.

A boy Logan didn’t recognize sat on the futon wearing an Iron Man T-shirt. He fiddled with loose bits of electronics, looking up at the sound of the door closing. His wide brown eyes were both scared and curious.

“Do you guys like mozzarella sticks?” Logan asked. She set the to-go box on the futon and delicately opened it. “They’re probably cold now, but . . .”

“You’re . . .” the Iron Man boy said.

"Logan. What's your name?"

"Nick." He dug into the mozzarella sticks. "We didn't write that thing on your dads' door."

"I know you didn't," Logan said.

Nick and Elexis shared a nervous glance.

"Did they write something else?" Elexis asked. He paced across the room and stood in front of the TV like he meant to hide the game he'd been playing. "I can tell you who did it. I saw John Paris's truck here the other night. Or, I heard it. It woke me up. And then I woke you up."

"Not surprising. I just ran into him at the bar and he seemed *lovely,*" Logan said. She waved a hand. "I was actually coming over to see if you guys wanted to hang out. Family's gotta stick together."

"I'm not related to you," Nick said.

"There's not a lot of kids our age around here." Logan pulled apart a mozzarella stick. "And my dinner date kinda ditched me."

"You had a date already?" Nick asked. "You just got here."

"Figure of speech."

"She was hanging out with Ashley Barton," Elexis interjected. "I saw you guys leaving town this morning."

"Correct." Logan smiled. "I was briefly hanging out with Ashley Barton."

"Why?"

"We're hunting ghosts."

Elexis and Nick both eyed her. After a moment, they laughed. Logan laughed, too, because sometimes it was easier to just tell the truth and let people make up their own minds about it. If Elexis and Nick thought she was joking, she wouldn't correct them. Convincing a couple of teenage boys that the impossible existed wasn't on her usual list of fun party activities. She barely believed it herself.

"What're you working on?" Logan asked, angling to get a better look at the contraption in Nick's hands.

"Making a computer," Nick said. "Are you and Ashley friends?"

"No. It's strictly professional."

After a long moment, Nick sighed and put down his bits of plastic and wiring. "You're so lucky. I wish *I* was friends with Ashley Barton."

"Well, she's single now." Logan shrugged. "You could probably make a move."

Elexis gasped. "That's not funny."

Logan sank onto the edge of Elexis's mattress and put her hands on her knees. "Sorry. Question, though—did you guys . . . *like* Tristan Granger? Gracia seemed like she hated him."

"Oh, that's just Nana," Elexis said. "She hates him because him and his friends used to pick on me. But they kinda picked on everyone. And it wasn't really Tristan."

"Yeah, Tristan never said anything to me," Nick chimed in. "Him and Ashley were always nice."

"But they let their friends pick on you?"

Elexis and Nick were quiet.

"Why'd you tell me about the thing on my dads' door?"

"I don't know," Elexis said. "Just felt like I should."

"Huh. Well, thanks." Logan slouched. "A lot of people here seem to really hate us. But not you guys. Why?"

Elexis shrugged. "Because I don't think your dad did anything?"

"Why?"

"He just . . . doesn't seem like he would." Elexis narrowed his eyes at his video game, quickly killing off a slew of masked bandits. "Besides, if I ratted out family my nana would kill me."

Logan blinked; she hadn't expected such relief. She gathered herself and smiled. "That's how us gays get you. You get distracted by the fancy button-ups and next thing you know, you're getting tossed in the dumpster out back."

Nick choked. "You're a lot weirder than you look."

Logan smiled. It was like she'd passed some kind of test—Elexis went back to his game while Nick dug into computer parts, explaining each one to Logan as he went. Logan listened and nodded, plucking snacks from her to-go box and, for the first time since she got to Snakebite, it felt like she could breathe. If Snakebite was war, Elexis's room was a single patch of sanctuary. The boys weren't the ultra-queer crowd of loose acquaintances she'd had back in LA, but Snakebite was a different world. In Snakebite, people were either allies or enemies. She wasn't sure what Ashley was, but Nick and Elexis were at least vaguely on her side.

She'd finally found allies.

14

Grief Like Seeds

"The girls didn't wanna join us?" Tammy asked from the kitchen, slipping a piece of sourdough into the toaster oven. Her bright blond curls were tucked up in a fitness headband, makeup done to perfection. She'd clearly expected guests. "I made enough for the whole gang."

"They were busy," Ashley lied. "It's okay. I'm glad it's just you and me."

Historically, Sunday morning brunches on the lake had the magic ability to fix any kind of sadness. This was the way she'd gotten over a failed math test and the first time the Ford broke down and the time Fran temporarily decided she didn't want to be friends anymore. It was a long shot to believe that brunch could solve the problem of her boyfriend's disappearance, but it was worth a try. At the very least, it was a chance to figure out what the cabin was all about.

While Tammy fixed a plate of toast and jelly, Ashley set the table on the back deck with silverware, mugs, and a fresh pot of coffee. The sky was still rosy with morning, the wind off the lake crisp and cool, but the sun was fat and low on the horizon, glaring at them through the heat. It was too early for it to be this hot outside, but that's how it had been ever since Tristan disappeared. Either too hot or too cold, always at the extreme. Tammy settled in with her coffee and a self-help book for "girl bosses." Ashley left her hibiscus tea to steep and leaned her head back against the chair, inspecting the tangled juniper limbs overhead. This was easy. Ashley inhaled and exhaled and it felt like the first time she'd done it in weeks.

"What's going on with you?" Tammy asked. She tucked a loose strand of Ashley's hair behind her ear. "You seem stressed."

Ashley cupped her hands around her mug for warmth. "Same as always. I'm fine."

"Tristan?"

Ashley looked out at the water.

"If he's out there, he'll come back," Tammy said. "You've got it all under control. That's how us Barton girls are. Calm under fire."

Ashley nodded.

"Not to make this about me, but I can tell you from experience, sometimes boys leave because they think they're gonna find themselves somewhere else." Tammy took a long drink of coffee. "Sometimes they come back different. If God wants to take them out of your life, he'll take them. Things always fall into place. Don't drive yourself crazy over it."

Ashley wished it was as easy as her mother made it sound. But this wasn't like her dad—Tristan wasn't off in some other city with a new family. He hadn't run off to avoid a life here. In fact, Tristan had been ready to make Snakebite his forever. Every time she closed her eyes, she saw him in the woods. She saw him choking, bruised, *dying*.

She saw him in her room. She remembered their last conversation, standing across the room from each other, and her chest ached. She wished she could undo that last moment, unspool it all and try again.

She needed to change the subject.

"It's not just Tristan stuff. I feel kinda bad about how we're all treating that new family," Ashley said. She stared intently into the stitching on the arm of her chair, ignoring the way her mother turned to look at her. Tammy's eyes raked over her, cool as ice. It was the signature intensity that had always served Barton women well.

"Oh, the Ortizes."

"Yeah. Ortiz-Woodley, actually," Ashley clarified. "I think they hyphenate it."

Tammy made a soft *hmm.* She glanced down at her book. "You think I'm being mean? If you knew them better, you'd understand."

"How *do* you know them?"

Tammy said nothing. Ashley didn't know much about the Ortiz-Woodleys, but Logan herself didn't seem to know much about them, either. Everyone else in Snakebite had some kind of ancient vendetta against the two men—and by extension, Logan—but no one was willing to explain it. It was an old thing, dormant and quiet and unmoving.

"You know, I read an article a while back about people like the daughter," Tammy continued as though she hadn't been asked a question. She leaned back in her chair and looked out over the gray lake. "Studies say they usually turn out just fine, actually. Totally normal. I thought the lack of balance at home would make it hard for them to grow up right. But the article said they're like those plants that grow in the dark. Resilient."

She said *resilient* with a punch in her voice, like Logan was a soldier marching against her oppressively gay fathers.

"I don't know," Ashley said. "She seems fine. I've barely met her dads."

Tammy shook her head. She cupped her mug of coffee and faced the wind off the lake with her eyes closed. She got like this sometimes when she was pulled into a memory so strong it briefly replaced reality. It was the face she made when she talked about Ashley's father. It was the face she made when she talked about learning ranch work from Grandma Addie. And now it was the face she made when she thought of the Ortiz-Woodleys.

"You're better off," Tammy said. "I don't believe in curses, but those two are a *curse.* They were when they lived here before, they are now, they always will be. I swear, everything they touch just falls apart. I wouldn't be surprised if more of you kids went missing before they leave."

"Mom . . ." Ashley breathed.

"I wish I was being dramatic." She inhaled, sharp and sudden. "If I were you, I'd stay away from that family altogether. Even if the daughter's normal, it's not worth it. They're poison. I don't know why we keep letting them back in."

"You told her dad you'd be nice."

"I said I'd be nice to the *girl,*" Tammy clarified, purposefully not saying Logan's name. "And Alejo knows me well enough to know that ignoring them *is* me being nice."

Ashley nodded. She wanted to ask *how* he knew her well enough, but she didn't press. She stared into the swirling surface of her tea and the hibiscus scent made her eyes water. Maybe her mother was right. The moment the Ortiz-Woodleys arrived, Snakebite had become a bitter, guarded thing. Ever since they'd arrived, the shadows had teeth. Even brunch felt tainted.

"Did they *do* something?" Ashley asked.

Tammy didn't look at her. "Yes. Sort of."

The lake rippled in the sunlight. The sky was wide and bright, but today it felt like a lie. An illusion of Snakebite from a time when it was simpler.

"I don't want you to worry." Tammy smiled. She took Ashley's hand and squeezed. "Snakebite's tougher than you'd think. They'll leave, or we'll spit them out all over again."

Ashley nodded. She carefully ran her finger along the arm of her chair. "Did you guys used to hang out at the cabin when you were my age?"

Tammy blinked. "The cabin?"

"Yeah. There's this cabin on the other side of the lake. It looks like it's been there forever." Ashley traced the floral design on the side of her mug. "Just wondering if you guys ever used to hang out there."

Tammy was quiet.

"Me and the others hang out there sometimes."

"I know of it."

Ashley's eyes widened. "Okay, cool. I was just wondering if you'd ever seen anyone there, or . . ."

"Or?"

"Or if you know who owns it?"

"My friends and I never 'hung out' there because it didn't

exist when I was your age," Tammy said. "The cabin wasn't built until I was . . . twenty-four? Maybe twenty-five?"

"Wait, really?" Ashley sat up straight. "It looks *ancient.*"

"I don't know what to tell you about that. But I'd really rather you kids not mess around out there."

"Why?"

"Because I said so."

Ashley ran fingers through the end of her ponytail. "Someone must've built it, though. Whose is it?"

Tammy took a long drink of coffee, eyes trained on the lake. For a moment, Ashley thought she wouldn't answer. The cabin would be just another secret Ashley didn't deserve. But Tammy set down her mug and shook her head. "The cabin is mine."

At the Bates, morning came without ceremony.

It wasn't like the cascading pink light of LA's slow-rolling dawns. In Snakebite, it was dark and then it was light. If Logan blinked, she was sure to miss it. When she put her coffee in the microwave, it was dark as midnight. When she stepped outside for a breath of fresh air only moments later, it was a cream-colored morning.

It probably didn't mean anything, but given everything she'd seen lately, it made her nervous.

Logan sat in the parking lot alone most mornings, microwave-nuked coffee in hand. The sunrise made it easier to think, but this morning she struggled to focus. She'd dreamed about being buried again, and the nightmare lingered like a second skin. It was different from the first time. This time, she'd clawed her way out of her tomb. She'd pulled herself from the earth, crawled to her stomach, and looked out into the tar-thick night.

She crawled out of her grave and ended up *here.*

In Snakebite.

At that stupid lake.

The door to room eight opened and Brandon stepped out into the sweltering morning. He was dressed in jeans that slouched at his ankles, and a backpack full of ghost-hunting equipment. His sweatshirt read BARTON LUMBER. He stopped in front of the Neon, apparently surprised to see Logan on the curb.

"Nice sweatshirt," Logan said. "I thought the Bartons were evil."

"When in Snakebite . . ." Brandon said, looking down at the logo. His grimace was small but impossible to miss. "You're up early."

"I'm up early every morning."

"Oh." Brandon stood there a moment longer. He tapped his foot on the pavement, searching for something to say.

Logan remained silent. Given what Ashley had seen at the cabin, she had no idea what to say to him. Then again, she *never* knew what to say to him. Even if he had nothing to do with Tristan's disappearance, even if the paint on his door was a joke, he was hiding something.

Brandon cleared his throat and said, "See you later, then."

She offered a quick wave and that was that. Brandon climbed into the Neon and carefully pulled away from the Bates. Logan watched him turn left toward the highway and made a mental note of it. Either he was making a trip into the city or he was heading out toward the lake. Toward the cabin.

Behind her, Alejo cleared his throat. He stood in the doorway of room eight dressed in a plaid robe, shoulder-length hair still wet from the shower. He motioned to the curb she squatted on. "That looks comfortable."

"It's great."

"You could make more of an effort."

Logan arched a brow. "To what?"

"Your dad just tried to have a conversation with you, or did you miss that?" Alejo leaned against the doorframe. "He's trying. You could try, too."

"Me and him are fine."

"Logan."

"What? Sorry I'm not super talkative all the time. I hate it here. I just sit around with nothing to do." Logan took another sip of coffee and stared out at the soft glow of the horizon. This wasn't usually how she talked to Alejo—this ire was usually reserved for homophobes on her dads' Twitter page—but she was tired of this. She was tired of being treated like she was the unreasonable one when she was being lied to and shut down left and right. She was tired of being the bad guy.

Alejo shifted. "I get that you're bored, but you don't *have* to sit around all day. You could apply for schools."

"To do what?"

"I don't know. You like history," Alejo said. "It's probably too late for fall term, but you could still get in for spring. I loved college. You might learn a lot about yourself."

"I already know all about me." Logan leaned back and closed her eyes. "And besides, I'm on my gap year."

"Jesus," Alejo said, covering his mouth to stifle a laugh. "Why don't you come inside for some coffee?"

Logan raised her mug. "Already got some."

"Let me rephrase—come inside. We need to talk."

Logan pushed herself up from the curb and followed Alejo inside. Where she'd at least made an effort to humanize her room, Brandon and Alejo had seemingly done the opposite. The walls were bare, beds clean and precisely made, motel toiletries untouched. It was the kind of room she'd seen in crime shows when a secret agent wanted to fly under the radar. They'd been at the Bates for almost a month, and Brandon had been here even longer.

Something was off.

Alejo pulled out a seat at their window-side table and motioned for Logan to sit. "I'm just making a pot. You want a refill?"

"Uh, sure," Logan said. "You guys are keeping it super clean in here."

"Yeah, well . . ." Alejo slid into the seat across from her. The sunlight was copper over his face. "I lived in this motel my whole life before I met your dad. I'm not exactly thrilled to be back here. This helps me remember it's temporary."

"Oh," Logan said. "I didn't know you lived *here* here."

"I told you Gracia is mi tía," Alejo said. "When I was a kid, this motel was mostly us Ortizes. Me and my parents lived on the other side of the motel." He looked around. "I don't remember if anyone lived in this one. Might've been empty back then."

"Wait." Logan's brow furrowed. "Do I have more family here?"

Alejo's expression was wistful. "Ah, well, my parents moved away from Snakebite a long time ago. I don't know where. They didn't tell me. But Gracia is our family. Elexis is your cousin. Nice to know we're not totally alone, right?"

"Wow . . ." Logan trailed off. "What about on Brandon's side?"

"Not anymore, I don't think," Alejo said. "His dad used to run a boat shop here, though. He taught my brother's algebra class before he retired. It's funny—me and your dad were actually in the same grade all through high school but I didn't get to know him until I came back from college."

He said it casually, but it was clear that *before* college was a different world from *after.* She'd never given much thought to her fathers' lives before her. She couldn't imagine what it was like for them in this town all by themselves for so long.

She finished off her cup of coffee. "You wanted to talk about something?"

"Right." Alejo poured himself a cup and refilled Logan's, but his expression was cautious. It was measured. Something made him nervous. "I haven't talked about it with your dad because it's a touchy subject, but I was catching up with an old buddy the other day and he told me you made a new friend . . ."

"Ashley?"

"I assume so," Alejo said. "Ashley Barton."

"Yeah. We're not friends, though."

"But you spent all day with her?" Alejo asked.

"Who was monitoring us that closely?"

Alejo waved a hand. "That doesn't matter."

"Did I do something wrong?"

"No, just . . . help me out," Alejo said. He pressed his fingertips to the bridge of his nose. "If you and Ashley aren't friends, why hang out with her?"

"Because there's, like, four kids my age in this town?"

"Yeah, well, if she's anything like her mother, I promise there are better choices."

Logan laughed. Alejo had always taught her that if she wanted the truth, she had to give the truth. People only owed you honesty if you were honest. So she shrugged. "We're hunting ghosts."

"Are you serious?" Alejo stared at her like he didn't understand. This shock was different from his overdramatic TV persona.

"Yeah. Weird stuff's been going on in Snakebite. Since you guys never tell me anything, I figured we'd get some answers on our own."

"Since when do I not tell you things?" Alejo asked, indignant.

"Okay, why are we here?"

"We're location scouting for the show."

Logan rolled her eyes. "And what case are you investigating?"

"Your dad already told you. You've noticed the weirdness here. Strange weather, dark omens . . ."

"I didn't realize you guys were meteorologists."

"If Ashley wants answers, she can ask her mother," Alejo said. He pressed his fingertips against the table, doing his best to hide his disdain. "I don't think Tammy Barton loves anything more than the sound of her own voice."

"What about *my* questions?"

"Ask away."

Logan took a deep breath. "Does the investigation have anything to do with Tristan Granger?"

"Who?"

"The missing kid."

"Listen," Alejo said. He pinched the bridge of his nose. "You know how it is in the early days. It might have something to do with the missing kid, it might not. You know that we never have much to go on at first. It's an investigation show."

"Well, your timing isn't great," Logan said. "Now everyone thinks you guys had something to do with it."

Alejo frowned. "What else did you want to ask?"

"Right." Logan almost wished she'd brought a notepad. She cleared her throat. "Uh, ghosts . . . what are they?"

Silence, and then Alejo laughed. He covered his mouth to hide a smug smile, then quickly sobered. "I'm not laughing at you, I'm just . . . how many years have we been doing the show? You know what ghosts are."

"*Real* ghosts."

Alejo gasped. "I don't like what you're implying."

"The stuff you guys hunt is . . ." Logan cleared her throat. "I just wanna know what the real thing is like. If there is a real thing."

Alejo looked into his mug. This was always his reaction when she talked skeptically about the show. To date, Logan couldn't tell if this was embarrassment at his TV antics or frustration that she questioned it. Probably both. No matter how ridiculous it was, Alejo seemed to truly love the show.

But loving the show and thinking it was real were two different things, and the things Ashley saw in the cabin were different from anything on *ParaSpectors*.

Alejo looked up. "Real ghosts aren't the kind of thing you put on TV."

"You've seen one?"

"I mean . . . yes? It's hard to explain without sounding like

I'm making it up." Alejo let out a gentle breath between his lips and looked out the window. "I've been able to see them my whole life."

Logan blinked. Not only could Alejo see ghosts—he'd been able to see them the *whole time.* The tightness in her chest wavered from anger to awe. She pushed her empty mug around the table. "So the ghosts on the show were . . . ?"

"The ghosts were real. In a way." Alejo tapped his fingers on the table. "Everywhere we went had real ghosts, but that's not a bad thing. *Everywhere* does. Real ghosts don't hurt you. They don't need to be exorcized. They're hardly even sentient. They're like . . . feelings. Or memories. I don't know."

"You don't know?"

"There's not really a guide on how it works."

Logan shook her head. "And all the gear?"

"The gear is real . . . to an extent."

"What do ghosts look like?" Logan asked, careful not to betray too much of her excitement. Maybe Alejo had meant it when he said you could trade honesty for honesty. He'd never talked about ghosts this plainly.

Alejo's hands were tight around his coffee mug, knuckles pale against the speckled ceramic. He crossed his legs and leaned forward like this was some kind of campfire story hour. "I don't want to freak you out."

"I don't get scared."

"You never did." Alejo's smile was only a flash before his expression darkened. "The ghosts I've seen are more like impressions left by the dead. Like a captured moment. It's not always visual. Sometimes it's a smell, or a voice, or a feeling. It's hard to describe."

"What do they do?"

"Not much, honestly. From what I can tell, they only really appear if they've left something behind. No one wants to stay here if they can move on. But if they weren't ready or they're not quite gone yet, *that's* when they show up. It's like they're reaching back, asking for help the only way they can."

"Can Brandon see them, too?" Logan asked.

"No. I don't know why people can or can't see them. I've met a few other people who could. Usually they're not big fans of the show." Alejo gave an uneasy laugh. "But, no. Your dad can't see them."

"And living people?" Logan asked. She traced a circle in the carpet under the table with her toe. "Did you guys ever see a ghost for a person that's still alive?"

Alejo narrowed his eyes at that, lips pressed in a flat line. Logan wondered if she'd overstepped now—if she'd gone too specific. Maybe he'd seen Brandon's ghost at the cabin, too. Maybe he was involved in all of it. He gently set his mug on the table, skepticism melting into a soft frown. The way he looked now was almost mournful.

"I don't have a for-sure answer. We know that spirits are made of unresolved pain that lingers somewhere between life and . . . beyond. Theoretically, I'd say pain that leaves a deep enough impact—pain that kills a piece of a person—could leave ghosts, too. Ghosts are death, but maybe death can mean different things. I don't know. If pain is the measure, I promise Snakebite is *full* of ghosts."

Logan sucked in a sharp breath. They'd never kept secrets from each other. At least, she'd *thought* they didn't, but now it seemed like Alejo was made of secrets. Just like Brandon. A part of Logan wanted to tell him about what she'd seen at the cabin. But she couldn't shake the creeping fear that he and Brandon had something to do with all of this. That whatever Brandon had done to cause the ghost in the cabin, Alejo was a part of it. Maybe there was a simple explanation, but maybe there wasn't.

Her curiosity curdled into fear. She emptied her mug with one swallow. "Was there anything else we needed to talk about?"

"Your dad." Alejo tentatively smiled. "He says you two had fun shopping the other day. Your room looks great."

"Yeah, it was fine."

"He's trying," Alejo said. "I know things can be . . . awkward. And the show hasn't helped. Just try to cut him some slack."

Logan nodded. "That's everything?"

"I guess so," Alejo said.

Logan checked her phone. She swiped open a series of texts from Ashley:

ashley b: party tonight at the cabin
ashley b: learned some stuff from my mom
ashley b: maybe we'll see some ghosts
ashley b: kidding
ashley b: we should actually investigate though
ashley b: i'll pick you up at nine

Logan smiled at the screen. She turned to Alejo and pocketed her phone. "I guess I should tell you I'm going to a party tonight?"

Alejo raised a brow. "A Snakebite party?"

"Yeah, at this abandoned cabin. It's very on-brand creepy for me."

Alejo's expression steeled. It wasn't just the party, it was the location. He *did* know about the cabin.

"It's not a *party* party," Logan continued. "It's a gathering of friends."

"All your good Snakebite friends?"

"Mm-hmm."

"The same friends that decorated our wall?"

Logan's stomach clenched.

"Actually, I'm taking Nick and Elexis from next door. They're my new friends," Logan said. "I'm helping Nick build a computer."

"You're helping him?"

"Okay, I'm *watching* him build a computer. My moral support means a lot to him."

"You're responsible," Alejo sighed. "I know you'll be fine. Just . . . make sure you have a way home. Don't stay out too late. And if you need help, please call me."

"I will," Logan said. She hesitated. "Dad?"

Alejo looked up.

"Thanks for telling me. About the ghosts and all that."

"Oh. Well, you know you can ask me anything." Alejo took a long drink of his coffee. "Have fun at your party."

15

The Cabin In The Woods

"You're kidding."

Ashley killed the engine on the Ford and slumped back in her seat. She'd expected to pick up Logan *singular* at the Bates on the way out to the cabin. She hadn't expected Logan to emerge from the Bates with a duo of creepy nerds that she had apparently befriended in the last week. Even after twelve years of going to the same school, Ashley doubted she'd ever spoken a word to either Elexis Carrillo or Nick Porter. They were just the guys who always smelled like Cheetos and Red Bull in math class and she was *not* walking into the cabin with them. As they climbed into the back seat, Logan leaned into the passenger-side window with a wine-colored grin. "Hope you don't mind I brought a plus one. Or two, I guess."

"Where'd you find the strays?" Ashley hissed.

"Don't be a bully," Logan said.

Ashley leaned across the truck and whispered, "I said *you* were invited."

"And I decided I didn't wanna hang out by myself with a

bunch of people that write slurs about my dads." Logan shook her hair from under the collar of her jean jacket. "Besides, you should be nicer. They have nothing but nice things to say about you."

Ashley grimaced.

Logan, Elexis, and Nick all climbed into the Ford and Ashley got a good look at the three of them. Logan looked like a character from a movie, dressed in a short black dress with a denim jacket and a face full of makeup. She was the type of person who arrived in a limo, not a thirty-year-old truck. Ashley suddenly regretted not explaining what these parties were like. They weren't even really parties. A feeling somewhere between awe and embarrassment welled in Ashley's chest.

"Thanks for the ride, Ashley," Nick said from the back seat.

"Yeah, thanks Ashley," Elexis echoed.

Ashley pried her grimace into a forced smile. It'd only been thirty seconds and her truck smelled like Mountain Dew. Elexis Carrillo wore his signature gray beanie and a flannel that was too tight for his arms, probably because he'd been wearing the same one since middle school. Nick Porter was in a hoodie with the Captain America shield in the center. He looked at her longer than she was comfortable with.

"Uh yeah, no problem," Ashley said.

"Elexis," Elexis said. He gestured to Nick. "This is Nick."

Ashley's smile was tight. "I know your names."

"Oh, you all hang out a lot?" Logan asked with no attempt to hide the sarcasm in her voice.

"Not really," Ashley said. "But you two are always welcome."

"We were never invited," Nick said, matter-of-fact.

Logan gasped. "The *drama*."

Ashley shot Logan another warning look. She was sure Logan had just invited them as revenge for being left at the Chokecherry, which Ashley guessed was fair. But *still.*

Logan returned her look with a knowing smile. The stabbing yellow light of the motel sign made the shadows on her face deeper and darker, blending into the sharp wings of her eyeliner. Her hair was down tonight, straightened to her shoulders, and Ashley was struck again by the *other*ness of her. Logan Ortiz-Woodley wasn't the kind of person who ended up in Snakebite. She wasn't the kind of person you'd find slouched in the worn passenger seat of Ashley's truck.

"You're staring," Logan said.

Ashley turned the ignition and the truck rattled to life. "You're making me look underdressed."

"I don't think so." Logan glanced at Ashley's legs, then pulled down the passenger-side mirror to wipe away a stray bit of lipstick. "Your shorts are cute."

Ashley smiled. She'd gone with her standard fare: a black tank top, denim shorts, and a flannel around her waist in case they ended up outside. She mostly thought of it as practical, but Tristan had always said she looked cute.

Guilt knotted in her stomach.

They drove out of town on the lakeside highway. The evening sky was the color of bruised knuckles as night crept in. The still lake glimmered white with moonlight, holding up the jagged black hills on the other shore. Orange blips of campfire radiated from the campground across the water, but it was all worlds away.

Ashley cleared her throat. Quietly, to Logan, she said, "So, the cabin . . . I asked my mom about it."

"What did Tammy say?" Logan asked, tapping idly at her phone.

"I found out who owns it—technically, *we* do." She waited for Logan to look up. "My grandma bought the land from the state, like, twenty years ago? She wanted my mom to turn it into a resort, but my mom didn't think it would make any money. She let some family build on the property back in the nineties."

"The nineties?" Logan asked. "It looks like it hasn't been touched since the Oregon Trail."

"I know. She doesn't know why it looks like that, either."

"Huh." Logan leaned into the back of her seat. "She hasn't gone out to see it?"

"Apparently not."

"Then it looks like we'll have to *investigate*."

"You . . ." Ashley scowled, eyeing Nick and Elexis through the rearview mirror. Softer, she said, "Do they know what we're doing?"

"They don't care," Logan whispered. "I'm pretty sure they think I'm joking. Seriously, relax about them. They'll probably hang out with each other the whole time. I just didn't wanna be totally alone at this thing."

"You wouldn't've been alone," Ashley said. "You're with me."

Logan said nothing.

By the time they pulled into the gravel turnout at the end of the highway, John's white Silverado was already parked. Through the trees, Ashley spotted the faint yellow glow of camping lanterns inside the bones of the old cabin. It felt like she was putting Logan on trial, or like she was putting herself on trial and Logan was the damning evidence. Either way, she was about to face the jury.

"Okay, guys," Ashley said. "It might be kinda weird at first, but that's just—"

Logan threw open the passenger door and hopped out of the truck. "Because we're losers? It's usually just you and your mean friends and you don't like outsiders. We appreciate the heads up. We'll be fine."

Elexis followed her out of the truck, but Nick remained buckled in the back seat. He looked at Ashley and cleared his throat. "*I* was listening to you."

Ashley flashed a tense smile through the rearview mirror. "Thanks, Nick."

The four of them made their way through the woods, following the thumping sound of country music to the cabin. Ashley shouldered her way to the front of their small group to open the door. She prayed it would be just another get-together and no one would bat an eye at the LA socialite and her accompanying nerds.

A wave of heat and beer smell greeted them on the other side of the door. For a moment, the cabin fell silent. John, Paul, and Fran were all crowded on the sofa in the corner of the room. Bug stood next to them, leaning on the old piano with a can of PBR and wide eyes. All four stared at Ashley with matching creased brows, waiting for some kind of explanation. She'd barely gotten permission to bring Logan—bringing Elexis and Nick was a mistake.

Maybe this whole thing was a mistake.

"Oh, it's *literally* a gathering of friends," Logan said, bouldering through the silence. She pushed in front of Ashley with a broad smile and hoisted a box of beer over her head. "Greetings, rednecks. I come in peace."

Ashley braced herself.

The silence in the cabin stretched for one more excruciating moment before Fran jumped up from the couch with a bright grin. She took the beer from Logan and pulled her into an awkward hug. "You look cute. I hope we're not too boring for you."

Logan laughed, short and sharp. "Anything's better than the motel."

Fran laughed too, brushing a curl behind her ear. She didn't want Logan here, clearly, but she was putting on a good face and trying to make it work. Ashley hoped everyone else would do the same.

They made their way back to the ratty sofa with the beers, Elexis and Nick trudging along behind Logan like they were lost. Ashley sat on the arm of the sofa, and Logan, Elexis, and Nick sat on the floor. There were usually six people, but now there were eight. Ashley wasn't sure how it was possible for the cabin to feel so empty and so overcrowded.

"I should probably introduce everyone," Ashley said once everyone was settled in. "Logan, this is Bug, Paul, John, and you know Fran."

Logan nodded with the vacant stare of a person who has not retained anyone's names. She gestured to Elexis and Nick. "Do you guys all know each other?"

"Yeah, kinda," Elexis said. "We go to school together."

John checked the time on his phone.

The tension was so thick Ashley could cut it with a knife. She pulled a beer from the pack in the center of their little circle and popped it open, eager to wash away some of her discomfort. Bug eyed her and shook her head, but Ashley didn't need the reminder. She'd caused this by inviting Logan. By not putting her foot down about Elexis and Nick. A Barton would've found a way to make this whole thing run smoothly. Her mother would've made this work. Country music thumped from John's Bluetooth speaker on the piano, not quite playing loud enough to cover up the awkward silence. Logan pulled a beer free and took a long drink.

"God, why is it so awkward?" Fran laughed uneasily. "Let's talk about something interesting."

"What kind of guys do you like?" Bug asked Logan.

Logan traced the lid of her beer can with her pointer finger and didn't look up. Somehow, Ashley understood the answer before Logan said a word. Logan's nose wrinkled up and she said, "Uh, none?"

Fran and Bug looked at Ashley with the quickness of vipers.

"Like . . ." Fran drawled.

"Like none. I'm a lesbian."

All at once, everyone took a drink. Blood rushed to Ashley's cheeks. For a moment, she thought Logan was kidding, but it felt true. It felt right in a way Ashley couldn't quite untangle. It was probably normal in LA, but people in Snakebite just . . . *weren't* gay. Ashley bit back her surprise and donned a smile.

"Wow, that's—"

She didn't have time to finish. John folded his arms over his chest and asked, "So, what, you like girls?"

"Yeah. That's generally what a lesbian is." Logan took a drink of beer without breaking eye contact. How she'd gone so quickly from semiembarrassment to unrelenting bravado was a mystery to Ashley.

"Is it . . . like, do you think it's a genetic thing?" Fran asked.

She wrinkled up her nose and looked around. "Is it okay to ask that?"

"First, I'm adopted," Logan scoffed. "Second, no, it's not."

"It's not genetic or it's not okay to ask?" Paul asked.

"Both."

The cabin was silent.

Bug looked at Ashley like she was going to be sick. Ashley closed her eyes and pictured her mother sitting in this circle. She tried to picture the perfect Tammy Barton solution.

"Hey, I have a party game for us to play," Ashley said. She put a hand on Bug's wrist to comfort her. "Let's all just drink until we're having fun, okay?"

Somehow, this worked.

Paul turned up the music on the speaker and everyone drank. Within an hour, it was a party just like any other before Tristan's disappearancc. As it turned out, the best way to make a room of people get along was to blur their heads with cheap beer until they couldn't remember why they were different in the first place. Fran ended up on John's lap, Bug seemed to actually *enjoy* talking to Paul for once, and Logan, Nick, and Elexis drifted into their own conversation about god knew what. It was all effortless again. The apprehension about Logan and the others melted into easy laughter, and everything was *okay.*

Ashley could almost picture Tristan here, laughing along with the others. She could imagine him and Logan joking together.

Everything was the same again, but Tristan was gone.

Quietly, Ashley moved to the cabin's old, worn-down kitchen. It was more like a crumbling wooden tunnel given the missing back wall. Wind whispered between the decayed planks, ruffling

Ashley's hair against her neck. She hadn't had more than two beers, but the room felt distant. The whole *world* felt distant. If she wandered into the woods right now, she wondered how long it would take the others to notice she was gone. Just as easily as they were moving on from Tristan, they'd move on from her. She could slip into the night and be a ghost just like him. The thought made her heart slog an empty rhythm against her ribs.

Under the sounds of the party, there was another noise. A quiet hum, throaty and low. When Ashley closed her eyes, it was all she could hear. It danced between the shifting trees. Almost like it was getting *closer.*

Without warning, the kitchen door burst open.

"There you are," Logan declared. "I was looking for you."

Logan staggered into the kitchen and ripped open another can of PBR. She'd smudged the corner of her lipstick, but she was otherwise surprisingly put together. She wasn't sharp and sarcastic like she'd been when they arrived. She seemed comfortable—happy, even. She fit in a little *too* well, like parties were her first language.

"Seems like you're having fun," Ashley said.

"Seems like you're not." Logan leaned against the decaying counter opposite Ashley. "You find anything interesting?"

Ashley arched a brow.

"The investigation. The whole reason we're here. Did you see any ghosts?"

Ashley exhaled. "Oh, yeah. Uh, no. I haven't seen anything."

"Have you been looking?"

"No. Not really."

Logan narrowed her eyes. The bass from the song in the main room thumped in the silence between them. After a moment,

Logan looked out the collapsed kitchen wall into the black night. "What've you been doing in here, then?"

Ashley shrugged. The thing she'd felt before—the loneliness that welled like a tide in her chest—was gone as quick as it had come. The junipers outside the kitchen rustled in the cool wind, and Ashley was back to earth. She fixed Logan with a look. "It's not like you've been investigating, either."

Logan scoffed, indignant. She held out a closed fist. "I have, too. I even found something."

"Are you gonna show me?" Ashley asked.

"I don't think you earned it," Logan slurred. "You didn't even look."

Ashley rolled her eyes. Against her better judgment, her lips curled into a reluctant smile. This Logan was different from the one she'd expected. For a moment, she was warm and open. Her laughter was real, dark and smooth as velvet.

"Please," Ashley said, "can I see what you found?"

Logan smirked. "Since you asked nicely."

She turned her fist over and revealed something small and shining on her palm. It was a thick gold ring with a cursive inscription inside: *Mark 10:9.* Ashley plucked it from Logan's palm and studied it. "What God has joined together let no one separate."

"It doesn't say that," Logan said.

"That's the verse."

Logan snorted. "I *knew* you were a church girl."

Ashley playfully shoved Logan in the arm. The ring was nondescript—no embellishments or jewels on the outside, and only the inscription on the inside. "It's not really a clue."

"Yes, it is," Logan said. "Look, there's no dirt on it."

"So?"

"So that means it was here recently."

Ashley handed the ring back. Someone had been to the cabin recently. Someone else had walked the decaying floors. Someone had crept here and lost a piece of themselves. "You think whoever was out here saw what we saw?"

"Maybe," Logan said. She tilted her head back, emptying the rest of her beer. When she finished, she crunched the can down and discarded it in the cracked kitchen sink.

"Are either of your dads missing a ring?"

"No. And they wouldn't have Bible shit on theirs, either." Logan's eyes widened with a sudden realization. "Oh, I found out something else."

Ashley waited.

"Breaking news—you're not the only one who can see stuff. Ghosts." Logan wiped her mouth, smearing her lipstick the rest of the way across her cheek. "My dad sees 'em, too."

Ashley's chest tightened. "What?"

"Yeah. He says he's always seen ghosts." Logan put on a mischievous smile. "Not so special *now,* are you?"

Ashley waved away the comment. "That's . . . a big deal. You're sure?"

Logan nodded. Before she could answer, she tripped over a loose plank in the floor and stumbled into a collapsed counter. Her eyes were glazed over, dark as the night outside and hazy. She was too drunk to talk about the disappearance; Ashley was pretty sure she was too drunk to be here at all. She propped a hand under her elbow and helped her sit down. The night wind skirted Logan's hair into her mouth and across her eyes.

Ashley pushed Logan's hair out of her face.

Something strange snagged her breath.

"I'm an amazing detective," Logan said, eyes half lidded. "I did a great job. Way better than you."

"Sure," Ashley breathed. "You did amazing."

Logan reached up and took Ashley's shoulder. The wind through the gaps in the kitchen walls grew colder by the minute. Logan's eyes watered in the crisp air. "Why're you in here by yourself?"

"I'm not by myself. I'm with you."

Logan blinked, then laughed. "Before that. You looked *so* sad."

"I . . ." Ashley trailed off. She looked back at the main room of the party. No one was looking for them, no one was listening in on them. She closed her eyes. "Honestly? I'm having a really hard time. I'm just really . . ."

". . . lonely," Logan finished.

Her eyes were closed when she said it. The word sounded too natural on her tongue. Too quick. Ashley recognized the same look on Logan's face that she'd seen in the mirror for months. They were adrift in the dark, senselessly paddling for shore.

"Yeah," Ashley said.

In the main room, someone thumped into a wall. Ashley recognized John's voice bellowing something about *my truck* or *my dad*. In approximately thirty seconds, he and Paul would start throwing punches. Fran would cry because she'd told John not to get so worked up. Bug would shut off the music. The party would be over.

Ashley took a sip of warm beer.

It already felt like it was over.

Ashley hooked Logan's arm over her shoulders. "Hey, let's get you some water."

"Get off, straighty," Logan moaned.

Ashley shook her head, biting back a quiet laugh. She poured out the rest of her beer and walked Logan out of the cabin toward the lake. She'd babysat Fran and Bug at a thousand of these parties; she was used to the fussy and unmanageable. The farther they walked from the cabin, the more sober she felt.

The walk had the opposite effect on Logan.

"Where're you taking me?" she said, all in one dump of words.

"To get water. And fresh air." Ashley readjusted Logan's arm on her shoulder. "Then sleep."

Logan's head lolled back against Ashley's shoulder, eyes closed. Her smoky gray eyeshadow was cloudy with sweat now. "We're going so far," she slurred. "*Ohmygod,* are you the murderer?"

"That's not funny."

They reached the lakeshore and Ashley propped Logan against a tree trunk. She filled her empty beer can with lake water and tilted it against Logan's lips. Logan drank slowly until her nose wrinkled up and she spat at Ashley's feet.

"Tastes like pee and grass," she said. "I'd rather have a hangover."

"C'mon," Ashley whispered. She pressed the can to Logan's lips again. "You don't want your dads to see you hungover."

Logan waved a dismissive hand. "My dads don't care."

Something in the way she said this made Ashley think she wished they did.

Farther down the shore, Ashley spotted Elexis and Nick

making their way to the water. She waved them down. "Hey, I'm taking her to the truck. Meet me there when you're ready."

Nick gave her a thumbs-up.

Ashley helped Logan to her feet. In the dark, they walked back to the gravel clearing where the trucks were parked. Ashley pulled a sleeping bag from the storage box in the back of the Ford and laid it across the bed of the truck. It was tradition to camp out for a few hours on nights when she was still too drunk to drive home. Logan was already most of the way passed out as Ashley tucked her in, muttering something about calling a "yee-haw Lyft." By the time Ashley climbed into a second sleeping bag, Logan was out cold. The quiet of the woods settled in and Ashley's heart stopped racing.

She'd spent countless nights in this truck bed, in this clearing, in this sleeping bag looking at the stars with Tristan. She'd spent more time than she could measure lying with him in silence just like this. She'd never felt as far away from him as she did now. She'd never felt so far away from everyone.

She would find him. They would have more nights under the stars.

They had skies left to see.

Interlude

The host is getting stronger.

Waiting in the woods tonight is *his* idea.

The night is wide and warm and full of wondrous noise. Voices echo through the trees. The host pushes his way through the dark, dodging roots and boulders with ease. Part of his quickness is memory—he has come out here a hundred times in the last few months—but the host is lither than he seems, too. He looks as unassuming as most humans do, but most humans don't have a viper coiled in their chest, hiding just under their skin. Most don't hunger like the host does.

This host's hunger is all his own.

He lurks in shadow, silently watching the cabin. Like a snake never regrets swallowing its prey, the host is learning to set aside his guilt. Before the Dark leaves him, the host will be unafraid of the shadowed corners of his heart.

A boy separates from the party. He drunkenly ambles away

from the light of the cabin into the twisted, swaying junipers along the shore. The host inhales the night air and it smells like fresh water and soil. It smells like peril.

The host is afraid.

He is excited.

"What if they catch us this time?" the host asks. "I shouldn't be here."

They cannot catch a shadow, the Dark breathes. *They cannot catch someone who was never here.*

The host nods. He knows how to hide. He's been doing it his whole life. He's been hiding the very nature of who he is. He's been hiding so long that indulging in this violence feels like a lie when it is his only truth.

The boy continues down the slope toward the water. He is oblivious to the woods around him because he believes he has nothing to fear. It is this kind of ignorance that makes it so easy for the host. The boy stops at the shore and faces the water.

The host stands behind him, just out of sight. The moonlight on the lake ripples white over the boy's face, but the host's face is shadowed by thick boughs of juniper.

His heart beats with fear and anticipation in equal measure.

Now is your chance, the Dark whispers. *Take it.*

The host hesitates when the boy turns to look at the trees. His eyes are wide and brown, but they do not fear.

Not yet.

The host's heart beats once, twice, and then he moves.

By the time the boy understands that he is not alone, the

host has him. By the time he understands that he will die, it is too late to scream. Farther in the trees, the cabin is emptying. The children laugh and, only feet away, the boy is gone.

The host has never felt stronger. The Dark has never felt stronger.

16

Sunny Side Up

The first thing Logan smelled in the morning was bacon. Bacon and cat hair and the faintly sweet scent of Red Bull. The ceiling looked like the crosshatched one in her motel room, but the lighting came in from the wrong side of the room.

She wasn't supposed to be in her room, anyway. She'd fallen asleep in the back of Ashley's truck. Or at least, she was pretty sure she had. Everything after the kitchen was hazy.

Logan sat up and a pile of blankets fell to the floor around her. She hadn't slept on a bed at all, apparently. The futon under her was mostly spring and no cushion. Elexis sat a few feet away playing a video game.

Like hers, Elexis's room was connected to the room next door. The door between them was wide open, and considering the lack of bacon or cats in Elexis's half, Logan guessed the smells were coming from the other room.

She stood, carefully clutching a blanket around her shoulders to hide the mussed black dress she'd worn out the night before. A mirror hung on the wall over the futon, forcing her to face the monstrous version of herself who'd spent a full night in makeup. Her eyeliner was smudged into a streak of black that made her look more like a demon than a girl.

"Morning," Elexis said. Logan couldn't see his face, but the smugness was clear in his voice. "Sleep okay?"

"I guess . . ." Logan trailed off. "Uh, how did I get here?"

"Your girlfriend dropped us off this morning. She didn't want any people in the truck bed when she got back to the ranch since her mom is evil."

"My . . ." Logan started. She scowled. "Hilarious. Where's *your* buddy?"

"Nick got a ride with John and the others."

"Climbing the social ladder. I thought he'd ride with Ashley considering he's, you know, in love."

Elexis shrugged and kept playing his video game.

Logan wandered to the open door between rooms and whispered, "Who lives in this one?"

Elexis cupped a hand over his mouth. "Nana, she's awake."

In the next room, a chair creaked. Logan followed the sound. The room attached to Elexis's was slightly different from the others she'd seen at the Bates. Instead of a second bed, there was a slab of mint-green countertop, complete with a sink and stove. A twin bed was pushed against the back wall, surrounded by framed pictures of a dark-haired family. Logan recognized the toddler in one photo as a much younger, much cuter Elexis. In another photo was a teenage boy in high-waisted shorts ordering pizza from the stand in the parking lot, presumably before it closed down. It took her a moment longer than it should've to recognize the teen as Alejo. In front of the TV, a crocheted doily was draped over the back of a rust-orange recliner. Gracia sat in the recliner with her feet elevated, spectacled gaze laser-focused on the TV.

She turned in the recliner and beamed. "Are you feeling better?"

"Totally." Logan patted sweat from her forehead. "I . . . thanks for letting me crash here. I really like the decorations."

Gracia held up her deep green doily in progress. "You want one? This is for your dad."

"I—"

"I think yours will be red."

Logan smiled. "You don't have to do that. But I'd love one."

"Give me a week." Gracia laughed. "I didn't know you and Elexis were friends. You must be a miracle worker. I can *never* get him out of his room."

"Happy to help," Logan said. A familiar voice rang from the TV screen. Logan spotted her fathers' faces, inverted by an infrared camera. She laughed under her breath. "You're a fan?"

"I watch every week. Even the repeats. When your dad left, he promised he'd call, but he never did. Never told me what was going on with you guys. This is the only way I saw him." Gracia motioned to a plate of cooked bacon on the counter. "Help yourself to some breakfast. You and me need to catch up."

"I should get back to—"

"You only want to see Elexis, not me?" Gracia asked.

Logan shook her head. Gracia's old-lady sympathy tactics were underhanded, but she had to respect them. She plucked a strip of bacon from the plate and sat at Gracia's window-side table. She vaguely recognized this episode of *ParaSpectors,* though the details escaped her. Maybe it was the one where their camera operator was possessed by Satan. After a while, they began to blur.

The show went to commercial and Gracia turned.

"You were so sick when you got here," she said. "Do you need anything? Juice? Water?"

"Sick," Logan repeated. A piece of her hoped Gracia thought it was a stomach bug and not too much beer. "I must've had a fever or something."

Gracia smiled.

She knew.

"Wait until her dads find out," Elexis called from his room.

Logan chewed on her bacon. "They don't care."

"They would have no room to judge." Gracia chuckled. "After the messes I saw back in the day, I could tell stories that would have them blushing."

Suddenly, Logan was paying attention. She leaned forward—she couldn't believe she hadn't thought to try Gracia for information sooner. She'd had an encyclopedia of Snakebite history living next door this whole time.

"Your dad never told you about when he was your age?"

Logan shook her head.

"Oh, he was always ending up in my room after crazy nights out. His parents—my sister and her husband—they were a lot stricter than your dads. If he came home sick they would've put him on the street. Which . . . well, never mind. I must've cleaned him up a thousand times before sending him back to his room."

"Wow," Logan breathed, immediately abandoning her attempt to figure out what kind of relative that made Gracia to her. "Brandon, too?"

Gracia pursed her lips in thought. A gnat buzzed around the rim of her coffee mug and, from Elexis's room, virtual gunfire echoed off the walls. "No," she said finally. "Not Brandon so much. Alejo was a party kid. I don't think they knew each other back then."

"So Dad was the wild one?"

"He was always a good boy," Gracia clarified. "It was that Tammy Barton who tried to make him bad. She was always dragging him everywhere, making him go to bars and parties with all that drinking. She wanted him to be a bad kid like her. Probably made her feel better about herself."

"Wait," Logan cut in. "Dad was friends with Ashley's mom?"

Gracia blinked. "Friends? They were dating. Always telling everyone they were so in love. But your dad was always causing trouble with his dating. First the Bartons were mad at him and Tammy, then *everyone* was mad at him and Brandon."

Logan choked.

"No one ever told you? You're making me into a chismosa," Gracia said. "Ask your dads to tell you more about Snakebite back then."

"What was Brandon like?" Logan pushed. "Tell me about him."

Gracia looked at her for a long moment. "I shouldn't say anything about it. It's not my business."

Logan tried to swallow her desperation for information. She wanted to know what Brandon had been like. In a way, she barely knew what he was like now. Before she could ask, Gracia shook her head.

"Honesty for honesty," she said. "I always tried to teach your daddy that when he was little. How about you tell *me* something?"

"Oh," Logan said. "Uh, sure."

Gracia popped a honey-lemon cough drop into her mouth and mulled over it quietly. Her salt-and-pepper hair fell in loose curls over her shoulder. "What case are those boys here for?"

"I don't really know," Logan admitted. "They said it's little stuff. Changes in the weather. Some weird sightings."

Gracia shook her head. "The weather didn't change until your dad came here."

"What?"

"It started in January," Gracia said. "It snowed. It doesn't snow here. In spring, it was floods. And now this heat. It wasn't like this before your dad arrived."

She didn't say *came home.*

"I . . ." Logan started. "Why is it changing now?"

"Good question." Gracia laughed. "I don't know. I want to know what your dads think. I could tell them my thoughts, but they don't listen to me. They never have."

Logan looked at her hands. She'd thought there was something off since she first got here, from the creepy mob at the cemetery to the strange heat to the cabin. But until now, it was like everyone else thought it was normal. Gracia said that Snakebite was wrong and Logan was flooded with a sudden crash of relief.

"Was it ever like this before?"

Gracia chewed on the question. "You know, for a long time I felt it. There was a thing under Snakebite, like a little buzzing. It was like it made people nervous, even if they didn't know it was there. It was quieter than it is now. But then, one day it was gone. None of us ever really talked about it, but I know we all felt it go. Like we could breathe again. The little buzzing sound went away the day your dads left Snakebite."

The last sentence dropped like a stone in Logan's stomach. "And it didn't come back until . . ."

"Until Brandon returned."

"So, wait—"

Gracia held up a hand. "In a minute. The show is back on."

BRANDON VOICEOVER: Alejo and I have never seen a haunted windmill before. The investigation this morning turned up nothing, but any good paranormal investigator knows that most ghosts come out at night.

BRANDON: Can we check this loose patch?

[Brandon walks to the side of the windmill and nudges the crumbled brick with the edge of his shoe.]

BRANDON: It looks like a crawl space, doesn't it?

[Alejo crouches and looks through the bricks.]

ALEJO: Too small for anything human.

[He looks at the camera.]

Gracia laughed and crunched on a burned strip of bacon. Logan wanted to laugh—her fathers were always overdramatic on the show, which Twitter loved for screencap potential—but Gracia's words still sat heavy in her gut.

[Brandon points to Alejo's satchel.]

BRANDON: Let's get the ThermoGeist on this. I have a good feeling.

[Alejo digs through his satchel and pulls out the ThermoGeist. He points it at the open night, waiting for it to calibrate. He swings it toward the hole in the windmill's side. As the ThermoGeist passes, it flickers blue.]

"Wait," Logan said. "Is this a recording?"

"Yes," Gracia said. "I love your dad, but this show comes on past my bedtime. I always record."

"Can I rewind it?"

Gracia arched a brow, but surrendered the remote. Logan sat up and rewound the episode by a few frames. The ThermoGeist was steady in Alejo's hand, dead quiet each inch of the way to the crawl space.

Except one.

It passed so quickly it was almost impossible to see. As the ThermoGeist passed Brandon, it flickered. Not soft like a glitch. Not small like a temperature difference. Not a mistake.

It passed Brandon and it flared the color of the dead.

17

Old Sins

Ashley yanked the Ford across the lakeside highway, knocking Logan against the passenger door. Elexis groaned in the back seat, tapping away at his phone. At first, this whole investigation thing had felt like a longshot. But now, with revelations unspooling themselves everywhere she looked, it felt real. Logan didn't know what they would find at the end of this—she didn't even know what they were trying to solve—but they were getting close.

She and Ashley weren't friends. They were just investigating Tristan Granger's disappearance together. But after the party at the cabin, there was something easy between them. Maybe it was just the comfort of knowing Ashley had already seen her messy drunk and passed out.

Logan wasn't sure.

"I found out something else," Logan said.

"What?" Ashley asked, clearly only halfway paying attention.

"Our parents used to date."

Ashley looked at her, then focused back on the road. "Wait, like my mom? No way, that's—"

"Guess which dad."

Ashley scrunched up her nose. "Alejo? I'm assuming. I heard them talking at the store one time and their conversation was *so* weird. They were saying they hated each other, but I don't know."

"I'm still in shock." Logan unfolded her legs, propping her feet up on the dash. "I just kinda assumed my dads were together since birth. They're so annoying about it."

Ashley slapped Logan's ankles. "Feet off the dash."

Logan rolled her eyes.

"Was he, *you know* . . . back then?"

"Was he bi?" Logan snorted. "Yeah, the whole time."

Ashley blinked. "Oh, he's both. I didn't know."

The truck hiccupped over one pothole, then another, and Logan restrained her laughter. "You're *so* straight."

Ashley opened her mouth, but nothing came out. She shoved Logan against the passenger door. "*Stop*—I'm trying. I get it. It's just all really new to me."

"Well I, for one, am glad we're not sisters. It would've made this whole thing weird."

Ashley paused. "Would've made what weird?"

Logan said nothing. She wasn't sure what she meant.

They reached the gravel turnout at the edge of the trees and Logan hopped out of the truck and stretched her arms. Ashley unfolded herself from the driver's seat while Elexis remained in the back seat, lying down with his jacket draped over his face. Logan knocked on his window.

"C'mon," she said. "We've got ghost busting to do."

Elexis groaned.

"I'm confused, though. If the thing lit up at your dad, shouldn't we be talking to him?" Ashley asked.

"Brandon is only part of it. I'm talking about the gear, though. I watched a few other episodes just to check, and they *never* point the ThermoGeist at Brandon. They point it at Alejo sometimes and nothing. But on Brandon it registered, like, *immediately.*"

Logan had spent the past few days holed up in her motel room with her eyes glued to the TV. Saying she'd watched "a few" episodes was an understatement. She'd known that they were potentially dealing with something paranormal, but she'd never thought Brandon himself was the source. She thought of the Brandon from her dream, garbed in strange darkness, voice deeper than an ocean. Maybe none of it was connected, maybe it was *all* connected.

She needed to get the ghosts at the cabin to talk.

She needed the truth.

Elexis hoisted himself out of the back seat. "Okay. Pretending that any of this is real, what does that mean?"

"It means the ThermoGeist flagged something paranormal on him. Maybe a spirit? Something bad." Logan shouldered her tote bag and locked the car door. The gravel turnout was quieter in the daytime. Logan shook off the feeling that she was trespassing. "Which means the gear *works.* We can use it on the ghosts in the cabin."

"And then we'll talk to Brandon?" Ashley asked.

"Maybe." Logan scratched the back of her head. "I don't know."

Ashley frowned.

"Why bring me?" Elexis asked. "I thought this was you guys' thing."

"We're family," Logan said. "Family helps each other."

"You don't help me with anything."

"I would if you *asked*."

Elexis shrugged and straightened his beanie. It wasn't just about family, though. Since the party, something had changed in Logan's chest. Looking at Ashley felt *different* now. There was the same irritation, the same skepticism, the same doubt she always felt. But it was like she'd been looking at a blurry photo before, and now the details had come into focus. She looked at Ashley and she saw eyes the color of clear water, lips that hinted at a phantom smile, the gentle way she turned her head when she looked at Logan. This dumb, tugging feeling about straight girls wasn't new, and it was never worth it. But Ashley wasn't just a straight girl. She was the daughter of a sworn enemy, she had the power to throw Logan out of town in the blink of an eye, and she was searching for her missing boyfriend, whom she still seemed very into.

Elexis wasn't just family—he was a buffer.

Logan cast a glance at Ashley. She stared into the trees, but her gaze was unfixed. She idly ran her fingers through the end of her ponytail without a word.

Logan inched closer. "Are you feeling okay?"

"What?" Ashley blinked to life. "Oh, yeah. I don't know. I feel like something's weird today."

"Yeah," Logan mused. She turned to Elexis. "Nick didn't wanna come with? I figured you guys were like a two-for-one kind of deal."

Elexis frowned. "I think he got grounded for going to that party."

Logan sucked in a breath. "Yikes."

She pulled the ThermoGeist reader from her bag and smacked

it until it turned on. She'd never actually held this one before, but she'd watched Alejo fire it up on TV a million times. It was a black plastic square with two silver rods protruding from its back. According to the show, the ThermoGeist was supposed to detect patches of disparate temperature in the atmosphere. Cold patches—patches that made the ThermoGeist's little screen flash blue—indicated the presence of spirits. She'd always assumed that the ThermoGeist's accuracy, like everything else on *ParaSpectors,* was exaggerated. But something about the quick way Alejo had angled the rods away from Brandon said he *knew* he'd unveiled a secret. Logan couldn't shake the image. The piercing cold of the blue.

So, she'd stolen it. Alejo and Brandon were in Ontario for the day getting groceries and making phone calls for the show. She'd packed a few other devices from their gear trunk just to be safe. The SonusX was a walkie-talkie-shaped device that emitted loud crashing sounds and could detect ghostly voices. The Umbro Illustrator was a scanner that rendered animation of any humanoid spirits in the vicinity. The Scripto8G was a chip that plugged into the headphone port of her phone. It was her favorite of her fathers' ridiculous devices—*apparently* it allowed them to receive texts from ghosts.

She'd mostly brought that one for fun.

They made their way to the cabin and Logan's stomach churned. Today, there was no piano music, no voices through the splintered wood, no breathing like Ashley had described. Logan calibrated the ThermoGeist and pointed it at the cabin, but the screen remained blank.

"It looks different," Elexis said. He wandered to the back of the cabin with his hands in his pockets. "There's a firepit back here."

"Do you guys know anything about the family who lived here?" Logan asked.

Elexis shrugged. He walked farther, pausing at the back of the cabin to admire the massive, smashed windows. "They had a cool view."

Logan unearthed a handful of devices from her tote bag, unsure where to start. She and Ashley made their way to the front porch and stepped into the main room. Ashley's quiet was deeper than usual. It was unsettling. Logan glanced at her every couple of seconds to make sure she hadn't left. She wasn't the only thing that was different; it was like the cabin was determined to be different from the last time Logan visited. Today it didn't feel like death or despair or magic or any of that. It felt like a wooden house in a clearing. Nothing more.

The ThermoGeist agreed. Logan cautiously paced the cabin floor, but the square screen on the device remained unlit. There was nothing paranormal here—at least, not for her.

Logan tasted the tang of disappointment on her tongue.

The air outside was light with birdsong and smelled sharp like soil. Sunlight filtered into the cabin through gaps in the roof, angled like sheets of gold through the sunbathed wood. She imagined how beautiful this place might've been once. How it might've felt to stand here and listen to the piano and taste the summer wind through the open windows. She imagined white linen curtains on the far wall, a basket of fruit on the kitchen counter, a wooden light fixture over her head. It was a vision so real it felt like a memory. Logan could almost see it when she closed her eyes.

"I feel like . . . I've been here before."

"You have," Elexis called. "Twice, right?"

"You know what I mean." She put a hand on her hip. "*Before* before."

But there was no before. She wasn't like Brandon and Alejo; she didn't have memories here. This wasn't her home. Snakebite was only supposed to be *now.*

"Well," she said, "whatever was here before, it's gone."

Logan wasn't sure she believed that.

Ashley said nothing.

"Hey." Logan waved a hand in front of Ashley's face. "Are you in there?"

"Sorry," Ashley said. For the first time, Logan noticed the deep circles under Ashley's eyes, dark as bruises. Her eyes were glassy and distant—even when she looked into Logan's face it was like she couldn't focus. "Sorry, I don't know what's . . ."

Elexis made his way into the cabin's main room. "Can we go home? My allergies are kicking in."

"No," Logan snapped.

"I feel kinda sick to my stomach," Ashley said. "I think something bad happened here. It wasn't like this before. I don't know why I . . ."

She sank onto the ratty sofa in the corner of the room and put her head in her hands. Her blond ponytail fell in waves down her back. Fear twisted like a knife in Logan's chest. The air was too still, the cabin was too empty. Ashley was a mess.

Something was wrong.

"Do you see anything?" Logan asked.

Ashley shook her head.

Logan nodded. "Okay. I wanna take a quick look outside, then we can leave. You just . . . stay here."

Elexis and Logan left the cabin and wandered farther into the trees toward the shore. The first time Ashley had seen Tristan, he was in the trees, not the cabin. Logan juggled devices, scanning the trees, but nothing registered. Nothing indicated that this was anything other than a regular patch of trees bordering a regular lake outside a regular town. Nothing indicated that the things they had seen before still lingered here.

They reached the water and Elexis froze.

A piece of clothing was caught along the dusty ridge of the shore, hooked under a flat rock. The water from the lake ebbed and retracted over a red sleeve. For a moment, Logan thought the thing was breathing.

"What's—"

Elexis snatched the thing from under the rock and unfurled it. A waterlogged Captain America symbol spanned the front of the hoodie.

It was Nick's.

"He'll be happy you found that." Logan laughed.

"No. He wouldn't leave it." Elexis draped the sweatshirt over his shoulder and began scouring the ground, panicked. "It's his favorite. He wouldn't leave it here."

"You guys were both out of it."

"Not *that* out of it."

"I—"

Elexis pointed to Logan's tote bag. A faint blue seared through the stitching. She fished through the bag and pulled the ThermoGeist to freedom, pointing it at the hoodie. Just like the windmill episode of *ParaSpectors,* the device blared solid blue. She turned it away from the hoodie and it went dark again.

"Have you talked to Nick?" Logan asked. Her tongue felt like lead in her mouth. "Since the party?"

Elexis shook his head.

Logan closed her eyes. She was sinking.

"Take that hoodie. We're going to the police."

18

Long Shadows

Logan slipped into the passenger seat of the Ford and let out a sigh. It was only her second trip to the Owyhee County police station, but she was already tired of it. Elexis was still inside, talking to Sheriff Paris and waiting for Gracia to pick him up. The moment they left the woods, Ashley seemed clearer. The dark circles under her eyes subsided, and she was back to being her annoyingly wholesome, doe-eyed self.

Logan, on the other hand, was hazier. Tristan Granger was a missing stranger; Nick Porter was a missing friend. Her stomach twisted until she thought she might puke.

"I think we should talk," Ashley said, climbing behind the steering wheel. "I'm still not . . . I'm just really confused."

Logan nodded. They pulled away from the station onto the lonely highway toward Barton Ranch, plucky guitar humming faintly from the radio.

Ashley chewed on her bottom lip, eyes trained on the road ahead. "Am I losing it? Like, this isn't normal. I *know* it's not normal to see ghosts and stuff. I don't even know if it's possible."

"You're not losing it."

"Then what's happening to me?"

Logan sighed. "I don't know. It's not just you, though. I've been off since I got here, too."

Ashley narrowed her eyes.

"I've been having these weird dreams." Logan looked out the window, tracing her finger along the rubber dust trap that bordered the glass. "It'll be like a regular dream, then out of nowhere, I have to start digging."

"Like you're looking for something?"

"No. I'm digging a grave." Logan shifted in her seat. "For myself. I crawl inside and someone starts throwing dirt on me. I can't breathe and then I just . . . wake up."

"Who's burying you?"

Logan looked at Ashley. Even now, in the truck, far away from the stifling world of her nightmares, it was like she couldn't breathe.

Ashley's mouth twisted into a careful frown. ". . . is it Brandon?"

Logan looked away.

The sun was just beyond the hills on the horizon when they made it to Barton Ranch, giving the sky an eerie red glow. All the lights in the house were off as far as Logan could tell, except for one window on the right side of the house facing the empty fields. The yellow light inside flickered.

"Is that your room? Logan asked.

"Yeah," Ashley said, "but I don't know why it'd be doing that."

"Huh. You're sure it's okay for me to come in?" Logan asked.

Something about the pristine front face of the house didn't sit well with her. "Your mom won't care?"

"She's not home." Ashley motioned lazily to the driveway. "No cars."

"Fair enough," Logan said. Her head spun. Between Ashley's strange nausea in the woods and her nightmares and Nick's disappearance, something was happening. It wasn't quiet and slow like the last few weeks. Something was happening *tonight.* She felt it in her bones, in the air, in the ground beneath her feet.

Maybe this fear was the dark thing in Snakebite that Gracia had mentioned.

They entered the house in silence. The main room was exactly what Logan had pictured—rural decorations and beige furniture and whitewashed walls. It was the kind of home that felt like a *home.* The kind of place they'd snap pictures of for cutesy magazines. It'd been a long time since Logan had been in a place like this. She tried to push down the jealousy that rose in her chest.

A crash sounded from down the hallway, clattering like metal on wood.

Ashley's eyes widened. "Sounded like my room."

Logan nodded and they made their way toward the sound.

Ashley's room was a surprise. It had a twin bed covered with a pink patchwork quilt, a kid-size desk against the wall, and a bookshelf lined with old textbooks whose only purpose was to collect dust. Ashley's room was humble and impersonal, like a preserved memory. Logan guessed this was how the room had looked for Ashley's whole life. It was the room of a girl who'd never known herself well enough to make it her own.

The air in the bedroom was so thick it was suffocating. Logan spotted the source of the crash. Ashley's bulletin board was facedown in the middle of the floor with a wreckage of Polaroid photos scattered around it: pictures of Ashley with Bug and Fran, Ashley on the ranch, Ashley and Tristan. The window above her bed was wide open. Wind whistled through the screen, buffeting the curtains like a ghost's breath. It was perfectly reasonable to assume the wind had knocked over the bulletin board.

It was perfectly reasonable, but Logan knew it hadn't.

Behind them, the bedroom door slammed shut.

The desk lamp's bulb flickered, then burned out.

Ashley stumbled away from Logan. She was hardly visible in the sudden darkness, but she was clearly afraid. Logan cautiously made her way over, stepping carefully to avoid the pictures.

"What's going on?" Logan asked.

"I think he's here," Ashley whispered. "I don't think he's alone."

"Who's here? Tristan?"

Ashley nodded. She sank to her bed and knotted her fist in her bedspread. "I think he's mad at me."

"Why would he be mad at you?"

"Because I . . ."

Tears dotted the corners of Ashley's eyes.

"Okay, never mind. We'll get back to that." Logan cleared her throat. She tried to put on a calm face, but there was nothing calm about this. Her heart raced. This wasn't like their first trip to the cabin. She could feel something happening here. "You said he's not alone. Who else is here?"

"I can't see them. It's just, like, a *feeling*." Ashley's hands shook. "Parts of it are Tristan. Other parts . . . I don't know."

Logan swallowed. "Try."

"I think it's . . . Nick?" Ashley's expression was complicated. It was tangled between hurt and fear, caught in the brambles of panic.

Logan imagined her own expression was similar. It was the crushing, spiraling dread that she was responsible for this. She'd invited Nick to go along with them. She hadn't made sure he was okay the next day. She hadn't even given him a second thought until they found the hoodie.

"It's my fault," Ashley whispered. "Both of them."

Logan hesitated. She was several things, but "comforting" was not one of them. Ashley's breath was shaky, eyes red and swollen with tears. It was fear and anger and grief all at once. Logan reached for Ashley's shoulder, but hesitated an inch away. She thought of what Brandon asked people on the show—she could at least do that.

"Tell me about Tristan. Not what he's like now. Before, when he was—"

"—alive?"

"When he was *here*," Logan clarified.

"Why?"

"Because it helps. I think."

Ashley's lips quivered. She wiped her eyes and nodded. "Okay. Um, he was really great. He was always super nice. We spent a lot of time together." She cleared her throat and whispered, "I'm sorry. I don't really know what to say."

"Tell me something specific."

"There was this one time he wanted to see a horror movie

together. It was about a nun or something." Ashley stopped for a moment, then laughed. "I'd just failed this math test so my mom said I couldn't go out. I was here by myself, and I heard this banging on the roof. When I opened the window, he was there. He'd downloaded the movie off some site and set it up on his computer so we could watch it on the roof. He said I wasn't breaking the rules if I never left the house."

Logan smiled.

"It was so stupid." Ashley wiped her eyes. "We should've just watched it inside. But he was just like that. He thought watching it on the roof made it a romantic thing. Once he got an idea, he had to make it happen."

Ashley looked into the distance—into where Logan assumed Tristan was—and another tear rolled down her cheek. This wasn't the kind of face a person made when they just missed someone, Logan thought. There was something else here, deeper and more painful than grief. There was guilt. Logan saw it in her eyes.

She braced herself.

"Why did you say it's your fault?"

Ashley closed her eyes. "I told you I was the last one who saw him the night he disappeared."

"Right."

"He was here because I told him I wanted to talk. Tristan was supposed to apply for college and move away. I thought he was going to." Ashley sucked in a deep breath. "But then he decided not to apply. He wanted to stay here. In Snakebite. With me."

Ashley's voice cracked.

Logan reached out and put a hand on her shoulder. She knew where this was going. The house was quiet except for Ashley's small, choked breaths.

"I didn't want him to stay. We broke up." Ashley spat the words out like they burned her tongue. "I thought we could still be friends like we were before. Everything was gonna be okay. But then his mom didn't see him. John didn't see him. No one saw him after that, and I just . . . if something happened to him. If he did something to himself, I—"

"Did you tell anyone?"

Ashley shook her head.

Logan gently took her wrist. "Hey, this is not on you."

Ashley rested her fingers softly against Logan's hand, breathing slow and quiet like she needed the silence to soak up the words. The breeze through her open window was sickly warm, too hot for nighttime. It hushed through the curtains like a whisper.

"What if they're both haunting me because they're . . ."

Logan squeezed her wrist. "You saw my dad at the cabin. He's alive."

"Tristan and Nick could be alive, too."

"Right," Logan said. She wished she believed it.

Suddenly, a crack sounded from the roof. Not a crack, a slow groan. It was weight against the wood, slow and deliberate. It was footsteps, each one measured as though the creature above them struggled to balance. The sound started at the center of Ashley's bedroom ceiling, getting closer to the window above her bed with each step.

Ashley closed her eyes. Logan felt her racing pulse through the inside of her wrist.

The footsteps arrived above the window, and then stopped. The night outside was thick and dark as molasses. Logan felt a pull toward it, briefly, when her tote bag buzzed. This time it wasn't the light of the ThermoGeist flashing. It was her phone.

Logan didn't recognize the ringtone. A message alert titled SCRIPTO8G popped up on her lock screen.

Ashley leaned over Logan's shoulder to read.

unknown: FOLLOW

A chill crept up Logan's spine. She looked at Ashley, but she couldn't find the words to explain what it meant. According to the part of her brain that believed in rational answers—in provable science—it made no sense.

"Is this Tristan?" Logan asked the empty room.

Silence, and then her phone buzzed.

unknown: TRISTAN

Ashley gasped. She took the phone from Logan's hands, staring at the screen like she thought he might appear to her. Her hands shook, but no messages came through.

"Tristan," Logan continued. "Where do you want us to go?"

unknown: GRAVE

"The cemetery," Ashley breathed. "Tristan, are we supposed to meet you there?"

unknown: OLD

They met each other's eyes. Logan listened, but she only heard the branches outside and the horses in the barn and the slow, lumbering groans of old wood. Ashley looked at the floor, slowly muttering the word *old* to herself like it would eventually make sense.

She looked up.

"Old grave. It's Pioneer Cemetery."

As it turned out, driving was much harder during a panic attack.

Ashley rolled along Main Street, following the dull shine of Snakebite's sparse streetlights. Most of the stores and restaurants along the main strip of town were closed for the night, but at the end of the road there was a blip of life. The Chokecherry still glowed faintly gold against the harsh blackness of the night. Ashley could just make out the thumps of classic rock pulsing from the jukebox inside.

Past the main stretch, the streetlights fell away and they were left in darkness. Storefronts gave way to the sprawling plateaus of farmland on one side and the black, ebbing mass of the lake on the other. Fog rolled in over the highway in a thin blanket of slate gray. Ashley turned on her low beams and pushed ahead, unable to shake the feeling that there was something hiding in the mist.

"Another message," Logan said from the passenger seat. "It says *CLOSE*."

"Yeah," Ashley said. Her heart hammered in her throat. "Pioneer Cemetery is just around the corner."

"I think we stopped here on the way into town."

"You did," Ashley said, maybe too quickly. She cleared her throat. "The day of Tristan's vigil. I saw you and your dad there."

Logan looked at her but said nothing.

They rounded a massive black hill and the Ford's headlights caught on the squat fence that enclosed Pioneer Cemetery. The graves here were especially pitiful at night—only mounds of dirt bathed in yellow headlight beams. Outside the truck, the wind moaned. It was heavier now than it had been when they left the ranch, heavier than it should be.

"Do you feel that?" Ashley asked.

Logan nodded. They climbed out of the truck and the packed dirt sounded hollow under their feet. The stone key stood resolute at the front of the graveyard, unflinching in the wind, the names etched into the stone almost as indistinguishable as the graves themselves. Beyond the key, the graveyard was black.

Ashley turned on her phone flashlight. Logan handed her the ThermoGeist.

At the back of the cemetery, the shadows moved. Not like the wind, but like an animal. Like some great, lumbering thing. Ashley narrowed her eyes, trying to track the shape of it.

The ThermoGeist lit up.

"Oh my god, *look*!" Ashley shouted over the wind. The ThermoGeist flared brighter than her phone, streaking the muck of the graveyard in blue. The light tugged her toward the back of the cemetery plot, toward the moving dark, with a magnetism she couldn't explain.

Ashley suddenly understood that she was standing alone.

"Logan?"

She whipped around. The white light from her phone glinted off Logan's hair. Logan, who was still standing at the front of the cemetery with her eyes trained on the stone key. Logan, who looked like a ghost herself. Logan, who was so still Ashley wondered if she was breathing. In the murky black of night, she was a shadow of a person. Her expression wasn't right—brows furrowed, eyes wide, neck strained forward as if she couldn't read the etched words. The ThermoGeist continued to flare, begging Ashley to follow it to the back of the cemetery.

"Logan?" Ashley called again. "What are you looking at?"

"I . . ." Logan glanced up, hauled out of her trance. The wind whipped her hair into a flurry of black at her shoulders. "There's a name on here, but it's . . ."

Ashley pocketed the ThermoGeist and made her way back to the key. They didn't have *time* for this. Logan's gaze was fixed on the engraved names in front of them, and Ashley followed her gaze to one in particular. For a moment, it didn't register, and then her heart snagged on the hyphen.

ORTIZ-WOODLEY, 2003–2007

"Wait, like . . ." Ashley breathed.

Logan pushed a hand into her hair to keep it out of her face. "I don't get it. What does this mean?"

Every device in Logan's tote bag began screeching.

Ashley cupped her hands over her ears. The wind through the graveyard picked up, piercing through the black night with a bite sharp enough to draw blood. The darkness at the back of the cemetery transformed. It was two masses now, both hunched over and swaying in the wind. They gathered at the very edge of the cemetery where the dirt met tufts of yellow grass, circling one mound of dirt just off the Pioneer Cemetery plot, hidden from the main walkway.

The ThermoGeist flared again, but instead of flashing the blue light, it was a steady, unflinching red.

It was the color of blood.

"Logan," Ashley said tentatively.

Her voice echoed back in the wind. She swung her flashlight back over the darkness behind her, and Logan shielded her eyes, face washed in the ThermoGeist's red.

"I've never seen it do *that* before."

They followed the light to the back of the cemetery. Ashley's hands shook, but she kept her grip on the ThermoGeist. It was as though Tristan stood directly behind her—she heard his breath, felt his hand hovering just above her shoulder. The truth was in front of her now, if she could just be brave enough to see it.

Ashley's jaw clenched. "What do you want me to do?"

"What?" Logan asked, before realizing that she meant Tristan. Logan showed Ashley the Scripto8G. "It says *DIRT*."

Ashley's breath caught in her chest. She could almost see him now, squatting in front of her, brushing his hand along the crumbling dirt. She could almost see his eyes, begging her to just do this one thing. She understood, but it was too much to ask. She tucked a strand of hair behind her ear and shook her head.

"I can't . . ."

"You can't what?" Logan asked.

Please, a voice groaned, carried along by the wind.

Logan's eyes widened. "Holy shit. I heard that."

This voice wasn't Tristan's. Logan's face said she recognized it, too. The voice was intensely familiar, but distorted as though the speaker stood miles away. Ashley had heard this voice, soft and bashful from the back seat of her truck.

It was Nick Porter's.

"Okay, okay . . ." Ashley breathed. She turned to Logan. "Can you help me dig?"

Logan stared at the dirt and her face drained of color. She shook her head, fist clutched to her chest. Even in the dark, Ashley recognized the fear in her eyes. Her pupils were shrunken, ragged breath fogging from her lips. She whispered, "I can't."

"Then call Paris."

Ashley fell to her knees and pressed her quivering fingers to the dirt. Her heart hammered and hammered, but she swept at the dirt anyway. She tucked her phone under her chin so it could soak the ground in white light. The night smelled like fear and the metallic scent of impending rain. She dug until her fingers brushed against something solid. And then Ashley's heart stopped. She pushed away a layer of dirt and there, beneath the earth, her fingers met skin as cold as stone. The skin was too human to have been buried long, and too close to the surface to have been buried right. She bit back a sob and kept brushing at the dirt until it gave way to the ridges of human knuckles. She stumbled back and collapsed in the dirt.

She'd wanted to find one of the missing kids alive.

Instead, she'd found a body.

19

The Body But Not The Soul

After the cemetery everything was a strange dream.

It was a dream with claws. A sweltering blur. A nightmare rippling over Snakebite in slow, aching waves. Windows were shut, blinds drawn, children ushered inside on hot afternoons when they would usually play in the lake. News about the body wasn't like the usual gossip—it wasn't discussed over coffee at the Moontide. This was the kind of thing that snatched the words from people's tongues. There was a killer on the loose. Snakebite was blanketed in a coat of silence, because now it was all real.

Nick Porter was dead.

Not missing, *dead.*

For the last two weeks, Ashley had been silent, too. The Owyhee County police had dug up one body in Pioneer Cemetery; Ashley had expected them to find two. More than ever, Snakebite was sure the Ortiz-Woodleys had something to do with it. Ashley wasn't sure. Tristan was still missing, which was as terrifying as it was hopeful. He wasn't dead, but he wasn't home, either.

Ashley didn't know how to feel. Mostly, she felt empty.

Nick was dead, Tristan was gone, and she still knew *nothing*.

It'd been two weeks since she'd spoken to Logan. Two weeks since their whole world had been turned inside out. She wasn't avoiding Logan—at least, not any more than she was avoiding everyone else—but something about reaching out scared her. If they kept looking, it meant everything they'd already found was real. It meant Snakebite could never go back to the way it had been.

More than anyone else, though, she'd wanted to text. To call. She wanted to drive out with Logan and keep looking. Ashley wasn't sure what to do with that.

The call came in while she lay on her bed, head hanging over the side, blond hair draped across the floor. Ashley stared at Logan's name a moment too long, then picked up.

"Hey," she said.

"Hey." Logan's voice was hoarse. After a moment, she cleared her throat. *"How're you doing after . . . yeah, how're you doing?"*

"I don't know."

For a moment, the line was quiet. *"I was gonna text you, but it's been weird. Obviously. But . . . I think we should keep going. If you still want to."*

"You wanna go back to the cabin?" Ashley asked.

"I do. I don't know. I feel like . . ."

". . . like we didn't find everything yet," Ashley finished. Her chest was tight with the need to know more. "Same."

Whatever fear sat in her, whatever was waiting for them, Logan was right. There was more to find.

And if Tristan was still out there, she couldn't give up.

The trip to the cabin was somber this time. The junipers blurred as Ashley drove down the lakefront highway, dead and brown from the sweltering heat. Logan curled up in the passenger seat with her knees tucked against her chest, probably to avoid the no-feet-on-the-dash rule.

"You weren't at the funeral," Ashley said.

Logan took a deep breath. "I know. I was gonna go, but it felt disrespectful. I don't know."

"It wouldn't have been disrespectful," Ashley said. "You were friends."

"Not like that. I mean it would've been a distraction. Everyone thinks my dads have something to do with it. If my little gay family showed up at the funeral, that's all anyone would've paid attention to. I didn't wanna distract from . . ." Logan pursed her lips. "It needed to be about Nick. That's all."

Ashley grimaced. She wished Logan weren't right. Something sat heavy in her chest. She blinked out at the sunny shore, blurry through the dirt-smeared window. "How did your dads react when you told them?"

"Uh, told them . . . ?" Logan trailed off.

"About, *you know*—"

"Okay, you have to stop calling it that." Logan ran a hand through her hair, shaking out the tangles. "You mean when I told them I'm gay?"

"Yeah. That."

"Um, I mean, they didn't really have room to be mad about it? They were definitely surprised, though." She idly messed with the air conditioner vents without looking up. "Alejo was worried I just thought I was gay because of them. Brandon was really freaked out, though. He said things were gonna be a lot harder for me. Which always seemed weird to me because I knew lots of queer kids back in LA. When I was there it was never really hard. It was just, I don't know, a *thing*."

Ashley nodded. She loosened her grip on the steering wheel; she couldn't remember when she'd clenched her knuckles.

"I get it now, though. They grew up *here*."

The trees thickened as they reached the gravel turnout. The sun on this side of the lake used to be gold, but now it was too close. It was blistering, sitting too low in the sky. Ashley stared at the trees and ached for the shade between them. The more time passed, the more she was sure there was something wrong here.

Logan kicked open the passenger door the moment they parked. She pulled her hair into a short black ponytail. "I feel it today. I feel like we'll figure something out."

They made their way to the cabin. Immediately, something was different. Not like the nauseated feeling she'd had the first time. Ashley paused at the cabin's front porch and held out an arm to keep Logan in place. The cabin was alive, but not as though with ghosts. Something rustled inside, groaning across the floorboards.

"Do you hear that?" Ashley whispered.

To her surprise, Logan nodded.

Ashley swallowed hard. She carefully made her way onto the porch and pressed open the front door of the cabin. She expected a wild animal or knocked-over furniture. Even ghosts seemed more likely than Sheriff Paris standing in the far corner of the room, inspecting the initials carved into the walls. His posture was careful, fingers delicate as they traced the decayed wood.

Paris stiffened at the sound of them. He turned, and his expression softened into a quiet laugh. "I thought I heard someone coming in."

"I . . ." Ashley started, but she wasn't sure what to say. She cleared her throat. "What're you doing out here?"

"I'm guessing probably the same as you," Paris mused. "Except looking for Tristan is my actual job."

Ashley looked out the shattered window to the other side of the lake. "I thought—"

"—that we weren't looking on this side of the lake?" Paris asked. "I said I didn't want you kids over here. There's not really any trails or landmarks. If I lost track of one of you, it'd be hard to find you again. I've already got one kid missing and another one dead."

"Oh," Ashley said.

"And, as your sheriff, I really don't like you girls being out here by yourselves," Paris said. "With everything going on, it's really not safe. I'll stick with you for now, but I'd really prefer you not to go anywhere without chaperones from now on."

Ashley and Logan nodded. For a moment, there was only silence.

Paris's expression brightened and he quickly made his way across the main room. He turned to face Logan and extended a hand. "You must be Alejo's kid. Nice to officially meet you."

Logan blinked. "You know my dad?"

"Oh yeah. Me and your dad were best friends in high school. Me, him, and Miss Tammy Barton."

Ashley shook her head. "I didn't realize you knew her that well."

"Yeah, Tammy's the best. She's a busy lady, though." Paris pulled off his cowboy hat and ran a hand through his straw-colored hair. "I try not to bother her much anymore."

"What tangled webs," Logan said quietly. "Did you know Brandon, too?"

Paris pulled the cloth off the piano. The keys beneath were decayed and brown around the edges. Logan looked at the piano and her expression changed. It was soft and almost mournful. Ashley thought she looked at the piano like someone else might look at a grave. Sunlight danced over her cheekbones, but her eyes were dark and faraway.

Ashley wondered how many times she'd caught herself staring at those eyes, deep and brown and dark enough to swallow sunlight whole. Ashley's chest felt tight. She tore herself away, focusing back on the cabin.

"Brandon . . ." Paris sighed. "Kind of? He was a quiet kid. There were only twelve of us in the class of '97. I knew him, but I didn't *know* him. I don't think anyone really did. I saw him every day but I think I only talked to him once."

"I know the feeling," Logan whispered under her breath.

"But yeah, me and Alejo go way back. We used to spend our summers out here on my dad's boat. We kind of drifted apart when he went off to a fancy college. I still love him, though. He was like Snakebite's golden child. *Everyone* loved him."

Ashley inched her way into the cabin and closed the front

door. Logan seemed wholly uninterested in using any of her dads' gear now. She only wanted to interrogate Paris. Ashley tried not to be vaguely irritated.

"Why'd you guys stop being friends?" Logan asked.

"We didn't stop being friends." Paris continued to pace the cabin before taking a seat on the ratty sofa. "Well, mostly. I don't know. It sounds so bad, but in a way, when your dad came home and told everyone the news about him being . . . you know . . . I was kinda grateful. Like, I was mad that people were so awful to him over it, but it was kind of a relief, too. I got to step out of his shadow." Paris shook his head. "Wow, that sounds terrible."

"Yeah," Logan said, "it does."

Paris eyed her. "I don't mean it in a bad way."

Ashley laughed uneasily. Logan shot her a look.

"What is this place?" Ashley asked. She was careful not to mention that John had found the cabin on his father's maps. Things with John were already tenuous enough—she didn't need to snitch on him, too.

"It used to be a gorgeous little cabin." Paris frowned. "Obviously, it's not in its prime anymore."

"Do you know who lived here?" Ashley asked.

Paris's brow furrowed in confusion. He looked at Logan. "I do. I thought you two . . . Well, now I don't feel it's my place to say."

Ashley and Logan eyed him impatiently.

"I guess it'll come out one way or another since it technically has to do with both of you. You can't tell your parents I told you about this." Paris put his cowboy hat back on. "I know the property is Tammy's. For whatever reason, she sold the place to your dads. Maybe she gave it to them. I don't know. But they're the ones who built it."

Ashley blinked.

Next to the piano, Logan exhaled. "They *built* it?"

"Yeah." Paris nodded, solemn. "I wasn't as close with your dad at that point. I think the two of them just wanted a way to get a little farther out of town."

Ashley eyed the walls, the crumbling ceilings, the shattered windows. Brandon and Alejo had built this place by hand, and this was what was left of it. It was as though the wood itself exhaled disappointment. "What happened to it?"

Paris shrugged. "No idea."

The three of them remained for a moment in silence. Logan's eyes were wide, but she said nothing. Ashley felt the urge to go to her side, to put a hand on her shoulder and make sure she was all right.

She didn't know why.

"If you girls don't mind, I'm gonna check down closer to the water." Paris stood and made his way out the front door, leaving it open behind him. "Hang tight until I get back."

When he was gone, Logan dropped her tote bag. It landed on the wood floor with a sickening *thud*. She said nothing. She only paced the main room, eyes closed as if trying to imagine what it looked like before the destruction. Ashley tried to picture it, too. There had been life here once. It felt miles away now.

When she opened her eyes, she froze.

Brandon sat on the couch in the corner of the room, looking out the window facing the lake. His expression was blank, eyes glassy and fixed on the distant shore.

It took Ashley a moment to realize that Logan didn't see him. The ghosts were back. The girls weren't alone.

Ashley braced herself against the wall.

Logan turned to face her. "What's going on?"

"I, uh—" Ashley swallowed and motioned to the couch. "He's here. Brandon. The ghost version. Something's weird."

The scene was dark and cold and *wrong*. The wrongness of it permeated the air, casting a shadow over the cabin so deep it was difficult to breathe. Ashley felt the darkness like an oily film on her skin.

Logan blinked. She moved to the couch and pulled several devices from her bag, methodically turning them all on.

Brandon's ghost was silent, just like the last time Ashley had seen him. He ran his hand through the space next to him, eyes fixed on the lake outside. His expression was steely. It wasn't an expression at all. He was a shell, as if there were nothing human in him.

A voice whispered, but she couldn't make out what it said.

"Do you feel that?" Ashley asked.

Logan arched a brow. "Feel what?"

Ashley's jaw chattered in the cold. It made no sense—outside the lakefront window, the sun shone warm and golden over the dirt. She'd just been outside, she'd just *felt* the heat. But inside the cabin it was as cold as winter. Voices whispered outside, soft as running water. Too many voices, as though there were a crowd gathered just outside. Ashley's stomach sank with the distinct feeling that something was circling them, pressing at the walls, looking for a way inside.

"He's just sitting there," Ashley said. "What's wrong with him?"

"Describe it," Logan said.

"I think he's . . ." *Grieving,* Ashley wanted to say. But the voices outside continued to hiss, circling the aching wood like vultures circling prey. "Close the door."

Logan ran to the door and closed it. She held her phone up like better service might give her a message from the Scripto8G. "Is he saying anything?"

Ashley looked down. Brandon Woodley wasn't vague like Tristan's scent or Nick's disembodied voice. Just like last time, he was unsettlingly present.

"*One day,*" a voice breathed, "*we'll be happy.*"

Brandon stiffened.

And then he looked at her.

Ashley jolted back, crashing into a collapsed table. Her knees buckled on the corner of the wood and Logan's palms flattened against her back to hold her upright. The floorboards cried out, but the sound was muddled like she heard it from underwater. She clutched her chest, but she didn't look away.

After a moment, Brandon blinked. He shook his head slightly and the room changed. The air loosened, shedding its shroud of cold as though it were shrugging off a blanket. Ashley felt Logan's hands at her back—*actually* felt them—and then she was in the cabin. Sunlight glinted through the shattered windows, but the skin of her forearms still prickled with goose bumps. The voices outside were gone. Instead, she heard the rustling of juniper branches high above the cabin's collapsing ceiling.

"What just happened?" Logan asked, trying to hide the shaking in her voice.

"He *saw* us," Ashley hissed. "I don't know how, but—"

Brandon pressed his fingers under his glasses to rub his eyes. *"I thought I saw something."*

"What's—" Logan started.

Ashley hushed her.

Brandon paused like he was listening, then shook his head. *"I can't be around them."*

Ashley let go of Logan's arm and stood in front of Brandon. Up close, his face was full of *nothing*. He looked out the window into the undefined void. She didn't know what a killer looked like, but if she had to picture their expression, she'd picture this.

Brandon paused again, listening, then nodded. He watched the space beside him—the space where Ashley had stood seconds earlier—and narrowed his eyes. After a moment of tense quiet, he swiped a hand through the empty air and closed his eyes.

"*Not real,*" he whispered.

Quietly, he made his way to the front door and out of sight.

Ashley let out a pent-up breath and wiped beads of sweat from her brow. "I'm . . . so confused."

"*You're* confused?" Logan snapped.

"Follow me."

They made their way out of the cabin and down to the lake, away from where Paris paced the shore. Once Logan was seated on a small boulder, Ashley recounted the moment as well as she could. But the *strangeness* of it was impossible to put into words. It was a feeling that settled in the pit of her stomach like stones. Even on the lakeshore, with the sun beating down on her and a warm breeze rustling through the trees, she felt the cold under her skin. She felt Brandon's stare, relentless and empty and dead.

"It's like he wasn't alone," Ashley said. "There was something else there. I could hear it outside, whispering."

Logan scratched her scalp. "Who would it be, though?"

"I don't think it was a person."

Logan arched a brow.

"I don't think it was *human*."

"I just don't get it," Logan said. She kicked a smooth oval stone into the lake. "Was it just Brandon?"

"Just Brandon that I could see. I heard something talk to him, though." Ashley closed her eyes, conjuring up the voice in her memory. "It said they'd be 'happy again.' I don't know why. It kinda . . . sounded like someone died."

"Is this just you filling in blanks?" Logan asked.

"What?" Ashley asked. "I'm not making it up. I'm just telling you what I saw. And what I saw looked like they were grieving someone."

Logan pressed her palm to her forehead. "Who, though?"

"Maybe family?"

Logan scoffed.

"When I heard our parents talking, my mom told your dad she was sorry for his loss," Ashley said. "Did your dads . . . ever mention someone dying? Maybe before you were adopted? I know you don't wanna talk about it, but—"

Logan stiffened.

"—that grave at Pioneer Cemetery."

"No."

"If they lost someone, maybe that's why they left."

Logan shook her head. "*No.* It's literally not possible. They would've told me. Alejo would've . . ."

Logan didn't finish her thought. They sat in silence for a

moment. The lake ebbed up along the shore, carrying dust out into the water with each pulse. Logan wanted to believe Brandon had nothing to do with the deaths, but his footsteps were everywhere they looked. He was the only thing that'd changed in Snakebite.

"I thought we were supposed to be looking for Tristan," Logan said. "We're supposed to be clearing this up, not making it worse."

"I don't think this is someone just killing people," Ashley said. "The voices I heard outside were . . . what if they're connected to all this?"

"You think something paranormal is behind it." Logan said this like a statement, not a question.

"It wouldn't be weirder than everything else going on."

Logan pinched the bridge of her nose. "I know it looks like Brandon is involved, but . . . let me talk to my dads and see what I can find out. I don't wanna jump to any conclusions. Please."

Ashley's frown was involuntary. There was desperation in Logan's face, but she wasn't sure if it was desperation for Brandon to be innocent or desperation because she thought he wasn't. Logan's straight black hair rippled with the wind. She cupped a hand over her mouth.

"Okay," Ashley said. "I can ask my mom some more stuff, too. But we don't know how long it'll be before someone else goes missing. There's not that many kids here. It could be one of my friends. It could be one of *us*."

"Promise me you won't do anything until I've talked to them," Logan said. "Just trust me."

Logan's eyes narrowed, glassy like she might cry. Ashley looked beyond her to the cabin. The cold under her skin was almost gone now, but the weight in her stomach still pushed her down. It felt like she was sinking. She closed her eyes.

"I promise."

20

A Whisper Soft And Staying

At the end of all of this, Snakebite would never be the same. A piece of Ashley already knew that, even if she pretended otherwise.

The sky was open wide and bright blue with morning. From the peak of the massive hill on the eastern edge of the Barton property, the rest of the hills were only gentle ripples reaching out to the horizon, the lake twisting between them like a vein. The wind carried the sweet scent of juniper up the hillside. This was the Snakebite etched into Ashley's bones. It was the one she saw when she closed her eyes. It was *her* Snakebite, just out of reach as darkness rolled into the valley like an impending storm.

It was just another thing she was losing.

Ashley had climbed to the grassy cap of this hill for picnics with Bug and Fran since they were in middle school. It'd been months since they'd been here together, but even with everything else changing, this was exactly how Ashley remembered it.

She was nervous about coming here. She was nervous about seeing Bug and Fran. She'd spoken to them a few times since

Nick's funeral, but this was different. Nothing between the three of them had ever made her nervous before. There was a silence that settled between them, holding them an arm's length from one another, wordlessly seeding doubt into Ashley's chest. With everything going on, hanging out with friends felt like a lie.

Ashley's horse reached the crest of the hill. Bug and Fran trotted up behind her on borrowed Barton horses. Quietly, the three of them made their way to a knotted juniper that stood alone on the hill's bald face. Bug laid a blanket across the dead grass, and Fran unlatched the picnic basket from her horse's saddle. They assembled turkey sandwiches and mason jars of lemonade like they had every summer, lying back on the blanket under the shade of the juniper tree. The air was crisp and clear and Ashley immediately wanted to sink into the ground if it meant she could stay here forever.

"I miss you guys," she said between bites of sandwich. "Like, *so* much."

"Whose fault is that?" Fran laughed. "You're the one always hanging out with Logan now."

"She means we miss you, too," Bug said.

"Yeah, sure."

Fran's attitude was justified, but Ashley had hoped everything would just be normal. Bug was harder to read—she was the nicest of the three of them, which meant she was the least likely to say how she really felt. Both she and Fran looked up at the sky and not at Ashley. She wondered how many worried conversations they'd had about her over the last few weeks.

"Sorry I've been weird," Ashley said. "There's just been a lot going on."

"Yeah. But you can talk to us," Fran said.

"I know."

"Good."

Ashley grimaced up at the withered branches overhead. It wasn't like she didn't trust Bug and Fran. It was just that they were her last patch of normalcy in Snakebite. They were the last thing left that was untouched by this looming shadow.

Ashley closed her eyes. "Okay. You know I've been out of it since Tristan. And you know I told you I was still kind of . . . *sensing* him, like he was still around."

"Sure," Fran said.

"Well, I think I can kind of . . . I don't know. I think I can see ghosts?"

Bug and Fran were silent.

"Not literally," Fran said.

"Literally."

She could feel Fran's frown radiating from next to her. Fran shifted onto an elbow to stare at the side of Ashley's face. "You wanna elaborate?"

The sun burned through the blue morning as Ashley explained it all, from the first sighting to the cabin to the body at Pioneer Cemetery. She explained the way she had smelled Tristan in the woods, the way he'd told her where to find Nick's body, the way he lingered with her, even now. She explained it while Bug and Fran listened and sipped their lemonades. She couldn't look at either of them. Her heart raced up her throat and tasted like iron. "I thought I was just losing it at first. So I asked Logan for help. Because, I don't know, she knows about this stuff."

"Jesus," Fran huffed. "Why didn't you tell *us*?"

"I don't know."

Fran sat up. "You told a stranger."

Ashley covered her face.

Bug was quiet—even quieter than usual. After a moment, she said, "Do you think it's really him?"

"Obviously not," Fran cut in. She flipped honey-brown curls over her shoulder. "Logan's whole thing is this ghost stuff. She's trying to make you think you're crazy, seeing ghosts and all that. It's disgusting."

Ashley narrowed her eyes. "I know what I saw."

"Being sad about Tristan doesn't make him a ghost."

"I *saw* him."

"Yeah, and if you told *me* that, I would've told you to see someone," Fran said. "That's what a good friend would do."

"If I didn't investigate it with Logan, I never would've seen all that other stuff." Ashley sat up and put her sandwich down on the blanket. Suddenly, she didn't have an appetite. "If Logan didn't believe me, we never would've found Nick."

"Finding a dead body isn't a *good* thing," Fran said. "None of this stuff is good. Do you know how messed up that is? You found a *dead body*. Of a person we *knew*. That's, like, a serious problem."

"Yeah. I found proof that someone is killing people," Ashley hissed. "I knew both people that went missing. It could be one of us next. I can't just . . . not do something."

"Police catch killers," Fran said.

"Paris gave up on Tristan. Everyone did."

"Are you serious?" Fran snapped. "We spent *hours* out there every morning looking for him. Paris, too. No one *gave up* on him."

"Yeah, but you didn't think we'd find him." Ashley swallowed the tears that barreled up her throat. She thought of the graffiti at the Bates. For months, everyone had assumed Tristan was dead. "What was I supposed to do?"

Fran's eyes widened. Ashley had never seen her angry like this before. Her fists clenched at her sides, jaw tight with rage. "Ash, Tristan is *gone.*"

"No, he isn't."

"Guys—" Bug tried.

"You know what, I'm not hungry." Fran stood and stormed over to her horse. "You guys have fun. I'll take the horse back. Just . . . whatever."

She ran the horse down the hillside toward Barton Ranch, leaving Bug and Ashley in silence. The warm wind blew between them, painfully quiet. Ashley lay back and waited for Bug to get up and leave her, too. She waited to be alone again.

But Bug stayed. She reached across the blanket and took Ashley's hand gently. "That was . . . intense."

"Yeah," Ashley croaked. "I shouldn't have said anything."

"I'm glad you did, though." Bug lay on the blanket next to Ashley and laced their fingers together. "I was really scared for you. Fran's just mad because she loves you a lot. We both do. You really think it's Tristan?"

"I do. I can't explain it. But it's *him.*"

"I believe you."

The three words were heavier than she expected. Ashley closed her eyes to keep from crying. They lay there in the quiet and Ashley slowly remembered how to breathe. "Thank you."

"I can help you look, too," Bug said. "Have you done any of your investigating at the motel?"

Ashley turned to face her. "Why?"

"Not trying to be mean," Bug said, "but Logan's dads are clearly part of this. Somehow. I don't know, they're . . ."

". . . suspicious," Ashley finished. "I know. But I promised Logan I would let her talk to them first."

"She doesn't think they'll just lie?" Bug asked.

"I don't know."

"I think Logan seems cool, but maybe she can't really see the obvious," Bug said. "I'm just saying it's worth a look."

"We'll see," Ashley said.

Maybe Bug was right. Either way, if she wanted her old life back, she needed to end this. She needed to find Tristan, find the killer, and find the old Ashley who didn't spend every day afraid of the dark. She wanted the old Snakebite back one way or another.

No more ghosts; she wanted this to end.

21

The Jukebox Knows Your Name

ALEJO: Something wrong?

[Alejo taps at his phone, pulling up the Scripto8G screen. He watches Brandon carefully. Something is clearly wrong.]

BRANDON: I just don't like it in here. It feels off.

ALEJO: Yeah, it's haunted.

[Brandon does not laugh. Alejo moves toward the stairs but stops when his phone screen lights up. He opens the message, moving his shoulder to shield it from Brandon's view. The camera zooms in to show that the Scripto8G reads *ALREADY HERE.]*

ALEJO: Already here?

[The cameraman gives a muffled response.]

BRANDON: Let me see that.

[Alejo hesitates. His hands tremble.]

ALEJO: It just says *already here.* Any ideas?

[The phone flashes again. This time, it reads *HERE ALL ALONG.*]

A knock sounded from the door to room eight.

Logan muted the TV and climbed out of bed, brushing stray potato chip crumbs from her shirt. In the past week, Alejo and Brandon had kept mostly to themselves, coming and going from the motel in near silence. She'd barely seen either of her fathers in days. At one point, she'd worried about Brandon and Alejo hearing her *ParaSpectors* marathon through the walls, but they acted almost *too* normal, like they had nothing to hide. Like the entire population of Snakebite didn't suspect them of murder. Like there weren't teenagers dropping around them.

She opened the door. Alejo wasn't alone. Brandon stood behind him, cleaning his glasses with the hem of his button-up, which she assumed was a strategy to avoid making eye contact.

"Can I help you?" Logan asked.

Alejo peeked into her room. "I thought I heard my voice."

"Oh, yeah." Logan grabbed the remote and shut off the motel TV. "It's the one where Brandon gets possessed and you guys have to exorcise him in the basement. Extremely good TV."

"A terrible episode," Brandon scoffed.

"I don't know—*I* had fun. I wasn't the one who had to writhe around on the floor for once." Alejo scanned the room. "I was gonna invite you to a little family dinner, but I don't want to break up this rager."

Logan let out a singular "ha." The concept of a family dinner in the middle of everything going on was so alien she thought Alejo had momentarily slipped out of English. Even before the murders, and before Snakebite, the Ortiz-Woodleys didn't do "family dinners." They did dinner shifts, which usually meant that Alejo cooked a huge batch of picadillo and ate alone, Logan took a serving to her room at some undetermined point in the night, and Brandon came home after everyone was asleep to microwave leftovers for himself.

But she'd promised Ashley she would talk to them about the cabin, the ghosts, all of it. It was now or never.

"Sounds fun," Logan said. "Maybe we could get fancy and push our tables together. We could even microwave a pizza."

"Very funny," Alejo said. He looked back at Brandon. "I think we're feeling diner food?"

"You don't think the mob will come out?" Logan asked.

"Don't worry about everyone else. You'll have us. We know how to take the heat off." Alejo nudged Brandon, who wordlessly nodded. "As long as me and your dad are there, no one will have time to bug you."

"That's true," Brandon said, rubbing the back of his neck.

"Nothing this town loves more than roasting a couple gays on the pyre," Alejo said. When Brandon and Logan both went silent, he laughed. "Sorry, that's a little intense. But what do you say—wanna grab some burgers before they get the pitchforks?"

Logan shrugged.

"Okay, fine, the real reason." Alejo's expression was somber. "I found my old hat and I wanna wear it in public before I'm banished."

He pulled a short-brimmed black cowboy hat from his bed and placed it squarely on his head. It had a musky leather scent, and Logan couldn't fight off a smile. Alejo dipped his head cowboy style and said, "I'd be much obliged if you came to dinner with us, ma'am."

"Oh my god." Logan laughed. "You're really gonna wear it?"

"I wish he wouldn't," Brandon said, almost too quiet to hear.

"Why not? My dad used to wear his everywhere." Alejo pulled the hat off and ran his thumb along the leather. "Let's call it assimilation. I'm blending in. Embracing Snakebite culture."

"My dad always had his, too." This was Brandon, forcing himself into the conversation like he feared he might fade out if he didn't contribute in time. He smiled, momentarily snagged in memory. "I didn't know he was bald on top until I was sixteen."

Logan looked between them and something behind her ribs sank. They were trying—both of them—and she was shutting them down. There was a piece of her that wanted this more than any answers. She wanted something easy—casual family dinners, nights on the town, movie mornings on the weekends. She wanted conversations that didn't feel like pulling teeth.

She put a hand on her hip. "Where's *my* hat? You guys are really robbing me of my cultural heritage."

Alejo plucked the hat from his head and clapped it on

Logan's, immediately mussing her hair. She took the brim between her fingers and tilted it over her brow like they did in old Westerns.

"Yeehaw—let's go."

When Logan and her fathers arrived at the Moontide, it was completely empty. They slid into a vinyl booth near the back of the diner without a word, each glancing over the other booths to make sure they were really alone. The diner didn't have the piles of memorabilia that the Chokecherry had, but it did have a sense of timelessness. It was at once a diner that could be anywhere and one that could only exist right here. Logan nestled into the booth and sank into the worn cushions.

A waitress emerged from the kitchen with a rosy smile and an armful of menus.

"Alejo." She beamed.

"Ronda," Alejo said. He stood and pulled the woman into a tight embrace. He was at least a foot taller than her, but she reached up and hugged him like he was a very tall child and not a forty-year-old man. Without letting her go, Alejo said, "You haven't aged a *day*."

"I think you say that to all the girls. Or"—Ronda looked at Brandon and her expression sobered—"maybe not."

"Good to see you," Brandon said stiffly.

"I tell you what, I did not expect to see you in here." Ronda laid menus on the table and pulled three sets of silverware from her apron. Her expression was hard to read, idling somewhere between curiosity and disappointment. "Still don't understand why you three are in town, but I'm glad to see you're all right. Anyway, let's get some food on the table." She turned to Alejo.

"It's been a bit, but I think I remember. Regular Moontide burger with no pickles or onions, extra cheddar?"

Alejo grinned. "You got it."

"I'm just glad you're not one of those California vegan types now." Ronda took Brandon's and Logan's orders and stuck her notepad back in her apron. "Sit tight. I'll be back with your food."

Brandon looked around the diner with a distant smile. He looked like he actually fit in here. Logan had never seen him actually settle into a place. No matter where they were, he always looked like he'd been cut out and pasted in, like he always existed somewhere else. But at the Moontide, he looked comfortable. He leaned against the vinyl booth like he'd spent years in it. Maybe he had. Logan knew next to nothing about Brandon's life here before the show. She'd gathered bits and pieces of Alejo's, but Brandon's was a blank.

It all felt crooked.

"Did you guys come here a lot before?" Logan asked.

Alejo looked at Brandon, who fixed him with a classic straight-lipped frown. "Uh, yeah. I'd say so. Not together, but I think we both came here a lot."

Logan wrinkled her nose. "Weird answer."

"We didn't really know each other then," Alejo said. "Me and your dad could've been sitting right next to each other but probably wouldn't've said a word."

"That's not true," Brandon said. "I knew who *you* were."

"Okay, well, that's because *I* was cool."

"And I was not," Brandon said. "I'm sure that's a surprise."

The jukebox, which Logan hadn't noticed before, started playing John Denver, and Alejo's face lit up. "Your dad used to be able to play this one on the piano," he said. He put a hand on

Brandon's forearm. "We should get a piano at the LA house. I bet she didn't even know you played."

"I doubt I'd remember how." Brandon grimaced at the jukebox, then softened and looked at Logan. "You wouldn't wanna see me play now. It'd be embarrassing."

Logan's chest felt tight. She thought of the piano in the cabin. It couldn't be a coincidence that Brandon's spirit had materialized there, that she'd heard piano music in the woods, that he apparently used to play. But this wasn't what she wanted to find out—she didn't want more reasons why Brandon was at the center of all this. She bit back the twinge of hurt in her chest. "How did you guys meet? I don't think I ever asked."

"Oh, uh . . ." Brandon eyed Alejo. "You're the better storyteller."

"I don't know," Alejo mused, "you apparently knew about me way before I knew about you."

The held each other's gaze a moment longer in a silent standoff. Finally, Brandon cleared his throat. "We met here, actually. In the diner. I was eating with my parents and he was here with—"

"No, we met at the lumberyard, remember?"

Brandon grimaced. "No. It was here."

Alejo's brow furrowed, searching for the memory.

"You were on a date?" Brandon tried. "It doesn't matter. It wasn't a long conversation. I don't even know why I remember it."

"Are you sure you met *me?*" Alejo asked. "I didn't meet you until I came back from Seattle. And I didn't really go on dates. I was . . ."

Logan groaned. "You were with Tammy, right?"

Alejo flushed. "Gracia . . . that chismosa. I was a different guy back then."

"I don't think you were that different," Brandon said. When Logan and Alejo fixed him with identical stares, he looked down. "When you came back, I was actually glad you were just how I remembered you."

"Oh, because you knew me *so well* from our one conversation?" Alejo's laugh was a pointed challenge.

Ronda came back from the kitchen and laid their burgers on the table, saving Brandon from having to elaborate. Before she could turn to leave, Alejo held up a hand. "Ronda, you have a great memory. Do you remember me and Brandon meeting here? For the first time?"

Ronda stared.

"I was in the booth by the door," Brandon said.

"I'm sorry. I don't remember." Ronda straightened and gestured to the table. "Do y'all have enough napkins?"

Alejo looked to Brandon and frowned. "Uh, we're good. Thanks."

Logan looked down at her lap. She waited for Ronda to disappear back into the kitchen, then took a deep breath. "Can I ask you guys something?"

"When have you ever asked permission?" Alejo scoffed.

Brandon watched her warily.

"I know you said you're investigating the weather and sightings and stuff, but . . . I was talking to Gracia a few weeks ago. She said this weird stuff didn't start until you got here. And you haven't been taking any notes or pictures. None of the crew has come out. I took you guys' gear, like, three weeks ago, and—"

"You what?" Brandon asked.

Logan was quiet.

"What do you mean, you took our gear?" Alejo asked.

"I . . ." Logan narrowed her eyes. "No, the point is that you guys didn't even notice it was gone. We're supposed to be here investigating, but you don't realize you're missing all your gear?"

"The *point* is that our gear is expensive," Alejo said. "And off-limits."

Brandon leaned forward. "What did you use it for?"

Logan looked between them. Alejo was upset, but Brandon was afraid. His hand was flat against the table, eyes wide behind his glasses. Because it wasn't about the gear; it was about what she'd found. Logan's heart raced. She felt fire in her cheeks.

"Logan," Brandon said, hard and cold. "What did you use the gear for?"

"That's what I wanna ask about. The cabin across the lake—"

Brandon exhaled.

"I know it was yours. And there's this grave I saw. It had our name on it." Logan looked at her hands. "I thought, if you guys could just start at the beginning. If you could just tell me what's going on here."

Brandon sank into his seat and shook his head. Alejo looked at him, then at Logan, and it was the first time she'd ever seen him speechless, unable to mediate. She wondered how the three of them looked, alone in this diner. Country ballads softly filled the silence between them, almost mocking.

After a moment, Brandon shifted out of the booth. His face was unreadable. He looked anywhere but at Logan. "I'm gonna go take a walk. I'll be back."

He made his way out of the diner into the swollen summer air. Guitar plucked from the jukebox and Logan thought she might be sick. It was Tulsa all over again—hate curdled in Brandon's voice, cloying and hot. Logan looked at Alejo, waited for him to explain, but he only stared at the diner door after Brandon, lips in a hard, thin line.

He gathered himself. "Did you put the gear back?"

"It's in my room," Logan sighed.

"Okay." He placed his hands palms-down on the diner table and slowly inhaled. "Everything's gonna be okay. I told you, if you want to know anything, you can just ask. You don't have to . . ."

"Does he have something to do with what's happening?" Logan asked. "Kids are dying. I just wanna know why."

"Your dad has done nothing wrong. Neither of us have. I . . . can't get into it right now, but I promise your dad is not responsible for this. It'll be easier to explain when we're out of here," Alejo said. "Until then, how about we make a deal. No more cabin, no more ghost hunting, no more taking things from our room. And when this is all over, me and your dad will explain everything."

"So I *can't* just ask, then?"

"Soon," Alejo said. "I promise."

"When?"

"When it's over," Alejo said again.

Logan leaned back in her seat. This was how it was going to be—she didn't deserve the truth. She could get close enough to taste it, but she could never have the real thing. She cleared her throat. "I guess it's a deal."

22

How To Breathe Underwater

Ashley parked the Ford haphazardly across three of the slim parking spots at the Bates Motel and climbed out of the truck. On most summer nights, she heard the distant moan of cars far down the highway, but tonight it was only the flickering bulbs of the Bates's fluorescent sign and the crackling of the Ford as it cooled down. Even at night, the heat was blistering and moist. The parking lot smelled like fuel and mildew.

She made her way to room seven. In the window, Logan's string lights glowed warm and gold through the blinds. Ashley knocked twice, and the door thumped as Logan pressed her eye to the peephole.

"Just me," Ashley said, waving.

The door opened. Logan's hair was pinned up in a messy bun. She wore an all-black sweater and skirt combo with black ankle socks. For the first time since Ashley had met her, Logan wasn't wearing any makeup. She almost glowed in the low light.

"How are you wearing a sweater?" Ashley asked.

"Beauty is pain." Logan leaned against her doorframe. "What're you doing here? Did you miss me?"

"I told my mom I'm staying at Bug's," Ashley said, ignoring Logan's comment. She wrapped her arms around herself. "She'd be pissed if she knew I was here. No offense."

"A *secret* meeting."

Past Logan's shoulders, Ashley caught a glimpse of the motel room. It was nicer than she'd imagined—Logan used string lights in lieu of the murky fluorescent bulb in the ceiling, and she'd carefully arranged canvas paintings of landscapes and skylines around the room like windows to better worlds. Ashley motioned to the door. "Can I come in?"

Logan paused. "I don't know. You're here way after office hours. Kinda unprofessional, to be honest."

Ashley rolled her eyes. "Ha."

"Unless . . ." Logan trailed off. "Is this for business or pleasure?"

Ashley's eyes widened. She shoved Logan's shoulder and muttered, "You're an idiot."

"Thank you for that." Logan smiled and lingered just a moment too long in the doorway before gesturing into the motel room. There was something off about her. Her humor was too sharp, too deflective. "You can come in. No judging, though."

Ashley stepped into the room. It was bigger than it looked from the outside, but it was irrefutably a motel room. The wallpaper was a sickly shade of green, chaotically patterned with brown roses. Ashley hadn't spent much time in the Bates, but Logan had clearly rearranged the furniture—the breakfast table was fashioned into a makeshift desk, the minifridge acted as a second end table, and a potted plant was precariously draped over the mounted TV, drooping sadly across the screen.

"It looks great," Ashley said.

"It looks *okay*," Logan corrected. She shut the door behind them and leaned against it, arms folded over her chest. "Not my fault, though. It's a million times better than it was when we checked in."

"It's gotta be expensive to stay this long."

"I think Gracia's charging my dads monthly rent? I'm not really the family treasurer." Logan shrugged. "Anyway, what's up?"

Ashley swallowed. She hadn't fully thought through *why* she was here. After the fight with Fran, it felt like the sky was closing in on her. She was like a tire stuck in the mud, spinning, trying to get free. Snakebite had never felt like this before. Now, it was like she'd forgotten how to breathe. She hadn't planned to come here—common sense said Logan would just make things worse—but it was like she was on autopilot. She couldn't have landed anywhere else.

"Things are weird," Ashley said. "I just needed some fresh air, I guess."

"So you came to a . . . motel room?"

"You know what I mean."

"Bug's house wasn't good enough?"

"Sorry. I can leave."

Logan sighed. "No, sorry, you can stay. It's a reflex. Hanging out just kinda seems like something *friends* do."

Ashley smiled. After all the investigating, all the days at the cabin, all the secrets, maybe they *were* friends. She turned to face the TV mounted on the wall. *Judge Judy* played on mute, and

Ashley wondered if this was the only channel at the Bates or if the show was on by choice. Either way, the room painted a picture of a certain kind of loneliness. She wondered how many nights Logan had spent like this, here and elsewhere.

"Looks like a party," Ashley said. "You're sure I'm not interrupting?"

"Nope, now you have to stay. I already used mental energy letting you in." Logan motioned to the bed. "You're free to stay over. I'd say sorry there's only one bed, but we're clearly in one of those dark, murdery romances. We should just lean into the cliché."

Ashley laughed and threw herself onto the bed. The mattress was stiff as stone, but it was covered in knit blankets and a plush black comforter to make it bearable. Logan wandered around to the other side of the bed and joined her without a word. There was something weird about Logan tonight, something weird about the quiet.

Something weird, but not something wrong.

"Did you have an update?" Logan asked.

Ashley frowned. "If it's okay, I don't really wanna talk about investigation stuff. I just wanna . . . I don't know, *talk*."

"Oh. Okay."

Outside, metal clattered against pavement. Ashley peeked through the motel blinds, squinting at the night. A shadow moved on the far side of the parking lot near the massive dumpster. For a moment, Ashley's chest tightened.

"Who's—"

"That's my dad," Logan interrupted. "Taking out the trash. You can wave."

Tentatively, Ashley waved.

Alejo turned toward the window and blinked. After a moment, he waved back, expression snagged somewhere between confusion and distaste.

Ashley cleared her throat. "It's okay I'm here?"

"My dads haven't cared about who I brought over since I was, like, thirteen."

"You brought a lot of people over?"

Ashley wasn't sure why she asked. Maybe it was the strangeness in the air. She thought it was probably the strangeness in her own chest.

"You should've seen me in LA." Logan smirked. "I was a *menace.*"

"I feel like that version of you would've been even worse."

Logan's nose crinkled up in protest. "*Worse* implies I'm bad now. Which . . . is actually fair."

"You're not as bad as you think you are," Ashley said.

"I think I'm a national treasure." Logan's eyes widened. "Oh my god, if a bunch of camera guys pop out at the end of this whole thing and it was a hidden intervention to make me nicer, I'm gonna be *pissed.*"

"I wouldn't," Ashley said. "That would mean no one is actually dead."

Logan pressed her lips together, squashing whatever she meant to say next. Just like that, Ashley knew she'd killed the easy tone of it all. She hadn't meant to bring up the disappearances—tonight was supposed to be murder-free—but it was always lingering in the air around her.

"Hey, we're not talking about dead people," Logan said.

"Right." Ashley closed her eyes. She didn't want to talk about investigating. She just wanted a friend. "When this is over, are you gonna go home?"

Logan hugged a pillow tight to her chest. "I don't know. To be honest, I don't really know if LA *is* home for me. When I was growing up, my dad said home wasn't a place we lived. It was when we were together. All three of us."

Her voice was quieter than usual, dark eyes tracing the criss-cross ceiling pattern in silence. It was only in quiet moments like this that the sadness came through. Because that was the thing about Logan—under the sharp one-liners and incredulous glares, there was always a sadness that felt so deep Ashley thought she could fall into it and never reach the bottom. It was a sadness Logan had sewn into her chest. That she'd fashioned into a piece of her personality.

"You don't think that anymore?"

Logan shook her head. "I don't know. Once we moved to LA, I was just alone all the time. I thought the show would end eventually and it would be the three of us again. But it was like I was always waiting. Even if we leave here and go back, I just . . . I don't know."

Ashley held her breath for a moment. "What's wrong?"

Logan looked at her. It felt like the first time she *really* looked at her. She pursed her lips for a moment like she was considering whether or not the truth was worth it. Then, she sighed. "I talked to my dads. About everything. Or, I *tried* to. But Brandon just shut down. He literally walked away."

"Oh." Ashley cleared her throat. "Why would he do that?"

"I don't know. But it's not like it's the first time. He just . . . shuts down." Logan wiped her nose. "They let me on the show once. Alejo wasn't there, it was just me and Brandon in Tulsa.

Everything was fine, and then we were in the tunnels and I kept asking him questions and he just *freaked.* He wouldn't even look at me. He told me to go home and leave him alone. And then that was it. They never let me on the show again. And he never . . . since Tulsa, this is how he's been."

Logan faced Ashley, but she stared past her at the motel wall. For a second, Ashley thought she might cry.

"That's so sad," Ashley said, and the words felt immature and wrong. "I'm sorry."

"Don't be," Logan said, voice quiet like a sigh. "I don't know if he hates me or whatever. Until then, I really was trying to make it work. But I've got other plans now. When I turn eighteen, I'm gonna pack up and hit the road. I'm gonna find a place that actually feels like home."

Logan looked at her. Her black hair fell at her neck, glowing with a warm sheen from the string lights. Ashley listened to the thrumming rhythm of her own heartbeat. She clutched the comforter between her fingers and inhaled the scent of air conditioner and musk. She was a different Ashley tonight.

What was *wrong* with her?

"You could stay in Snakebite," Ashley said.

Logan's brow furrowed. "I really can't."

"People will get better after we figure all this stuff out. You'd just be one of us." The wall behind Logan was a blur of green and brown. Ashley stared at it instead of looking Logan in her eyes. "You wouldn't have to keep moving around. You could stay here."

Logan smiled, but it was bitter and cool. "Cute idea, but I wanna go somewhere that people don't default hate me. In fact, I'd love to live somewhere they actually *like* me."

"Where?"

"I don't know yet." Logan shrugged. "There's lots of places. I'll find one."

Ashley looked down. As much as she wanted to believe there was a place like that—a place where people didn't feel so alone all the time—it was starting to feel like it wasn't about the town itself. Before Tristan's disappearance, Ashley had loved everything about Snakebite. This had been home. She'd never felt alone here.

"Here's a thought," Logan said. She pointedly avoided eye contact. "You could come with me."

Ashley's throat was tight. "You mean leave Snakebite?"

"Sorry, that's stupid." Logan cleared her throat and tilted her head to face the ceiling. "Obviously you'd wanna stay here. You've got the farm and all that."

Ashley's grip on the comforter tightened. There was something strange about Logan's suggestion, like she'd pulled open the curtains and revealed a horizon Ashley had never seen. In all her years in Snakebite, no one had ever asked if she wanted to leave. It had never occurred to her that she could just . . . *go.* But Logan said it like it was easy. The thought almost made Ashley laugh.

"It's not stupid," Ashley said. "I just don't think I could—"

"No worries. I take it back." Logan ran a hand through her hair. "I always say stuff that makes no sense when I'm tired. That's all. When I leave Snakebite, I wanna leave by myself."

"Oh."

"I mean, you meet tons of stray cats on the road, but that doesn't mean you take them all with you."

"I'm the stray cat?"

"Obviously."

"I feel like *you'd* be the stray cat," Ashley said. "You're, like, two steps from being a cat lady now."

"What're you trying to say about me?" Logan scoffed.

Ashley arched a brow at her and they both burst into laughter. The sound echoed off the motel walls and that heavy feeling in her chest—that *dread*—quietly dissolved until Ashley could breathe again.

Logan's smile was easy. She was only inches from Ashley now, cheek pressed into the mattress, eyes half lidded with sleepiness. It was the first time Ashley had seen laughter make it all the way to her eyes. They danced in the half-light, black and endless as the night outside. Ashley couldn't remember Logan inching this close to her. Maybe Ashley was the one who'd moved. There was something restless in Logan, magnetic and dark and impossible to ignore. She'd lain across from Tristan like this a hundred times, but she'd never felt this *pull.*

Ashley held her breath.

"You okay?" Logan asked.

"Yeah, I'm . . ."

Ashley didn't know what she was.

Logan's expression deepened, her smile fading like a dimmed bulb. She propped herself up on one elbow, hovering just above Ashley's face. Her black hair fell in a curtain between them, brushing gently against Ashley's cheek. Ashley tasted her heartbeat, tangy and electric on her tongue. She let out one ragged breath, then another. It would be so easy to reach up, to pull Logan to her. She wondered if kissing Logan would make her forget about everything else.

This was a bad idea.

Before Logan could close the space between them, Ashley sat up. Her mind raced between panic and embarrassment.

"I . . ." Logan collapsed back onto the mattress and covered her face with her hands. "Oh my god, why did I—"

"It's okay," Ashley said, too quickly.

Even in the dim light, Logan's cheeks burned brilliant red. She buried her face in her pillow and let out a long groan.

Ashley tucked her hair behind her ears. She didn't know what to do with her hands. All at once, the motel room was too small. It was suffocating. The rose-patterned walls were too close, the air was too hot, the ceiling was too low.

"I thought you were . . ." Logan said.

Ashley fixed her eyes on a shadow in the far corner of the room. Logan's stare bored into her. "I'm not into girls like that."

Logan said nothing.

"I'm not into you like that."

"Cool," Logan said flatly. "*Super* cool. Got it the first time."

They sat there for a moment that felt like a year. Ashley's heart barreled up her throat, threatened to choke her with panic. Because, for a second, she'd wanted it. She'd wanted it more than she'd wanted anything in a long time. She hadn't kissed anyone since Tristan. Even now, something tugged in her stomach and she wanted to reach across the bed and kiss Logan like she'd meant to.

"I'm so embarrassed," Ashley said finally.

"Why are *you* embarrassed?" Logan cleared her throat. "You're not the one who . . . you're fine. We're fine. Let's just forget about it."

"I should go," Ashley said.

Logan shook her head. "No way. Not with everything going on. Just crash here and leave in the morning. It's fine."

"You're sure?"

Logan sighed and buried herself under her comforter.

From the nightstand, Ashley's phone buzzed. She reached across Logan to silence it, and even that felt like too much contact. It felt like danger. The silence was molten. The motel room buzzed with quiet anxiety. It burned in Ashley's cheeks.

"Good night," Ashley said.

Logan hummed something that sounded like *night* from under the comforter. She curled into a ball, pointedly facing away from Ashley like she could minimize physical contact. Ashley reached out and unplugged the string lights and they were left in the hot, stifling dark.

23

The Witching Hour

Beatrice Ursula Gunderson didn't believe in ghosts.

That said, she *did* believe her best friend. And if Ashley Barton said the ghost of her missing boyfriend was haunting her, it was at least worth a look.

Bug had tried Ashley's cell phone at least a dozen times over the last half hour, but she had no luck. Maybe that was for the best, since Ashley refused to look into the *real* suspects. The Ortiz-Woodley clan had something to do with all of this. Logan's dads were cult-level weird, sneaking around all over Snakebite, lurking at the library, at the grocery store, at the park. They always whispered like everything they said was a secret.

Once, when she was boating on the lake, Bug was sure she'd seen the one with the glasses just wandering around at the cabin in broad daylight.

The neon BATES MOTEL sign had a brilliant yellow glow at night. For the most part, the lights in the motel rooms were off, but one window on the inside corner was ringed with a halo of soft light. It was probably Logan's. Bug wondered if Ashley had ever been inside. She couldn't pretend to understand what Ashley was getting from this friendship.

Bug tried Ashley's phone again. It rang a handful of times before dumping her into voice mail. "Hey, it's me again. I texted you. You're probably asleep. I'm at the motel to do some spy work and thought you might wanna come help." Bug looked at her phone and frowned. "Anyway, uh, see you tomorrow."

And then she spotted it.

Parked over three spots on the far end of the Bates parking lot. A massive red truck gleamed in the yellow light, tucked into the shadows like it thought it could hide. Bug narrowed her eyes, because she *knew* that truck, and it wasn't supposed to be here. Not at this hour. And not if Ashley wasn't answering her phone. Bug scowled and opened her text window.

BUG: are you HERE???
BUG: i see your truck in the parking lot

She prepared to call Ashley again, but something rustled in the bushes at the far side of the motel. Bug pocketed her phone and warily approached the noise. There were all kinds of animals that prowled around Snakebite at night, but Bug didn't think this was an animal. Its rustling was sporadic, more like the sounds of a person adjusting their limbs than a lost animal. She cast a glance at the room she assumed was Logan's.

Maybe Ashley was in there now.

Maybe she knew what was creeping outside the motel.

Maybe *that* was why she was here.

Bug held up her phone flashlight and scanned over the

bushes. In the murky yellow light, she finally saw the source of the rustling. A creature squatted near the lit window, half shrouded in bushes. Bug squinted and realized the thing wasn't a creature—it was a man. He stooped along the motel wall with his fingers latched on the windowsill.

Bug's heart came to a crashing halt.

She took a step back, trying her best not to breathe.

Her car was only a few feet away. She'd had nightmares like this before, meandering through the dark only to realize she wasn't alone. But she wasn't asleep now. The oil-slick pavement was real under her sneakers. The night air was warm and sweet, carrying the whistling moans of the wind through the valley. This was real, and so was the strange man staring into the motel.

He was real, and he was moving again.

If the tremor in her heart meant anything—if the instinctual twisting in her gut was real—it meant he was the killer.

Bug ducked around the abandoned pizza stand and sank onto the pavement. The night wasn't just *night,* now. She felt something here in the dark. The shadows were thick, smeared across the pavement like molasses. Bug clasped a hand over her mouth to keep quiet.

There was no more rustling in the bushes.

There was no sound at all.

Bug pulled her phone from her back pocket and typed a text to Ashley.

BUG: there's a man out here please come outside

She stared at the message for a moment, eyes fixed on the flickering cursor at the end of the text. She backspaced the message and tried again.

BUG: `there's a man out here. don't come outside.`

She sent the text and closed her eyes. If she was quick, she could make it to the car before the man saw her. But he wasn't alone out here. The night was heavy, and the shadows were on his side.

It occurred to Bug that this might be it.

Without another thought, she ran.

Or, she began to. Before she made it to her feet, a fist knotted in the back of her T-shirt and threw her to the ground. Her skull cracked against the pavement and she gasped at the shock of pain, blinking up into the yellow light. A silhouette hovered over her, at once a man and a shadow. Bug fought to sit up, but the man wrapped his hands around her neck, thumbs pressed into her throat. Her scream came out as a croak.

"No," the man huffed, not to Bug but to someone else. Someone she couldn't see. He closed his eyes and snapped, "*No.*"

Bug Gunderson hadn't given much thought to how she would die. She especially hadn't pictured it like this: alone, writhing against the pavement of the Bates Motel parking lot, watching the white stars overhead blur and slip away into the dark. Bug gasped once, twice, and then there was no more.

She had one thought before she faded away.

She recognized her killer's face.

24

On A Cold, Bleak Morning

Logan was aware of two things when she woke up. The first was Ashley's limbs, warm and soft and tangled with hers under the comforter. The second was blue-and-red lights flashing against her closed blinds. In her hazy half-dream, she wasn't sure which was more alarming. She pressed her face into her pillow and burrowed under her blankets. The motel room was cool and dewy with morning, gray shadows casting sharp lines across the wall. It was red, then blue, then red.

Logan abruptly sat up.

Police lights were *definitely* the more alarming thing.

She threw the blankets back and gave herself a quick once-over. She was still dressed in the clothes she'd been wearing the day before, though her sweater was crumpled and her skirt had rotated halfway around her waist.

Ashley sat up and slowly blinked to life.

"What . . . ?" She trailed off. Logan wasn't sure if the confusion stemmed from the police lights or the room she'd woken up in.

Logan motioned to the closed blinds. "Apparently we have visitors."

"I don't—" Ashley wearily peeled away the blankets and looked down at her legs. Her lips twisted into a scowl. "I slept in *jeans.*"

"We all make mistakes," Logan said, parting the blinds. The police cruiser in the parking lot wasn't alone. A square van was squeezed into the narrow space between Ashley's truck and the abandoned pizza stand. The back of the van was open and a steel cart was loaded into the back. It was hard to tell for sure, but the cloth-covered object on the cart looked uncannily like a body.

Logan cleared her throat. "I think this is serious."

Gracia stood outside, talking to the sheriff. She dabbed at her eyes with the sleeve of her blouse and shook her head in disbelief.

"I have to go," Ashley said. There was a fearful edge to her voice. "How do I get out of here?"

"Out the front door?"

Ashley stared at Logan for a second like she thought she was joking. Slowly, Logan understood what she meant, and embarrassment coiled in her stomach. Ashley couldn't be *seen* leaving the motel room. No one could know she had been here overnight, and more specifically, that she was here with Logan. Even though they hadn't done anything but talk, the mere implication of it would be too much for her reputation. Logan had to be a secret.

It wasn't a great feeling.

She cleared her throat. "Right. Wouldn't want anyone to see you."

"Sorry," Ashley said. She snatched her phone from the nightstand and unlocked it. Her hands shook. This was something more than embarrassment. "I had such a creepy dream last night."

Somehow, the fact that Ashley didn't get how rude it was made Logan even angrier. She grabbed the rest of Ashley's things—a purse, a hair tie, and a set of car keys—from the breakfast table and shoved them into Ashley's hands. "There's a window in the bathroom if you wanna sneak out. Maybe if you—"

Ashley scrolled through the notifications on her phone. "Wait."

"No, really, it's cool. I don't think it's super rude to act like you're embarrassed to be here."

"Wait." Ashley's eyes were fixed on her phone screen, wide with panic. Before Logan could ask what was wrong, Ashley slammed her phone on the nightstand and tore open the motel door. Logan hesitated behind her. She tapped Ashley's phone and read the stream of messages:

BUG: i'm checking out the motel wanna come?

BUG: just got here

BUG: are you asleep?

BUG: just called

BUG: are you HERE???

BUG: i see your truck in the parking lot

BUG: there's a man out here. don't come outside.

"Shit," Logan muttered. She threw on a pair of sandals and rushed outside.

The motel parking lot was at once chaos and dead silence.

Two police cruisers were parked in the lot, and now that she was outside, it was clear that the gray van she'd seen earlier read OWYHEE COUNTY CORONER across the side. Logan spotted Ashley on a bench near the pizza stand, eyes fixed on a point in the distance like she'd been powered down. Sheriff Paris sat next to her with a hand on her shoulder. He shook his head and said nothing.

Ashley didn't move.

The wind off the lake rang in Logan's ears. She'd been right inside; she would've *heard* something. She would've known there was someone dying just outside her room. The door behind Logan opened and a hand grabbed her wrist. She pushed the stranger away before recognizing it was Alejo.

"Logan," Alejo said. He tenderly squeezed her wrist, tugging her back to reality. "Come back inside. You don't need to be out here."

"What happened?" Logan mumbled.

An Owyhee County deputy strung caution tape across the length of the parking lot. A man she didn't recognize paced the area, snapping photos.

"It's all gonna be okay," Alejo said, "but we need to stay inside."

Logan tugged her wrist free. "What *happened?*"

"Is everything okay over here?" Another deputy approached cautiously. He was at least ten years younger than Sheriff Paris. The tag on his uniform shirt read GOLDEN, like the police receptionist.

"Everything's fine, Tommy," Alejo said. "We just wanna get out of your way."

"Actually, I need to talk to your daughter." Tommy Golden

put a hand on his hip. "I know it's a lot to take in right now. We can talk here or at the station. Up to you."

"Can I talk to Ashley?" Logan asked. Her voice was muddled in the wind. She felt like she was drowning.

"You can in a bit. Ashley has some questions to answer, too."

"I wanna talk to her now."

"Logan," Alejo warned.

"You're not in trouble, Miss Ortiz." Golden gave her a weary, half-baked smile. He wore his grief plain on his face. "I just need to know if you heard anything last night. If you maybe saw anyone outside."

"We understand," Alejo said. He took Logan's hand again. "You could question all three of us at once. Maybe it'd save you some time."

"No can do." Golden turned to Logan. "Gotta talk to each of you separately. It'll only take a second."

"She's a minor," Alejo said.

Deputy Golden hesitated. After a moment, he said, "I'm sorry. Sheriff's orders."

Logan swallowed. "Was it Bug?"

Deputy Golden said nothing, which meant it was.

Shadows danced at the edge of Logan's vision. She was about to pass out. Across the parking lot, Sheriff Paris helped Ashley from the bench and took her to his police cruiser. They left the Bates in silence, disappearing on the highway toward the police station. The sky was heavy with gray cloud cover; it weighed down on her, pressing like fists to her shoulders.

". . . What do you need to know?" Logan croaked.

Deputy Golden motioned to Logan's motel room. They entered, and Logan fought the urge to hide the evidence that

Ashley had been here. That they'd been here together when Bug died. That, for a second, things had been okay. She wanted to make the bed, to go back to the beginning of the night, to scrub the memory from the walls.

Deputy Golden shut the door behind them.

"Let's start from the beginning."

25

Let The Survey Show

"Should I get state police on the line?"

"I tried. They're sending someone out this week."

"This is an emergency."

"They don't think so."

"Have we notified the family?"

"God, not yet. What do I say? Frank's always done the notifications."

"Frank, the county coroner is on the other line. Can you take him now?"

"Put him through to my voice mail. I'll do the notification, I just need to talk to . . ."

Silence. Ashley felt Sheriff Paris turn his eyes on her. Everyone in the station turned their eyes on her. She kept staring into the brick wall across from her, tracing the mortar lines from the floor to the ceiling in aching detail. She needed to focus. Needed to block the rest of it out. She needed to keep her eyes open, because if she closed them, she'd see it again.

It'd only been a moment; she'd thought it was a nightmare at first, but now she knew. In the dark of the motel room, sometime between when she'd fallen asleep and when the police arrived, she'd seen her.

Bug.

Across the room, leaning against the makeshift desk in her dark green flannel, a braid of red hair drooped lazily over her shoulder. The room was laced with her—it even smelled like that perfume she bought from the mall in Ontario. She'd mouthed a word that Ashley couldn't quite understand. Over and over, her mouth was long like a vowel, and then thin as a smile. She'd thought it was a name. But maybe Bug was still alive when she'd seen it, just outside the room, struggling to breathe. Maybe she was mouthing *Help me.*

Ashley was going to be sick.

"Ashley?" Becky said. She came around her desk and sat on the chair next to Ashley, lingering just on the edge of the seat like she wasn't sure she was allowed. "Your mom is here. She wants to go with you for the questions. Is that okay with you?"

Ashley closed her eyes. Tammy Barton was going to skin her alive for lying about where she was last night, but that was better than being alone right now.

She nodded.

Becky stood and motioned to the front door of the station. A warm draft funneled into the lobby, accompanied by the signature *click* of Tammy's heels. In a flurry, Tammy swept Ashley into a hug so tight it threatened to cut off Ashley's airway.

It wasn't the right reaction. There was supposed to be anger. There was supposed to be yelling. Instead, Tammy just rocked her back and forth, whispering *It's okay* into her ear.

"I . . ." Ashley trailed off. The weight of it all punched its way up her chest like a stampede. Her tears were hot behind her eyes. Her head was going to explode. She knotted a fist in the back of Tammy's shirt and breathed, "I'm so sorry."

"Hey, look at me."

Ashley nodded and looked up. Tammy took her face between her hands and fixed her with an intense stare.

"You did *nothing* wrong." She tucked a strand of hair behind Ashley's ear. She was gentler now than Ashley had ever seen her. She struggled to reconcile this Tammy with the one she'd pictured on the way to the station—brow etched with fury, angry at her for lying, for being *there* of all places. Instead, Tammy gave her a small, quiet smile. "And Paris is gonna find who did this. Just breathe."

"I was there," Ashley croaked.

"I know." Her mother pulled her into another hug. "It could've been you."

Ashley exhaled, pushing back the first words that came to her: *it should've been me.* Bug had been there because Ashley told her about the investigation. Bug had died because of her, just like all the others. She wrapped her arms around her mother and held her tight, like she was the only thing keeping her from sinking.

"Ashley, Tammy, why don't you come on back?" Sheriff Paris asked.

They followed Paris deeper into the police station. It wasn't particularly large—behind the lobby was a closed-off holding cell, two desks, and an office with a wooden desk and a wall of bookshelves. Ashley followed Paris into the office and took a seat on the visitors' side of his desk. His office was surprisingly calming—white light streamed in through the blinds at the back, streaking the mahogany paneling on the walls.

Paris shut the door and circled to his desk chair. "I figured it'd be better to talk somewhere quiet."

"We appreciate it," Tammy said. "So? Do you know who did it?"

Paris frowned. "Not yet. I'm hoping Ashley can help me."

"I didn't see anything," Ashley said.

"Maybe not, but you can still help." Paris leaned forward and propped his elbows on his desk. "First, I have to know what you were doing at the motel."

Ashley nodded. She felt Tammy's eyes bore into her. "I was just visiting Logan."

"And you two were in there all night? You never went outside?"

"No."

"When I called your mom to let her know what happened, she said you were staying at Bug's house. I haven't talked to Bug's mom yet. Were you at Bug's house at any point last night?"

Bug's mom. He would have to tell Bug's family that their oldest daughter was gone. They would hate Ashley when they found out she was feet away when it happened and did nothing. They trusted her, and she'd failed them. Snakebite trusted the Bartons, and she'd already let three kids disappear. Ashley's throat felt swollen. She clutched the front of her T-shirt and tried to swallow her tears before they surfaced.

"Maybe if you didn't act like you're accusing her of murder, Frank," Tammy spat. She cupped a hand on Ashley's shoulder.

"I'm—" Paris straightened his spine and tried again. "Why don't you tell me what you did after you left your house?"

Ashley nodded. "I drove to the motel. Me and Logan just hung out. I fell asleep. I didn't look at my phone. I didn't see . . ."

"And Logan's dads? Did you see them, too?"

Tammy grimaced.

"No, I didn't see them."

Paris nodded. "Did you hear anything from their room?"

"No."

"Did you see their car in the parking lot?"

"I . . ." Ashley paused. "I didn't look."

"I understand." Paris straightened a stack of paperwork and put it in a box at the corner of his desk. "Do you think it's possible either Brandon Woodley or Alejo Ortiz left their room while you were there last night?"

Ashley was quiet. She understood now, maybe too late, what Paris was saying. And even though her instinct was to say no, it wasn't possible that the Ortiz-Woodleys had done this, it felt like a lie. People were still dying, and Tristan was still missing. She had promised Logan she wouldn't jump to conclusions. That felt like years ago now.

And she *had* seen someone outside the motel.

"I . . . yeah. It's possible."

"Frank, you don't think *they* . . . ?" Tammy said. Her expression was complicated—Ashley thought her mother would be more excited that the Ortiz-Woodleys were finally on the table. Tammy just looked disappointed.

"We've had suspicions for a while, but without a credible witness, we can't make an arrest." Sheriff Paris fixed Ashley with a hard stare. "I know how hard this is. You're still in shock. Logan is your friend. I'm friends with the family, too. But you were there when it happened. You're our only chance to get it right."

"Tell him the *truth,* Ashley," Tammy warned.

Ashley closed her eyes. There were two paths ahead of her, both tugging at her and both pushing her away. When she looked ahead, she saw nothing but darkness. She'd lost so much already—Tristan, Nick, Bug, and something more than them. She'd lost the Snakebite she knew. She'd lost the feeling of *home.* She wondered how much more pain she could take.

She thought of Logan.

She wished she'd had a chance to say goodbye, because she was about to lose Logan, too.

"Ashley," Sheriff Paris said, fist clenched on his desk, "do you know who could've been in that parking lot?"

Ashley took a deep breath and opened her eyes.

"Yes."

26

An Apple Off The Cleaven Trunk

"This is Ashley. I'm not here. Leave a message!"

It was Logan's fifth time hearing Ashley's stupid outgoing voice mail message. It'd been hours and there was no way she was still at the police station. "Hey, can you just text me to say you're okay? I need you to be okay."

Her room was empty now. Shadows clung to the walls like drapes. This room was always empty, but without Ashley it *felt* empty. Deputy Golden had finished questioning her within a couple minutes and moved on to her fathers.

Tires screeched across the pavement outside. Logan pried her blinds open in time to catch Sheriff Paris climbing out of his cruiser. He stood in the parking lot, cautiously eyeing the door to Brandon and Alejo's room with a blank expression. He steeled himself and marched to the door, quietly pushing his way inside.

Logan scrambled out to the parking lot.

"I'm almost done with the questions," Deputy Golden started. "I—"

"Yeah, well, something came up," Paris said. "We'll finish this at the station."

"Hey, *stop.*"

This was Brandon's voice from inside the motel room. A series of thumps sounded against the wall, followed by metal clinking against metal. Logan pressed her palms to her forehead. It was finally happening—after months of speculation, they finally had enough proof to arrest Brandon. They thought he was responsible for the deaths. After all the slurs, the whispers, the glares, Paris was finally going to do it. He was going to take Brandon away.

Except it wasn't Brandon being led from the motel room.

Alejo emerged with Sheriff Paris close behind him. His hands were pinned behind his back, balled into fists like all his fear was concentrated in his fingers. Brandon followed them out of the room and wedged himself between Alejo and the cruiser. His chest rose and fell rapidly, eyes wild with quiet panic. Behind them, Deputy Golden stood at the motel room door, brow furrowed in quiet confusion.

"Woodley," Paris sighed. "You gotta move."

"You know he didn't do anything," Brandon said. "You *know* he didn't."

"How would I know that?" Paris asked.

"He wasn't here for the first one."

"We haven't found Tristan Granger's body. He could still be alive," Paris said. "Which is the point of questioning. Unless you have information I don't."

"He wasn't here."

"Is there something you wanna tell me?"

Brandon grimaced.

This was all wrong. It wasn't supposed to be *Alejo.* It made no sense. Brandon was right—Alejo wasn't in Snakebite when Tristan disappeared. Alejo wouldn't kill anyone. This was the same man who got emotional when someone cried on his favorite cooking show. The same dad who had to turn off the news if there was too much violence.

Alejo looked at Brandon with a quiet expression she couldn't read.

"It's okay," he said. "It's gonna be okay."

"If he didn't do it, he has nothing to worry about," Paris said. He patted Alejo squarely on the back. "You know me and him are friends."

Quietly, Deputy Golden stepped to Paris's side. "We're okay to take him in? Just . . . like that?"

Paris's jaw clenched. "I don't want to do this, either. But there's a witness."

Logan blinked. Alejo narrowed his eyes. Brandon's face drained of color.

"How could there be a witness?" Brandon asked.

"Woodley, *move.*"

Brandon stepped aside.

"No," Logan muttered. "No, he didn't do anything."

Paris paused. He glanced at Logan over his shoulder and his expression was complicated; concern and confusion tugged at his focus. He motioned to Brandon and said, "Why don't you take Logan inside. She shouldn't be out here for this."

Logan's heart hammered in her chest. This was wrong. This wasn't how it was supposed to go.

Brandon approached her tentatively, hands raised in front of him as if she were some kind of wild animal he had to calm. The fear in his face made her sick. He was supposed to be fighting for Alejo, not talking her down. Even if he didn't care about her, he was supposed to fight for Alejo.

He offered her a small frown. "Let's go inside."

"You're just gonna let this happen?" Logan asked.

"What else is he supposed to do?" Alejo said as Sheriff Paris ducked him into the back seat of the cruiser. His expression softened. "Go back inside with your dad. I'll be okay."

Logan clenched her fists.

Paris fixed them each with a skeptical look before walking to the driver's side of the car. He pulled out of the Bates parking lot with Deputy Golden's cruiser trailing behind. Logan watched Alejo in the back seat, his eyes trained forward, jaw tight like he was swallowing his panic.

The morning was thick with hanging clouds. The sky was blank white and too bright to look at. Logan squinted into the empty horizon.

This was the end of them.

Brandon turned back toward room eight in silence. Logan followed him inside and slammed the door. Before she could speak, Brandon tore off his glasses and threw them against his nightstand. He pressed his palms over his eyes and turned his back to Logan, taking one measured breath and then another.

"Okay," Logan said, "what's the plan?"

Brandon moved his hands to look at her. His expression was as empty as the sky outside. He looked at her like he'd just realized she was in the room. His eyes were wide and glassy with a fear that went deeper than Alejo's arrest. It was fear of something else, deeper than false accusations, like an animal trapped in a net.

"I know you didn't let them take Dad without a plan to get him back."

"I don't know."

"We have money from the show."

"We do."

Logan leaned in expectantly. "So . . . we should use it to get Dad out of jail. What do we have to do?"

"I don't know," Brandon said again. He fixed his gaze on the floor and massaged the back of his neck.

"I'll look it up and—"

"No." Brandon sat on his bed and curled his fingers around the edge of the mattress, knuckles white with tension. "We should . . . we should leave him. The person is still out there. They'll know it isn't him."

Logan shook her head. "In jail. You think we should leave him in *jail*."

"Until we know what's going on," Brandon said. "He'll be safer."

"Oh, cool, so you're hoping more kids die." Logan clenched her jaw. "There's, like, forty *total* kids in this town. We just got here and there's already been three murders. I knew two of them. The next one could be Ashley. Or me."

"It won't be you."

"How do you know?"

Brandon was quiet. He gripped the mattress harder. "There won't be anyone else. We'll catch them."

"You know who it is?"

Brandon stared.

The motel room was quiet, but it was alive with a current that made Logan's heart race. Because, for just a second, she'd thought everything would be okay. She and Ashley were friends, Brandon and Alejo had promised to tell her everything when this was over, and even if everything hurt, the clues were slowly coming together. There was a light at the end of this—the promise that she would make it out of this town in one piece. But now it was all wrong. Bug was dead, Ashley was gone, Alejo was on his way to jail for a crime he didn't commit.

And Brandon was all she had.

Brandon, who stared at the wall now like his husband hadn't just been hauled away in handcuffs. Brandon, who couldn't speak more than a few words without disappearing into himself, who wouldn't look her in the eyes, whose whole plan was to just *wait*. Something boiled in her chest, electric and blinding and new. It was a rage she'd never let herself feel before because it was too big, too hot, too much. It was a fire that sparked its way over her skin now. Her breath caught.

"I thought they'd come for you, not Dad."

"So did I," Brandon breathed.

Logan swallowed and closed her eyes. She remembered the Brandon from her dreams—the one who buried her, who spoke in a voice as deep as an ocean, whose eyes shone dark and glossy like an oil slick. She remembered the Brandon who couldn't look at her in Tulsa. The one so full of anger it choked her.

"Was it you?"

Brandon lifted his face from his hands. His eyes were foggy with tears. His hands shook, hovering in front of him in a silent question. The gray morning light crept in through his drawn blinds, painting his face sickly and pale. "Logan . . ."

"Me and Dad weren't here when Tristan went missing. He didn't do it. But you were already here."

"I wouldn't—"

"Everyone thinks you did it."

Brandon's brow furrowed. "You think I *killed* those kids?"

"Did you?"

"You know me. We're family."

Logan sucked in a ragged breath. "I don't know you."

Brandon stood, but not as though he meant to come after her. He looked out the motel window and shook his head. "I *can't* explain it to you. Please trust me."

She couldn't. She wondered if she ever had.

"I have to . . . I have to make sure Ashley is okay," Logan said. She plucked the keys to the minivan from Brandon's bedside table.

"Logan," Brandon said, quiet as a breeze. "I promise we'll explain everything when this is over. I promise. We'll be okay again."

She doubted they had ever been okay in the first place. Brandon stood behind her, lips parted like he had a thousand more words tucked under his tongue. Like he wanted to let it all spill out into the silence between them.

But he said nothing.

Logan stepped out into the morning and closed the door behind her.

For the thousandth time since coming to Snakebite, Logan was suffocating. She pushed down her rising panic attack and drove across town. The morning was petrichor and musk, rain fighting to split from the gray clouds overhead. Snakebite was unsettlingly quiet as though it were already in mourning. The minivan tore down Barton Ranch's gravel driveway, leaving a cloud of dust in its wake.

The Ford was parked in the driveway, spattered with mud and dirt. Logan stormed past it to the back of the house. The windows were shut, blinds drawn, and for a moment Logan hoped no one was home.

She sucked in a sharp breath and knocked on Ashley's window.

Nothing.

Logan knocked again. Her heart hammered in her chest because Ashley was all she had left. The wind from the lake was biting as the slate gray sky.

She slammed her fist against the window again.

The window tore open. Ashley pushed her curtains aside and then they were face-to-face. Ashley's eyes were red rimmed with tears. Her expression wasn't grief, it was anger. She leaned out the window, fingers clenched on the windowsill.

"Are you okay?" Logan asked.

"What are you doing here?" Ashley snapped. "Go home."

Logan blinked. "I'm sorry about Bug. I just wanted to . . ."

Ashley's eyes narrowed. Through the window, her bedroom floor was littered with clothes and blankets. Her bulletin board was stripped bare, and pictures of Bug, Fran, and Tristan were scattered across the room. The cool wind fluttered Ashley's curtains against her arms.

"What happened?" Logan asked.

Ashley exhaled. "I got asked a million times why I was there. At the motel. Why I didn't . . . *hear* anything."

"I'm so sorry."

"You already said that."

"I . . ." Logan started, but she didn't know what else to say.

She hadn't expected Ashley to be angry like this. She hadn't really expected to see Ashley at all. "What did you tell them?"

"I don't know."

"You don't know?" Logan folded her arms. "You were at the motel. You could just say we're friends. It's not weird."

Ashley said nothing.

"Can I come in?" Logan asked.

Ashley glanced back at her room, then reluctantly nodded. Logan climbed in through the window and surveyed the damage. It wasn't just clothes and photos on the floor. Ashley's chair was knocked sideways, the contents of her desk swept to the floor, her closet emptied. It was worse than she'd thought.

"What do you want?" Ashley asked.

"I . . ." Logan pressed a palm to her forehead. "I just wanted to make sure you're okay. You weren't responding to texts or calls. And—"

She paused. She couldn't get the sound of handcuffs clinking around Alejo's wrists out of her head. She couldn't wipe away the police lights on the blinds, the sound of Brandon's glasses hitting his nightstand, the look on Alejo's face when he realized what was happening.

"Paris arrested my dad."

Ashley eyed the clutter on her floor. Slowly, she began picking up her pictures and piling them on her desk. She was unsettlingly calm about the arrest. Her jaw was tight, her movements cold and rigid. A breeze wafted into the room and fanned over Logan's back and, suddenly, it clicked.

"He said there was a witness."

Ashley paused.

"I'm going through the list of people who were at the Bates, but it's pretty small. Gracia and Elexis are family. They wouldn't throw my dad under the bus."

Ashley folded her quilt and tossed it on the bed. "The Bates is pretty much apartments. Lots of people live there."

"Ashley."

She turned, eyes glassy with impending tears. "I don't wanna talk to you about this. I wanna be alone."

Logan's heart crashed and she wondered if it was breaking. Her pulse was heavy, slow, deep. It labored with the weight of this grief, but she wasn't angry like she was at Brandon. It was like someone had come up behind her and snatched her world right out of her palms. It left her cold in its wake. Ashley's expression said everything—it was anger and sadness, but more than that, it was *guilt*. It was the same look she'd had when she admitted she'd broken up with Tristan.

"You didn't even see anything. Why'd you—"

"I did."

Logan paused. "Oh my god, you mean when he was taking out the garbage?"

Ashley looked away.

"You know it wasn't him," Logan croaked. "Why'd you say it?"

"He could've—"

"He *didn't*." Logan sank to the edge of Ashley's bed and cupped her hands over her nose and mouth. "Me and Dad weren't even *in* Snakebite when Tristan went missing."

Ashley huffed. "Maybe they worked together. Like a team."

"Oh my god." Logan's voice was too loud for the room. She closed her eyes and exhaled. "I told you it wasn't him. You *prom-*

ised you wouldn't say anything unless we were sure. Did you not trust me at all?"

"I trust you," Ashley said. A tear rolled down the curve of her cheek. "I don't trust them."

"Oh, don't start crying."

"How am I not supposed to . . . ?" Ashley sat down at her desk. She rubbed her swollen eyes with the heels of her hands. "Before all this, nobody died in Snakebite. It was perfect."

"Careful . . ." Logan warned.

"You guys showed up and everything fell apart."

"So, you *do* think they did it," Logan scoffed.

"Can you blame me?"

"Yes."

Ashley's expression wrinkled in frustration. "What do you want from me? I ignored the obvious because I trusted you, but . . . I can't let this keep happening. I'm losing *everyone*."

"You haven't lost me."

"I lost my home."

Something snapped in Logan. She stood, red-faced and breathless. "Oh, like Snakebite was so great before." Anger crept up her throat and threatened to choke her. "I've heard lots of stories. It sucked then and it sucks now. You thought it was perfect because this stuff didn't matter to you, but it's *always* sucked for people like me."

"That is not true."

"There's a reason people like my dads have to leave. Alejo said you'd turn on me just like your mom turned on him," Logan said. "But this fucking sucks."

Floorboards groaned outside Ashley's room. Tammy Barton peeked around the bedroom door and surveyed the room. Her gaze landed on Logan and her expression soured. "What is going on in here?"

"I was just leaving, Ms. Barton," Logan said. She approached the window and opened it. She wanted to spit on both of them. She wanted to let them know that they'd torn her whole world apart. Instead, she laughed. "In case you didn't hear, my dad's in jail. Maybe you can go tell all your friends. You can have a party."

Tammy's eyes widened, but she said nothing. Under the stern layers of her town matriarch persona, she looked more confused than relieved. "I don't—"

"*Logan,*" Ashley snapped.

She didn't wait to hear more excuses. Ashley was supposed to be her ally, but she was the same as Brandon. Too afraid to do the right thing, too afraid to admit what she'd done wrong. Logan climbed out the window and rushed back to the minivan. She pulled away from Barton Ranch in a blur, because this was it. This was the end. Alejo was gone, Brandon was silent, and Ashley was a traitor. After everything, she was alone.

She was alone.

27

Chokecherry And Other Menacing Flora

Logan was not okay.

Maybe she'd never been okay. It'd been two weeks since the fight with Ashley. Two weeks since Alejo was arrested. Two weeks of visiting him in the holding cell at the Owyhee County police station, talking about nothing, waiting for something to come to a head. Two weeks since her dreams of being buried alive had become a nightly occurrence. And for the last two weeks, Brandon was hardly more than a ghost in her life. No—given everything, ghost wasn't the right word.

He was nothing at all.

Logan sat alone in the back booth of the Chokecherry. It was the same as always: mildly populated, playing country a little too loud with the lights a little too low. It didn't set her on edge like it had the first time Ashley walked her through these doors. In a way, it was almost comforting. It was familiar.

"Can I have another porter?" Logan asked as Gus approached her table.

He slapped a plastic cup of water on the table and fixed her with an arched brow. "You're drinking water."

"Ugh, this sucks."

"I don't think you like beer much, anyway," Gus said. "Your dad used to order beers and he always made that same pinched-up face you do."

"Huh."

Logan was decidedly *not* into dad talk.

"Brandon was always doing stuff like that. Trying to order stuff to make him look normal."

Logan blinked. This was maybe the first time she'd heard someone tell a story about her fathers that wasn't about Alejo. She'd given up on the idea of an investigation the day Bug died, but she still wanted to understand. She cleared her throat. "Did Brandon come here a lot?"

Gus threw his dish towel over his shoulder. "Let me get the dishwasher running, then I can tell you all about it."

He made his way back behind the bar.

The bell at the front door rang and the door swung open. Late-afternoon light spilled into the Chokecherry, painting the cracked cement floor a sickly shade of yellow. The first to enter the bar was John Paris with Fran hanging on his arm, honey-brown curls bouncing at her shoulders. John's glorified shadow, Paul, tagged along behind them. He sneered at the dark corners of the bar.

Logan shrank into the shadows and held her water cup close to her chest. She'd never been one to hide, but she was already at rock bottom. She didn't have the mental fortitude to fight anyone anymore.

"The booth at the back is empty," Fran said.

"No," Paul said. "There's someone—"

Hefty footsteps clapped over the cement floor, each one louder than the last. Logan braced herself.

"Haven't seen *you* in a bit," John Paris scoffed.

He slid into the booth opposite Logan. Fran and Paul hung back, watching the scene unfold with a strange mix of fear and admiration. Logan gave a fleeting glance to the rest of the bar, but no one did anything. No one said anything. They just watched.

She was alone.

"Yeah, haven't been out much," Logan said. She took a sip of water and avoided eye contact. "No offense, but I was really hoping to just sit by myself today."

John laughed. "Ashley couldn't make it?"

Logan grimaced.

"Uh-oh, trouble in paradise?" Paul asked.

"Probably she didn't like your dad killing her best friend," John said.

"John," Fran warned. This was apparently an argument they'd had before. Fran crossed her arms and tapped her foot. "Let's just sit somewhere else."

John held up a hand to quiet her. "Why did he do it? What was the reason? I've been trying to figure it out for weeks."

"*John,*" Fran snapped.

Logan's hands curled into fists under the table. "As much as I'd love to sit and theorize, how about you fuck off?"

John reached across the table and grabbed Logan sharply by the elbow. "Tristan was my friend. Bug was my friend. Ashley's my friend, too. If you people do anything else to my friends, I'll kill you."

Logan swallowed. The bar was silent. The handful of other people in the room watched quietly, eyes wide, lips parted in surprise. But they weren't outraged for *her*. It was like the store all over again. People in this town didn't care what happened to her. Logan wanted to kick herself for the sinking feeling of disappointment in her chest. She was still the enemy. In Snakebite, she always would be.

A whistle sounded from behind the bar.

Gus made his way out of the kitchen with the Chokecherry's decorative double-barreled shotgun in hand. "Not in my bar," he said. "Get out of here."

"You couldn't fire that if you wanted to," John scoffed.

"I could," Gus said. He gestured toward the door. "Now get."

John rolled his eyes. Reluctantly, he pushed himself out of the booth and made his way to the door. Fran and Paul followed behind him—Fran cast a glance over her shoulder, torn somewhere between sympathy and anger.

Once the three of them were gone, Logan exhaled.

"Mind if I sit?" Gus asked.

Logan motioned to the seat opposite her. Banjo plucked from the speaker mounted on the wall, but other than that, the bar was quiet. Unrest simmered in the air. The rest of the bar patrons were apparently too afraid to speak. Logan didn't like the idea of someone having to protect her, but she didn't fight it. Gus returned his shotgun to its mount behind the bar, then slid into the seat across from her, pressing the table away to make room. He watched the sidewalk outside until John and the others disappeared around the corner, then leaned across the table.

"You okay?"

"Mostly, yeah." Logan laughed uneasily. "Uh, sorry for causing problems in your bar. And thanks for sticking up for me."

"Didn't mean to embarrass you."

Logan waved dismissively. "I'd rather be embarrassed than get the shit kicked out of me."

"It doesn't help when you sass back at them," Gus said. "Your dad was always the same way. I had to break up his fights, too."

"Which one?"

"Alejo," Gus said. "Whatever people say about your dads, they sure balance each other out. Alejo never knew when to shut up. Always said exactly what he was thinking, even if it turned right around and bit him. Brandon was always quiet, though. The day the two of them met was the first time I ever heard him say more than two words."

"Wait—you were there when they met?" Logan asked.

"Oh yeah," Gus said. "Well, I don't know if it was the first time they met. Me and Brandon used to work together at Barton Lumber. He never talked to anyone. Just showed up on time, did his work, and went home."

"That sounds about right," Logan mused.

"He only worked there for a few years, though. Tammy hired a new site manager and the guy's first move was firing him."

"What?"

"Yeah, it was bullshit. But a lot of the guys agreed with him. They wanted your dad out." Gus sat back. "I'd already opened the bar at that point, so I wasn't there anymore. I would've said something."

Logan shook her head. "Is that why you helped me?"

Gus exhaled sharply. "The way we pushed your dads out of

town never sat right with me. I don't know how I feel about all that gay marriage stuff, but they weren't hurting anyone. Even their little cabin across the lake wasn't far enough for some folks."

Logan shook her head. "Just because they were together?"

"Mostly, yeah. We don't like change around here. They were asking everyone to change a lot."

Logan rolled her eyes. "It doesn't sound like they were asking anyone to do anything but leave them alone."

"Maybe not," Gus said with a shrug.

"Thank you for telling me," Logan said. "I just wish I knew why they left."

"I'm not sure why, either," Gus said. "Probably . . . well, you know. They tried to be as quiet about it as possible, but losing a kid isn't easy. And they had to handle that on their own. I'm sure leaving felt easier than staying here. A fresh start."

Logan paused with her water cup halfway to her lips. "Wait, *what?*"

"Me and my wife lost our boy just before he turned six. It's the hardest thing that ever happened to us. After that, all I could think about was your dads." Gus wiped his mouth. "Didn't have any family or friends to mourn their kid. They didn't even have a plot on the hill. They buried the girl at Pioneer Cemetery. I still think about it. All the time."

"Gus." Logan pressed her palm flat to the table. Her head spun. There was another child—one her fathers had never told her about. Whatever had happened—whatever she didn't understand about her fathers—this was the missing piece. "What happened?"

"Can't say for sure," Gus said. "I know it was back a ways. 2006? Maybe 2007?"

"Thirteen years ago," Logan breathed.

"Right," Gus said. "They must've adopted you after they left. I know it doesn't ever make up for losing a kid, but I'm glad those two got to have a family in the end."

Logan could taste her heartbeat. "Hey, thanks for this. I'm gonna head out."

"Wait," Gus said. "Didn't you have questions about your dads?"

"I think you answered everything." Logan stepped out of the booth and shouldered her purse.

"You're heading back to the Bates?"

"Straight home," Logan lied.

"I can give you a ride."

"Nope. I'm good." She put a twenty on the table. "Thanks again for sticking up for me. See you around."

Logan stormed out of the Chokecherry and turned right. Away from the Bates. Away from Snakebite. She walked down the sidewalk until it ended, and then stumbled along the gravel shoulder. Lake water slapped at the shore to her left, gray and endless along the valley. Between two massive hills, she saw the iron fence, the mounds of dirt, the dusty road up to Snakebite Memorial, and her stomach twisted in knots. It was finally time for the truth.

She'd waited long enough.

28

And Then There Was One

BRANDON VOICEOVER: Tonight on *ParaSpectors,* there's no way out but down. The team heads to Tulsa, Oklahoma, where we'll be tracking down the infamous Tulsa Devil. Local legend says that the Tulsa Devil isn't your everyday demon. Everyone in this city has been touched by the Devil in some way or another. Alejo is out sick this week, but I won't be investigating alone. Along for the ride is super-fan and detective-in-training Logan.

[A young girl is shown at Brandon's side with a bag of gear. She wears a black T-shirt that reads WHO'S AFRAID OF THE DARK? A nametag appears across the screen: LOGAN ORTIZ-WOODLEY, INVESTIGATOR/DAUGHTER.]

BRANDON: I don't know what we'll find down here. But I bet you'll be less scared than your dad.

LOGAN: Anyone would be less scared than Dad.

Ashley wasn't sure why she was watching this. It burrowed into her like claws, reminding her of what she'd done. How she'd taken Alejo away from his family. How she'd probably ensured that this happy, excited Logan Ortiz-Woodley would never exist again. Her mother said that the Ortiz-Woodleys were a poison. Ashley wondered if Snakebite was the poison; if *she* was the poison.

[Logan smacks the SonusX against her palm. They stand in the basement of a Tulsa hotel waiting for the voice-detection box to power up.]

LOGAN: It doesn't work.

[Brandon crouches beside her.]

BRANDON: It's a button on the side here. It gets jammed all the time.

[Logan slides her finger along the side of the device and the noises begin. She jolts back. Brandon laughs.]

BRANDON: It still scares me sometimes, too.

For Ashley, it had been two weeks of radio silence. She'd gone to Bug's funeral with her mother and spoke to no one. It was two weeks of no Logan, no Fran, no anyone but Tammy occasionally bringing meals to her room to make sure she was still eating. She wasn't sure what made her turn on this episode of *ParaSpectors* other than an aching, rotting sense of loneliness.

She wasn't sure what the Logan-shaped hole in her chest meant. This episode was the thing that ate at Logan, and Logan was the thing that ate at her.

Ashley missed her old world. She missed Logan.

She wasn't sure how to reconcile the two.

Tonight, Tammy was at a community dinner to raise money for the cattle ranchers outside town, which meant Ashley had the ranch to herself. Normally, it would've been her curled up on the couch between Fran and Bug watching something stupid on TV until they all fell asleep. Before that, it might've been her and Tristan planted in the chairs on the lakeshore roasting hot dogs over the firepit. She wasn't supposed to be alone like this. She'd *never* been alone like this.

She couldn't take being alone like this anymore.

She scrolled to Logan's name in her contacts and hovered there a moment too long. She'd considered calling Logan a dozen times since their fight, but couldn't bring herself to do it. If Logan's life was ruined, it was her fault. But losing Logan felt like another death. Another person who she'd never get to talk to again. Just like Tristan, Logan would be another person gone and Ashley had spent their last moments saying all the wrong things.

Ashley scrolled away from Logan and pressed Fran's name. Almost immediately, the other end of the line clicked. *"Ashley?"*

"I didn't think you'd pick up," Ashley breathed.

"I didn't, either." Fran was so quiet that, for a moment, Ashley thought she'd hung up. Fran cleared her throat. *"It's late."*

Ashley glanced at the clock on her nightstand. It was only 6:32 p.m.

"Sorry."

After another pause, Fran sighed and said, *"I'm gonna go, then."*

"Wait." Ashley knotted her comforter in her fist. "I just wanna talk. We haven't talked since—"

"Since Bug, yeah." Fran's inhale was sharp. *"I can't talk about it right now."*

The surge of tears behind Ashley's eyes was sudden and overwhelming. She bit her lip to keep from crying. Just like everyone else, Fran was going to slip away like water between her fingers. "Do you think it's my fault?"

"God, I don't know." Fran sucked in another breath and Ashley realized she was on the verge of tears, too. *"What were you doing there?"*

"I—"

"Visiting Logan, right?"

"Yeah . . ." Ashley sighed. "I was with Logan. And Bug called me so many times. She texted me. I didn't see until after . . . I was right there. I don't know what happened."

Fran was quiet.

"Why didn't she call me?" Fran asked. *"I would've gone with her. Or talked her out of it, or . . . It's because I said I didn't believe any of it. She thought she couldn't ask me for help. She thought I wouldn't care."*

"She only went because of what I said."

Fran was silent.

"Fran—" Ashley started.

"I'm sorry," Fran said, sharp as a knife's edge. *"I can't talk to you about this."*

"Fran, I'm . . ."

"Night, Ashley."

There was a beep, and the call ended.

Ashley sank to her mattress and stared at the window. She couldn't remember what it felt like to breathe without this knotted mess of anxiety between her lungs. This town was wrong; this *world* was wrong.

There was a shift in the air of the room. It brought the quiet close to Ashley's throat, smothering the sound of the wind. Ashley turned to face the door. She couldn't quite see him, but Tristan was there. In the weeks after Bug's death, his spirit lingered all the time, watching her, waiting for something she didn't know how to give him. Maybe he wanted to lead her somewhere again. Maybe there was another body. If so, she ignored it. She'd found enough bodies in this town—someone else could find it this time.

"What do you *want?*" Ashley asked. She didn't have the Scripto8G this time, so there was no real way for him to respond. But she asked anyway.

The air shifted. It crackled, alive with static for a moment, and then it loosened. For the first time since he'd started visiting her, it was like he listened. He was leaving.

"Wait." Ashley clambered to the end of her bed. "Don't go."

The air came alive again. The pungent scent of fuel blossomed under her nose, flickering like a dying flame. For a moment, Ashley could almost see him. She saw the shape of him, at least. A cool draft blew through the window, skirting Ashley's hair over her shoulder, but Tristan was undisturbed.

"You're the only one left," Ashley said.

The air lost pressure like a plane in turbulence. There was only silence. Ashley lay back across her bed. The blankets smelled like stale detergent and dust and she wished she could just sink down through the mattress, through the floorboards, and into the dirt. She wished she could cover herself in soil and burrow until this was all over. She wished she could emerge back in January and do it all differently.

When she spoke, it was only a whisper. "I think you might be dead."

Tristan's reaction to this was strange. Like smoke from a field fire, Tristan emerged from the dark. His hands were balled into fists, jaw sharp with tension like he was fighting to hold something back. He walked toward her, stilted and jarring like he could hardly manage it. The sight of him made fear catch in Ashley's throat, but she stayed calm.

"I wish I could do our last night over," Ashley said, pushing past the way her voice shook and her eyes watered. "I would explain it differently so you'd understand. I wish I could talk to you back then."

Tristan's ghost was silent, as always. He stood at the end of her bed and cocked his head to the side in a curious gesture that was so Tristan it hurt.

"I would've made sure you knew how much I loved you. I said I didn't, but that's not what I meant. I just didn't love you like I thought I was supposed to. You were my best friend. Just because it wasn't like—"

Ashley blinked. The house was silent with night and she was left dizzy and breathless. She didn't know what she'd meant to compare it to. Or, she did know, but she didn't mean to think it. It was too quick, too easy to say her name.

"It's not fair," Ashley said. "You and me should've worked . . ."

Tristan looked at her, and she imagined him like he was before. He would sit at the edge of her bed with his hands on his knees. He'd laugh at the roundabout way she explained everything. *You're being so vague,* he'd tell her. *Just say what you mean.*

But she didn't know what she meant. Trying to have feelings for Tristan had been this slow-rolling thing like waves on the lake in summertime. It was happy and it was calm and she thought she could spend her whole life building up to it. They would be okay; they would last long enough for it to be real.

This other thing was too fast. It gripped her and wouldn't let go. It crushed her under its weight and didn't wait for her to catch her breath. It shoved her to the bottom of the lake and didn't care if she made it up for air. It was like she was always running out of time.

"You know how I said I wanted to break up because I didn't feel like you did?" Ashley swallowed. "I feel it now. I didn't know how scary it was. I'm so sorry."

Tristan's fists clenched. Ashley wished she could see his face. The Tristan she knew always wore his whole heart in his expression, but this Tristan was only a shadow. His face was nothing but a trick of light, impossible to see clearly. He recoiled, sharp and sudden, slamming against the bedroom door. The ceiling light flickered and the curtains flapped against the window. Ashley clambered back in her bed until she bumped into her headboard. After a moment, Tristan calmed. He was fighting to stay solid, to stay with her, to stay *here.*

Ashley sucked in a breath.

"Do you wanna come back?" she asked.

Tristan flickered. Maybe it was an answer; if so, Ashley couldn't understand it. It was almost dizzying sometimes, the way Tristan filled up the room. It wasn't just sensory anymore—every memory of him sat at the surface like a coat of moss on the wood floor. Things she didn't even realize she remembered, things she'd pushed to the back of her mind, things she'd tried to forget. "I'm glad I get to see you again."

Tristan wavered. He reached for her, his movements stilted and jagged.

The sound of the TV broke through the quiet. When Ashley blinked, Tristan was gone. Her hand lingered in the empty air. Brandon's and Logan's voices droned on and the rest of the room was empty.

Ashley turned back to the TV.

Brandon and Logan had made their way down into the tunnels now. Brandon was several feet ahead of Logan, scanning the graffiti-laden walls with a device Ashley didn't recognize.

Logan called to Brandon, fiddling with another device.

When the camera caught Brandon, everything was wrong.

Ashley narrowed her eyes at the screen. It was only a flicker of static at the edges of the TV. The infrared space was distorted, just warped enough to notice. Ashley nudged her TV, but the static remained. At Brandon's feet, something black pooled like oil. He stood completely still, eyes wide, and Ashley recognized his expression.

He'd looked at her like this in the cabin.

He was afraid.

"Dad?" Logan asked. She tried to hide it, but fear snuck into her voice. Her small fist was clamped around the ThermoGeist.

Ashley wondered if Logan could see the shadows at Brandon's feet. If she could feel the way the tunnel seemed to contract now, a throat swallowing them whole. Logan had told her about the moment in Tulsa, but she hadn't mentioned *this*.

And then Brandon spoke.

"Stay back," he said.

Brandon wasn't alone. Something else spoke, too. The second voice was deeper than Brandon's, empty and cold. It roiled like thunder. It was indecipherable and wrong. The voice didn't say the same words as Brandon; Ashley couldn't make out if it was saying *words* at all. Something about it pried beneath her skin.

The darkness at Brandon's feet spread until it was everywhere. Until only Logan and Brandon were left on the screen, distorted and melted and wrong. The picture continued to decay, and Ashley couldn't look away.

"Dad?" Logan said again.

Her voice was impossibly small.

"Get *out*, Logan," Brandon snapped at her.

The second voice groaned beneath the sound. Ashley touched her TV screen and it was hot.

Brandon closed his eyes. When he turned to Logan, he didn't look at her. The dark substance crashed over him like a wave and, for a moment, the screen went black. The only sound was Brandon's ragged breathing.

And then the screen roared to life. A commercial for tires. Ashley exhaled and her lungs ached. She wondered how long she'd been holding her breath. Her phone vibrated from the table next to her bed.

"Hello?" she said.

"Ashley." A man's voice. *"It's Gus. From the Chokecherry."*

Ashley blinked. She wasn't sure who she'd been expecting, but it wasn't Gus. "Oh. Hi, Gus. What's going on?"

"I don't wanna bother you. But I just saw your friend Logan in here. She said she was heading home, but I don't know. She seemed kind of down. I think she's heading to the old cemetery."

"Why?" Ashley asked.

"She was pretty hung up on one of the graves. I don't wanna get too much into it. Don't know if you two are getting along, but she was looking a little worse for wear. I'd go make sure she's okay, but I gotta close up."

"Wait," Ashley breathed. "The Ortiz-Woodley grave, right?"

"That's the one." Gus cleared his throat. *"She . . . a couple of your friends gave her a hard time. I think she was pretty shook up. And then we got to talking about her dads and the grave. It's my fault."*

"I'll be right there," Ashley said.

There was one thing they'd seen that they'd never talked about. One thing that had haunted Logan since the night they found Nick. And if Logan was going to visit the grave, it meant she wasn't waiting for ghosts to find *her* anymore. Ashley clenched the fabric of her shirt between her fingers.

The logo for *ParaSpectors* crashed back onto the TV.

Ashley stared at Brandon's face on the screen. This Brandon was different from the one she'd seen in Snakebite. His face was gaunt, eyes wide, hands trembling. The dark thing she'd seen coiling around him was gone, and now he was alone. There was nothing in his eyes.

He was empty.

Maybe whatever was wrong with Brandon was connected to

everything going on. It was connected to the grave. It was connected to *Logan*—Ashley was sure of it. And if she wasn't fast, she was sure it was going to kill again. Ashley turned off the TV and grabbed her purse.

If Logan was going to find the truth, she wasn't going to do it alone.

29

Hands Made For Hurting

Ashley parked the Ford along the highway shoulder. On one side of the road, the lake beat against the shore. The clouds overhead were deep gray, bruised and swollen with an approaching storm. Ashley could taste the musky scent of impending rain on the tip of her tongue.

On the other side of the highway, Ashley spotted Logan. She sat in the dirt beside one of the graves with her face cupped in her hands.

"Hey," Ashley called.

Logan looked up and her expression changed, brow furrowed in anger. "Oh my god, are you serious? Leave me alone."

Ashley's jaw tightened. Cautiously, she walked around the iron fence that enclosed the cemetery and made her way to Logan as the dust under her feet spotted with rain. She didn't check the stone key to see if this mound of dirt was the one marked ORTIZ-WOODLEY, but she didn't need to. Bits of the dirt had been swept away by deft hands, hardly scratching the surface. Dozens of dried white lily petals littered the ground. Ashley recognized them as the flowers Alejo had left when they first arrived.

Logan leaned against the iron fence, knees curled to her chest.

"Are you okay?" Ashley asked.

"No," Logan snapped. "I don't want your help."

"Gus called and said you were in trouble."

"Gus is full of shit."

Ashley frowned and motioned to the grave. "You were trying to dig this up? You can't just . . ."

Logan ducked her forehead against her legs and folded her arms over her knees. For a moment, Ashley thought she was crying. But she was quiet. Dirt caked her fingernails and smeared her wrists. The rain freckled the dust around them, catching in Logan's straight black hair.

"You probably hate me—"

"Correct."

Ashley steeled herself. "—but I wanna help."

"Then get my dad out of jail," Logan said. She looked up. "That's what you can do to help."

"What do you think you're gonna find?" Ashley asked. "It's a grave."

"Gus says they had a kid that died. They never told me about that." Logan wiped her cheeks, leaving a streak of gray dirt behind.

Ashley swallowed and crouched beside Logan. "So you're gonna dig up their body? What would that prove?"

Logan's expression softened. She was afraid. Raindrops dotted her cheeks and speckled her scalp. Somewhere far behind them, thunder groaned.

"What if it's exactly what it should be?" Ashley asked. "What if you're just digging up a kid's bones? There are better ways to figure this out. You could just ask Brandon."

Logan shook her head. "I can't."

"Then you could visit Alejo and ask him," Ashley said, swallowing the guilt welling in her chest.

"You don't get to talk about him."

Ashley nodded. "I'm sorry."

"If you wanna help, you have to help me do this," Logan whispered. She wiped her nose with the hem of her sleeve. "I . . . feel like I'm losing it. I don't know what's real. I don't know if I'm remembering things right. I don't know if I'm supposed to trust my dads or if they've been lying to me the whole time."

Ashley touched Logan's hand.

"What if there was never a second kid?" Logan said.

"What?"

"What if it's . . ." Logan clutched the front of her jacket. "I told you about my dreams. When I'm being buried, it feels so real. It's like at the cabin. There are all these things in Snakebite that I *remember*, but I shouldn't. I've never been here before."

"You think you're connected to whatever's buried here?" Ashley asked.

"I don't know."

Ashley stared into the mound of dirt.

"In my dreams, Brandon's the one burying me."

Ashley grimaced. Logan was right; it didn't make sense that the Ortiz-Woodleys had a child they never mentioned. It didn't make sense that this grave was down here with Snakebite's unnamed ancestors and not up on the hill with the rest of the town. The more they unraveled Snakebite, the less sense it made. Fear grew in Ashley, warning her that if they unraveled too far, there would be no more Snakebite left.

Ashley swallowed. "Okay."

She made her way back to the Ford and opened the tool chest in the trunk. She pulled out two worn shovels and returned to the grave. Logan took one of the shovels and pressed it against the mound of dirt.

"Are you sure about this?" Ashley asked.

"No." Logan bit her lip. "But I don't know what else to do."

They went to work. There was a strange hum on the wind, low and quiet like at the cabin, but now it was everywhere. The earth in Pioneer Cemetery was drier than the soil on top of the hill. It was caked together and hardened like brick. The hillside echoed with roiling thunder and the clang of metal against stone, but slowly, they made progress. Eventually, a layer of the dusty earth fell away, revealing a small wooden box in the grave. It took a moment for the strange object to register—Ashley had expected to find bones or nothing at all. The box wasn't big enough or buried deep enough to be a casket.

Logan didn't hesitate. The rain graduated from droplets to thick splatters of warm water bursting over the grave, swirling the dirt into a paste. Logan plucked the wooden box from the grave and pulled open the lid. Inside was a folded piece of paper.

Logan looked at Ashley. Ashley looked back. A truck whirred past on the highway behind them and Ashley was suddenly reminded that there was a world beyond this moment. She held her hands over Logan's piece of paper to protect it from the rain.

"There's writing on it," Logan said.

"Can you read it?"

Logan's hands shook but she nodded. She brushed dirt from the paper, crumpling its edges in her grip. "It's . . . to me."

She scanned the paper again and again, and each time her tear-rimmed eyes widened. She exhaled and pressed her wrist to her eyes. The damp wind through the cemetery was colder than it had any right to be. Whatever was on the paper, it was unspooling Logan from the inside.

"I don't get it . . ." she breathed.

Tenderly, she handed the paper to Ashley. The writing was brief, scrawled as if it'd been written quickly. It read:

Logan,

I tried everything. I tried to live quietly, but that was too loud. I tried to raise a family right, but I lost it. I tried to live without you, but I couldn't. I tried to save you, but I lost myself. Maybe this was all a mistake and things won't ever be the same.

I'm happy I got to see you again.

Love,

B

Ashley shook her head. She read it over again but the words swam without meaning. She turned the paper over but the other side was blank, dotted with bits of dirt and rain. There was nothing else in the box, nothing else in the grave, nothing else at all.

"What does it mean?" Ashley asked.

Logan snatched the letter back and read it again.

"It's from Brandon." Logan took a deep breath and closed her eyes. "I think this grave was mine."

30

Game Over

Elexis Carrillo was lonelier than he'd ever been.

It'd been a month since Nick's funeral. A month since Logan dropped off the face of the earth. A month since his nana started acting like going outside was suicide. It'd been a month since his world was flipped upside down and shaken until all the good fell from its pockets.

"It stinks in here, Nana," Elexis said. He shut off his PS4 and leaned across the doorway into Gracia's room. "I'm gonna take out the trash."

Gracia spun her recliner away from the TV screen and fixed him with one of her *looks.* She narrowed her eyes and the wrinkles at the corners bunched up like a thousand tiny frowns. Her room reeked of cigarette smoke and honey-lemon cough drops. "We took out the garbage yesterday. It doesn't stink so bad."

"It does in my room," Elexis groaned. "And I want some fresh air."

"You need a buddy. It's too dark to go alone." She leaned back and pointed across the parking lot. Logan's light was off and the

Neon was missing from the lot, though Gracia didn't seem to notice. "Ask your prima."

Elexis grimaced. "She's not there. Not like she'd come out of her room, anyway."

"If you ask nicely she would."

Elexis rolled his eyes. He pulled on his sweatshirt and sighed. "Okay, okay. I'll ask her."

He had no plans to ask Logan anything. He grabbed the trash bag from Gracia's room, then gathered up the empty chip bags and frozen food boxes from his floor. The Bates Motel dumpster was only a few feet from his room. It'd be a longer walk to Logan's door than it was to take out the trash. It was ridiculous to think he couldn't handle walking even that far on his own.

He stepped into the night and closed the door behind him. Without the rambling of the TV or the groaning air conditioner, the air was quiet. The silence was like a cool balm to Elexis's racing brain, smoothing the nerves that the motel room made jagged. Without Nick, he'd spent the last month playing video games until it felt like his eyes were going to cave in.

The truth was, since Nick, it felt like the world was moving too fast. Elexis had stayed upright for now, but Nick was the one person in Snakebite he'd been able to call anytime without worrying that he was being annoying. Nick was the only person who made him feel less lonely.

Nick made Snakebite feel like home.

He'd died alone, and now Elexis was alive alone. It wasn't fair to be mad, but sometimes Elexis wasn't sure where to put the hurt in his chest. On nights like this, he took a moment to lay his head against the motel door and just breathe.

He made it all the way to the dumpster before he heard it.

Boots echoed hard and fast off the pavement.

Elexis turned, but the stranger grabbed him before he could scream and clapped a hand over his mouth. He pushed Elexis hard against the dumpster, crushing his cheek into the sticky metal. He was bigger than Elexis, but not by much. When he finally spoke, his voice was hoarse.

"Calm down," the man muttered. "You're not gonna die."

Elexis writhed against the stranger. He wanted to scream, but the sound died in his throat. His heart beat so fast he thought a heart attack might kill him before the stranger ever got a chance.

This was how Nick had died.

This was how Elexis was going to die.

"Hold still," the man said.

Something crawled over Elexis's back, cool and slick as oil. He kicked at the dumpster, searching the parking lot frantically for someone who could help him, but no one came. No one could hear him. The substance at his neck snaked along his collarbone and then, slowly, seeped into his skin.

He shuddered, but the urge to scream stopped.

Everything stopped.

Do not be afraid, a voice whispered to him. The voice had the timbre and depth of a great ocean. It lured Elexis into its waters, and before he understood it, he was submerged. It continued, *I only want to help you. Don't you want to fix your lonely heart?*

He did. He wanted nothing else.

He wasn't sure why.

You want a place for your hurt. I know whose fault it is that you're alone, the voice breathed as though it were coming from the dark itself. *You want this town to feel what you feel. You want them to feel alone. You want them to feel like the last people alive.*

"I . . . do," Elexis murmured.

Good. The dark wrapped around Elexis's chest, and then poured itself into his heart. It was thicker than blood and it pumped through him like tar. It was all he could feel. Overhead, the stormy sky was streaked with gray and pinpricks of lightning, but Elexis only saw dark. *You're going to help me, Elexis Carrillo. But right now, you're going to sleep.*

The last thing Elexis saw before he slipped into darkness was his nana watching TV in the window and the vicious blur of the sky as he fell and fell and fell.

31

The Great Stage Of Fools

From the cemetery, it was a short trek to the lakeshore. Logan stumbled along the highway shoulder, stopping at a small slab of concrete stuck in the earth. A picnic table was bolted to the concrete, rusted and discolored as though it had never been used. Ashley paused somewhere behind her; Logan sensed her there, cautious and afraid as if she thought speaking were dangerous. Wind whipped Logan's hair across her face, sticking it to the rainwater on her cheeks.

Logan exhaled. "Can we sit for a second?"

Ashley nodded. They climbed onto the picnic table at the water's edge and let silence pour over them. It was all wrong. The world was unsteady under Logan's feet, like one too many stones had been pulled from the foundation. The grave was supposed to contain answers, but she'd dug it up and only had more questions.

She pressed her face into her palms. "It doesn't feel real."

"The letter?" Ashley asked. "Or . . . ?"

"God, *any* of it." Logan reached for the rain-spotted paper in her pocket. The handwriting was Brandon's, but she couldn't untangle the meaning. An apology, but it didn't say what Brandon was sorry *for*. Logan traced the letters—they were jagged and misshapen, like he'd scrawled them in a panic. The letters were shaped like they hurt. "Whatever's doing all this, I think you were right. Brandon's connected to it. So am I."

Ashley looked down. "I shouldn't have said that."

Logan waved a dismissive hand.

Dusk settled into the valley as the storm clouds burned away. The horizon was a crown of black hills blanketed in shadow and, beyond that, the sky was bloodred and bright as fire. Specks of white starlight crept through the sunset, promising that night was only minutes away. Dark water lapped at the gravelly shore, rhythmic and calm as a heartbeat. Other than the crickets and the water and the tender, cautious sound of Ashley's breathing, there was quiet. The night smelled like juniper and gentle anticipation.

Logan closed her eyes.

"I bet people used to think this was paradise."

"Yeah." Ashley stared at the hills across the water and her eyes were full of sunset. "I did. Maybe I still do. I don't know. I look at it and there's nowhere else I wanna be."

"Not me," Logan said.

"I wish you saw it before all this," Ashley said. "It wasn't like this before. I used to actually *like* how it felt like we were the only people in the world. There's no one around for hours. You could do anything you wanted here and it would never matter to anyone else."

Logan's laugh was a bitter stab. She hadn't expected to laugh. The sound felt hollow in her chest. "That's terrifying. It explains how you've got three dead kids and no one outside Snakebite cares."

Ashley's expression darkened and Logan realized what she'd said a moment too late.

"You think he's dead?"

Logan started to speak, but she didn't have the right words.

Ashley looked out at the water. Her eyes were the color of freshwater in the hazy half-light. The breeze buffeted her hair over her shoulders. "I don't wanna give up, but I don't think he's coming back."

"Hey," Logan said. She cleared her throat, reshaping herself into someone with a softness she'd never had. "I didn't mean it. He could still be out there."

"You don't think he is, though."

Logan grimaced. No, she didn't think Tristan was alive. But stranger things had happened in this town. She hardly knew who she was anymore—hardly knew what being *alive* even meant. Who was she to say Tristan was gone for good?

"I just don't know anymore," Logan said finally. "When I got here, I thought people were alive or dead. I thought you remembered things or you didn't." She traced the veins along her wrist. "I don't know if we're ever gonna figure out what's going on. Every time I think I'm getting there, it gets more confusing."

"I made it worse," Ashley said. "I don't know what I thought it would fix. I'm so sorry."

Logan grimaced but said nothing. For a long time, Alejo had been the glue holding their family together. Without him, Logan understood how alone she truly was. How many days she could go without speaking, without leaving her room, without *doing* anything. "They'll realize he didn't do it soon, and then they have to let him go. But I wanted to solve this for me. I just wanted to understand."

Ashley ran her thumb along the picnic table, considering. "What if you didn't solve it?"

"I don't know," Logan said. "I'll keep trying, but—"

"No, I mean what if you didn't *try* to solve it?" Ashley shifted to face Logan, eyes wide with either fear or excitement. "What if we just gave up?"

Logan narrowed her eyes. The breeze off the lake was warm now. The suggestion sounded like nonsense, but Ashley seemed genuine. Something small and hopeful sparked in Logan's chest. "What do you mean?"

"I could go to Paris and tell him Alejo didn't do it," Ashley said. "It's the least I can do. I know we keep thinking we have to fix Snakebite, but what if we just . . . didn't? What if we just left?"

"I . . ." Logan wiped rainwater from her cheek. "Are you serious?"

Ashley nodded.

Logan stared into her face—*really* stared—and tried not to cry. Because, for the first time since she'd been dropped into this hellscape, there was a way out. She wanted to understand everything happening here, but more than that, she wanted out. She wanted to breathe again. She didn't want to be alone.

"Yeah . . ." Logan breathed. She laughed and dabbed at the hot tears welling in her eyes. "I think I'd like that."

Ashley's gaze fluttered to Logan's lips. With surprising force, she leaned across the table and pulled Logan into her. The kiss was only a guess; it was a gentle hand reaching through the dark, wondering what it might meet on the other side. It was careful and quiet and unassuming. Logan held still, because this wasn't the way it ever went. She was the black hole, the one always reaching, the one always starving. She wasn't wanted—not in a real way. She wasn't kissed in a way she felt.

She pulled away, eyes still closed. Her lips tingled in the cool wind.

"Was that . . . ?" Ashley trailed off. Logan didn't need to see her face to know it was contorted in panic. "I'm sorry. I shouldn't have—"

Logan cupped the back of Ashley's neck with both hands and pulled her into another kiss. Unlike the first, this one was purposeful. It was shaking hands and ragged breath. It was Ashley's fingers knotting in the back of Logan's sweater. It was Ashley's lips that tasted like freshwater and hibiscus tea. Logan pushed a loose strand of Ashley's blond hair out of her face just to brush knuckles over her skin. Her fingertips left a gray smear of dirt on Ashley's cheek, but it didn't matter. Ashley's lips parted and Logan sank into her, kissing her like it was more important than breathing.

Ashley put her hands on Logan's shoulders and shifted to straddle her waist. Her lips moved against Logan's frantically, desperately, like it was all she knew. She kissed like someone who'd never meant it before. Logan wrapped her arms around Ashley's back and held her closer. She snaked a hand under Ashley's T-shirt, raked fingernails over the hot skin of Ashley's back, and her heart raced too fast. The world raced too fast.

Behind them, truck wheels crunched over the loose gravel on the highway shoulder. The steady thump of a country song was muffled inside the vehicle.

Ashley went stiff.

Logan pulled away and glanced over her shoulder. Her head still spun from the kiss, but the white truck parked behind them sent her crashing back to earth. She'd seen it on the gravel turn-out to the cabin, outside the Chokecherry, outside the police station. John Paris jumped out of the driver's seat and slammed the door shut behind him. Paul climbed out of the passenger's side.

She gripped the side of the picnic table and forced herself to breathe.

"John," Ashley said tentatively. She climbed off the picnic table—off Logan's lap—and approached the boys. Her hands were raised in semisurrender as though she were a frightened hunter talking down a charging bear. "What're you doing here?"

"Saving you." John strode toward them with a confidence that made Logan's stomach turn. He pushed past Ashley and leaned against the picnic table. Logan expected him to be angry, but he wore a strange, almost dreamy smile. He was looking forward to this. He eyed Logan and said, "I warned you."

"Last I checked, people don't have to listen to you," Logan spat.

She wished she felt as brave as she sounded. Maybe Gus was right; maybe she needed to learn to shut her mouth.

"Warned her about what?" Ashley asked.

John kept eye contact with Logan. "I told her to back off from my friends. She's supposed to leave you alone."

"I don't think she knows how." Paul snorted.

"She didn't do anything," Ashley said. "I started it. And it's not your business, anyway. I can make my own decisions."

John turned to Ashley with such ferocity Logan thought he might charge at her. "I hope Tristan can't see this, wherever he is. He loved you so much, Ash. And now you're out here with the bitch that helped kill him."

"I . . ." This stopped Ashley for a moment. "It's not about Tristan."

"It should be." John turned back to Logan. His eyes were darker than the night creeping in on the horizon. "He was my best friend. Then you people show up and kill him and nobody cares. Everyone just forgets him. But I didn't forget, and I'm not letting you kill anyone else."

"John, what are you—?" Ashley started.

In an instant, John lunged across the table and grabbed Logan, dragging her to the dirt by the collar of her sweater. Logan fought against his grip, but it was pointless. The sweater tugged against her neck like a noose, cutting off her airway. Her calves skidded along the rocks, rubbing her skin raw and bloody. Somewhere behind her, Logan heard the lapping waves of the lake against the shore, but all she saw was starlight. Starlight and John's face, contorted with hate and anger and grief and pain.

She was going to die.

She'd thought she was getting out, but this was how she was going to die.

"Let *go* of her," Ashley screamed, but she was far away now.

John threw Logan down in the gravel, but before she could scramble to her feet, he reached down and grabbed a fistful of her hair. He pulled her into the cool Lake Owyhee water.

It was a crash in her ears—against her face—and then silence. No more Ashley screaming, no more of John's raspy breath, no more crickets chirping in the evening. Just the slow, sucking sound of water fanning over her skin.

Logan clawed at John's fist in her hair, but it made no difference. She couldn't breathe. Somewhere, just beyond her memory, it came back to her.

She'd done this before.

Just as hard as he'd shoved her into the water, John pulled her back out. The night wind was hot and sharp as a whip on her cheeks and she screamed for help. She screamed until her throat was raw.

"That's so loud," Paul said from somewhere far away.

John laughed, hoarse and smug, and Logan knew he wouldn't stop until he'd killed her. He was beyond stopping now, twisted up with rage and hurt. Logan couldn't see anything but the water. John held her head steadily an inch above the water. She only saw black waves and nothingness.

"I'm calling the cops!" Ashley screamed. "If you don't let her go, I'm—"

"Do it," John thundered.

He said something else, but it was lost. John shoved Logan's head back under the water with enough force to scrape her cheek over the rocks along the lake floor. Her lips parted in a gasp and her mouth filled with lake water. It rushed to the back of her throat and she was going to *die.* Black water closed over her vision, pulling her farther and farther into the waves.

And then, Logan was somewhere else.

She looked up at the surface of the water. It rippled like a sheet of glass overhead, distorting the moon into nothing but white light. The sounds of the lake disappeared and only starlight covered her eyes. There was no water anymore—she didn't need to breathe.

The voice that spoke to her was cool and sweet.

You cannot die here. I still need you.

Logan was ripped out of the water again. Behind her, Paul and John laughed in chorus. John turned her over, and his laughter died on his face.

"What the hell?" he breathed.

Logan touched her cheek. Warm blood dotted her fingertips, but other than the small cut, she was okay. She wasn't sure how long she'd been under the water, but judging by John's shock, it should've been long enough. She kicked at John's legs in another vain attempt to break free. Behind him, she heard Ashley's muffled voice yelling into her phone.

John pushed Logan back into the water.

Come back to the place this all started, the voice from before whispered through the lake. Logan felt suspended. She was a weightless, untethered thing. She floated under the water's surface for only a moment, but she felt time swirl past her in the black current. The voice sang, *I saved you once. Let me save you again.*

Logan was pulled from the water again, breathing and alive.

"Shit," John muttered.

He released Logan and stepped away from her. She rolled to her side and spit water into the gravel. The sky was black with night now; red and blue flashed against the dark, and Logan realized that the police had arrived. She shivered, wet hair clinging to her neck. The sky and the black hills and the lake all spun around her.

Footsteps struck the gravel, and then a hand wiped the blood from her cheek.

"Hey," Ashley breathed. "Hey, stay with me, it's gonna be okay."

Logan blinked up at her, but her vision was spotted with wild color. She lolled back on the gravel and took Ashley's hand.

"We're gonna be okay," Ashley continued to whisper. "We're gonna be okay, we're gonna be . . ."

Logan's eyes fluttered shut and she slipped into the dark.

32

At The Bottom Of Below

"You're sure that's everything?" Deputy Golden asked. "You're making it sound like they had her underwater for over fifteen minutes."

"They *did*," Ashley snapped.

"And there's nothing you're leaving out?"

Ashley pulled her blanket tighter around her shoulders. She hated this: hated Deputy Golden, hated Snakebite, hated the hot wind, hated the churning dread in her gut. She sat on the same picnic table she'd been sitting on with Logan only half an hour ago, but now everything was different. The bench was sweaty, the wind was hot, her fingertips were numb. Dry tears made the skin on her cheeks tight. Her throat was raw from yelling, filling her mouth with the tang of iron. The sky was only night now, stripped of the last dregs of sunset the moment John shoved Logan's head under the water.

And she'd done *nothing*.

"Yeah, that's everything," Ashley said.

She didn't mention the escape plans. She didn't mention the

grave. She didn't mention the kiss. She didn't need to. This was Snakebite—if John Paris had seen it, then everyone already knew.

She didn't mention the voice she'd heard, softer than the wind. While Logan fought for air, a voice whispered over the water. *Come back to the place where this all started.* It was a low groan, just like the one she'd heard on the TV. Just like she'd heard at the cabin.

Sheriff Paris was parked on the other side of the highway. He delicately loaded Logan into the back of his cruiser wrapped in a wool blanket and gave Ashley a quick, uncomfortable wave. Even from the shore, Ashley could see the blood crusted on Logan's cheek, the black hair matted to her neck, her smeared eyeliner. She'd warned Ashley a thousand times that Snakebite was wrong. Now, it had almost killed her.

Paris promised that John and Paul would pay for what they'd done here, but given that they had been allowed to drive themselves home, Ashley seriously doubted it.

Logan had been right all along.

There was something *wrong* with this place.

"Can I go home?" Ashley asked. She pressed the heels of her hands to her eyes until the backs of her eyelids spotted with color. "I just wanna go home."

"Ah, um . . . you seem pretty shook up." Deputy Golden checked his watch. "Paris didn't think you'd be okay to drive yourself. And with some of the legal stuff, he just wanted to make sure nothing bad happened."

Ashley's eyes narrowed. She prayed he wasn't saying what she thought he was saying. "I'm eighteen. I'm a legal adult."

Deputy Golden gave her a thin grimace, then glanced over his shoulder. As Paris pulled away from the lake and drove down the highway, a white Land Rover parked along the shoulder in its place. It wasn't just any mammoth-size vehicle; Tammy Barton's car was complete with a WORLD'S BEST MOM decal and a license plate frame that read OWYHEE COUNTY FARMER'S UNION. She threw the beast of a car into park, climbed out, and thundered down the gravel shoulder toward the picnic bench.

Ashley braced herself.

"Is she okay?" Tammy demanded.

"Yeah, she wasn't hurt," Deputy Golden said. "Paris is taking the other one back to the station, but Ashley's free to go."

"She's not being arrested?"

Ashley gripped her blanket. "I didn't do anything wrong."

Tammy turned on her with a fire in her eyes Ashley had never seen before. This wasn't like with Bug. Her mother wasn't just happy she was alive. Tammy turned back to Deputy Golden and softened. "Well, I appreciate the call. We'll head home. Call me if you need anything else."

"Will do."

Tammy motioned Ashley toward the car and Ashley followed.

The ride back to Barton Ranch was quiet as the night outside. Ashley sank into the passenger seat and watched the hills streak past her. Usually, they listened to Christian hits on the radio with the air conditioner on full blast, but tonight, the car was silent. Even the sound of Tammy's breathing was subdued. This Tammy Barton was the one Ashley feared. She wasn't soft and supportive. She seethed with a smoldering anger that was slowly working its way to the surface. Ashley felt it like a brand against her skin.

They parked in the driveway and Tammy threw open her door. She stormed into the house with Ashley at her heels.

"I've never been this embarrassed in my life," Tammy barked once they were both inside. She swept into the entryway like a hurricane, tossing her purse at the console table. The key dish clattered to the floor, but Tammy didn't give it even a second glance. She turned to face Ashley. "In my *life*."

Ashley stood in the open doorway, eyes fixed on her mother's face. A warm, sickly breeze gusted into the hallway, but Ashley had long since forgotten how to breathe. The Tammy Barton Ashley knew was a monument—she was carved of marble, unshakeable against the storm—but now, bathed in sallow half-light, she slouched against the kitchen counter and peeled off her black heels, discarding them across the room like *they'd* just been caught kissing the town pariah. Like *they'd* disgraced the Barton legacy she'd worked so hard to cultivate. Tammy's voice was small in the same way a star was small moments before exploding.

But this wasn't fair.

The fear and guilt that'd been bunching up in Ashley's stomach since the lake began to unfold into something else. It crawled up Ashley's throat, forcing her to bite back angry tears. Her hands curled into fists at her sides. "You're embarrassed of me?"

Tammy considered.

"You know what? Yes. I mean, am I the *last* person in town to know about this? People have probably been talking about it behind my back for weeks."

"Behind *your* back?"

"Yes, behind *my* back. We're the backbone of this town. And you turned us into a joke."

Ashley wiped her eyes. "Me and Logan aren't a joke."

"If it was serious, you would've told me."

Ashley shook her head. Because telling her mother about Logan wasn't like telling her about Tristan. It wasn't like telling her about a failed test or a party she felt guilty about going to. There was an unspoken rule in Snakebite that said that this truth was different and dangerous. It was self-exile. It wasn't the kind of thing Snakebite knew how to forgive.

"I couldn't tell you."

"Really?" Tammy asked, incredulous. "Why not?"

"I saw how you treated Logan's dads."

"Oh, you *saw* how I treated them? I guess you were a really observant toddler, then." Tammy exhaled and her rage transformed into a bitter chill. Her perfectly maintained blond curls bobbed at her shoulders. "If you knew anything about it, you'd know I *saved* them."

"You kicked them out."

"And they're lucky I did."

Ashley arched a brow.

"You think they would've had a great life here?" Tammy asked. "You think they would've been happy?"

"It's their home."

"I love Snakebite, but I know what it is and it was never gonna be home for them." Tammy leaned against the kitchen island, grip tight on the edge of the counter. "They were so *stupid.* They thought because they were from here it wouldn't hurt them and they could just do whatever they wanted. People were ready to literally *kill* them and they wouldn't leave. They have no idea how many nights I spent convincing people to put the pitchforks away."

Ashley cleared her throat. Cautiously, she approached the counter and slipped onto a barstool across from her mother. The storm hadn't passed yet—Tammy's eyes were glassy with tears she refused to let loose—but her grip on the counter was slack. Soon, she'd reach into the fridge for a bottle of cheap pinot grigio and the worst would be over. But it wouldn't be over for Ashley. A new storm raged in her chest full of pain and anger and even more questions.

"And now you're making the same mistake," Tammy said. She wiped her eyes, streaking eyeliner across her cheek. "Snakebite . . . it doesn't change. They love you, but they won't change their minds for you."

"Do you hate me?" Ashley croaked.

Tammy's eyes widened. She reached across the counter for Ashley's hand, gently running her thumb over Ashley's knuckles. "I could *never* hate you. I will love you no matter what." She cleared her throat. "But this isn't you. This isn't how you are. You've just been through so much these last few months—"

Ashley winced. "It *is* me, though."

Tammy closed her eyes. "No, it's that family. They ruin everything they touch. They come in here, and—"

"Mom," Ashley warned.

"Or maybe it's me. Maybe I'm just cursed."

"Mom." Ashley stood.

Tammy looked at her for a moment, and Ashley understood with crushing clarity that everything was different now. Her mother looked at her like she was a puzzle that needed to be pieced together to make any sense. Like there was a mistake tangled deep in her veins that her mother was trying to unravel.

Behind her, the floorboards groaned.

Ashley turned. Tristan stood behind her, fists clenched, eyes impossible to see under the shadow that obscured his face.

"What?" Tammy asked.

Ashley's heart stopped. This was different from the other times he'd visited her. Every haunting felt urgent, but this one felt final. Tristan wasn't waiting for her—he was begging her to listen. He wavered between Ashley and the front door and she knew she had to follow him.

"Ashley, what are—" Tammy started.

"I have to go."

Tammy gave an incredulous laugh. "You aren't going anywhere. You're grounded."

"What?"

"You don't get a free pass for sneaking around and causing trouble for weeks." Tammy ran a hand through her hair. "At least until roundup next month, you're staying home."

Tristan continued to fade in and out of the space near the door. Dread twisted in her chest. He was trying to warn her that Logan was in trouble—somehow she understood.

"Okay," Ashley said. "Okay, fine."

"Get some rest," Tammy said. She threw open the fridge door and searched the shelves for a bottle of wine. "You and me have a lot to talk about tomorrow."

Ashley tentatively made her way toward the front door and closed her eyes. It was time to be brave. For once in her life, she needed to be braver than the Ashley she had been. Tristan watched her, flickering in the low light. At his feet, the key dish was still toppled from where Tammy had knocked it over, leaving various keyrings strewn across the hardwood floor.

Her Ford was still parked at the cemetery, but the Land Rover was in the driveway.

Ashley stooped near the front door and picked up the key

dish. She slowly, methodically placed each set of keys back in the bowl as though she were just cleaning up. She reached into Tammy's purse and gently hooked a finger in Tammy's keyring.

When Tammy turned to pour herself a glass of wine, Ashley ran.

She bolted into the driveway and threw open the Land Rover's driver's-side door. Behind her, Tammy stumbled onto the front porch. She watched, wide-eyed, as Ashley tore out of the driveway and into the night. Down the road, Tristan flickered in the Land Rover's headlights, guiding Ashley into town.

Wherever she was going now, there was no turning back.

33

The Devil, The Devil

When Logan woke up, she was fairly certain she was dead.

Slowly, pieces of the world around her came together like a mosaic in the back of her skull. The surface she lay on was too narrow to be a bed, the walls too close. She rocked up and down, each bump searing her muscles. Outside, trees blurred into a mass of green and black.

She was in a car.

She was in the back seat of Paris's car.

Logan pushed herself up and rubbed her eyes. The seat under her head was damp with lake water. She was being taken to either the police station or the hospital, but either way, she was being taken by the father of the boy who'd just tried to kill her. It was possible that John and Paul had been arrested, too, but something told her they'd probably been released with a slap on the wrist and nothing else. Even attempted murder was a forgivable offense in this hell town.

"Logan," Paris said from the front seat. "How're you holding up?"

Logan stabilized herself, dizzied by the force of sitting up. Wet hair clung to the back of her neck. She brushed fingertips along her cheek and it throbbed at the touch, swollen and crusted with blood. "I, uh . . ." She trailed off. "Where am I?"

"On your way to the hospital. You got pretty scratched up back there." Paris didn't look back at her. "It's a long drive into the city. I was hoping I could ask you a few questions on the way in."

Logan blinked out the front windshield. The road was narrower than the highway she remembered. The trees closed in like a tunnel, headlights cutting through the filmy dark. She'd driven into the city with Brandon once and it hadn't looked like this. "Sure, I guess. How long was I out?"

"Only about fifteen minutes. Are you feeling okay?"

"Uh, yeah. I'm fine," she lied. She wasn't okay, but she hadn't been in a long time. "Did you arrest the guys who did it?"

Paris gave her a thin-lipped smile through the rearview mirror. "John's at home. He'll be getting a talk when I get back."

Logan swallowed. "Like, a parent talk or a police talk?"

"You're funny," Paris said.

Logan was no expert on the law, but she was fairly certain she'd just been the victim of a verifiable crime. The kind that people went to prison for on TV. Instead of arresting everyone involved, Paris had just sent them all home. All but her. Paris hadn't called an ambulance. She shrank into the back seat and clutched the seatbelt.

"Why don't you tell me what happened," Paris said. "From the beginning."

"Okay." Logan cleared her throat. "Me and Ashley were at the lake, just talking. Then John and Paul showed up and—"

Paris shook his head. "Before that. John says he saw you two at the graveyard. What were you doing there?"

Logan narrowed her eyes.

"There were shovels against the fence. I found one of the graves partially dug up. Did you two find anything?"

Logan peered into the front seat. Paris's knuckles were a sickly yellow with bruising, and red welts like claw marks tracked all the way up his forearm. On his ring finger, a puckered indent was purple where a wedding ring should have been. He kept his eyes trained forward on the road, but his stare was miles long. She shook off the swelling sense of dread that curdled in her chest and focused on breathing. "We weren't at the graveyard."

"Huh." Paris turned the cruiser along the curve of the road. It skidded off of pavement and onto gravel. "Do you know what prompted the attack?"

"No."

"You have no idea?"

Logan cleared her throat. "I was at the Chokecherry earlier today and John threatened me . . ."

"Gotcha."

Logan swallowed again. Between the scratches on Paris's arms, there were red half-moons like fingernail indents. His thousand-mile stare was fixed on her now, and she understood. The truth was a slow thing, but the fog was burning away second by second. Logan met Paris's eyes and there was nothing there. He smiled, but there was nothing, nothing, *nothing*.

She'd seen a face like that before in her dreams. She'd seen it behind Brandon's spectacles, piercing and cold and empty. She could taste her heartbeat.

"You're sure this is the way to the hospital?" Logan asked. "It seems pretty dark for the highway."

"Yep. Almost there."

This was not the way to the hospital. Logan had driven on this road before. She'd seen these trees at night. She'd seen the black hills across the lake, the blips of campfire, the scratches of road on the distant shore. This was the way around the lake.

Paris was taking her to the cabin.

It was him.

He was the killer.

Paris leaned back in his seat. "You've been through a lot since you got to Snakebite. Can't be easy coming here, where things are so different from the big city. We've got good hearts, but we keep things traditional. Maybe that's a bad thing—I don't know—but it must be hard on you."

Logan could only stare at his hands. They looked strong enough to choke the life out of her like they'd done to all the others. Maybe that was why he was taking her to the cabin: to kill her. She kept her arms at her sides to hide her shaking. She was going to throw up.

"You probably think I'm backward, or that I hate gays. I'm not like that, Logan. I never had a problem with your dads. It hurt me to see all that hate just as much as it hurt them. Alejo and me were always good friends, and I never had a problem with Brandon. The two of them always kept to themselves. To see people accusing them of crimes we both know they didn't commit . . . it's a shame. I really wanted to keep your family out of this." Paris sighed. "But I think you've figured out by now that the three of you are always gonna be connected to all this."

"What do you mean?" Logan asked, voice shaking.

Paris arched a brow. "You still cold? You're shaking."

"A little."

Paris reached into his passenger seat and handed her a towel. Logan wrung out her hair and covered her face with the towel. She counted her breaths to keep from panicking. There had to be a way out of this car, off of this road, back to safety. She patted her back pocket for her phone, but it was gone.

Paris gave a low *hmm* and looked at her in the rearview mirror. Suddenly, his expression changed and he shook his head. "Looking for your phone? I've got it up here."

"Can I have it back?"

"No, I don't think so." He let out a disappointed sigh. "Wouldn't matter much. There's no service out here."

Logan blinked. Her heart climbed up her throat. Somewhere, miles away, she hoped Ashley was looking for her. She hoped *someone* was looking for her. There had to be a way to tell them where she was. Who she was with. What he'd done.

"Where are we actually going?" Logan asked.

"You know where we're going," Paris said. "You kids have been out here a dozen times already."

"The cabin, right?"

"I *am* sorry," Paris said. "I would've kept you out of it if I could."

Logan closed her eyes. "Are you gonna kill me?"

"No."

Paris signaled his way off the main road and pulled into the gravel turnout. His headlights cut through the trees. Deep in the woods, Logan could just see the outline of the cabin. Inside, a single lantern glowed orange against the night.

The ghosts, the deaths, her fathers: it all started here.

Logan let out a shuddering breath. A piece of her had thought the voice she heard in the water was a hallucination. That it was something her mind had created to keep her from dying. But it had told her she needed to go to the place where everything began. And for one reason or another, that place was here. Something told her that the cabin was where it would end, too.

"Why are we here?" Logan asked.

"Because it says I've gotta do one more thing, then I'm good." Paris turned in his seat to face her. His eyes shone like glassy obsidian in the dark night. "Look, I don't know what it wants with you or the kid from the Bates. Carrillo."

Elexis. Logan's eyes widened.

"Anyway, I'm supposed to tell you that, if you want your answers, you gotta head into the cabin. The Carrillo kid's inside. You think you can do that?"

Logan swallowed. It was probably a trap. It was probably dangerous. But she'd left Nick at this cabin and he'd been killed. She couldn't leave Elexis, too. They could find a way to signal someone from town. There had to be a way out of this.

"Just go to him?" Logan asked. "You won't hurt us?"

"I won't." Paris unlocked the doors and pushed Logan's door open. "Now get in there."

Logan swallowed her fear and nodded. She stepped into the night and waited for her dizziness to pass. Without a flashlight, she only had Paris's headlights and the light in the cabin to follow. She tripped over roots and stumps, scraping her arms against the rough juniper trunks as she went, but she didn't stop. Behind her, Paris's headlights seared yellow against the dusty forest floor.

And then they didn't.

She turned in time to watch Paris's cruiser reverse out of the gravel turnout and drive away.

He was gone; he'd *left* her here.

Something wasn't adding up. If he wanted to kill her, why would he leave?

Logan made her way onto the cabin's porch and placed her hand against the front door. Inside, she heard the strangled sound of Elexis's breathing. Logan sighed in relief. "Elexis. Hey. It's me."

"Don't come—" Elexis started. He choked on the rest of his sentence as if the words were too big for him. "I can't . . ."

"It's okay," Logan said. She pushed open the front door and stepped into the cabin. The wind followed her inside, gusting against the old wood like a whistle. "I'm not gonna leave you. We're gonna get out of here."

Elexis sat against the back wall of the cabin, tied to the piano. Other than the rope, he looked unharmed. Logan scanned the room for some sign of danger, but it was exactly the same as she remembered it. Another wave of wind gusted into the cabin again and snuffed out the lantern.

"Hello?" Logan asked in the darkness.

"Logan, you—"

Something crawled over her skin, and she was frozen. The sensation was the same one she'd had underwater. It was the same creeping blackness, the same cloying, thick tar crawling up her throat. Logan could just see Elexis across the room, and he shook his head. The long shadows of the room crawled over her skin like icy fingers, pressing into the exposed skin of her neck. She willed her legs to move, but they didn't answer to her anymore.

I am glad you could join us, a voice whispered. She felt its sickly breath against her throat. *It has been a very long time.*

"What . . . ?" she began.

She couldn't remember what she meant to ask.

You want to know why you dream of death. You want to know why your bones reach for the earth. You have spent your nights starving for the truth.

Logan's stomach churned. She nodded. The voice's words were true, but they were true in a way she'd never felt before. They were true in a way that had no alternatives. Logan was peeled away and something else took her place. The truth was the only thing she wanted; she couldn't remember wanting anything else.

"The truth . . ."

The dark rested just above her skin like gathered cloth. Sweetly, the dark breathed, *Would you like me to show you?*

Logan didn't answer. She didn't *need* to answer. The dark swallowed her whole and she was gone, hurtled out of time.

34

If The Truth Is A Lie

Ashley followed Tristan to the police station with her heart in her throat.

As soon as she killed the engine on the Land Rover, Tristan's silhouette disappeared and she was left in the yellow glow of the station lights. She'd followed Tristan because there was supposed to be an answer at the end of the road, but the station was empty. None of the police cruisers were parked outside. The only car in the lot was the scuffed-up *ParaSpectors* minivan.

Ashley climbed out of the Land Rover and ran into the station. The front desk was empty, but all of the lights were on. Behind the reception desk, she heard clattering and scraping like someone was digging around in the drawers. The overhead lights flickered, and it struck Ashley that it was too bright, too *alive* in here to be empty.

"Hello?" Ashley asked.

The clattering stopped. A man stood up behind the counter. She immediately recognized his short crop of dark hair and thick-rimmed spectacles. He'd been living in this town for months, but this was the first time Ashley saw him face-to-face. The first time she saw him alive.

Brandon Woodley rolled his eyes. "Are you serious? I don't have time for this."

"Mr. Woodley?" Ashley asked. "Are you here for Logan?"

He stared. "I was. She's gone. Her phone is off."

"But she . . ." Ashley trailed off.

"Your *mother* called and said she would be here." Brandon dug into the drawers again like Ashley wasn't there. His hair was disheveled, fingers fumbling over sticky notes and highlighters like he was running out of time. "Didn't even say what she was arrested for. I swear to god, this town never fails to—"

"Did you find it?" another voice called.

This was Alejo from somewhere in the back of the station. Guilt bunched up in Ashley's stomach. While she'd been wallowing in her grief for the last two weeks, Alejo had been stuck here.

"Not yet." Brandon pulled open another drawer and scanned its contents. "Becky would have the keys, right?"

"I don't know." Alejo laughed. "They don't really show prisoners where the keys are."

Brandon gave a short, strangled laugh.

Ashley cleared her throat. She'd seen keys before, but not at Becky's desk. She made her way back into the station, past the wooden desks, and into Sheriff Paris's office. The holding cell was carved into the wall behind her. She felt Alejo watch her through the bars, puzzling through where she was going. A mounted rack near Paris's desk held several sets of keys. Ashley plucked the ones labeled HOLDING CELL from their hook and stepped back into the lobby.

"How about these?"

Brandon stared at her, then wordlessly snatched the keys from her grasp. He frantically undid the lock on Alejo's cell and stepped aside. Alejo ambled out into the light and rubbed his eyes. In a blur of motion, he tumbled forward and threw his arms around Brandon.

Brandon hugged him back, releasing a ragged breath into Alejo's shoulder.

The guilt in Ashley's stomach tightened.

"Can't wait to leave a one-star review for this one." Alejo chuckled, though it didn't reach his eyes. Dark shadows bored deep into his face. He let go of Brandon and stretched his arms. "The bed was *really* uncomfortable. No complimentary pillows."

"You look pretty okay for a guy who's been in jail for two weeks," Brandon said.

"You flatter me." Alejo straightened. "Becky brought me food and shower stuff from home. I'm supposed to be waiting for a transfer to county jail next week."

"Well," Brandon said, but he didn't finish the thought.

Alejo gave the station a cursory glance. "No one came in recently. If Logan's not here, where is she?"

"I don't know, but we need a plan." Brandon adjusted his glasses. "We have to get out of here. We just broke you out of jail, which is an *actual* crime. I don't think Paris will overlook that one, even if you guys are friends."

Alejo shrugged. "We reinvented ourselves before. We can do it again."

Ashley looked at the two men in awe. This was the same Brandon and Alejo she'd seen on TV, but now they were here in the flesh. They weren't full of darkness and secrets and pain like she'd thought. They spoke to each other like any two people did. Brandon rubbed the back of his neck. Alejo touched Brandon's shoulder to comfort him, and Ashley felt like a monster.

"Let's go," Brandon said. "We find her and then we pack up tonight."

"Wait," Ashley said.

Both men turned to look at her like they'd just remembered she was there. She couldn't blame Brandon for the disdain plain on his face, but it was Alejo's expression that was more difficult. It was calm, like he wasn't even angry. Like he didn't blame her for the last two weeks. Maybe he didn't know it was her.

"I wanna help," Ashley said. "I wanna find her. I was with her when she . . ."

Brandon's eyes narrowed. "When she what?"

"Paris might've taken her to the hospital in Ontario."

"Hospital?" Alejo asked. "What happened?"

"We were kind of attacked," Ashley said. "Well, *she* was."

"By who?" Brandon asked. Rage flamed behind his expression. "Is she hurt?"

"A little. I don't know." Ashley swallowed. "I didn't get to talk to her before Sherriff Paris took her. It was John Paris and Paul Miller. They tried to . . . drown her."

Brandon met Alejo's eyes. Ashley watched their hearts break. She clenched and unclenched her fists.

"Me and Logan were trying to find out who's doing all of this. Who's hurting people."

"And you landed on Alejo?" Brandon asked.

"I'm so sorry." Ashley shook her head. "I know it isn't you.

Me and Logan think it's . . . we don't know what it is. I don't even think it's human."

Brandon and Alejo were quiet again. They communicated in a silent language Ashley didn't understand, then slowly nodded.

"Come with us," Alejo said.

They exited the police station and crowded into the minivan, Brandon and Alejo in the front with Ashley in the back seat. The sky above the parking lot was speckled with faint starlight. Silence filled the tiny space, searing and thick.

"Why do you think it's not human?" Brandon asked.

"I . . . we went out to the cabin a lot. The one across the lake. And we kept seeing things there." Ashley swallowed hard. It was too late to skirt around the truth. "I've been seeing people that died. Tristan, Nick, Bug . . . they've been trying to tell me something. Logan told me you see them, too."

Alejo gave her a small smile. "No fun, is it?"

"What does it mean?" Ashley asked. "If we can find out what the thing is that's killing people, we can stop it. I just don't know—"

"We've been looking into the same thing this whole time," Brandon said. "Tracking the same deaths. The same killer."

Alejo fixed his hair in the passenger-side mirror. "Maybe we should've swapped notes."

"What did you find?" Brandon asked.

"It's something to do with the cabin. I think the thing comes from there. When Logan . . . when she was underwater, I heard a voice saying we had to go back to where it all started. Maybe if we figure out how it started, we can get rid of it."

Alejo watched Brandon, but Brandon continued to stare out the windshield with a grimace. His eyes were wide, fingers clenched too tight around the steering wheel. “Finally,” he said, “something I can explain.”

“Brandon,” Alejo warned.

Brandon looked at Ashley and the shadows on his face were sharp as a knife. “The thing you’re looking for is called the Dark, and I created it.”

35

The Dead And The Dark

1997

Brandon Woodley was a ghost in his own life.

Moontide Diner was unusually busy for a Sunday morning. Brandon sat in a red vinyl booth opposite his parents as they split a Moontide Breakfast. Like usual, they smiled at each other and ate in gross, contented silence. Brandon ate a singular waffle and wished his parents had just let him stay home. The diner radio played something upbeat and swingy. It smelled like hot grease and burned meat.

"Baby, you don't have to sit there all bored," his mother said. She popped another bite of egg into her mouth. "Why don't you talk to your friends over there? We're just figuring out the move, anyway."

Brandon shrugged. He didn't *have* friends. You had to be a person to have friends, and he was pretty sure he didn't count. He was a shadow on the wall, a thought that never quite surfaced, a phantom of what a boy should be. He was like a stranger posted outside the room that the rest of the world lived in, and no matter how hard he pressed his fingers to the window, he wasn't getting in.

He wasn't an outcast; he didn't exist at all.

Brandon looked across the diner anyway. In a booth identical to theirs, Tammy Barton and Alejo Ortiz shared their own Moontide Breakfast. They looked disgustingly happy together, a study in contrasts. Tammy's hair was platinum blond and fell in loose curls down her back. Alejo's hair was cropped close on the sides and, as always, he looked like the kind of person who meant it when he smiled. Frank Paris sat opposite them, shoulders broad as a brick wall. He said something to Tammy and Alejo and all three of them erupted into laughter.

That was the problem—they were too perfect to hate.

Brandon's mother frowned. She glanced across the diner at the golden trio and her expression hardened. "Well, I guess *I'll* say hello." Before Brandon had a chance to stop her, she waved across the diner to the other booth. "Tammy Barton, is that you?"

The three teens stopped eating and looked over. Immediately, Tammy's face lit up and she climbed out of her booth. "Mrs. Woodley, how *are* you?"

"Doing just great. You?"

"So great, Mrs. Woodley. I love that you guys go for family breakfast—it's *so* cute. God, we haven't caught up in forever."

Brandon looked at his plate.

His mother reached out of the booth and pulled Tammy into an amiable side-hug. "I don't think we've really caught up since I was your sitter. You've grown so much. How's the ranch?"

"You know, lots of cows." Tammy clearly had no idea how her own ranch worked. And she didn't have to yet. Her mother still ran the ranch—Tammy had a whole lifetime to learn. She turned around and motioned for Alejo and Frank to join her. "You guys know these two, right?"

Alejo joined them with one of those smiles that went all the way up to his eyes, and Brandon's heart sank. Alejo turned to Brandon's father. "I haven't met you, Mr. Woodley, but you taught my brother algebra. I love the boat shop."

"And it loves your business," Brandon's father mused. He sat a little taller in his seat, reaching out to give Alejo a firm handshake. There weren't many people who still visited Woodley Fish and Boating. It was one of several things Brandon's parents planned to sell before they left this town behind. "You all go to school with Brandon?"

Tammy, Alejo, and Frank all turned their eyes on Brandon, and he wanted to fall through the floor. He took a deep breath, fixed his glasses, and extended his hand to Tammy to shake. Which was stupid, because he already knew her and this wasn't an introduction.

Tammy turned to his parents, button nose wrinkled up in a silent laugh. "Yeah, we know Brandon. He's so funny."

"Hey, man," Frank Paris said.

"I don't think you and me ever talked," Alejo said, shaking Brandon's hand with an easy smile as if socializing weren't the hardest thing in the world. As if he weren't everything Brandon wished he could be. "I see you around all the time, though. Hard to miss anyone in a class of twelve."

Brandon's mother leaned across the table, nearly spilling her coffee in Brandon's lap. "Kids, honestly, Brandon is painfully shy. I thought I'd call you over, make some introductions, see if I can get him out of the house. I know he could make some friends if he just branched out more. And you three are so nice."

Brandon thought his heart might stop. "Mom . . ."

Tammy and Frank blinked at him, their expressions so full of pity it stung. But Alejo laughed, smooth and bright as running water. "Your mom is a killer wingwoman. You should take her everywhere."

Brandon's mother smiled, graciously accepting the compliment.

"Well, Brandon, you're welcome to hang out with us whenever," Tammy said. But her voice was hollow. She was already skipping ahead to when they got to sit back down and talk about how weird this was. How weird *he* was. She glanced over her shoulder at the half-eaten breakfasts on her table. "We better go before our food gets cold. It was so nice to catch up."

She and Frank made their way back across the diner.

Alejo lingered a moment longer. He clapped Brandon on the back, then half turned to his table. "Seriously, let me know if you wanna hang."

"I will," Brandon lied.

He didn't.

It didn't matter. Within the year, Alejo Ortiz left Snakebite for college in Seattle. Tammy Barton took over Barton Ranch. Frank Paris got a job with the Owyhee County police. Brandon's parents moved to Portland to get away from "small-town politics."

And Brandon stayed in Snakebite because he didn't know how to do anything but *remain.* He remained like a stone stuck to the bottom of a lake. Currents washed over him, rolling him haplessly against the muck, but never to shore. Never to the sun. It was easy this way. He imagined how simple it might be to walk into the trees and disappear. He would be a pinprick of disruption, and then he would be gone.

His loneliness was a darkness. It spread over him like shadows at dusk. He felt it under the earth, under his skin, wrapped delicately around his bones. Snakebite held him in place.

Because no matter what time unleashed on Snakebite, it would never change.

Until Alejo Ortiz came home.

2001

For the first time in years, it was raining in Snakebite.

Brandon squared his hips and kicked another log onto the industrial saw, smearing a mix of sweat and rain across his brow. While most of the other men in the yard shuffled to the shed to mingle and sort wood, Brandon kept running the saw. He preferred working, even in the rain.

He preferred working *alone*.

His parents had long since made good on their promise to get out of this place. They'd sold the store to a local—Gus Harrison—who'd reopened it as a pub. Brandon spent most nights tucked into a booth at the back of the Chokecherry. He pictured the old kayaks his father had nailed to the walls, now replaced by football jerseys and stuffed fish. The building had changed faces, but it was all the same.

That was Snakebite; they painted over it, but it never changed.

His parents had superficially offered to bring him along, but Brandon had decided to stay. He could only picture himself here. The dark, shadowed feeling that crept under his skin like ink blots on paper told him that this was where he needed to stay.

If he was going to be lost, he might as well be lost in Snakebite.

Barton Lumber fell quiet, pulling Brandon back to reality.

Through the dust and the rain, Brandon could just make out the person who'd shocked the others into silence. The man stood just outside the woodshed dressed in an oversize sweater, straight-legged jeans, and a deep green parka. His hair was longer than Brandon remembered, tied in a low ponytail that ended just between his shoulder blades. He wiped the rain from his face and tenderly pulled a bundle of papers from under his sweater.

The yard foreman approached Alejo cautiously and snatched the papers from his hands. Behind him, a handful of men stifled laughter. The foreman gave the papers a cursory look—not long enough to read even the first page—then shoved them back into Alejo's chest.

Brandon didn't need to hear to understand what'd just happened.

For a moment, Alejo stared at the group of men, all facing him like they hoped he'd retaliate. Like they hoped he'd make a scene. But he didn't. Alejo's shoulders slumped. He pocketed his papers and trudged out of the yard, away from the men, into the rain.

Brandon's heart came alive with a strange fear. For a reason he couldn't pinpoint, it was like he *knew* Alejo. It wasn't as though their brief talk in the diner had made them friends, but in the blur of his memories, Alejo stuck out. Brandon was different from the rest of Snakebite, a fact he was painfully aware of. He was different in a way that went deeper than being awkward, being poor, being quiet. He was different in a way Snakebite would never allow. But something told him Alejo might understand.

He left the saw and scrambled down the ramp, through the muck, and farther into the rain. Outside Barton Lumber's domineering wood fence, Alejo paused in the parking lot and stared up at the sky, letting thick drops of rain coat his face.

"Hey," Brandon called. "Hey, I'm sorry about that. They shouldn't have . . . well, I don't know what they said. But I'm sorry."

Alejo turned and cupped a hand over his brow, blinking away the rain. He was just how Brandon remembered. He cleared his throat and said, "I appreciate it."

Brandon held out a slightly damp hand. "Brandon Woodley."

"From the boat shop." Alejo shook his hand. He smiled in the way a person smiled when they were waiting for a better explanation. "I always wanted to buy a boat there. Seems like lots of things are different around here now."

"I don't know." Brandon looked away from the yard toward town. "It feels about the same to me."

"Ah," Alejo sighed. "Maybe I changed."

"What was that about?" Brandon asked, motioning back to the yard.

"You didn't hear?" Alejo mused. "Snakebite's never seen a queer before. There'll probably be a mob at the motel when I get back."

Brandon's eyes widened. Before he'd left for college, Alejo Ortiz was Snakebite's golden child. He had everything: perfect grades, a perfect girlfriend, a perfect life. He had a laugh that lit up a room. When people talked, he actually listened. Alejo was the promise of everything Snakebite should be. He was the kind of person Brandon wished he could be around. The kind of person Brandon wished he could become.

Alejo looked different now. His expression was darker, like

he was always one step from a frown. But his eyes were the same. His laugh made Brandon's stomach drop.

"Well," Brandon said, "I think you're really brave. That's all."

"Cool." Alejo's expression soured. "Did you run out here just to tell me that?"

"I . . ."

The rain continued to fall around them, soaking the parking lot in a sheen of black. He wasn't sure *why* he'd come out here. He could've just let Alejo leave. He didn't need to stand here, soaking wet with his heart jumping up his throat. He'd always known he was different—he'd always known he was gay—but for the first time, he wasn't alone. There was someone else like him. Someone who'd gone out into the world and come back alive.

"Why did you come back?" Brandon asked.

Alejo eyed him warily. "I can't tell if you're nosy or if you're trying to tell me we, uh . . . have something in common."

Brandon took a deep breath. He was going to be brave. Just for once in his life, he was not going to roll under the tide. He was going to reach for the shore. "I just want to talk to you. I guess I have for a long time."

"We're talking now."

"You didn't have to come back here. You could've stayed in Seattle. Why did you come back?"

"You know a lot about my life, dude." Alejo shook his head, but slowly his expression twisted into an amused smile. "It was a lot easier up there. I don't know why I thought everyone here would let it slide. I guess because it's me."

"Does Tammy know?"

Alejo laughed. "I guess she does now. We broke up two years ago. She probably thinks this is why."

"What about Frank?"

Alejo waved a hand. "Frank is Frank. He doesn't care. He's probably the only friend I've got left around here."

"Are you gonna leave?"

Alejo folded his arms. "Should I? Seems like you've stuck around."

Brandon chewed on the question; people didn't usually ask him questions about himself. "I can't go. I . . . this is home. I don't know how to explain it. There's something here that I just can't—"

"—get away from?" Alejo asked. He leaned against his car and his dark eyes shone with the light from the passing storm clouds. "There's things I feel in Snakebite that I don't feel anywhere else. I could've stayed in Seattle, but it felt like running away. It's like there's stuff I still have to do."

"Yeah," Brandon sighed. *"Yeah."*

"So you don't wanna leave," Alejo said. "I don't, either."

"Which means we're just stuck."

"Fun," Alejo said. He laughed, and it was as quiet and easy as Brandon remembered. "I assume you're telling me all this for a reason?"

"I . . ." Brandon rubbed the back of his neck. Talking was hard, and putting words to the unidentified years of tumult in his gut was even harder. What *did* he want? There was a reason he'd chased Alejo out here, but now that he was standing here in the rain, he couldn't remember. The dark loneliness that always lingered in the ground under him was quiet around Alejo. "I remember you from before all this. You were . . . I don't know. Everyone was always happy around you. You paid attention. It always felt like you actually cared."

Alejo laughed. "Discriminated against one second and hit on the next. Snakebite is really full of surprises."

Brandon flushed. "Oh, no, I wasn't—"

"I wish you were," Alejo said. His dark eyes warmed, just slightly. "If I don't get murdered outside my motel room, let's get drinks sometime."

"I'd . . ." Brandon steeled himself. "I'd like that."

And from there, it was as easy as breathing.

It had never seemed easy to Brandon before. In fact, falling in love had seemed like the most impossible thing in the world. He'd built fortresses on the concept of being alone; loneliness was his blood, his bones, his heartbeat. Without it, he wasn't sure who Brandon Woodley even was.

But Alejo didn't mind. On their first night out, he told Brandon he dreamed of a family and a house with a porch and a garden where he could grow "one good tomato." On their second date, he held Brandon's hand and asked if he thought there was anywhere in Snakebite that they could carve out for themselves. Brandon didn't know the answer to that. After their third time out, Alejo walked him to his door, slipped a hand into his back pocket, and kissed him square on the mouth. Kissed him like he meant it. Like he wanted to.

Maybe it was a dream. Whatever it was, it didn't belong anywhere near Brandon's world. None of it was right. Brandon was Brandon—he was a stone knocking ceaselessly against the lake floor. He hadn't expected Alejo to reach in and pluck him from the water like it was nothing. He hadn't expected to feel the sun. Alejo pulled him to freedom and it terrified Brandon how easily he'd done it.

Outside, there was a swarm of people who hated them.

Under his feet, there was a darkness that crept into Brandon's bones. But for a moment, he wasn't alone. The shadows were quiet.

Now that he knew what it felt like to be loved, he could never go back.

2002

It was strange how much could change over a single year.

Brandon was by himself and then he wasn't. Alejo had a family and then it was gone. They were together, but they were completely alone.

Rumors about Brandon and Alejo curled through Snakebite like weeds, choking out everything else. For someone who'd been a ghost his whole life, it was a strange thing being the name on everyone's tongues. Within a month, a new foreman was hired at Barton Lumber and his first order of business was cutting Brandon loose to save the face of the company. Without money, without allies, without family, Brandon was lost.

But heroes came from surprising places.

Their hero came in the form of the newly minted head of Barton Ranch. It was Tammy Barton, married and divorced with a blond infant permanently glued to her hip. It was Tammy who just happened to review her family's books and find a patch of land her father had bought across the lake decades earlier. Who said, in her typical apathetic drawl, *If you guys want the land, you can have it. Build something on it, I don't care. I'm honestly just tired of seeing you around here.*

And for the first time since meeting, Brandon and Alejo were free.

They were six months into their new life across the lake when things changed. Summer turned to fall, the bristled ends of the junipers by the lake fell bare, and a cold wind settled into the Owyhee valley. The cabin wasn't perfect, but stepping away from Snakebite was like breathing for the first time. It was a taste of what life could be. It was the good things, like afternoons lying by the lake, nights by the fire with a book, waking each morning to birdsong and rustling leaves. And it was the rest—Post-it Notes about forgotten dishes, blankets hogged on one side of the bed, days where each other's company was simultaneously *too much* and *not enough.*

On a trip into town for eggs and kindling, Brandon heard the first whispers: . . . *left at the church . . . just a baby, and they left her right on the front step . . . who was even pregnant? . . . Pastor Briggs says it was a camper . . . foster care, probably. What else can they do?*

But like everything in Snakebite, the wonder died just as quickly as it came. After a week of talk about the mysterious baby girl dropped on the steps of Snakebite First Baptist Church, gossip shifted its gaze to a group of teens caught smoking pot outside the grocery store. And while Brandon was ready to move on just as quickly, something about the story caught Alejo like a snag on splintered wood.

"We have to see her," Alejo said. "It's a sign."

"A sign of what?" Brandon was generally good at weeding the skepticism from his voice, but not this time. He sat in their half-built kitchen, wedged between the fridge and a cabinet-to-be.

Alejo stepped inside from the back porch, but his gaze lingered on Snakebite's hazy outline across the shore. "We talk about wanting a family one day and then a baby girl gets randomly dropped at the church. You don't think that's destiny?"

"I think it's sad."

If Alejo hadn't been raised Catholic, Brandon might've noted that the god *he* knew didn't typically act as a stork for small-town gay pariahs. But he had to admit there was a piece of him, small and afraid, that dared to want this: a *family*. Even a year ago, it had been too impossible to imagine. A year ago, he'd resigned himself to a life alone. But now he could almost picture it when he closed his eyes.

"We could be her family," Alejo said. "Isn't that what our little unit is supposed to be? A collection of things other people threw away?"

"You can't pick up a baby like you're grabbing scrap metal off the side of the road." Brandon rubbed the back of his neck. "There's so much you have to do. Paperwork. Money. I don't know if we can do it."

"I'm not asking you to commit right now," Alejo said. "I'm just asking to see her."

So they did.

Snakebite First Baptist Church was painted cool by the late-fall sun, but the moment they stepped into the church's nursery, the cold melted away. Brandon wasn't religious, and he'd never been fond of chalking things up to destiny or divine purpose, but when they approached the girl's crib and he saw her for the first time—wide eyes as dark as wood smoke, fingers too little to be real, a single tuft of black hair jutting from the top of her head—it was all over.

Alejo's breath hitched in his chest. "I would never force you to do anything this important, obviously. And I know it's a big deal, but—"

Brandon leaned into the crib and pressed his thumb into the girl's impossibly small hand. Her fingers curled around his knuckle and she looked at him with eyes that unmade him. That unraveled him from the inside. He shook his head, but he didn't pull his hand away. "She needs us."

And then their family of two was a family of three.

Brandon had been right. It wasn't easy. It was months of paperwork, interviews, and nonstop work on the cabin to prove that the girl would have a home worth living in. The search for the girl's parents came up empty, leaving her nameless and alone. She was a mystery—another stone at the bottom of the lake. But this time, Brandon was on the shore. This time, *he* could do the saving.

By February, they signed the paperwork in the living room of a finished cabin. They called their daughter Logan.

And everything was perfect.

Brandon Woodley once thought of himself as a man in two parts. He was alone and then not. He was the Brandon before Alejo, and the Brandon after. He was the Brandon who sensed shadows under his feet, and then he was the Brandon who felt the sun. But things were different with Logan. His life was not in two parts, or even three—it was a song, and all along it had been swelling toward this. He sat at the piano bench most afternoons and watched sunlight ripple across the floorboards. He watched Alejo on the couch, on the rocking chair, on the front porch with Logan tucked in his arms. He watched Logan grow taller, watched her smile, watched her skip between low-hanging junipers along the lakeshore. Brandon felt the sun on his face and the cool piano keys under his fingers and breathing was *easy*.

There was a small tremor in his chest that promised it would end soon.

2007

By the time they took Logan to the hospital, there was nothing to be done. The doctors said sometimes, this happened. Children got sick. It could happen to anyone. People lost their daughters all the time—sometimes, there wasn't a reason why.

Brandon did not cry.

There were no tears in him—there was nothing at all. He was hollow without her. They'd been so close to having a life and he'd made the mistake of thinking it could last. They'd fought through thickets of hate and isolation just to end up *here*. Childless and alone again. Everything was carved away, scraped from his bones, left bare and numb. There had been warmth in him once that sounded like piano strings and Logan's laughter and water on the lakeshore, but it was all black and twisted now.

Logan was five years old.

She would never make it to six.

"We'll be happy again," Alejo breathed into Brandon's chest. They sat alone in the cabin; it had never felt lonely before Logan, but without her, he felt every inch of the aching space they'd built. "One day, we'll be happy."

But Brandon wouldn't be happy. He would *never* be happy if she was gone. The articles that Alejo read told him that the pain would subside eventually, but Brandon Woodley had been in pain his whole life. He'd never loved anyone like he'd loved her—losing her wasn't a pain that would ever subside. It was endlessly consuming, this *hate*. He hated this cabin, hated Snakebite, hated Tammy Barton and her perfect blond child who was so, *so* alive. Tammy would see her daughter grow old, but Brandon wouldn't. He hated every person who lived while his daughter was gone. The hate welled up in him like a stain. It changed everything in him until it was the only thing left.

Brandon Woodley knew he would never feel the sun again.

They continued on like this—Alejo slowly learning to heal and Brandon simply *not*. Snakebite First Baptist Church staunchly refused to sell them a plot in Snakebite Memorial, claiming they were only for members of the church, and the hate in Brandon's chest grew. They buried their daughter in Pioneer Cemetery among the decades-dead founders of Snakebite. She had no headstone, no service, no one to mourn her but her fathers.

Parents weren't supposed to see their children's graves. They weren't supposed to feel darkness under the earth, coiling around their daughter's corpse. Alejo said they would be happy again, and maybe *he* would. Of the two of them, he'd always been better at being a person.

But Brandon wasn't a person anymore—the darkness that lingered under Snakebite grabbed him at his every step. He felt it there.

On the night it happened, he stood in the center of the cabin facing the window that looked over the lake. He couldn't remember why he stood there, only that it was right. He'd had weeks of this—seeing faces just beyond his peripheral vision, hearing voices too quiet to understand, feeling fingertips on his skin—but tonight was different.

In the next room, Alejo slept in their bed. The night was black and full of something like magic, but darker. It wasn't under the ground anymore. It pressed against the glass, begging to enter the cabin. It was dark and ravenous. He felt it in his chest, pulsing with death and anger and hate. The cabin reeked of smoke and rot.

Beyond the window, he couldn't see the water. He couldn't see the trees. He couldn't see the glowing campfires on the other shore. He could only see the dark.

"I can't take this," he whispered into the empty room. "I can't take this anymore."

I know, the Dark breathed between the floorboards. *It kills you.*

Brandon's breath was a ragged gasp. He'd spoken his grief into the night for months, but it had never spoken back. The cabin was colder than the night outside and darker than black. He wondered if Alejo could hear him talking. He wondered if Alejo was *here* at all. Brandon felt as though he'd slipped away, suspended between one life and another; between what was and what *could* be.

Things were supposed to be different, the Dark moaned.

Something opened like a pit in Brandon's stomach. "I wanted a family. I wanted to be happy."

What would make you happy?

"My daughter," Brandon croaked. "My daughter is gone."

The wooden walls groaned in the wind. The floor beneath Brandon's feet shifted. Something inside him shifted, too, and he thought he might be sick. The unknowable thing slithered through him, coiling in his stomach, wrapping around his heart like an oily noose. He hadn't thought to be afraid, but now the fear and the ache were all he had.

Your daughter is buried in my arms, the Dark whispered. *Would you like her back?*

Brandon sucked in a quivering breath. For the first time since he'd lost her, hot tears stung at his eyes. He knew it was wrong—it couldn't be that simple—but just the thought was enough. "How?"

I can bring her back to you, just as she was, the Dark offered. *For a simple favor, your world could be right again.*

"What kind of favor?"

Carry me with you, the Dark whispered, hushed like a breeze. *I have lived under this town for years. I want to see the light of day. I want to roam. Give a little of yourself to me—let me come up for air—and I can bring your daughter back.*

Brandon wiped at the tears that rolled down his cheeks. It wasn't true, or it was too good to be true, but he didn't care. He didn't know what the Dark was, but he would let it consume him until there was nothing left if it meant she was alive. Brandon felt her little hand wrapped around his finger like a phantom limb.

"What *are* you?" Brandon asked.

I am the dark created from everything. I am the memories of this place come to life—anger, grief, hate. You know these feelings well. You have felt me here your whole life. In a sense, I am *Snakebite.* When the Dark stopped speaking, the world was quiet. *But I want to be more than a shadow. I want to help you. Will you let me?*

Before he could answer, the Dark crept into Brandon's lungs and ran in his blood. Its tendrils spread into his skull like ivy. The Dark wasn't Snakebite, anymore; it was *him.* Its thoughts, its movements were his. It shifted in him, quiet and black as the night, and he shuddered.

"Yes," he said. He closed his eyes. "Please bring her back."

And then the world exploded.

The blast was enough to shatter the lakefront window. The cabin's roof and walls split, banging against each other in the impact. The ceiling lights flickered on, then collapsed from their bolts and crashed to the floor. The world was a spiraling storm around Brandon, but he was the eye. The *calm.* The trees shook and the lake rippled out for miles. The shadows around him were thick with magic, suspending splinters of wood and dirt in the air.

The door to the next room crashed open before collapsing from its hinges. Alejo stood in the dark, half dressed, eyes wide with terror. He surveyed the room as though he thought he might be dreaming.

"Brandon?" he asked.

Brandon turned slowly to face him. Draped across his arms, hidden from the debris, a girl with dark hair and unusually dark eyes blinked awake. She looked into her father's face—into Brandon's face—and smiled. And though he was full of darkness, Brandon smiled too. He'd *done* it. Nothing else mattered.

He was the Dark, and he was whole again.

Alejo looked at Logan and his eyes welled with tears. His expression was recognition and fear and love all at once. Slowly, cautiously, he stepped into the room and reached for Logan. She reached back and wrapped her arms around his neck. Alejo's laugh was sharp with a sob. He shook his head.

His dark eyes met Brandon's.

"Brandon . . ." he breathed. "What did you do?"

36

A Goodbye Of The Forever Kind

"Wait," Ashley said. "So . . . *you're* the Dark?"

Brandon rubbed the back of his neck. "Until a few months ago, yeah. Kind of. I was more like a host for it. I carried it around for years, but I never *killed* anyone. That's new."

"Then how is it killing people now?" Ashley asked.

"Not sure."

"How are you not sure?"

Alejo scoffed. "I think Logan's rubbing off on her."

Ashley flushed.

Brandon took off his glasses and cleaned them with the hem of his shirt. "I don't know as much about it as you'd think. It doesn't really talk about itself. After Logan . . . after the incident, we packed up and left. There'd be too many questions about the cabin if we stayed. People would ask how she was back. We couldn't explain any of it, and we knew no one *here* would take our word for it."

"Plus, we had to get rid of the Dark," Alejo said.

"Well . . ." Brandon trailed off. He looked away from Alejo

and cleared his throat. "At first, it *did* help me. It said it would keep us afloat. It wanted to help us find a new home."

"Logan said you guys lived on the road," Ashley said.

"Not on purpose. We ended up in different small towns that were a lot like Snakebite. Which meant we ran into the same problems. People didn't like outsiders, and a couple of guys rolling into town with a five-year-old girl in the back seat made them nervous. Everywhere we went, we ended up leaving again. The longer we went without settling down, the pushier the Dark got. It was like it was getting weaker. More desperate. The angrier it got, the more of *me* it took up. I spent months in a blur, just driving, not really knowing where I was going. It wanted more to feed on. For years, it'd had all of Snakebite. Now it only had me."

"Why would it do that?"

Brandon shrugged. "I have my guesses. It might've wanted me to do something it needed a physical body for. My best guess, though, is that it wanted a new town to infect. It needed a way to move on. It wanted me to lay down roots in a new little town. And if we'd stopped moving, it would've started all over again."

"But it made a mistake," Alejo said.

Brandon nodded. "We'd been driving for two weeks straight, living on the last bit of a loan from my mom. I remember putting gas in the car while Alejo was in the store buying some water. And I remember hearing it whispering right at the back of my neck. It said to take the car seat out of the back and leave it on the curb. To just . . . take the car and go."

Alejo shook his head. "It wanted him to leave us behind."

"It wanted to find a new home, I guess. Obviously I didn't do it, but I remember *wanting* to. And I remember knowing that the need wasn't mine. It was the first time I felt it trying to . . . *overwrite* me. The Dark didn't want to help me, it just wanted to use me. It wanted to find a new home that was just as hateful as Snakebite so it could start all over again."

Ashley's stomach sank. This spiraling dread, these uneasy shadows, this black-tar fear that'd burrowed its way into her since January—it was the Dark. It was all the years of hatred Snakebite had built up, sticky and black and cloying. She'd loved this town her whole life, but *this* was what it had created.

"From then on, we were just looking for ways to get rid of it," Alejo said. "We knew we couldn't stay in one place for long or the Dark would find a way out. I've been able to see spirits since I was little. But Brandon and I realized that we could use this . . . *whatever* to find people who might have some answers. We helped people talk to dead relatives, scooted lingering spirits out of people's houses, exorcised haunted objects, but we were always looking for information on the Dark."

"Eventually, we started to make a name for ourselves," Brandon said. "We were approached by a network that wanted to make a show about what we did. It was a perfect setup—we could move around the country without worrying about money, and we'd reach a bigger audience. Someone would know about the Dark and how to get rid of it. We found lots of people who could see ghosts—"

"Who, by the way, were *not* fans of the show," Alejo interjected.

"—but no one knew about the Dark."

Ashley looked out the window, head reeling. She and Logan had spent weeks trying to understand what was plaguing Snakebite, and here it was, laid out in front of her. Logan had been an arm's length from the Dark her whole life and she'd never known it. Ashley thought of Tulsa. Of the way a single moment had haunted Logan for years.

"What happened in Tulsa?" Ashley asked. She sat forward, leaning against the back of Alejo's seat. "Did the Dark threaten her?"

"Not so much threaten. More like . . ." Brandon sighed.

"It asked what would happen to Logan if we got rid of it," Alejo said. "It just put that out there. We didn't know if getting rid of the Dark meant getting rid of Logan."

"But obviously we couldn't risk it," Brandon said. "I had to put distance between Logan and the Dark. Which meant putting distance between Logan and me. It knew we'd do anything to keep her safe."

Ashley nodded.

Alejo turned in his seat to look at her. His expression was strangely calm. "You're taking this all really well, by the way."

"I've had a really weird year," Ashley mused.

"Yeah," Alejo said. "We know the feeling."

Ashley traced the back of Alejo's seat with her pointer finger. Something about all of this still didn't add up. She closed her eyes. "Why did you come back to Snakebite?"

"It was a bad idea, but I couldn't think of what else to do," Brandon said. "I couldn't kill the Dark without the risk of losing Logan. And I didn't even know *how* to kill it. So I thought I'd come back to Snakebite and stay for a week or so. Let the Dark settle back into the place where it came from. Then I'd leave."

Ashley sucked in a breath. Brandon had brought the Dark back here on purpose. "You let it—"

"—get away from me?" Brandon said. "I did. It was way too

easy. The first morning I woke up in Snakebite, everything was so quiet. There was a solid few days where I wandered around Snakebite and thought maybe I did get rid of it. Maybe it was really that easy. I even booked tickets back to LA."

He put his face in his hands.

"Then your friend went missing."

Ashley's stomach sank.

"I *knew* it was the Dark. It never really felt gone."

"You think it picked someone else?" Ashley asked. She thumped her head back against the seat. She wasn't sure her head even had enough room for all this information. Brandon wasn't a killer, but he'd brought back the monster that was. He'd done it to save Logan, and that might be why Tristan was gone.

Logan was dead.

The two men sat silently in the front seat, Alejo's hand over Brandon's. Ashley wondered if Brandon had ever admitted this truth to anyone. After all the time Logan had spent searching for these answers, Ashley felt like she'd stolen them. These secrets weren't hers to hear.

"I thought if I could find the new host, I could convince the Dark to come back." Brandon cleared his throat. "I thought if I could get it back, the killing would stop."

"You'd take it back?" Ashley asked. "Even though you don't know how to kill it?"

"Better than letting innocent kids die."

"Why didn't you tell Logan?"

"What would that change?"

"We didn't know where to start." Alejo shook his head. "We didn't even understand how she came back. It would've traumatized her. We wanted her to have a normal life."

Ashley looked at Brandon. "She would've known why you weren't around."

"But it wouldn't've changed anything." Brandon stared at the palms of his hands. "I appreciate your concern. But knowing *why* I was gone wouldn't have changed that I was gone. She would've . . . I would've had to leave her just as much."

Brandon slumped back in his seat and, for the first time, Ashley noticed how *tired* he was. The stubble at his jaw hadn't been shaved in days, his clothes were disheveled, his eyes were rung with half-moons as dark as bruises. She thought of the nights he'd spent alone in the cabin, wandering the woods, looking for the Dark. How he'd been willing to take it on all over again if it meant the killing in Snakebite would stop. He'd hurl himself back into misery and loneliness to save the town that cast him out. She'd always thought of Snakebite as one big, tangled family, but she couldn't think of a single person willing to lose what Brandon had lost to keep it safe.

"I still think you should've told her," Ashley said. "Then she wouldn't think you hate her."

"She . . ." Brandon turned in his seat to face her. "She what?"

"No," Alejo said, as though he were trying to convince himself more than anyone else. "No, she doesn't think you . . ."

Ashley wished she hadn't said anything.

Brandon's expression sank. Of all the things he'd learned tonight, this one seemed to cut him the deepest. He pressed his palm over his heart and closed his eyes. She thought of the sadness Logan wore under her wry smiles. The way she longed for her family, even if she denied it.

"And now it was all for nothing," Brandon said. "Because we can't even kill it."

"The place where it all started," Alejo said. "We could just go to the cabin. Head it off at the pass."

"We could," Brandon said. "If the killer's there, we can at least *try* to reason with them. Or the Dark."

"Does it usually listen?" Ashley asked.

Brandon and Alejo scoffed in unison.

A strange, prickling sensation crept over Ashley's neck. She looked out the window and, outside the police station, she saw a shadowy figure flickering in the yellow light. She squinted, waiting for it to take shape. The faint scent of fuel wafted in through the air conditioner.

"Tristan," Ashley whispered.

Alejo turned to look outside the window. His eyes widened, and he looked at Ashley. "So this is Tristan. I've seen him a few times."

"I thought he was bringing me to you guys," Ashley said. "But I think I'm still supposed to follow him."

She climbed out of the car into the empty night. Behind her, the passenger door opened and Alejo stepped out. He pulled a jacket from the minivan and threw it on over his T-shirt. "Has he made you follow him before?"

"He hasn't *made* me do anything," Ashley said. "But he led me to Nick's body. And he led me here."

"Interesting."

Brandon leaned across the front seat. "We have to get to the cabin."

Ashley shook her head. "You guys go. I have to follow Tristan."

"She can't go alone. She's a kid," Alejo said quietly, like he thought Ashley wouldn't hear him. He stood with his hands on his hips, brow furrowed in frustration. His gaze traced Tristan's outline, lips quivering. "I'll go with her. You go to the cabin. Find Logan."

Brandon shook his head. "No, I can't—"

"She needs you."

"She doesn't need *me*." Brandon's eyes were wide, magnified by his glasses. His knuckles on the steering wheel were white.

Ashley looked between them. It didn't matter who came with her and who went to the cabin; they needed to *go*. Tonight was the night this all ended. Tristan was already gliding out of the parking lot, fading quickly into the night. He turned to look over his shoulder, but Ashley couldn't see his eyes. They were running out of time.

"I'm going," Ashley said.

"Hold on," Alejo snapped. He closed his eyes and slipped a hand over Brandon's clenched fist. "You're the only one who knows the Dark. You can stop it. You can *do* this."

Brandon stared.

"It's stronger than it ever was with me. I don't know what it'll do." He cleared his throat. Black clouds rolled past the moon above them, scattering silver light over the road. In the dark, Ashley heard Brandon breathing, slow and methodical and weary. "If it's too strong . . . I don't know who will come back."

"*You* will." Alejo shakily laughed. He wore an easy expression for Brandon's sake, but Ashley saw the way his grip shook against the passenger door. "Because I'm not doing taxes with that thing again."

"A fate worse than death."

This wasn't a normal send-off. Ashley understood, suddenly, that they'd expected this day. They'd known it would eventually come down to this moment. They'd known Brandon would have to face the Dark alone. After everything, they were always going to have this goodbye. The kind that might be forever.

"I love you," Alejo said.

Brandon nodded. "We'll be okay, right?"

"One day," Alejo breathed.

Brandon smiled. "See you when it's all over."

Alejo reached into the minivan and took Brandon's face in his hands. He kissed him, soft and lingering and mournful. When he drew away, he held Brandon's face and looked into his eyes.

With that, Brandon closed the door, threw the van into drive, and tore down the highway toward the woods. Down the road, Tristan lingered. He waited, hovering along the pavement, both there and gone at once. In the night, he looked more smoke than human, but she knew the shape of him, no matter how gone he was. Wind howled through the valley, whistling off the water like a scream. There was death in the air. The night was swollen with it.

Alejo lingered, eyes fixed on Brandon's headlights until they disappeared around the bend of the highway. "Well then, let's follow your ghost."

They climbed into the Land Rover and drove into Snakebite proper. Tristan's ghost was hard to make out in the dark, but between the two of them, they tracked him from street to street. He paused in front of a squat, green house behind the Chokecherry, spinning like he had in Pioneer Cemetery.

Ashley recognized this house.

Alejo shook his head. "This is Frank Paris's house, right? Why would he take us here?"

"I don't know."

Ashley unbuckled and took off. She and Alejo followed Tristan to the front door, hesitating on the porch. Inside, Ashley heard the muffled sound of the TV and murmured voices talking alongside it. Ashley met Alejo's eyes, then tentatively knocked.

The door opened and Ashley found herself face-to-face with John Paris. The same John Paris who had tried to drown Logan. Anger boiled up in her, but she suppressed it. Tristan shifted behind John, making his way deeper into the house.

"Ashley," John said. "And . . . ?"

Alejo donned a surprisingly easy smile and gave John a curt wave. "Alejo Ortiz. We haven't met. You're Frank's son?"

John narrowed his eyes. "What're you doing here?"

"Can I come in?" Ashley asked.

John looked over his shoulder, then opened the door and motioned her inside. She nodded at Alejo, promising him that she'd be okay on her own, then stepped into the Parises' living room. An action movie crashed on the TV. On the couch, Fran was curled up under a blanket, scrolling idly through her phone. She looked up and caught sight of Ashley, and her expression soured.

"Ash?" Fran asked. "What're you . . . ?"

"I just need a second," Ashley said. Tristan lingered at a door off the living room. "Uh, what's through there?"

"What's this about?" John asked.

Panic bubbled up in Ashley's chest. Tristan continued to spin near the door. "I just need to go in there. I promise I'll leave after that."

"No."

"John, *please,*" Ashley tried.

"No. Shouldn't you be with your girlfriend?" John asked. He donned an overconfident sneer. "I'm gonna need you to get out of my house."

Ashley turned toward Fran, because it wasn't John Paris she was appealing to. Fran looked back down at her phone, but she was listening. "I would be with her if you hadn't just tried to *kill* her."

At the word *kill,* Fran looked at John.

"What's she talking about?"

"She's fine," John scoffed. "Ash is just overreacting."

"I'm not overreacting," Ashley snapped. "You held her head underwater for fifteen minutes. You're lucky she's alive."

"Is that true?" Fran asked again. Her eyes were wide, expression something like a scared animal's. John looked at Fran, but said nothing, and she knew. Her mouth quivered, but she didn't speak. She looked at Ashley and her unspoken words were clear.

I'm sorry.

John clicked off the TV. "Get out of my house, Ash."

Tristan looked at Ashley, then at John, then at the door. Something was on the other side, and whatever it was, he needed her to see it. It was the thing he'd wanted all along. She was only steps from understanding why he'd been haunting her for months, and John Paris was not going to snatch it away.

"I can't," she said. "It's Tristan, he's—"

"Are you serious?" John boomed. "I thought Fran was exaggerating about you and this ghost thing. I'm so glad Tristan's not here to see this shit. You're out of your fuckin' mind."

Tristan moved from the door now. He hovered at John's side, and Ashley pictured the two of them like they used to be. John's hatred was deeper than anger; it was pain. He wasn't the only one who hadn't gotten to say goodbye. She looked at Tristan, but he had no answers. His stance was slouched. Mournful. He was sad for John—sad for what his friend had become.

"I can't explain it, but Tristan's trying to show me something." Ashley took a deep breath. "If you let me follow him, I promise I'll leave you alone. If I'm wrong, it doesn't hurt anything."

"I don't want you to leave us alone, Ash," John said. "I want you to go back to normal."

Tristan moved back to the door and faded through it. Ashley couldn't wait for John to cooperate anymore. She had to make a move. She darted for the door, but John was quicker. He lunged for her, balled-up fist aimed for her face. Ashley flinched, braced for impact, but there was none. A heavy *thump* sounded in front of her. She opened her eyes just as Alejo threw open the front door. Between them, John Paris crumpled to the living room floor, unconscious.

Ashley blinked.

Fran stood behind him, shaking fingers clenched around a hefty wooden bookend. She dropped it and clapped her hands over her mouth. "Oh my god. *Oh my god.*"

"Fran . . ." Ashley trailed off. "I'm . . ."

"Just go," Fran said. Her voice shook. "I'll stay here."

Ashley nodded. She and Alejo opened the door to a shoddily carpeted staircase. They made their way into the basement and Alejo pulled a ThermoGeist from his back pocket, holding it in front of him. It lit up bright red, just like it had at the cemetery, and his lips curled into a grimace.

Tristan hovered midway down the stairs and turned to face the far wall. He was *less*, suddenly—only a whisper of the Tristan who had been with them upstairs. Ashley squinted her eyes to see him properly. She thought he looked afraid.

"It was here," she whispered. "This is where you—"

"Died," Alejo breathed. He held a hand to his chest. "I'm not a perfect psychic, but this . . . I feel it here."

"I do, too," Ashley said, though she wasn't sure what it was she felt. It was deep and dark and cold. It sat in her chest like mildew and made it hard to breathe. She tried to see Tristan's face, but he was more shadow than human. She wasn't sure if her fear was her own or if it was his. She tasted the tang of it on her tongue. Tristan quivered, too weak to hold his fear inside. It seeped out of him and into Ashley. In this basement, death was all there was.

"Tristan," Alejo said. He rubbed at his jaw, like he was waiting for the right words to come to him. "I . . . thank you for bringing us here. I know you're afraid. But you're so brave, too."

Tristan turned to face them. It was hard to tell if he meant to block them from going any further into the basement or if he wanted them to go on without him. His gaze moved from Ashley to Alejo, and she wished the two of them could've met when Tristan was alive. She wished that Brandon and Alejo could've saved him before he disappeared. She wished they weren't always working in reverse, trying to understand what was already done.

Finally, Tristan drifted the rest of the way down the stairs and paused. Ashley followed, and the basement opened up around her. It was a basement like any other. A TV was mounted on the wall, faced by a plaid love seat and a plain coffee table. A washer and dryer were pushed against the staircase. On the far wall, the Paris family had a tool bench and an ironing board. It was all normal, except for the cloying dread that wedged its way up Ashley's throat.

Alejo was right. Death permeated the air here, thick enough to taste.

"I'm so sorry," Alejo said to her. "You shouldn't have to—"

"What's going on down here?"

Ashley spun to face the staircase. Sheriff Paris stood at the top of the stairs. He made his way down, and Ashley understood all at once why Tristan had led her here.

Because now, they were looking at the man who had killed him.

Tristan's ghost turned to face the staircase again. In an instant, he was reduced to nothing but an outline. He doubled over and collapsed to the floor. In all of his visits, Ashley had never heard Tristan make a sound.

But as Paris reached the bottom of the stairs, Tristan screamed.

37

And Then You Find Your Way

"No." Alejo backed away from the stairs toward the tool bench. "It's not you. It can't . . . that doesn't make any sense."

Ashley could hardly hear over the sound of Tristan's screams. She watched Paris's face; this was the same man who had helped with months of searches, who had wept at Tristan's vigil, who had treated Tristan like a second son. His expression was blank now, distant and unmoved by Alejo's shock. Between his short crop of blond hair and his sun-kissed skin, he was Snakebite personified. It *couldn't* be him.

He arched a brow.

"I'm pretty sure *you're* supposed to be in a cell."

"We were neighbors at the Bates," Alejo croaked. In the harsh basement light, his face was almost gray. "We hung out every day. You're the first person I told about . . . I know you didn't do this. I know you didn't hurt those kids."

Sheriff Paris said nothing.

Ashley was going to be sick.

"We've talked since . . . I would've known."

Tristan's screams stopped. The ThermoGeist went blank. For the moment, Tristan was gone, leaving Ashley and Alejo alone to face the devil. Maybe this was all he'd wanted them to find—the truth. But now that they'd found it, Ashley wasn't sure what to do. There was no one to tell. It wasn't like Paris would let them leave this basement knowing what they knew.

Paris's stance relaxed. "You didn't know? I thought for sure you did. How long did you live with it—thirteen years? Maybe you didn't know it as well as you thought."

Alejo cupped a hand over his mouth. "They were kids, Frank. They were your son's friends."

"Speaking of John," Paris said, "which one of you knocked him out?"

Ashley met Alejo's eyes. So Fran had left the house. They really were alone down here. Ashley could only hope Fran was getting help.

"It doesn't really matter." Paris eyed the tool bench. "You know I can't let either of you out of here."

"It's not too late," Alejo said. "The Dark is strong, but you can shut it out. Brandon did."

"Not too late for what? I killed people, Alejo." Paris cleared his throat. "Besides, the thing's gone. It's just me now. This is who I was always supposed to be."

Alejo shook his head, eyes wide. "If it's not with you, where is it?"

"It should be with your daughter now, actually. Said something about coming full circle. I didn't understand what that meant. It had a real grudge against your family for some reason. I tried to stay out of it."

Alejo's exhale was sharp. His fists clenched, but his expression wasn't angry. It was a sad thing, teetering just on the edge of grief. He'd lost his daughter once, and now he might lose her again and there was nothing he could do about it. It weighed on Ashley, too. If she and Logan had just left Snakebite, none of this would've happened. Logan would've been safe.

"You helped us look for Tristan," Ashley said. "Why?"

Paris frowned, and it felt like a knife in Ashley's stomach. "It's my job."

Alejo slowly reached for the phone in his back pocket. "You're gonna kill us? No one will be left in Snakebite by the time you're done. You think people won't find that suspicious?"

"I figure after you two, I'll hit the road." Paris rested his hand on the gun holstered at his belt. "John doesn't know yet, but he'll understand."

John Paris was a certain kind of monster, but Ashley doubted he was the type of monster that would understand *this.* Tristan and Bug had been John's friends. Until recently, John had been Ashley's friend, too. When he learned that his father was the one who had killed all of them—when he learned that his father was the reason he was left friendless—it would destroy him. This man was miles beyond the Paris she knew, living in a different world.

He pulled the gun from his belt.

Alejo gasped.

The ThermoGeist clattered against the basement floor, echoing from the walls with a stale clap. The red light along the top of the device clicked to a startling blue, then back to red as coils of black smoke curled through the plastic shell. Alejo gingerly gripped his palm, pressing his thumb against a strip of burned skin beneath his fingers.

"What . . . ?" Ashley started.

Suddenly, the air was heavy as though a layer of sound had dropped away, opening an endless chasm of silence beneath it. Her ears rang with the quiet. Alejo felt it, too—he stumbled back, clutching the railing along the basement stairs for balance. The ThermoGeist on the floor continued to smoke, rattling and popping with sparks. She smelled Tristan, like she always did at first. Gasoline and fresh cut grass and the quiet, indistinct scent of sunlight. There was one more thing he had to do before he was gone. He'd been waiting.

Sheriff Paris massaged the place where his jaw met his throat. His brow furrowed in quiet fury. "What *is* that?"

Ashley tasted electricity on her tongue. The room was charged with screaming grief. Tristan's rage filled her up until she couldn't breathe, until she couldn't see through her own eyes, until she couldn't remember her own name. She felt hands around her throat, wide-palmed and callused like leather. She saw Paris's slate-blue eyes staring into hers, felt snow under the ridge of her spine, felt dizzy with the realization that she was going to die.

On the night he had died, Tristan was so alone.

This was the last thing he felt.

Fingers gently closed around Ashley's wrist. Alejo leaned forward until his eyes were at her level, and his smile was bitter and warm at once. "Come back. These memories are his," he said. "Don't follow him."

Ashley swallowed.

Even if Paris didn't see what she saw, he felt what she felt. His eyes wildly searched the corners of the basement as though he might spot Tristan in the shadows; as if seeing him would stop him. Ashley wondered if he even understood it was Tristan. He backed against the basement wall, palms pressed to the concrete, but it was too late.

Tristan surfaced in the space between Ashley and Alejo and, for just a moment, he was himself. Between them, shoulders just broad enough to fill the gap, he was so much more than a memory. It was as though he'd been plucked from that last moment in Ashley's bedroom, alive and well. It was as though, with Ashley and Alejo here, seeing him, he was strong enough to finally become real. He was honey-colored hair and bright blue eyes and dimples at the corners of his mouth.

Ashley's chest ached because it was like none of this had ever happened. For a moment, Tristan stood next to her and turned back time.

His expression sobered. He moved across the room in a single stride, and then he wasn't Tristan anymore. He was a blur of white, shifting across the empty space like a small hurricane. He twisted around Sheriff Paris and, just beyond the blur, Ashley saw Paris's eyes.

Fear.

He knew that this was how he would die.

The static in the air spiked, and Ashley crumpled to her knees with her palms cupped over her ears. Somewhere in the static, there was a scream, low and guttural and deadly.

A body thumped against the floor.

The charge in the air died.

There was only quiet.

"Jesus," Alejo whispered.

Ashley opened her eyes and saw it. Sheriff Paris's body was slumped against the basement wall, neck crooked, arms splayed out at his sides. He looked at nothing and his eyes were wide with fear. She didn't need to check Paris's pulse to know he was dead. In the last few weeks, she'd seen more than her share of corpses.

Tristan reemerged. His shoulders sagged as he materialized in the frigid basement air. He settled in the middle of the floor like a cold draft of air, and he looked *tired.*

Alejo's back pocket buzzed, breaking the silence. Shakily, he pulled out his phone and Ashley recognized the Scripto8G clipped to the back of the case. He tapped the screen, and then his eyes widened. Tentatively, he angled the phone screen toward Ashley. "It's for you."

She blinked. The phone screen was stark white with two words in bold black: **STILL HERE.**

Tristan knelt in front of Ashley. He took her shaking hands in his and his eyes were still his own. Under the gray, misshapen flesh, they were bright blue and full of tears. His skin felt like a cool breeze against her fingertips, but it was enough. He was still here, still with her, still at her side for a little bit longer. Her lips quivered and her breath was ragged. Even now, she was afraid.

Ashley closed her eyes. "Do you have to go now?"

Tristan looked across the length of the basement and his expression twisted in pain. He let go of her hands and drifted to the far wall, lingering beside a boarded-up section of crawl space.

"What's wrong?"

Alejo put a hand on Ashley's shoulder. "Something's keeping him here."

The smell of mildew burned in her nostrils. Tristan continued to hover near the crawl space. When she squinted, Ashley saw that he was shaking. Between the mismatched boards, she saw the deep blackness inside and her stomach dropped. She closed her eyes.

"The, uh, the crawl space." Ashley pointed to the boards. She felt numb, head reeling. Dark crept into the corners of her vision. "I think he wants us to open it?"

Alejo nodded. He dragged his palm down the front of his face. "It shouldn't be you. I . . . I'll do it. I'm—"

He pressed his palm to his forehead and sucked in a sharp breath. Beyond the smell of dust and decay, there was something pungent and sweet permeating the air. Alejo moved to the crawl space and Tristan stood beside him. He looked at Ashley as if to make sure she was watching. Alejo grabbed a crowbar from the tool bench. His breath was short, hands fidgeting at his sides.

"You want us to open it?" Alejo asked Tristan.

Alejo's phone buzzed between Ashley's palms. The Scripto8G simply read YES. Ashley looked at Alejo and nodded.

"Okay." Alejo grimaced. "Can you please call the state police?"

Ashley dialed the Oregon State Police while Alejo pried the first plank from the crawl space. The darkness opened up behind the wood, stretching several feet back into the wall. Alejo pressed his foot to the wall and pried away the second board. It fell away, and the contents of the crawl space were visible. A small patch of dirt, flecks of dust and debris swirling in the blackness. She thought she saw something jutting through the stale surface of the dirt, round and rubbery like the toe of a tennis shoe.

Alejo covered his nose and mouth with the collar of his shirt and stifled a cough. "Oh my god. Ashley, don't look."

She didn't need to look to understand what was in the

crawl space. Tristan stared at the body, fading in and out of the light. He stared at it, and everything about him folded inward, shrunken down like paper kindling on a fire. There was a piece of Ashley, small and quiet, that had still hoped he was alive. That had still hoped that Tristan was the exception.

He wasn't the exception, though. He was the first victim.

Ashley could barely see Tristan now through her searing tears, but she felt him approach. She felt him pull her close. It wasn't like it had been—he was barely here now—but it was something. When she closed her eyes, she could almost feel the trembling beat of his heart. Ashley wrapped her arms around Tristan and pushed her forehead into his shoulder.

"Thank you," she breathed. "I'm so sorry."

Tristan's embrace tightened. She was sure it did. For just a moment, everything was warm. It smelled like diesel fuel and mown grass and eighteen years of memory. The world Tristan had created for them overtook her and they were lying in the bed of her truck, laughing and whispering and staring at the stars. The whole sky was open above them and they were home. Ashley breathed it in one last time, and then it faded away.

She didn't need to open her eyes to know he was gone.

Tristan Granger was dead, and he was gone.

Interlude

In the beginning, the Dark is only a thought.

It is impossible to say when it begins. It is only a smudge at first, only a spot of ink in the soil, only an idea. It is not a single thing that creates the Dark. If the gold hills and bright skies of Snakebite are hope, the Dark is the opposite. It is hope turned inside out. It is curdled anger, spite like tar, residue that sits on the lake water like a film. When a man kills his brother here, the Dark grows stronger. When a flood washes away graves in Pioneer Cemetery, the Dark nestles into them and makes a home. When, for a moment, all the hate in this town is concentrated in one point—one man grieving a lost daughter—the Dark finds an escape. It has existed in Snakebite as long as memory, but in the man it sees new horizons.

It is the shadows, the shifting boughs, the deeps of the lake. It has existed here as long as hate has clouded the hearts of Snakebite like black smog.

It is impossible to say when the Dark begins.

But this is where it ends.

The girl is mostly Dark now. It is easy to change her. Beneath layers of cynicism, she aches only for home. For happiness. For someone to love her. The Dark whittles away the light in her: a father with dark eyes full of laughter, a girl with sunlit hair and soft lips, memories of clear water and bright skies and the never-ending road. She remembers the bittersweet melody of a piano that now lies rotted.

The Dark is stronger than it has ever been, and this is what it has waited for. The girl is the sharp knife aimed to kill. In a way, she was always going to be the end.

She is the undoing thing.

Pick up the gun, the Dark breathes into her.

She complies because it is the only thing she can do. She wants only what the Dark wants now. No more convincing. No more groveling, begging idiotic men to listen. The girl's eyes are closed, heart marching an irregular beat against her ribs. Somewhere inside, she fights it, but she cannot break free. She trembles under the weight of the things the Dark has shown her. The years she forgot. Her memories flutter in the shadows like motes of dust and ash. She recalls what it was like to die once, to be buried, and she understands the world of her nightmares.

"Logan?"

It is the boy on the floor. His voice is weak, and the Dark has half a mind to make the girl kill him. The Dark wraps itself around the girl's neck. *Hit him hard. He will sleep until we are done. It will be better for him.*

The girl's jaw clenches, but she does as she is told. She steps forward and hits the boy hard across the face with the handle of the gun. The boy crumples back against the wall and falls to his side, glasses clattering to the floorboards. She regrets this—it is an emotion that tastes like rot and sorrow—but she does not help him. She cannot.

He will be here soon, the Dark reminds the girl. *I can hear him among the trees.*

The man's approaching heartbeat is quick now. It is erratic with fear. He is an animal afraid of a predator, yet he still runs toward it.

As if on cue, the man bursts through the cabin the door and the Dark shudders. It has pictured this moment all these months. The man is the original host. He is the one who pulled the Dark from the ether, who gave it a form. He is the only one who can unmake the Dark, and the Dark will *not* be unmade.

Say hello to your father.

"Logan," the man gasps, nearly collapsing with relief. He takes a step toward her, but he senses that she is wrong. He hesitates and his eyes land on the gun in her hand. His face drains of color.

The girl sucks in a sharp breath. "Hello."

The man is frozen. He looks at her, and he recognizes it. He didn't recognize it in the sheriff, but he recognizes it in her. He sees the shadows he is so familiar with in her eyes. He has seen these shadows in the mirror a thousand times. It pleases the Dark that the man remembers so well. As hard as the man has tried to cut it away, the Dark's presence still lingers in him.

"Logan, what happened?" the man asks. "Did it—?"

Tell him what will happen now, the Dark hisses into the girl's ear. *Tell him what he will pay for.*

The girl steels herself. Her grip on the gun tightens, slick with sweat. "You're gonna finish what you started," she chokes. "You knew it wouldn't last. We weren't both gonna make it."

Almost too quickly, this breaks the man. It is so much easier than the Dark thought. Behind thick lenses, his eyes close to keep from clouding with tears. The man's sun rises and sets with the girl. The Dark remembers that the girl wrapping her small fingers around the man's thumb was the first time he had ever felt truly alive. It is only right that she end him. It is only right that the girl the Dark brought back for him be the one to take his life.

A life for a life, the Dark whispers to her.

"Logan," the man says, "I know it's so strong. And it doesn't feel like you can fight it. But just . . . think about who *you* are."

The girl's brow twitches in a small act of resistance. The Dark doubles down in her bones. It scrapes against her skull, filling up her head so there's no room for anything else. It finds the small, trembling part of her that it needs; it finds the part of her that *hates* the man standing in front of her. It finds memories of forgotten birthdays, of nights spent watching his face on the TV, of dinners all by herself. It finds the tunnel in Tulsa, the hateful way her father looked at her, the fear that filled her up. It finds the lonely, quaking beat of her heart and takes hold.

He doesn't love you, the Dark reminds her. *He didn't save you. I did.*

The girl raises the gun. Her hand shakes.

"Hey, hey," the man says, hands raised in defense. "Logan, listen to me. It seems louder than everything else. But you can ignore it. If you just—"

Shoot him.

The girl does.

She hesitates at the last moment, swinging to the left to avoid the man's chest. The bullet pierces his shoulder and he collapses to his knees. He groans in pain and it sounds like music to the Dark. It is much better than piano song. Blood pools in the man's hand, and he bites his lip to keep from crying out.

"How are you *here?*" the man demands. His gentleness dissipates and he is only frantic agony, voice rasping with pain. "Why didn't you die? It was *years*."

The man still doesn't understand. He doesn't understand how the Dark came to be in the first place. He doesn't understand why he was chosen to be the Dark's first host. He doesn't understand what sustains it now.

The girl understands, because she feels the place where the Dark holds her. It fastens its grip on a knotted, misshapen piece of her heart that was supposed to hold her absent father. She has always known that this piece of her is blackened and rotted. She understands what feeds the Dark in a way the man never could.

Tell him why, the Dark whispers.

"It chose you because you hated Snakebite so much. When you didn't hate Snakebite anymore, it had to find something else. . . . It stayed alive because . . ."

The man remembers now. He remembers the quiet motel rooms and the long, empty stretches of highway. He remembers his husband's voice, choked with static through the phone. He remembers closing his eyes trying to remember the details of his daughter's face. He remembers the exhaustion aching in his bones as he forced himself to keep going, treading water to stay alive. He understands the Dark the way a stone understands a dam released over it.

The man looks at his hands.

". . . because I hated myself."

Again, the Dark commands. *Kill him.*

The girl grips the handle of the gun. Instead of the lonely memories the Dark feeds her, she recalls a moment spent with the man: a quiet car ride into town, a birthday party where her fathers dressed as Ghostbusters, a trip to an amusement park filled with smiles and laughter. The memories are ancient, buried under hurt and longing, but she clings to them like the sun-bleached bones of what her life could have been. She lives in the memories, pushing back against the Dark. Wind whistles through the loose boards of the cabin and raises pinpricks on the girl's flesh. She shakes. Beads of sweat collect at her brow, but she does not bend.

The man looks at her and smiles. "I did everything wrong. I get it."

"No, you don't," the girl says through clenched teeth.

"It's probably too late, but can I tell you some things about us?" the man asks. "Not when we were in LA or on the road. Before that, when we lived here. Do you remember that? Five years of just you, me, and your dad."

The girl's head reels. Even with all the Dark has shown her, she does not remember this place. But the Dark remembers. It remembers pulling the girl's bones from the dirt and piecing her back together—marrow to muscle, skin to skin, blood rushing through her veins. It remembers placing her in the man's arms in the place where she now stands alone.

It hurts her that she does not remember this. She wants to claw at her mind until it gives her memories back to her.

"We were so happy when we lived here. I wanted it to be like that forever—just the three of us. Me and your dad were in love, but the day I saw *you*, it all clicked." The man is still smiling with tears in his eyes, and the sight confuses the girl. She has never heard the man speak of love and happiness. She has never seen him cry. She doesn't understand what these things mean.

He continues.

"You got sick. You went too fast. We couldn't—*I* couldn't—live without you." The man tries to stand, but his arm won't support him. He grits his teeth in pain and keeps himself from toppling to the floor. "I'm the one who gave this thing power. I let it feed on me for years. And I was so stupid, because I didn't know what it could do. I didn't know if it would start poisoning another town. I didn't know if it would make me hurt people. I didn't know if it would make me hurt *you*. I thought you would be safer without me."

Enough of this, the Dark hisses, *kill him and be done with it. The things he says now do not make up for your loneliness. He cannot undo the pain.*

The girl closes her eyes and presses her palm to her forehead. It is a gesture the man recognizes as hers, not the Dark's. He smiles, frail but hopeful, because he thinks he can draw her out. He thinks he can separate his daughter from the Dark. He forgets that the Dark does not capture, it becomes.

The Dark presses against the girl's ear, warm and quiet and calm. *He cannot erase the way you hurt, but I can. I only want to take away your pain. I become stronger when* you *are stronger. Be strong now.*

"Logan," the man says again. He shudders and his fingers are slick with his own blood. "I let this thing out, but I don't regret it. I would do it again. I would let it kill me to keep you alive."

The Dark takes the girl by the throat. She can hardly breathe. Her heart trembles in the Dark's grip. Hot tears cloud her eyes as she looks into the man's face. She hates him, but she loves him, too. Both emotions rage like wildfire in her gut—they come from the same place. To the girl, they feel the same.

"No, that's not . . . that doesn't make any sense." With tears muddled in her throat, the girl asks, "If it was all for me, why did you leave me alone?"

The man's expression shatters. He reaches for his daughter's hand and she raises the gun again. This is how the man will die. After his years of wandering, of avoiding his family, of hating himself for his mistakes, this is how it will end. She will forever remember the way he sounded when he died—just flesh against wood, and then nothing.

"I'm so sorry," the man says. He closes his eyes and braces himself. "If you have to do it, I . . ."

He cannot finish his sentence.

This is the end.

"I never wanted you to go away," the girl croaks. She has never told the truth of it; she has never said the words out loud. She closes her eyes and hot tears rush down her face. "I wanted you to *love* me."

"I do love you." The man takes the girl's hand. His palm is wet with sweat and blood. He shakes with fear, but he holds her and breathes, "I love you more than anything. I love you and I'm so sorry."

He does not love you, the Dark tears into her. *This is what you have always wanted. You hated him from the beginning—*

"No."

The girl shakes.

Kill him.

The girl drops the gun and something inside her erupts. The

cabin explodes in a shockwave of nothing. Broken glass clatters against rotted wood and the ceiling groans, shifting in its wake. The man topples backward and slams against the cabin's front door.

The Dark scrambles for a foothold in the girl's mind. In an instant, the blackened, rotted place it nestled is gone. She is flooded with light, and it burns the Dark. There is nowhere to hide, nowhere to hold, nowhere to whisper. There is no hate here and the Dark is left scrambling in the unrelenting light. The cabin is all at once a ruin, a home, and a memory. The man is both young and old. The Dark unravels, fluttering around them like flakes of ash.

And then it is nothing.

It tears itself from the girl's mind, slowly evaporating in the untethered air. The girl's eyes shut and her knees buckle. Her vision turns black as she falls and falls.

38

Swimming In The Smoke

Logan never hit the ground.

Brandon's arms—her father's arms—were there to catch her. The cabin spun and spun and, for a moment, she saw it all. Not the strained, filmy past the Dark had showed her; *everything.* Every memory she had concentrated into one moment. Golden sunlight pouring through the lakefront window, the ceilings vaulted by massive wood beams, the air that smelled like wood-smoke and apple cider. Just faintly, the piano played a lullaby. It was everything she'd lost, drifting back to her like a sheet of falling dust.

Brandon was different. He smiled at her, but he was younger than the Brandon she knew. His eyes were alive with a joy she'd never seen, bright and dancing as sunlit water. He laughed and his eyes clouded with tears.

They were alive.

"I'm so sorry," Brandon whispered.

And then he was Brandon again; the *real* Brandon. The one who was both alive and dead, both here and gone. The cabin righted itself in a single moment. The Dark's residue ebbed away and they were left there on the floor, surrounded by rotting wood and silence. Somewhere far away, lake water lapped ashore. Somewhere farther away, the last of the Dark scuttled into the shadows until there was nothing left.

It was over.

Brandon's eyes were half obscured by a deep crack in his glasses. Blood spotted the ridge of his jaw, but he was smiling. He wrapped his good arm around Logan's back and pulled her against his chest. Logan's arms hung at her sides in disbelief. This had to be a dream. The weight of it crashed over her with sudden, unrelenting force. She wasn't dead, she wasn't dreaming, she was alive and there was no Dark left in her because there was no Dark anywhere.

Before she could help it, she was crying. Brandon held her, cautious at first like he wasn't sure he was allowed, and then he was crying, too. They held each other and shook and cried because they were *alive.*

Beside them, the floorboards groaned. Elexis stirred, massaging the purple welt on his brow. His expression pinched. "I . . . where am I?"

Logan blinked. She untangled herself from Brandon's arms and clambered to Elexis's side, fumbling to untie the rope binding him to the piano. "Oh my god. Please say you're okay."

Elexis groped along the cabin floor for his glasses. Other than the knotted bruise at his brow, he looked unharmed. Logan plucked his glasses from the rubble and grimaced. One lens was missing and the wire frame was bent. She held the glasses between them and laughed uneasily. Elexis groaned. "Awesome."

Logan hugged him. "I'll buy you, like, a thousand new pairs. I'm so happy you're alive."

"Whoa," Elexis breathed. He looked over Logan's shoulder. "Mr. Woodley, are you okay?"

Brandon cradled his injured arm and offered a pained smile. Blood stained his hand and soaked into his frayed jeans. It was worse than Logan had realized; guilt knotted in her stomach like a clenched fist.

She'd done this. She'd pulled the trigger.

"I'm fine." Brandon glanced at his arm. "But . . . maybe we should get out of here?"

Logan nodded to Elexis. Slowly, they hoisted Brandon from the ground with his good arm over Logan's shoulders. Brandon winced at the pressure, but slowly, they hobbled out of the cabin.

The sky was splashed with pale dawn and the trees were quiet, leaning in the wind like they were forming a way out. Logan's breath stung her chest with the effort of keeping Brandon upright. In the distance, the trees flashed red and blue. The gravel turnout was littered with state police, and at the front of the pack, Logan recognized Ashley, Alejo, and Gracia.

It took everything she had not to break into a sprint.

Logan and Elexis hauled Brandon the rest of the way to the gravel before Alejo rushed to meet them. He pressed one hand on Logan's back and used the other to hold Brandon in place. Brandon slumped into his shoulder, breath rasping. He threw his head back against Alejo's arm and laughed into the dawn.

"What happened?" Alejo asked. "There are paramedics. Someone will—"

"It's gone." Brandon lolled his forehead against Alejo's neck.

Blood from his shoulder painted Alejo's denim jacket red. "It's *gone.*"

Alejo didn't speak. He stared, knuckles turning white as his grip on Brandon tightened. He looked into Logan's eyes, silently begging her to confirm it.

She nodded.

"Oh my god," Alejo breathed. He inhaled sharply and covered his mouth with a shaking hand. When he blinked, he was crying, too. The morning wind was cold and bitter, but Alejo pulled them together in a hug tight enough to block out the chill. He shook until his tears melted into laughter.

"It's okay. It didn't take her," Brandon croaked. "We're finally gonna be okay."

Logan looked over Alejo's shoulder. Gracia had swept Elexis into a hug so tight she was shocked Elexis could breathe. Gracia peppered his face with kisses, muttering inaudibly in his ear. Ashley stood behind them, hesitant like she wasn't sure if she deserved to celebrate. Her eyes were red and swollen. She looked at the horizon with a smile that was relieved and pained at once.

"I'll be right back," Logan whispered.

She made her way to Ashley. Paramedics quickly swarmed Brandon, working to patch up his shoulder. It was a surreal scene—for the first time since she'd come to Snakebite, it was like there was a world outside. There were people beyond this little town. Someone in the real world cared about what happened here. They weren't stuck in a cage. They hadn't just come here to die.

"Hey," Logan said.

Ashley blinked away from the horizon and focused on Logan's face. She wiped tears from her eyes and smiled wearily. "Hey."

"I hope your night was a little less eventful than mine," Logan mused.

"I don't think it was."

Logan gestured to the crowd of police cars. "Did you call the cavalry?"

"I did. Actually, I think Fran called them first." Ashley looked at the ground. "I, uh . . . we found Tristan."

Logan's eyes widened. She knew better than to ask, but she couldn't help herself. There was still a piece of hope lodged in her chest, small and trembling. "Alive?"

Ashley gave her a tight-lipped frown. Slowly, she shook her head. Her lips quivered and the tears she'd clearly been fighting resurfaced.

"I'm sorry," Logan said. She felt selfish for a moment for being so happy that her family had survived this. Logan took Ashley's hand tentatively. "I'm so sorry."

They both looked out at the hills in silence. Earlier tonight—or yesterday, Logan guessed—she'd thought this place was a prison. And it was, in a sense. But without the Dark, there was beauty in it. There was hope.

Ashley took Logan's face in her hands. She pulled Logan to her and kissed her like they were the only people in the turnout. Like they were the only people in the world. Logan held Ashley's shoulders and kissed her back. She didn't know what they would do next—where they would go—but Logan kissed her and kissed her.

They were alive.

For now, that was enough.

39

Only Homesick Ghosts

It was a quiet morning in Snakebite.

It had been two weeks since Paris's basement. Two weeks since Snakebite learned their sheriff had killed three children. Two weeks of people asking questions before promptly realizing they didn't want the answers. Two weeks since Ashley had seen Tristan for the last time. His funeral was a quiet, hard thing. But it was a relief. Winter would come again and Tristan would still be gone, but at least he wasn't lost.

At least he was home.

Ashley wasn't sure she could ever call Snakebite home again.

The wind was quick over Snakebite Memorial and Ashley still tasted the Dark on her tongue like iron. She sat in the bed of the Ford, knees tucked against her chest, and let the breeze roll over her. It felt like she'd been here a thousand times since this all started. She'd already said a thousand goodbyes.

From the top of the hill, she could see them all: *Nicholas Porter, Beatrice Gunderson, Tristan Granger.* Ashley's eyes traced the letters etched into Tristan's headstone. His grave was almost completely obscured with bouquets of flowers. The first victim and the last one found.

TRISTAN ARTHUR GRANGER

2001–2020

"SLEEP ON NOW, AND TAKE YOUR REST."—MATTHEW 26:45

In the parking spot next to her, a car door shut. Ashley didn't look at who it was—probably another person here to lay flowers for the victims. News had spread outside of Snakebite in crashing waves. Frank Paris's face was on every news station in the state. Under his picture were always smiling pictures of Nick, Bug, and Tristan. People drove from all over to pay their respects and to see where it all happened.

"Can I come up?"

The voice wasn't a stranger's. Tammy Barton stood next to the Ford, one hand resting on the tailgate. Like always, she was the perfect portrait of what Snakebite was supposed to be. Her short blond hair was ironed into easy waves, her long lashes perfectly curled, her lips painted a subtle mauve. Before all this, when Ashley looked at her mother she had seen what she wanted to be in twenty years. She had seen the kind of woman who held Snakebite on her shoulders. She had seen the best parts of this town—the strength, the loyalty, the pride.

But Snakebite was wrong. Maybe Tammy Barton was wrong, too.

Ashley nodded and motioned to the space next to her in the truck bed. Tammy carefully climbed up and nestled against her in silence. She placed her hand gently on Ashley's knee and looked out at the lake, the hills, the bright gold horizon. After a moment, she unearthed a thermos from her bag and passed it to Ashley.

Ashley unscrewed the lid and a cloud of hibiscus steam wafted out. Even here, even after everything, the scent was home.

"How'd you know I was here?" Ashley asked finally.

"I've known you for a while now," Tammy said. She hesitated, then added, "Well, I've known *most* of you, I guess."

Ashley's stomach sank. "I don't wanna talk about that."

"Okay. We don't have to." Tammy paused. "But we can."

Ashley hugged her knees tighter to her chest. In the two weeks since Paris's basement, she and her mother had talked about a lot of things. They'd talked about what Snakebite would do now, what Ashley needed to recover from this, what Barton Ranch would do to stay afloat amidst the scandal. But they hadn't talked about this. They hadn't talked about the sinking feeling in her chest.

They hadn't talked about the way Logan made her feel incredibly, impossibly alive. The way Snakebite had tried to kill her piece by piece, and Logan had put her back together.

A few months ago, Snakebite had been her home.

Now home was something else.

"You mind if I talk at you for a second?" Tammy asked.

Ashley said nothing.

"I'm not gonna pretend to get it. I didn't get it with Alejo, either. But back then, I didn't really try. You've been through a lot these past few months. More than I ever went through at your age. And I know that's gonna change things for you." Tammy squeezed Ashley's knee. "If this is something you want, I can't stop you. But I've never seen it make someone's life easier. And after all this, I just want your life to be easy."

"Yeah, well that's kind of impossible now," Ashley said. She didn't want to snap, but anger boiled in her chest. For the last few weeks—last few *months*—it had been like she was trying to breathe underwater. "My friends are dead. How could it be easy now?"

"I lost my friends, too," Tammy said. "One of my best friends broke up with me and left. The other one . . ." She gestured to the cemetery.

"It's not the same."

"It's not. But I get it."

Ashley closed her eyes. She felt the hot tears before she could stop them. She pressed the heels of her hands to her eyes, but she cried anyway. This pain came from deeper than any she'd ever felt. It wracked her, scraped her inside out, made her hollow and cold. Snakebite was the only place she'd ever known, and now she didn't know it at all.

She was lost.

Tammy pulled Ashley's head against her chest and ran a hand through her hair. They sat alone for what felt like hours, Ashley crying quietly and Tammy letting her.

"When is she leaving?" Tammy asked.

"Next week."

"What do you want to do?"

Ashley sucked in a ragged breath. "I don't know."

Tammy ran a hand through her hair again. The horizon was cream-colored and light as a feather. It was the clearest the sky had been in months. The sun wasn't blistering like before. Even if the sky was back to normal, even if Snakebite was settling down, Ashley couldn't go back.

"Do you want to leave?"

Ashley sat up and wiped tears from her eyes. Tammy's expression was genuine. Her eyes were clear and blue and pained. Ashley shook her head. "I can't."

"You're eighteen," Tammy said. "I can't . . . I wouldn't stop you."

"The ranch . . ." Ashley trailed off.

". . . will go on one way or another. It always does."

Ashley's heart raced. She'd spent years imagining a future, and it was always here. It was always in Snakebite, always on the ranch, always married with two kids and a dog, always quiet and predictable. Since all of this, she hadn't imagined a future at all.

Now, she saw it. Sunset roads and forests she'd never seen. The truck rumbling under her, a soft hand folded in hers, dark eyes always watching.

"I don't wanna leave you," Ashley said.

Tammy smiled, bitter and soft at once. "You're not. It's not like you'll never come back. It's not like I'll never see you."

"Are you sure?"

"No," Tammy said. She laughed under her breath. "It sounds like a horrible idea. But I know you, and you don't want to stay here. You want to go with her. It's not the first time this has happened to me. Or to people I love. Staying here would be worse, I think."

Ashley nodded. She pulled her phone from her pocket and eyed Logan's number. Tammy looked her in the eyes for a long moment, and then she smiled. She squeezed Ashley's wrist once, then climbed out of the truck bed and made her way back to the Land Rover.

Only the quiet and the dead remained.

Ashley clicked Logan's name and pressed the phone to her ear.

At the Bates Motel, the world was anything but quiet.

The door between rooms seven and eight was wide open, a warm breeze sifting between the two. Brandon leaned over the breakfast table, needling a map of the US with the sharp end of his pencil. Alejo shoved the last of his floral-patterned shirts into a duffel bag and hauled it to the minivan, humming a Johnny Cash song under his breath.

Logan sat on the bed. They casually moved through their morning, and Logan could almost pretend this was how they always were. A collection of three lost things that had cobbled together a life they could be happy in. A *family.*

"Gimme another thing," Brandon said, tapping the eraser of his pencil against his glasses.

"Uh, how about America's oldest cemetery?" Logan asked.

Brandon frowned and circled a spot on the map. "You can also pick fun places. America's biggest mall. The tallest place you can drive to. The—"

"What about that big rubber band ball?" Alejo cut in, clapping dust from his hands. He closed the back of the minivan and strode back into the motel room, yellow sun bouncing from the aviators perched at his hairline.

"Do I look like a tourist?" Logan scoffed.

Brandon and Alejo made eye contact and said nothing.

"You guys are rude."

"I like that tree you can drive through," Alejo suggested.

Brandon grimaced. "Yeah, but it fell down in that storm."

"There's other ones."

"But it's not the same."

"You are *such* a downer."

Brandon shook his head. His lips hinted at a smile. It was a frequent expression now, but something in Logan still sank each time she saw it. How many smiles had the Dark swallowed whole? How many years had he lived in a blur of gray, waiting for the end? Even now, they were making up for lost time. She could spend every day with her fathers for the rest of her life, but it would never fill the hole the Dark had left. There was no fixing things; they could only move on.

Alejo and Brandon were packing to take off back to LA. They'd decided not to expose Snakebite to the *ParaSpectors* canon, but that didn't stop news cycles from associating them with the mystery. Even after police cleared them of any involvement in the deaths, Brandon and Alejo were inextricably linked to the crime. Clickbait news sites screamed headlines like:

KILLER IN RURAL OREGON: WHAT TV GHOSTHUNTERS HAVE TO DO WITH THE INVESTIGATION!

***PARASPECTORS* COUPLE SOLVE MURDERS?**

BRANDON WOODLEY AND ALEJO ORTIZ HELP POLICE SOLVE COLD CASES IN OREGON

The sudden publicity meant there was damage control to do. There was another season of *ParaSpectors* to film, and they had to come up with locations to fill it. There was a life to live—something they hadn't thought possible with the Dark always looming over them. Despite everything that'd happened, Brandon and Alejo were going to move on.

They were going to move on alone.

Logan had dreamed of cruising the US on her own for years, but now that it was the next thing on the horizon, it felt empty. She was going to be alone again. At the end of all of this, she was still going to be alone. She was going to have to meet new people. She was going to carry this darkness in her chest—the truth about Snakebite, about Brandon, about *herself*—and no one would know.

"Once we figure out filming locations, maybe we can meet up for a few episodes," Alejo suggested. He tucked the beige motel comforter under his chin and folded it. "You could be a guest investigator. An in-*guest*-igator."

He laughed at his own joke.

"Maybe," Logan said. And maybe she *would* meet up with them and film a few episodes. Maybe she would roll into a town a few months down the road and realize it was perfect. Maybe she would lay down roots somewhere and figure out how to build a life from the ground up. It all felt impossibly far away.

Her phone rang.

Logan rolled off the bed and wandered to her motel room. She and Ashley had spoken a few times since everything went down, but the world had fallen apart from under them. Whatever plans they'd made, whatever promises they'd exchanged, it was all in the wind now.

Ashley deserved to be happy again, whatever that looked like. Logan would learn to be okay with that.

"Hey," Logan said, shutting the dividing door behind her.

"Hey," Ashley said on the other end of the line. *"Do you have a minute to talk?"*

"Yeah, sure." Logan lay back on her bed. She and Ashley had lain here one night, hours before the world fell to pieces. "What's up? Where are you?"

"Visiting Tristan and the others." Her voice cracked. *"Are you packing up?"*

"Kind of. Brandon's helping me plan my stops."

"Oh, cool. You're still leaving next week?"

Logan swallowed. "Yeah."

"Okay."

Ashley was quiet for a long moment. Wind rattled like a long sigh from the other end of the call. Around Logan, the room sank. She hadn't said goodbye yet; she hadn't figured out how. Because all the years she'd spent picturing her life on the road felt hazy now. The only thing she pictured was Ashley next to her, Ashley smiling again, Ashley playfully shoving her when she said something stupid. At some point, something had shifted in her.

She didn't want to be alone. She wanted to be loved.

And she didn't want to say goodbye.

"Ashley . . ." Logan said.

Ashley cleared her throat. *"Do you want some company?"*

40

In The Morning Hour She Calls Me

On the last day of August, Snakebite was a dream. It was bathed in gold sunlight and bright under the wide-open sky, crisp and cool as summer tilted into fall. It was different than it had been when Logan first arrived. Or *she* was different, which felt just as likely. The sun had calmed the day the Dark died, like the town was freed from a paranormal vise grip. The endless hills that held Snakebite in place were softer now, rolling out to the horizon like ripples on the lake. From the beginning, she'd intended to follow the tide out of Snakebite and as far away as it could take her. That much hadn't changed.

But now, she wouldn't be alone.

The Ford dipped as she tossed the last of her overnight bags into the truck bed. Ashley fastened a bungee cord to keep their luggage in place. Even after everything, the sun in Snakebite treated Ashley differently than it treated everyone else. She ran the back of her hand over her brow and her freckled skin glowed in the late-summer light.

"You've got underwear?" Tammy Barton asked, leaning

against the driver's side of the truck. "Phone charger? Gas money? GPS?"

Ashley clapped on a baseball cap. "Check, check, check, and check."

Tammy eyed Logan and pursed her lips. She'd been trying to conceal her disdain for the last week. She wasn't succeeding, but Logan appreciated the effort. "Do you two have any idea where you're *going?*"

Logan and Ashley exchanged a smile. They had a couple of spots on the road, a couple of sights to take in, but no destination. That was the point of it. Logan had been everywhere, but she'd never felt at home. Ashley had only known one home her whole life, but it wasn't home anymore.

They had a thousand new skies to see.

Before either of them could answer, Alejo ambled from the front porch of the Barton Ranch house with the last box of Ashley's things nestled in his arms. Brandon followed close behind him, tapping incessantly at his phone screen. As Alejo loaded the box into the truck bed, Brandon sidled up beside Logan and turned his phone so she could see it. It was a compact map of the US, pocked with virtual red thumbtacks in almost every state.

"I added a few places in Missouri," he said. "Weirdly, there's lots of cool stuff there. It's probably my favorite place we visited."

"Also the most depressing place we visited." Alejo snorted. "So that checks out."

Brandon scoffed. "Obviously you don't have to stop *everywhere,* but it's a start. If you follow the ninety-five east out of Snakebite, you'll wind up in Idaho. Nothing much to see there, but I highlighted a few spots you can check out. I'd say head north from there until you hit Coeur d'Alene, then . . ."

Logan nodded. The map didn't matter, but the fact that he'd helped her make it was perfect. She was trying and he was trying. They had years ahead of them—they had time to heal.

". . . sound like a plan?" Brandon asked.

Logan smiled. "Sounds like a plan."

"Cool." Brandon rubbed the back of his neck. "Me and your dad are taking off tomorrow morning. I know it'll be hard to check in with each other, but we'll at least let you know when we're back in LA."

Logan nodded. She pulled Brandon into a hug.

Alejo rammed into them, joining the group hug with the ferocity of an excited golden retriever. "No goodbyes without me. It's illegal."

"I'm gonna miss you guys," Logan said. "I mean it."

"Can't miss us if we FaceTime every night," Alejo joked.

She *hoped* he was joking.

On the other side of the truck, Ashley wrapped her arms around her mother. The Bartons' goodbye was quieter. It was more solemn. Ashley let go of Tammy and tightened her ponytail, looking out at the lake behind the house like she thought she might never see it again.

"I know things are . . . hard," Tammy said. "But I love you. No matter what."

"I love you too, Mom," Ashley said.

Tammy gave her a terse kiss on the forehead and squeezed her shoulder. "If this doesn't work out, the ranch will always be here for you. You can always come home."

"And they're always welcome to crash with us, wherever we are," Alejo said. "You too, Tammy. We can have a big sleepover."

Tammy rolled her eyes. "Hilarious."

"I'm serious. We'll be like a big family now." Alejo ran a hand through his hair. "A big family that probably needs a lot of therapy."

Ashley climbed into the driver's side of the Ford, and Logan silently climbed into the passenger seat. They settled in, staring at the driveway that stretched out ahead of them like a doorway to another world. Ashley jammed her keys into the ignition and the truck roared to life. They pulled out of the driveway slowly, waving a final goodbye to their respective parents until they rounded the corner onto the highway. Logan pulled out Brandon's map and gave it a cursory glance.

"Where are we going first?" Logan asked. She threw her feet up on the dash and swiped her round black sunglasses over her eyes.

"East, to the highway."

"Then?"

Ashley smiled. The sun was golden over her freckled cheeks. "Another highway. Probably some mountains. A lot of nothing."

Logan slipped a hand over Ashley's thigh, fingertips tracing circles against her skin. "And then?"

"Somewhere, eventually. You ready for it?"

Ashley's smile was brighter than the sun.

The truck rattled on, shaking clouds of dust loose into the haze. The soft, gold hills of Snakebite cradled the girls in their palms, pouring them out of the lake valley and into the world beyond. Snakebite had been a nightmare for Logan; for Ashley, it'd been home. Logan touched the knuckles of Ashley's hand. Home didn't have to be a place anymore. It didn't need four walls or a rocky shore or stars over the hills. It was a feeling.

It felt like this.

"Home," Logan said, tasting the word. "Weird concept."

Ashley smiled. She leaned across the center panel and gave Logan a soft, short kiss on the lips.

The road stretched ahead of them, twisting into nowhere. Logan's heart skipped a little faster with each mile. Even without the Dark, it would be a long road ahead. Ashley settled into the driver's seat with sunlight caught in her hair and it was hard to believe she was real. There would be pain and there would be hope, and Logan wasn't sure which scared her more. But she wasn't alone anymore.

And wherever the road took them, they'd been through worse.

Acknowledgments

The thing they never tell you in writing class is how many people it takes to make a book. Growing up, I always thought writing a book meant sitting down, cranking out a novel, and then hurling it into the world. It's so much more than that, though. I have been beyond privileged to work with an entire team of absolute rock stars over the last two years who have all been dedicated to making *The Dead and the Dark* a real book. I can't even begin to cover all the help I've received, but I can at least try to thank you all.

First of all, a huge thank-you to my incredible editor, Jennie Conway. From our first phone call where you yelled at me for the contents of chapter twenty-five and told me the whole thing was "like *Riverdale,* but good," I knew we were going to be a great match. You have been an amazing champion for me and my girls, and I feel so lucky to be working with someone who so deeply understands what I'm trying to say, even when I don't. Thank you to the entire team at Wednesday Books and St. Martin's Press. To Mary Moates, Melanie Sanders, Alexis

Neuville, Lauren Hougen, Jeremy Haiting, Omar Chapa, and Elizabeth Catalano. Thank you to Kerri Resnick and Peter Strain for my mind-blowingly gorgeous cover. I stare at it every day and imagine I will until the end of time.

My second thank-you goes to Claire Friedman and Jessica Mileo, my tireless agents. Thank you for always answering my panicked midnight questions, for reassuring me through many anxiety spirals, for always encouraging even the most out-there of my ideas, and for sending me *Red Dead Redemption* memes to keep me grounded. I cannot imagine a duo better suited for me and all my creepy, unnerving stories. Here's to this first story and to many more to come. Thank you to the rest of the InkWell team, too. *The Dead and the Dark* wouldn't be here without you all.

Thank you to my CPs: Lachelle Seville, who has been writing with me for almost a decade now and still doesn't hate me. To Emily Khilfeh, who saw the very first spark of this idea and helped me kindle it every step of the way. To Cayla Keenan, who is an unrelentingly positive cheerleader and fierce supporter of all things queer. To Alex Clayton, who is the most supportive, kind, and loyal person I know. I wouldn't be here without you, and I am forever grateful for your friendship and love. Thank you to Sadie Graham, Allison Saft, Ava Reid, and Rachel Morris for being such incredible friends through this journey. We all have to stick together through this tough process. I look forward to backing one another up for years to come.

Thank you to Kelly Jones, my Writing in the Margins mentor, who has always held the door open for aspiring writers. Thank you for listening to all my venting and for always offering to connect me with writers who really know what's going on. Doing this whole thing one time was exhausting; I can't imagine how you've done it a dozen times!

Thank you to Trisha Kelly, Adrienne Tooley, and Ashley Schumacher for being early readers and supporters of this odd little story. Thank you to Andrea Gomez for your help pushing this book to a deeper level. Thank you to the Tea Time crew: Rachel Diebel, Anna Loose, Ingrid Clark, Maylen Anthony, Lauren Cashman, Adrian Mayoral, Camille Adams, Sylvie Creekmore, and Mike Traner. Thank you to Courtney Summers, Dahlia Adler, Emma Berquist, Francesca Zappia, and Erica Waters for reading and loving *The Dead and the Dark*. You're all incredible writers and it means the world to hear your kind words about my girls.

Thank you to *Red Dead Redemption, Riverdale, Sharp Objects, Holes,* Johnny Cash, *Westworld,* and all the other strange pieces of media I devoured while trying to figure this book out. Thank you to the towns of eastern Oregon I visited while trying to bring Snakebite to life—I hope you see yourselves represented in these pages.

Lastly, my family. Thank you to Carly for being the original hype-man for my creative pursuits. Thank you to Dad and Grandma for your patience while waiting to see if this writing thing would pay off. Thank you to Davis for always believing I could do this. Thank you to Mom for always saying this dream was practical, for sacrificing so much for us, and for always being home for me. I am beyond lucky to have you. This book is for you.

Thank you to everyone who helped create this story about two girls looking for love in a world of hate. I hope you like what it's become.